# Teaching Eliza

## RIANA EVERLY

*Cover design by Mae Phillips at* <u>*coverfreshdesigns.com*</u>

ISBN-13: 978-1-7751283-2-8

# Dedication

For my family, who made this possible

# Contents

# Acknowledgements

No book is the product of only one mind. For *Teaching Eliza*, I have to include in my acknowledgements Jane Austen and George Bernard Shaw, whose brilliant writings have given me so much joy and so much inspiration. I wish I could thank them personally.

The first of those I *can* thank in person is my husband, Mikael, who never once said, "Aren't you done writing yet?" I also wish to thank Gavriel and Hadassah, who cheered me on; my various friends and relatives, who listened to me blather on about my latest project and even read some of my scribblings; the terrific JAFF community I have found; and to a wonderfully encouraging group of fellow authors whose names I dare not write down in case I inadvertently miss someone!

Special thanks to Ginger Monette, for her invaluable advice, Mae Phillips for her amazing art work, Donna Kraus for all those little things that add up to something big, and to Sophia Meredith, without whose insight, editing, and guidance at every step of this project, *Teaching Eliza* would never have seen the light of day.

Cover design by Mae Phillips at coverfreshdesigns.com

RIANA EVERLY

"The great secret, Eliza, is not having bad manners or good manners or any other particular sort of manners, but having the same manner for all human souls: in short, behaving as if you were in Heaven, where there are no third-class carriages, and one soul is as good as another."
(G.B. Shaw, *Pygmalion*, Act V)

⊰⊱

PICKERING. We're always talking Eliza.
HIGGINS. Teaching Eliza.
PICKERING. Dressing Eliza.
MRS. HIGGINS. What!
HIGGINS. Inventing new Elizas.
(G. B. Shaw, *Pygmalion*, Act III)

# One
## An Auspicious Encounter

Autumn, 1811

"It is a truth universally acknowledged," said the gentleman as he stretched out his long legs and crossed them at the ankle, "that a single man in possession of a good fortune, must be in want of a wife." Fitzwilliam Darcy paused, sighed dramatically, then snorted, and took a large sip from the delicate crystal glass cradled in his large hand. Turning back to his friend, he added, "And yet, Charles, here I am, a single gentleman indeed, and rather suitably wealthy, but wanting nothing more than to be left alone with my studies. Oh, how I loathe the endless parade of young women, led through ballrooms and evening salons and even my very own parlour when my aunt thinks she might influence me, all hoping to catch my eye and tempt me into matrimony. It is a veritable curse, I tell you." Despite a very definite edge of displeasure, his enunciation was beautiful and precise, his voice melodious and smooth.

Charles Bingley shook his head vigorously in denial and sputtered some syllables of disavowal, but his companion ignored them all and lapsed into a silence broken only by the quiet sound of his breath as he contemplated the contents of his glass.

Darcy glowered in the subdued light of the lounge in which they sat and he took another sip of his brandy. His eyes roved across the dark woods and greens of the luxurious space, which absorbed candlelight from the numerous chandeliers and reflected back the opulent glow of elegance and restraint, then moved back to his companion. He snorted again. "Why do they not accept that I am not interested in being leg-shackled to one of these vacuous girls? That my interests in the affairs of society are nil? That I want only to be left alone? I am a grumpy old man, Charles, and wish to remain so." He turned his head heavenwards and sank back into the upholstery of his large chair.

With an ill-concealed smile and a half-stifled laugh, Bingley replied. "Grumpy, indeed, Darcy! That I would never contradict. But old? Even you must admit that seven and twenty hardly counts as old. For the schoolroom, perhaps, but whilst you do spend your time there, I own, it is as professor and not pupil. Indeed, you are remarkably young to have achieved your rank."

"I am still young in years, perhaps, but oh so old in spirit." He sat bolt upright and leaned forward in his chair, hands clenched on his knees as he levelled his dark brown eyes at his friend. "I have no interest in what my contemporaries enjoy. Yes, I include you in that group, for all that you seem to understand me better than most and bring out my less curmudgeonly side on the rare occasion. But even you, for all your unaccountably cheerful disposition and propensity to be pleased with every *one* and every *thing*, must admit that I am simply not like most men of my years."

He reached for his glass once more, nearly knocking it from the low table in his suppressed agitation. "Bah!" he huffed as he straightened the crystal before pouring the remaining liquid into his mouth. "I have no interest in horse races or gaming or cosying up with the dandies who surround the Prince. I have serious concerns: my estate, my books, my work." He swept his hand around, gesturing at the refined and restrained furnishings of his club. "Even this place I tolerate only because it is quiet and not fashionable amongst those of my own age. I require calm and intelligent conversation. Let them dance and drink and raise what havoc they will. I am satisfied with my lot. If only the mothers of those husband-hunting girls would accept this!"

His eyes scanned the scattering of tables occupied by groups of two or three, the thick carpet muffling the ambient noise until there remained merely the quietest hum of conversation to cushion one's thoughts. Indeed, those who wished to carouse and make a scene found other, more suitable locations for their revelries. He and Bingley were by far the youngest men he could see in the room. Most were the age his father would have been had he lived. Even the grizzled soldier hidden in the shadows of the alcove just past his own table seemed, by his posture and solitude, at least ten years Darcy's senior. Let the others attend their parties and balls. He was satisfied with more sedate and sober choices.

At a gesture from Bingley, a liveried attendant, smart in his dark green suit, brought over two more glasses of the fine brandy. When the man had walked away, Bingley asked, "Is that why you have holed up here, then? To avoid the predatory mamas on the hunt? The knocker on the door of your townhouse is down, and you have informed no one else, other than myself, of your presence in Town. Do you begin to hope that this will dissuade them all?"

"That is one reason, yes. The look in their eyes when my name is mentioned is positively predatory. They look upon me and see not a man, but carriages and jewels, dresses and my estates. But it is not only them. I am also seeking to avoid my aunt."

"Lady Catherine?" Bingley's head snapped up, his eyebrows rising in surprise. The solitary soldier at the nearby table shifted in his chair at the volume of Bingley's exclamation, and Darcy caught the glimmer of candlelight as it reflected off the gold braid on the man's uniform.

Ignoring the soldier, Darcy exhaled heavily and nodded. "Yes. Lady Catherine. She still believes that I shall marry her daughter and had the temerity to send a message to my rooms at Oxford informing me that since I am not wed, nor do I seem to be interested in finding my own wife, she would announce an engagement between Anne and myself at the start of the next Season. I sent back an immediate response insisting that she do nothing of the sort, and then... well, to make no bones about it, I fled. If she does not know where I am, she cannot find me, and if she cannot find me, she cannot make unreasonable demands of me. To all appearances, I am not in town, and I would have it remain thus."

"Then, Darcy, it seems that in order to dissuade both these mamas-on-the-hunt and your own aunt, you need a bride!"

"Are you mad?" he spat with a huff, drawing the eyes from patrons of several nearby tables. These glares he returned with his own until they retreated, then he lowered his voice. "You cannot possibly have meant that, Bingley. Have I not just said...?"

His friend pushed the crystal glass closer to Darcy's hand, and as Darcy raised it to drink, Bingley smirked, "Perhaps not an actual bride, but the rumour of one. Let it be known that you are married, or even betrothed, and perhaps you shall be let alone. At least, that is, until the hounds sniff out the truth about their prey."

The glass did not quite reach Darcy's lips. He placed it back on the table in an ominously controlled motion and stared suspiciously first at the glass and then at his companion. "There must be something in the food at this estate you have let, Bingley. Perhaps your chef is drugging your meals. You speak nonsense."

Bingley merely smiled serenely and murmured, "Perhaps. But think on it, Darcy." He took a healthy drink from his own glass, before changing the topic. "How goes your recent project? You had been most interested in some new specimens of dialect when last we spoke on the subject."

Darcy brightened. "Yes! It was most fascinating. I was in the north of Wales doing research on that odd little Quaker-like commune that has settled there—I believe I have told you about them. When I heard mention of this small cluster of fishing villages on the islands off the coast, of course I had to pay a visit. My Welsh is only passable, but these villagers' English was positively atrocious. Those vowels," he groaned, "Oh, Bingley, you cannot imagine those vowels. I was ready to ask them to speak to me in French, my poor ears ached so from such desecration of the King's English.

Charles laughed.

Darcy scowled. "You are amused, but ought not to be. You have done much work to eliminate the north from your own speech, but I still detect a trace of Scarborough in your accent. Most would not, of course, but my ears are most particularly sensitive and attuned to these matters. Even should I not know this from our years of friendship, I should be aware that your father was from Scarborough, born into a wealthy merchant family but educated at Oxford, and that your mother was from an estate near Flamborough. Your own youth was spent in Scarborough, albeit with fine enough tutors, and I can detect the trace of Cambridge in your alveolar consonants. The work we have done together, you and I, has erased much of this from what the common ear hears, but I still detect it. Therefore, do not laugh at me when I cringe at the sounds issuing from the mouths of the fisherfolk of the Irish Sea."

The old soldier at the neighbouring table shifted and interjected, "You seem to think you know a lot about this, sir. Pray tell, whence comes the arrogance that precedes your pronouncements on the origins of your fellow man?"

Darcy narrowed his eyes and addressed the shape in the shadows. "I shall ignore your rude intrusion, sir, and instead shall deign to answer your question. I do not imagine you have heard of me. I am Professor Fitzwilliam Henry Darcy, late of Cambridge and Wittenberg, now lecturing at Oxford. My expertise in linguistics and phonetics is sought after by my colleagues at the Sorbonne and Cambridge as well, and I have published several treatises on my chosen subject. Therefore, sir, you may take issue with my arrogance but not with my skill and knowledge."

"You speak very proudly for such a young man," the soldier mumbled. "I have not the information to refute your credentials, but would be curious to put your self-professed expertise to the test. Whence, sir, come I?"

Darcy peered intently at the brazen stranger, still mostly obscured by shadow. He could see little of the man's features, for his long hair fell heavily over his face and one eye was obscured by a patch. Much of the rest of the man's face was hidden beneath an unkempt beard, most unfashionable amongst anyone who might be able to afford membership in this exclusive club.

Stroking his own clean-shaven chin, Darcy pondered for a moment, then slowly uttered his assessment. "You are well born. Very well born. I would imagine your sire is an aristocrat—perhaps a baron or an earl. You were born and raised on an estate north of London, near Northampton if I am correct (which I always am), and were sent to Harrow at the age of eleven. From there you went to Cambridge, and then into the army. Your mother, too, is of aristocratic birth, from an estate near Basingstoke. You have recently returned from Jamaica, where you have spent at least three years. You have also, in the past, spent some considerable time in Kent, but have never resided there. You may now tell me how accurate I am."

The soldier laughed. "Where in Kent, my friend?"

Darcy blinked. "Hunsford..." He stopped. "Wait, sir. Ask me that again."

The soldier did so, and Darcy let loose a roar of laughter. "Brush back your mane, sir, and let me see your face." The soldier did so, and Darcy leapt to his feet and grasped the soldier's hand. "By God, Bingley, do you know who this man is? Charles, please allow me to introduce to you my cousin, Colonel Richard Fitzwilliam." Then he stood back and surveyed his cousin's countenance. "Richard, what on earth has happened to you? It has been five years since last you were on English soil if I am correct. That beard... your eye!"

"I tried my hand at pirating the seven seas, but I was mocked by all I tried to rob until I thought of this clever disguise! A pirate with two good eyes and no beard is a sorry sight indeed." Darcy chortled at his cousin's joke; ah, how he missed Richard's quick humour.

"But tell me, am I that changed, Darcy?"

"For one not expecting to meet you in this club, you are indeed. You seem much the worse for battle. I should, at first, have taken you for forty, at least, with that pirate's disguise you seek to exhibit. But now, seeing you in better light, I fancy I should alter my estimate by some five or seven years, which still marks you older than your years. Now, meet my friend and relinquish your lonely table." A wave of Darcy's hand quickly summoned the liveried attendant, and in short order a third chair and another glass of brandy were brought to the table.

Bingley raised his glass and toasted the cousins, "To the family we like!" The men cheered and drank deeply.

"As I look between you, I see that you do rather resemble my friend," Bingley commented between sips. "There is something about the eyes and brows, and you both share a noble wide forehead. 'Tis also unlined, which puts your age much closer to that of Darcy here than I had initially guessed."

"Ah yes, the noble forehead," Richard nodded, "so much more handsome on my face than on my cousin's. It is attributed to the great Fitzwilliam family."

Darcy raised an eyebrow and asked, "But to what do you attribute that atrocious beard? Surely not to my dear mother!"

Richard laughed. "This *atrocious* beard was the result of a particularly rough sea voyage back from the West Indies, during which I had no desire to subject my delicate throat to the whims of the rolling sea and my batman's unsteady hand. I would have shaved it upon returning to solid land, but it bothered my mother to such an extent and to such loud objections that I decided to let it remain some days."

Darcy smiled, "How does the countess?"

"Mother is well," Richard smirked, "delighting in her success with my younger sister and eagerly anticipating the arrival of a grandchild, no matter that we have had no news concerning any potential offspring: Laetitia is married, and to a viscount, and thus it is only a matter of time before she produces the expected heir. And yes, before you ask, Mother is in Town, and no, I shall not inform her as to your presence here."

"And your eye? Surely the state of your facial hair is nothing compared to the necessity of covering your eye with that patch."

"This, too, looks more dire than it is. On that same rough voyage, just before we made port, I received a nasty knock to the face, which scratched my eye and bruised the area around it rather severely. The doctors assure me it will heal completely in time, but it is very painful to keep open, and is most sensitive to light. Within a week, however, I shall most likely look once more as you remember me."

"Pity the world," Darcy teased, his voice light. "It is wonderful to have you back, Richard, it truly is. I have missed your company."

"I say, gentlemen," Bingley leaned forward, "Why not come and spend some time at my estate in the country. Darcy, it will provide you with convenient lodgings not in London, Pemberley, or Oxford. You may read or write up your recent studies, or whatever it is you do, in peace. And you, Colonel, may enjoy the countryside and the very pleasant society I have met there. My house, Netherfield, is more than adequate to provide you with all the company or solitude you desire, and I should be delighted to have you as my first guests."

"You shall inform no one as to my presence?" Darcy asked, at the same time as the affable colonel inquired, "Pleasant company?"

Bingley chuckled. "No, Darcy, your presence shall remain as secret as you desire. The society there cares little for the goings-on of the *ton*. We might even find you an alias, should you so desire. And Colonel, the society there is most pleasant. At a recent public assembly—Darcy, stop grimacing so!—I dare say I had never seen so many pretty girls in all my life! Oh, their manners are country manners to be sure, but they are no less delightful for the lack of pretence and formality. And..." he paused, unsure whether to continue, before spitting out, "I have met the most delightful angel there! I have requested and been granted permission to court her, Darcy, and expect soon to announce our engagement."

"*That* is why you suggested I take a wife," Darcy growled. "You wish for company in your misery."

Bingley winced and shook his head. "No! Not at all! There is no misery where my Miss Bennet is concerned. And as for you, Darcy, I suggested that the rumour of a lady might suffice as well as the actuality of one, if you recall. But Miss Bennet does have four pretty sisters." He raised his brows and beamed widely at his friend. Darcy scowled, while his cousin laughed.

"You shall not join the matchmakers, Bingley! Is that understood? But yes, thank you. I shall accept your kind offer of asylum in the country, and look forward to visiting Netherfield."

CRSO

Darcy and his cousin had been pleased to accept Bingley's invitation to his country estate, and within days the three men were galloping across the fields towards Netherfield Park. The sun was warm on his shoulders, despite the growing chill of autumn, and Darcy was pleased to be out of the confines of his self-imposed solitude in the city. "It is good to ride," he announced to the air, certain that his friends would not hear him as they tore across the meadows.

After a time, Bingley pulled his horse to a halt at the top of a rise of land and gazed out across the open countryside with a satisfied smile. "What think you?" Bingley presented the scene with a sweeping motion of his hand. "The vista is most pleasant, is it not?"

"Most pleasant indeed," the colonel replied. "I understand now your obvious satisfaction in your choice, as well as your suggestion to ride these last few miles cross-country."

"Aye," Bingley's voice was smug. "The carriage can take the roads with our trunks. This is my preferred manner of travelling."

Darcy could not help but agree. "This is a most pleasant prospect. I was also pleased to be out of the carriage." He wondered if his friend had heard his silent admission after all. He surveyed the lands around him with a practiced eye. "The land seems prosperous. Tell me about the neighbourhood."

Bingley was pleased to comply. The closest town, he explained, was Meryton, home to a small but vibrant community of wealthy merchants and country squires. The men had ridden through its streets on their journey, and they nodded as Bingley described its prominence in the area. "The closest house of any importance is Longbourn," he crowed, "home to my angel, Jane, and her four sisters. Our properties abut, but the manor houses lie three miles apart."

"Very good," Colonel Fitzwilliam supplied. "You will be happy here, I believe." He straightened and stretched his neck to better see something in the distance through his one good eye. "Is that a stream yonder? It looks a fair spot to do some fishing. Let us ride some more."

Bingley's chosen route led the men across the bubbling brook and then along the boundary between his estate and the Bennets'. Pulling once more to a stop, Darcy commented absently that Longbourn seemed to be a fairly prosperous estate, but it also carried a faint aura of neglect, as if the master of the estate were happy to enjoy the riches of his land, but cared little for improving it for future generations.

"Does the landowner not ride out across his property?" Darcy peered across an expanse of field from atop his horse, then set off in a gallop towards a rather poorly maintained stretch of fence. "See here," he explained when Bingley and the colonel had caught up with him, "this small stream marks the boundary between Netherfield's extent and Longbourn's. Here, where the fence is on your side of the stream, it is well tended and newly painted. But there, where it is on Longbourn's side, the planks are half rotten and the boards poorly attached to their posts. One good gale and the fence will be down." He dismounted and leapt across the small stream to further examine the run-down structure. With a gentle tug, he pulled a board clean from its posts and held it up to Bingley. "This is what you must watch for on your own estate, Charles. It may seem trivial, but it is symptomatic of the general health of the estate."

He returned to his steed and swung up in an easy motion. "You must know the man," he turned to Bingley, "if you are to marry his daughter. Why should he care so little for his family's land?"

"That is the crux of the matter," Bingley glanced back across the fields, "for the land is not truly his. That is, the estate will not go to his family. It is entailed, so my Miss Bennet tells me, to a distant relative. He is the son of Mr. Bennet's rather despised cousin, and since the daughters will not be able to inherit, Bennet sees little reason to impoverish himself to enrich the usurper."

"I see," Richard shifted in his saddle. "The daughters, then, will be left without a home."

"Perhaps, but they need not worry, for I can take care of them all once I marry dear Jane," Bingley smiled.

Darcy huffed. "Be sure the lady likes you, Charles, and not merely your fortune. Whilst you and I are very different, I would not have you wedded to one who seeks only the security of her family."

"She likes me, Darcy. Grant me the ability to discern the sincerity in her heart. You have not even met the lady and already you are casting her with the parade of young women you seek to avoid in London."

The colonel brought his horse alongside Bingley's, nodding his agreement. "My cousin is rather unforgiving in his nature. If you fancy her, and she you, what ill is there in being able to give her the peace of mind of knowing that her mother and sisters should not starve were they to lose their home?" He slowed his horse and turned towards Darcy. "Let us wait to meet the girl, Fitz, and then decide about her."

Darcy grunted.

Laughing, Richard turned away and shook his head, then squinted into the distance. "I say, Bingley, is that your acquisition?" He pointed to a manor house at the far edge of wide pasture.

"Indeed!"

"Very fine! Onward men!" Richard spurred his mount and began racing towards the house.

Darcy shook his head with a wry smile. The colonel managed his horse better with one eye than many men could boast with two, and Darcy was proud to be able to keep up with him on most occasions. A dash of childish competitiveness overcame him and he took flight as well, hoping to catch his cousin. He was aware of Bingley racing behind him, but his singular goal was to catch Richard. Yes, perhaps this sojourn in the country would be very good for him indeed.

Grinning with the rush of adrenaline that accompanied the gallop, Darcy closed the distance between himself and Richard, slowing only when he rounded the final bend in the drive, mere feet behind his cousin. Then all at once his unaccustomed satisfaction was destroyed by the sound of a familiar and most unwelcome voice singing from across the expansive drive. He glanced up to confirm his fears, and was greeted by the sight of a very pretty young woman standing at the entrance to the house, eyes fixed firmly upon him.

"Caroline Bingley!" he groaned under his breath, and immediately turned his horse towards the stable hands ready to take possession of the steed.

"Charles!" he sneered as his friend rose up and dismounted, "Why did you not tell me Caroline was here? Your sister is hardly conducive to my peace of mind. Surely you must have known..."

But his words were cut off by the woman's overly-effusive greetings, and all further conversation was necessarily delayed. Richard cocked his head in question, but Darcy merely scowled and whispered, "Later."

It was, so it turned out, much later indeed that the men were alone once more. Caroline had gushed over them, proudly shown them their rooms, paraded around the house, commented ceaselessly about her skills at managing a household, and finally led them in to a rather more substantial dinner than any of them had the appetite to consume. Richard said everything polite and pleasant, but Darcy, misanthropic and generally ready to be put out by all events, merely glowered.

At last the meal was over and the sun had set, and the men had escaped to the billiards room, a much-welcomed bastion of masculine solitude. Bingley's butler had brought up a rather fine claret from the cellars, and as he stared into its ruby depths, Darcy levelled his accusatory gaze at his friend and asked once more, "Why did you not tell me Caroline was here? She is one of the husband-hunters I had wished to avoid!"

Richard swirled his own wine in the firelight as he asked, "Miss Bingley seems a genteel lady, and seemingly fond of you, but not you of her. I beg you, Fitz, to explain matters."

Darcy put his glass on the mantelpiece and paced around the room as he spoke. "Charles' sister, attractive and accomplished though she may be, is one of the many women who aspire to be Mrs. Darcy," he informed his cousin, "and she presses the matter more than most. Forgive me for speaking so bluntly, Charles, but you know this is so. I do believe, in her mind, we are as good as already wed." Bingley waved away his concerns. "The way she talks, one would imagine her to be most intimately connected to me. She and I have no interests in common, nor can we speak more than two words to each other, but she manages to look past our glaring incompatibility and reflects only on how fine it would be to be mistress of Pemberley."

"Now Darcy," Bingley interjected, "surely she is not that bad. She does like you, although I admit she is somewhat taken with your wealth. She would not be a bad wife..."

"Merely a selfish one, and one whom I would ever be forced to avoid. No, I'm sorry to say this, Bingley, but she hopes in vain."

"Might she be convinced to play your betrothed, Darcy?" The colonel leaned forwards over the billiards table and lined up a shot with his cue. "The more I think on the matter, the more I believe that Bingley's idea of creating an amour for you is not a bad one. I know I have teased you mercilessly, but you must admit it has some merit." He rubbed his fingers across his freshly shaven chin and returned to his claret.

"Not a chance, Richard. She would not accept the illusory nature of it, and I would likely find myself bound hand and foot and dragged into a church by my boots were she to get the notion into her head."

"She is a most elegant lady, though," the colonel let his eyebrows rise, "and more than pretty too. Is she that bad, Darcy? Would she be interested in an old soldier, recovering from his wounds?"

The colonel rose and moved towards the mirror above the mantel. "See, my hair is trimmed and my face shorn of that awful beard. I am not so bad a catch. I may not be quite the handsome gallant the ladies dream about, but I am the son of an earl and am quite presentable, I do believe. I should disgrace no woman." He ran a hand through his neat hair and let his fingers rest on the patch that still covered his injured eye. "Even this scrap lends me a rakish charm that the ladies admire, do they not?"

"Alas, Colonel," Bingley sighed, "as drawn as she might be to you for your proximity to nobility, she will not settle for anything less than a title or a fine estate to manage. Your pitiable situation as a second son leaves you with little to attract her interest."

Richard laughed. "In truth, that is well, for if I were to wed below my exalted station, what little income I have from my family would surely be denied me. I am glad to know, then, that should I ever find myself fortunate enough to draw a lady's eye, her affection will be for myself and not my fortune." Bingley joined the laughter.

Darcy merely scowled with a huff.

"Save the foul mood for tomorrow night, Darcy, for we are to go to the village assembly. I mentioned as much in the carriage as we left London."

"I had forced myself to forget," Darcy groaned.

"You tease me! We shall go, and we shall enjoy ourselves, and you shall meet my Jane! Colonel," he turned to his other guest, "You at least will join me, will you not? You are much more sociable than your dour cousin."

"Without reservation, Bingley! I should be delighted to join you. I have been promised pleasant company, and where better to find it than at an assembly?" The colonel stood and executed a rather elegant bow and chasse step. "Besides, I have not had the pleasure of dancing in a long while. There was precious little dancing in the barracks in Kingston, and none on the ship. As well," he teased, "as much as I admired the men who served under me while I was in command there, I felt little desire to hold any of them in my arms as we twirled around the tent to the sounds of mosquitoes and drums."

"Was there no local society?" Bingley asked as he moved backwards to make room for the dancing colonel. "Surely there were good men and women in the town, some of whom might enjoy some entertainment of an evening?"

"I do not know what the society there did for their balls, but I heard hardly a melodious sound all the while I was on the island, save for the songs and drum beats of the native and slave populations."

"Aye, but every savage can dance," Darcy looked down his nose.

With little regard for his cousin's disdain, Richard continued on enthusiastically about his hopes for the assembly.

"Darcy, you will come as well, of course," Bingley said when the colonel had finished. "No, no, that was not a request. I know full well your preference to stay at home and do... whatever it is that keeps you from society, but that shall not be tolerated. You are my guest, and as such it is incumbent upon you to grace the assembly with your presence, if not your winning smiles. Besides, I would have you meet my angel. You will like her, Darcy, I know you will. There is no artifice in her at all. She is all that is sweet and good. And please, make no disparaging comments on the country fashions and manners. I have enough of that from Caroline."

Charles beamed, and his good nature almost seeped through Darcy's stony edifice. "Yes, yes, very well, Charles. I shall come. But I cannot guarantee that I shan't offend. I have a remarkable talent for giving offence wherever I go, and as much as I may strive otherwise, I am almost certain to do likewise at your assembly."

"That's my cousin," Richard muttered. "Always optimistic and ready to enjoy himself."

Darcy's eyes cut to his cousin. "Don't say I did not warn you."

# Two
## The Assembly

A very different conversation was underway in the manor house at Longbourn. Elizabeth Bennet stood by the mirror in her sister Jane's bedroom, watching as Jane sat before her and pulled the silver comb through her hair. Jane was all anticipation to attend the upcoming assembly, and she talked eagerly on the subject. Her aim, Elizabeth knew, was to find yet another opportunity to be with Mr. Bingley, and Lizzy was hard pressed to find a reason to dissuade her. "Here, let me help you with that tangle, Jane," she offered as she took possession of the brush and guided it through the slight knot left over from Jane's morning hairstyle.

Jane was particularly lovely, this Elizabeth had always known. She regarded her sister as she smoothed the tress of hair and began plaiting it in preparation for the style to be attempted this evening. Jane's features were fine and regular, with the glow of youth and a classical symmetry that would mature into ageless beauty. "You look exceptionally pretty tonight, Jane," she cooed as she twisted the plait. "It must be love that adds the sparkle in your eyes. Mr. Bingley will not be able to take his eyes off of you."

Jane blushed and lowered her gaze. "You look very nice tonight too, Lizzy," she insisted. "I imagine there will be more than one gentleman at the ball who would be only too pleased to have his eyes upon you."

Lizzy laughed as she regarded her reflection in the mirror. Although she lacked Jane's graceful height and classical poise, she privately quite liked her rounder figure. Not the Grecian ideal that was Jane, she was nonetheless still very pretty, or at least she had been called so in the past, despite her mother's disapproving remarks. *You spend too much time in the sun, Lizzy, and will grow brown and freckled.* She could hear her mother's voice in her head and she chuckled at the notion. *Look at Jane, so perfectly suited for candlelight, as a lady ought to be. Why can you not be more like Jane?*

"What are you laughing at, Lizzy?" Jane's voice roused her from her private amusement. "You will come tonight, will you not? I know you wish to answer Aunt Gardiner's letter, but I need you by my side. If he speaks to me tonight, I shall not know what to say if you are not there to guide me!"

Lizzy smiled indulgently. "Oh, Jane, what is there to say but what your heart tells you? Do you love him?" Jane nodded enthusiastically. "Then what can you do but accept him? The whole village is waiting merely for you to smile before we all begin with the celebrations."

"Then you will come?"

"Yes, dearest, I shall come. No one shall dance with me, and I shall have to spend all evening trying to make polite conversation with Mrs. Long, but yes, I shall come."

Jane turned her head away from the looking glass and half-whispered, "Mr. Bingley is bringing two guests this evening. They came down from London yesterday to stay for some time. One, I heard tell, is a colonel lately from the islands of the West Indies. If he is at all pleasant company, he might provide some entertainment."

This caught Elizabeth's interest and she felt her eyes widen at the prospect. "Indeed! That might very well be amusing! And who, pray tell, is the other?"

Jane paused for a moment, then replied, "I am not certain. A friend, I believe. I have only heard the news from the village, and we know how those stories can vary from truth! Some rumours have it that he is a man of some fortune, but others suggest that he has taken employment as a teacher somewhere, so that cannot be so. But he, too, might be an interesting partner in conversation if not in dance."

"Very well then, Jane!" Lizzy smiled happily, "you have quite convinced me! I shall come and enjoy myself immensely, and if your Mr. Bingley should take you aside, I shall endeavour to make certain that no one disturbs you."

The sisters continued their preparations for the dance, and the subject turned to that of the letter from their aunt. "Tell me again, Lizzy, what Aunt Gardiner wrote. Can she have truly meant it?"

Aunt Gardiner was wife to their mother's much younger brother. She was only ten years older than Lizzy, and the two had developed a friendship that went beyond the familial affection of aunt and niece. Mrs. Gardiner, in turn, had cultivated a similar friendship with her own brother's wife, a lady now of nine and twenty years, and during Lizzy and Jane's frequent visits to the Gardiners in London, the distant relations had met and decided that they rather liked each other. Mrs. Grant—for that was the brother's wife's name—had taken fondly to the two elder Bennet sisters and had suggested for some time that the girls have a season in Town as her particular friends.

"The content of our aunt's letter has not changed since I read it to you this morning!" Lizzy teased. "It contains a renewal—and a rather insistent one—of Mrs. Grant's offer. Or, rather, I must call her Lady Grant now! How wonderful that our aunt's brother was raised to a baronet! I shall never become accustomed to calling him Sir Harrison, let alone Sir Harry, as he insists. Shall we now have to kneel before him and offer him tribute, do you think?" Her eyes flashed in amusement.

"Cease teasing!" Jane tossed her head and then quickly turned to the mirror to ensure that her coiffure was unspoiled by the action. "Sir Harry is the same man he was, no matter that he has been granted a title and new estate for his service to the crown. He has ever been a kind and humble man, and so he shall remain, I am certain. But the letter, Lizzy, the letter!"

"Very well," she smiled and gazed affectionately at her favourite sister. "To repeat, Lady Grant has reiterated her pleasure at sponsoring the elder Bennet sisters for a season in London. She has written to Papa, who has reluctantly given his approval, and now she awaits only our own acceptance."

"Surely that is not all."

Lizzy withdrew the letter from her pocket and scanned it anew. "Aunt Gardiner says that Lady Grant talks of nothing but how we shall enjoy a full season in Town. She insists that we shall enjoy the best of everything London has to offer, from the theatre and the galleries to the most sought-after invitations and introductions to the most eligible young men in society. She cares little that Mama is from a family in trade, and suggests that Papa's status as a gentleman, as well as the dowry she mentions bestowing upon us, will more than atone for any inconveniently trade-born relatives. After all, Uncle Gardiner is in trade, and Sir Harry considers him the best of friends."

"It really is too much, is it not, Lizzy?" Jane asked her sister. "The offer of a season is more than generous, but to add to our dowries, that is beyond what we can accept!"

Lizzy was suddenly serious. "You speak truly, Jane. And yet, with the pittance Papa has to settle upon us, if we do not accept, our options shall be limited indeed. Or," her eyes lit up once more in mirth, "mine shall be. Your future seems rather settled, and awaits only Mr. Bingley's offer."

"Do not tease me, Lizzy!" Jane blushed, the delicate pink that spread over her cheeks only adding to her ethereal beauty. "Until it is done, I shall rely on nothing."

"It shall be done, dearest Jane. Now, let us finish your hair, so you leave Mr. Bingley absolutely no choice in the matter!"

By the time the Bennet sisters had completed their preparations and Jane's hair met with Lizzy's approval, it was time to summon the carriage and depart for the village. Mr. Bennet, the patriarch of this fine family of females, had announced that he had no interest in subjecting himself to several hours of raucous noise and shouted inanities, but the rest of the family were eager for the evening's proceedings to begin. Mrs. Bennet, still an attractive woman with more than a hint of her youthful beauty, fussed around her five daughters like a mother hen inspecting her chicks, offering comments, advice and chastisement with little regard for their content or intended audience. "Jane, stand up straight, dear, or no one will look at you. Lizzy, surely you aren't wearing those shoes? Oh well, it is too late to change them now. Kitty, dear, try not to trail Lydia all evening. Leave your sister some freedom to flirt. Mary, if you smile more, it will distract from your spots. Lydia, the lace on your fichu is uneven. Pull it down a bit. There, don't you look the lady now!"

At last the carriage arrived and the six women bundled inside. The younger girls, primarily Lydia and Kitty, chatted ceaselessly about who might attend, how many feathers Mr. Bingley's sister would have in her coiffure, and whether there would be ice served. Mary attempted to involve herself in the conversation, but was ignored by her younger sisters, and she resorted to staring out of the window, only to be chastised afresh by her mother. Jane seemed unusually silent during the short drive, although Lizzy surmised the cause of her dear sister's distraction, and resolved to let her be.

At a distance of only one mile, the drive took very little time, and within moments the Bennet ladies were standing in the great hall, greeting acquaintances and awaiting the first chords of music that would announce the dancing. Lizzy immediately spotted her dear friend Charlotte Lucas, standing by her mother, and with a pat on Jane's forearm, left her sister to make her way to her friend.

"Have you heard, Lizzy?" Charlotte gushed. "Mr. Bingley has company staying with him at Netherfield Park, and he is to bring them this evening. One is the son of an earl, no less! How splendid if he were to ask one of us to dance! Do you think I look suitably elegant to dance with the son of an earl?"

She spun in a slow circle, allowing her companion to admire her dress. Charlotte would never be considered beautiful, or even pretty, and she had passed by the years when youth can atone for lack of pulchritude; but her plain face was not unappealing in its own way, and her poise and good sense made up for her unremarkable features. And her dress, Lizzy gladly admitted, was lovely indeed. A skilled seamstress, Charlotte was able to copy the fashions she saw in the magazines from London, and could transform the simplest shift into a stunning gown.

"You look well indeed, Charlotte!" Lizzy hugged her friend, careful not to crush the gown. "An earl's son could do worse than ask you to partner him on the dance floor. If he is a man of education and sense, he will certainly wish for a second dance as well, for you would be sure to charm him with your conversation."

"You tease me, Lizzy! But I should be happy to be asked for a dance at least once this evening, even if not by the honourable gentleman, whoever he may be!" She paused to scan the room. "I do not see anybody from the Netherfield party yet. I do hope they arrive soon, for I am most curious to see who else arrives with Mr. Bingley. Shall he offer for Jane tonight, do you think? She had best accept him immediately. I know some ladies think it fashion to refuse at first the man they mean to accept, but that would never do. He might be discouraged and seek elsewhere without giving her the chance to reconsider and change her mind."

Lizzy laughed, "Oh, Charlotte, always the practical one! I am certain that should Mr. Bingley ask, Jane will be only too happy to accept him at once. Indeed, even should her lips form the word 'No,' her eyes would surely give away her true thoughts."

At that moment, the band leader raised his fiddle and the musicians began the strains leading into the first dance. As she had expected, Lizzy had not been asked to dance. There were more ladies than men present that evening, and she had been standing in a corner, talking to Charlotte, whilst people were forming into couples. She felt content to remain by the wall and watch, since she had no pressing desire to stand up with any one particular person, no matter how much she might enjoy dancing as an activity. The music swelled, just barely audible above the growing hum of conversation, and the dancers in the centre of the room formed and reformed the patterns of their well-learned steps. Lizzy thought she spied Jane in the midst of the crowds on the floor, possibly dancing with Charlotte's older brother, but the room was crowded and she could not be certain.

Then, as the final chords of the first dance faded away, the great doors to the assembly room were flung open and Mr. Bingley stepped brightly into the space, his usual smile affixed to his face, his eyes alight with good humour and delight. His sister, looking less pleased at her situation, stood beside him, garbed in the finest frock from London and ornamented with dazzling jewels. Lizzy heard one of her younger sisters whisper loudly, "Seven feathers! I was right!" but her attention was drawn, rather, to the two men standing just behind Mr. Bingley.

The first of the two to catch her eye was a splendidly dressed officer, the gold braid and brass buttons reflecting the light of the many candles that illuminated the room, his epaulets calling attention to broad shoulders. He did not wear his sword, as befit the activities of the dance floor, but fading bruises on his face and a black patch over one eye announced to the world that this was not a back-office soldier, but rather a man who had seen action. Although not quite handsome, his golden hair and broad smile nevertheless made him an immediate favourite amongst everyone who sought a partner for a dance or for a daughter.

To his side, and a step or two behind, stood a tall dour-looking man. Dark hair and eyes topped a handsome face, but his expression was nothing like the officer's. His brow was furrowed and his eyes narrow, and no trace of a smile could be seen. Suddenly intrigued by this brooding spectre, Lizzy could not help but observe his stance. Lingering behind the others and leaning slightly backwards with his arms rigidly at his sides, he seemed most reluctant to enter the room. He would be no happy addition to the assembly!

"Which is the earl's son?" Lizzy whispered into Charlotte's ear. "Surely not the officer. He seems much too pleased to be seen in such a fashion-poor place as this! It must be the other one, the tall gentleman. His is exactly the face I should expect from an overbred aristocrat accustomed only to the finest frills of London's society!"

But her supposition was soon countered when Mr. Bingley descended upon the small group after the set had concluded. Jane's partner had brought her to where Lizzy and Charlotte were talking, and it was thither that Bingley rushed as soon as the floor cleared.

"Miss Bennet," he bowed deeply and took Jane's hand to kiss. "Miss Elizabeth, Miss Lucas," he greeted the ladies, then turned to Charlotte's brother and shook his hand. "You must meet my companions, come,

come!" He placed Jane's hand on his forearm and covered it firmly with his own and led the ladies and John Lucas to where the newcomers still stood near the door to make the introductions.

The cheerful officer was, contrary to Lizzy's expectations, the earl's son. "Colonel Fitzwilliam," Bingley presented his friend, "recently returned to England's fine shores from Kingston, Jamaica."

The colonel bowed deeply and smiled even more widely. Bingley then introduced his other companion, and once more Lizzy's interest was piqued. The tall man's face was no less handsome in closer proximity, but neither was it less forbidding. He practically scowled, and hardly bowed his head as Bingley presented him as "Professor Darcy, of Oxford and Pemberley." Then he continued, "Colonel, Darcy, allow me to introduce to you Miss Charlotte Lucas, daughter of Sir William, whom you have just met, and Miss Elizabeth Bennet, sister to Jane." He beamed at Jane and placed a hand over hers once more as it rested on his forearm.

The colonel's greeting was everything polite and amiable, and he kissed each lady on the back of the hand as if they were duchesses. Both blushed. He then turned to Charlotte, clearly the senior of the two, and requested a set of dances. She wasted no time in accepting and sent a quick and radiant grin to Lizzy. If the others had expected the professor to request Lizzy's hand for a set, they were disappointed. He merely stood, ill at ease and stony in demeanour, until Jane said something to make the others smile, turning the conversation to something pleasant until the next set began and the colonel led a very pleased Charlotte to join the dance.

Elizabeth had only half-expected the professor to ask her to dance. It would, of course, have been the polite and customary thing to do, but it was clear at once to Lizzy that *customary* and *expected* were terms seldom applied to the dour man. Bingley's eyes bored into the professor's own and he gestured slightly with his head, but Darcy merely wrinkled his nose and straightened his back before staring into the distance. For a moment Lizzy wondered if he were a cleric, unused to the company of women, but the man's very fashionable and elegant garb did not quite conform to that notion. Perhaps, she mused as she schooled her expression, he was merely rude.

Bingley had the good grace to turn white and whisper something rather short in his friend's ear, but to no avail. Darcy merely stood as still as a rock within a burbling river. Bingley rolled his eyes heavenward and grinned in apology to Elizabeth, and seemed about to ask her to partner him for the set when Caroline appeared beside him as if from nowhere.

Beside her elegant and beautifully dressed form, Lizzy was all too aware of her own inadequacies. Her dress was pretty and expertly cut to best display her figure, but it was not the product of London's finest dressmakers. The sleeves were the wrong length, the lace trim last season's colours. Nor was her hair done up in the elaborate twists and coils that must have taken Caroline's maid hours to accomplish. This was not Elizabeth's first encounter with Miss Bingley, but on each occasion that they were in each other's company, Caroline made certain somehow to disparage her. Lizzy found these constant attempts mildly amusing, but they annoyed her nonetheless.

Now Caroline's eyes scraped over Lizzy's form, then alighted with more pleasure on the others in the party. "Oh, Charles, there you are. How lovely to see you, Jane," she curtseyed gracefully, "and Eliza," less gracefully. She scanned Lizzy once more and turned up her nose before addressing her brother. "Charles, you must speak at once to Sir William about some questions he had about the management of your livestock on the estate. He asked me to find you." She then, at last, faced the final member of the small group. "And Professor Darcy," she batted her kohl-blackened eyelashes at the stern man, "I believe it is our dance." She stared at him with a fixed and determined smile.

Darcy reared back subtly and blinked his eyes. This dance was as much a surprise to him as to everyone else in the room, but he dutifully offered Miss Bingley his arm and escorted her to join the others in their neat rows. Bingley bowed and scurried off to find Sir William, Jane's hand still firmly attached to his arm, leaving Lizzy alone. She rolled her eyes, and not being one formed for melancholy, laughed at her situation.

"Such is your lot, Elizabeth!" she chuckled to herself, "Always to be on the outside staring in. Perhaps if I accept Lady Grant's offer, I shall not be forced to remain always at the sides."

As she enjoyed the music and watched the dancers, she contemplated further her aunt's invitation. Spending that much time with her beloved relation and the charming Lady Grant was an incentive in itself. For such a treat alone she would happily leave her family home for some months. Further, she would enjoy a season in London, for the music and art and lectures and libraries more, perhaps, than for the possibility of finding a husband. Convinced that only the deepest love would tempt her into matrimony, she had long resigned herself to being her sisters' children's favourite aunt instead of being a wife and mother to her own family. Still, in the greater society of London, who knows what charming men might be waiting to captivate her with their wit and intelligence. With the addition to her dowry, thanks to the Grants, she would be seen as an eligible match for many a well-heeled young man. If such men existed, she would certainly not pass up the opportunity to meet them, even if she were not quite as committed to the hunt as some might be.

Yes, she had decided, she would definitely accept the invitation. The only questions remaining were whether Jane would join her, and what she might wear until a new wardrobe could be procured that would meet the standards of the *bon ton*.

The dance ended and Colonel Fitzwilliam escorted Charlotte back to Lizzy's side. "If I am so fortunate as to find a spot on your card, Miss Elizabeth, may I request a set of you as well?" he asked. His smile had not left his face for a moment, and Lizzy could see genuine good cheer in his regard, not the feigned simpers and smiles that graced Caroline Bingley's visage. The expression worn by her friend, Charlotte, also suggested that the colonel was very good company, and Lizzy most happily accepted.

"I shall procure some refreshments for both of you," the colonel purred, "and then shall come to claim my dance. Ladies," he offered a deep bow and melted into the crowd in pursuit of something to drink.

"He is certainly charming!" Lizzy commented to her friend. "Does he dance as well as he flirts?"

Charlotte smiled. "I have stood up with worse, to be sure! I would not say 'no' were he to ask again. And yes, he is most pleasant to converse with. I shall have to ensure that he is invited to all the card parties and soirees I can, so I can hear more about his adventures in the West Indies."

Lizzy closed her eyes and smiled. "I am certain he has so much of interest to say, and I have no doubts that he is fascinating and witty, but I could sit and listen to his voice for hours, no matter what he were saying. He speaks so beautifully, does he not? I wonder if he sings as well."

"The colonel does speak most beautifully," Charlotte agreed. "Even I dared comment upon it. He admitted to being singled out to sing in his church as a lad and having some training in matters musical."

"You spoke of this whilst you danced? I am surprised you had time to contemplate the steps."

"Silly Lizzy!" Charlotte blushed. "We talked of that and more. It seems his vocal training and quick ear has done much for his career. He is most interested in philology and dialect, and one reason he was posted to Jamaica is his ability to learn languages and converse with people of different tongues and classes. He explained it in rather technical terms, but it seems the colonel is something of an actor and a mimic."

"An actor, I can well believe," Lizzy grinned, "but he seems rather too sincere to be a mimic."

"You wilfully mistake me, Lizzy!" Charlotte flicked playfully at her friend's arm. "It is a bit of a family trait, it seems. Did you know that Professor Darcy is his cousin?" Lizzy's eyes widened in surprise, but she bade Charlotte continue. "The professor is an expert in accent and dialect, and has published several treatises, and is invited to lecture here in England as well as in France and Germany, on his area of speciality."

"Well," Lizzy countered, "it is a good thing that he is proficient in his field, for were he to be a supposed expert on etiquette, he should be the biggest charlatan that ever lived."

"Colonel Fitzwilliam told me," Charlotte added *sotto voce*, "that the professor also tutors members of the merchant class to affect the speech patterns and manners of the elite. Even with great funds, those who wish to rise into the gentry face significant disdain at the hands of the upper classes when they attempt to enter into society. They are sneered at for their dirt-covered manners and low accents. Professor Darcy teaches them these skills, that they may better ease their way into the society they desire."

"How fascinating!" Lizzy replied. "He clearly knows his manners, then, even if he does not mind them." She looked up. "Ah, here comes the colonel with our drinks. I believe I should prefer *his* company, even though he is not a professor."

Charlotte was correct. The colonel was a fine dancer and a charming companion. During their two dances, he inquired most politely after Lizzy's family, learned about her favourite books, and complimented her on her poise and grace. As well, he confirmed her supposition that he was known to sing when slightly drunk, and was able to tell her enough about his time in the Indies that she, too, was eager to hear more.

Although he flirted shamelessly with her, it was all within the bounds of taste and propriety, never crossing that intangible boundary. She knew she would certainly enjoy the colonel's company as long as he resided at Netherfield, while also being quite certain that any flirtation would remain purely within the realm of friendliness. A man such as he must have little independent income, and his family would insist that as well as being wealthy, any lady whom he might consider could be no less than the daughter of a baronet. This satisfied her, for having resolved to accept the offer of a London season, she had no wish to muddy the waters with an attraction. More than pleased with the situation, she returned at last to Charlotte's side with a great smile and only complimentary words about the colonel.

She was happily contemplating these matters when she heard to the side door to the supper room open a short distance away. Turning her head to determine the import of the sound, she noticed Jane emerge, followed closely by Mr. Bingley. Jane's glowing smile and bright eyes left no doubt as to what had transpired, and Mr. Bingley's grin, if it was at all possible, was even wider than usual. Spying Lizzy, Jane hurried over to her side, leaving Mr. Bingley to defend himself against his friend, the professor, who stood disapprovingly by the wall.

"Oh, Lizzy! Dear Charlotte!" Jane gushed as she approached, "I am so happy! Why can every one not be this happy? Oh, it is wonderful, so wonderful. He said he had thought to wait some days, until we might be alone at Longbourn, but he saw me tonight and could wait no longer before asking for my hand! He had no planned speech, no fancy words, but he spoke simply and from the heart, and oh, how I love him, Lizzy! We shall be so happy together!"

Hugs and congratulations ensued, but Jane urged restraint. "We cannot be public about our engagement until Charles speaks to Papa," she cautioned. "I know I do not require his consent, but Charles insists. He wishes to be the ideal son-in-law."

"Of that you need never fear! He will do everything to oblige Papa through his good and happy manners, and merely by marrying you and being rich will he forever enamour himself to Mama!"

Jane paled. "Oh, Mama... Yes, I had better warn him!"

"Come, lead me to your intended," Lizzy begged her sister. "Although it is not yet official, I feel I must congratulate him as soon as I might. I could not be happier for you!"

"Later, perhaps, Lizzy. Whilst we know this will not remain secret, if you seek him out now, the news will be about the room within a minute. But I shall tell him you wish to speak to him, and of what, and he will be pleased. Oh, he is the best of men! I am so happy!"

Letting her sister float off on her cloud of elation, Elizabeth and Charlotte wandered off in the direction of the refreshments table, hoping for another glass of something cool to offset the heat of the over-populated room. They had achieved their aim, and were seeking chairs upon which to sit whilst enjoying their drinks when they heard, and then saw, Mr. Bingley a short distance away, talking to the professor.

"Come, Darcy," said he, "I must have you dance, or at least try to engage someone in conversation. I hate to see you standing about by yourself in this stupid manner. You had much better dance."

"I certainly shall not," came the clipped reply. With Charlotte's revelations about the colonel still fresh in her mind, Lizzy found herself paying close attention to the professor's voice. To her chagrin, she found it most mellifluous and rich, his accent ideal, each syllable pure and perfect.

But his words were cold and bitter. "You know how I detest dancing," he said, "unless I am particularly acquainted with my partner, and even then it is a chore. At such an assembly as this, it would be insupportable. Your sister is engaged, and I should not wish to dance with her a second time, lest I raise expectations where there ought to be none. There is not another woman in the room whom it would not be a punishment to me to stand up with."

"You are being ridiculous!" cried Bingley, "Upon my honour I never met with so many pleasant girls in my life. They are not only uncommonly pretty, but lively and pleasant company as well. None as sweet as my Jane, perhaps, but—"

"*Your* Jane," Darcy emphasised the word, "is the only handsome girl in the room, and I will grant, the sweetest. I shall even overlook her atrocious accent in favour of her pleasant nature, for she seems to make you happy."

"You, my friend, are a snob!" Bingley huffed, although his smile never faltered. "I find nothing amiss in her accent, for she has no need to be ashamed of her country home. And before you begin, her country manners are delightful as well. When I am with her, I realise how I always feel I am an actor on a stage when in London. Here, with dear Jane and in this friendly village, I can be myself without a care to who might be judging me or trying to catch out some hints to my low origins. And Jane, Jane... Oh, Darcy, is she not the most beautiful creature you have ever beheld? But look, there is one of her sisters. You met Miss Elizabeth earlier. She is sitting down behind you. She is very pretty too, and very agreeable. Do ask her to dance. She is most lively and shall keep you amused if you allow yourself to enjoy her company. At least talk to her, take the measure of her accent, if such things are what pass for your entertainment. Come, let us approach her."

Turning around, Darcy looked for a moment at Elizabeth, till catching her eye. He withdrew his own and said coldly, "She is tolerable, but her accent is not interesting enough to tempt me, nor do I wish to suffer through a dance with her country manners. And those rhotic vowels, while hardly an interesting specimen in these parts, are painful to my ears. Why, oh why can't the English teach their children how to speak? Look, Bingley, I am in no humour at present to give consequence to young ladies who are slighted by other men, no matter their regional dialects. You had better return to your betrothed and enjoy her smiles, for you are wasting your time with me."

With an exasperated huff, and a slight lessening of his smile, Bingley did just as his friend bade him, and Professor Darcy, too, soon stalked off, leaving Elizabeth alone with Charlotte, and with no good opinion of the great professor.

# Three
## An Uncomfortable Revelation

Mr. Bingley arrived at Longbourn early the following morning. Lizzy and Jane were in the garden gathering flowers, and Lizzy stepped back to allow her sister a moment with her intended before the gentleman entered the house to deal with a very important matter. Bingley's interview with Mr. Bennet was conducted with great alacrity and to the satisfaction of all parties, and Jane was soon surrounded by the mob of her sisters all singing their good wishes, governed over by their mother, singing of her own great fortune in her eldest daughter's success, whilst Lizzy cringed at every syllable.

"Oh, we are saved, we are saved! When your father dies, Jane, we shall not be cast out into the hedgerows, but your Mr. Bingley will save us all. I shall have to ensure that I have enough black lace and trim to mourn suitably in such a grand house as his. Oh, how clever you were to be born so beautiful that Mr. Bingley should wish to marry you. Oh, we are saved!"

All the while, the man in question stood off to the side, blushing and looking a bit aghast at his future mother's pronouncements. Seeing his discomfort, Lizzy strove to assure him that Mrs. Bennet's words were seldom thought through. "She has been so worried for so long that all she can think of now is a happier future. She really is most delighted to have you for a son. And I know you shall make my dear sister very happy, and that delights me." Bingley's answering smile did not quite reach his eyes and Lizzy could see his discomfort remained, but he acknowledged the situation with the good grace that was his nature.

Seeing her mother draw breath to engage upon another ill-advised speech, Lizzy attempted to rescue the situation. "Oh, are those dark clouds I see in the distance? Come, let us all enjoy this wonderful day outside, for the sky above is still clear. Once the rains begin, it might be many days before we have the opportunity to walk again." Jane sighed her relief, and Bingley immediately proclaimed this a splendid idea as he dashed off to retrieve his hat.

The group had walked no more than a few yards when Lydia suggested that she and Kitty might walk into town. This, the older sisters encouraged, for the girls' fussing had not ceased with the remove to the outdoors. Neither did Lizzy object when Mary took herself to the bench under the parlour window to read. Now Lizzy only had to find her own excuse to wander off and the two lovers would at last be left in some semblance of privacy.

As she began to mention something about needing to respond to her aunt's letter, however, Jane burst out, "Oh, the invitation to London! Now that Charles and I are engaged, of course I will not go, but you must, Lizzy! Think of what an adventure it will be." She quickly summarised the circumstances behind the invitation to her betrothed, who commented that Lizzy must go indeed.

"We shall likely spend time in London after our wedding, and we would be most forlorn should you not visit us often and join us as we enjoy the city. I shall be proud to introduce you as my sister."

"Yes, I know I shall miss you greatly," Jane added, "but I shall be so much comforted were you to be in Town as well."

Lizzy offered an easy smile. "I had already resolved to accept, but your entreaties have redoubled my commitment to agree to the plan. And now I should not worry about whether to wait for your decision before writing my reply. We need only settle on the specifics. But..." she paused for a moment and her brow furrowed. "Do you really think the plan wise? I do long to spend the time in London, but surely there is no hope for Aunt Gardiner and Lady Grant to find me a husband. I am, after all, a country girl, and not one of the sophisticated ladies any worthwhile gentleman would expect in the city. I should be a rough stone in a field of polished diamonds." Professor Darcy's comments at the assembly about her Hertfordshire accent still rang in her ears, no matter how she strove to ignore them.

"Lizzy," Jane sounded concerned, "What has come over you? You know that anyone who is worthy of you will care little for your country ways once he sees the gem that is inside you. You will see. And your manners are perfectly proper, if not the style of the city."

Bingley added his agreement, and at last Elizabeth was able to return to the house to write her letter, and to leave Jane and Charles alone in the garden.

In due time the letter was written and sent. An enthusiastic reply came within days: Lady Grant was delighted to hear about Jane's engagement, and she now had determined even more strongly to find a wonderful husband for Lizzy. To that end, she proposed that Lizzy be presented at court, to ensure a spectacular London debut. The letter outlined in some detail the preparations required for such a grand occasion, and the lengthy litany rather horrified Lizzy. She had been prepared for a series of balls and card parties and soirees; the very thought of these new plans set her heart racing and sent ice through her veins. The notion of all that fuss and ado was somehow rather alarming, and she felt, for the first time, a semblance of real inadequacy and trepidation.

It was only the recollection of London's other delights—the museums and libraries and concerts and public lectures—that settled her mind somewhat, and she resolved to think seriously of Lady Grant's latest suggestion. *It is all your choice, of course, but think how it will secure your place in society*, her friend had written. With a deep breath, Lizzy resigned herself to her fate.

⊂⊃⊂⊃

The family were partaking of breakfast early the following week when a note arrived for Jane. "Oh, do read it, for it must be from dear Mr. Bingley!" Mrs. Bennet exclaimed over her eggs.

"Mama, it might be a personal matter, or some subject requiring privacy!" Lizzy warned. But her mother waved her hand dismissively.

"Nonsense, Lizzy. Let us hear what Mr. Bingley has to say. He will be brother to you all, and nothing he can write need be kept from us. Read it, Jane."

Nothing Lizzy could say would satisfy her mother, and consequently the note was read.

"Dearest Jane..."

"Oh, he calls you 'dearest.' How romantic! He declares himself so openly!" Mrs. Bennet interrupted almost before Jane could complete the salutation.

"No, Mama, it is not from Charles, but from Caroline."

"Oh. Well, I am certain he told her to call you dearest."

Lizzy rolled her eyes, but Jane continued reading with a calm and pleasant expression.

"'Dearest Jane,'" she read, "'My sister, Mrs. Hurst, has arrived at Netherfield from London and wishes to be made known to me immediately. Charles cannot speak a word of ill of you, and so she must see you for herself.'"

"What is that supposed to mean?" Lizzy whispered. Jane ignored her and continued reading.

"'It would please us were you to come to Netherfield to pass the day with us. Mr. Hurst proposes to go out hunting with the other men; perhaps if there is a good port or some fine vintage of wine at dinner, he will join us at that time. I am finding myself quite taxed in my role keeping house for Charles; Netherfield is rather busy, but I shall prove myself more than adequate to the task. We expect you this morning.

"'Your future sister,

"'Caroline'"

"She really means you to come at once, with no previous arrangement? What if you had already made plans?" Lizzy wrinkled her nose in displeasure. "She is no lady, despite the airs she gives herself!"

"Now Lizzy," her sister placated, "I have no other engagements, and I shall be part of the family soon. Caroline means no ill; it is only that she is not accustomed to our manners."

"You are too good and sweet, Jane!"

Mrs. Bennet had listened to the exchange with narrowed eyes, and she now peered out through the lace window-dressing. "You had better go at once, Jane, for the weather is rainy of late. It is clear now, but if you tarry, you will surely be caught outside. I see heavy clouds approaching."

"I was to ask Papa for the carriage."

"There is no need to impress Mr. Bingley now, for it is too late for him to withdraw his offer. I am going to visit Lady Lucas in the carriage. You may ride."

Jane left as soon as she was able, but the rains came quickly upon her departure, and Lizzy was not surprised to hear a messenger arrive some hours later with a note from Caroline Bingley. Jane had been caught in the shower and had taken mildly ill; a valise with her night clothes and some necessities was requested. The messenger soon departed with the bag, but Lizzy felt ill at ease, and could not rest until she had had resolved to see for herself how Jane fared the moment the weather cleared.

Fortunately for her plans, the following morning saw a break in the rain. After several days of sporadically inclement weather, she found herself more than happy to take her exercise and walk the three miles between the houses to ask after her sister, caring little about the muddy fields and pastures. She arrived as the residents of Netherfield were finishing their breakfast. She was ushered into the parlour by a butler with a stern face but a glint in his eye, and there she greeted the Bingleys and their guests and made her inquiries.

Mr. Bingley leapt to his feet. "Oh, my poor Jane! Caroline said that she is in good spirits, but is still feverish, with a very sore throat and head. Come, let me take you to her room, where she is being tended by a maid." He called over a servant to request that a tray be brought for Miss Elizabeth and hastened to lead her upstairs.

Lizzy curtseyed and offered her thanks, and was requested by Colonel Fitzwilliam and Professor Darcy to convey their best wishes to the patient. Caroline Bingley and the Hursts said nothing at all.

RIANA EVERLY
Darcy watched the door close behind Elizabeth. Her words rang in his ears, but somehow her accent did not bother him this morning. He reflected with a start that he had rather taken pleasure in the sound of her voice.

These musings were cut short, for the moment the door clicked shut, Caroline began to exclaim over Miss Elizabeth's atrocious appearance. "I would hardly have believed it if I had not seen it!" She smoothed a hand over her perfectly dressed hair. "To have walked all that distance so early in the day, and in such dirty weather, and all alone—why, it is almost incredible. And to think that she should deign to appear before Charles, the master of the house, and us, his guests, in such disarray even more so! Oh, what a sorry lot those Bennets are. But it is," she condescended, "commendable that such compassion should exist between sisters, and I suppose I will forgive Eliza all her other faults on that basis alone." She batted her eyes at Darcy, as if to recommend herself to him on the basis of her charitable words.

Having once spoken so magnanimously, Caroline returned to her conversation with Mrs. Hurst.

"And you, Darcy?" asked his cousin. "What thought you of Miss Elizabeth this morning? She is really rather pretty, I find."

Darcy was feeling slightly less grumpy than usual, having slept quite well in the extremely comfortable bed in his chambers. A ride at dawn through the countryside—which he was nearly ready to admit was quite lovely—followed by hot, fresh coffee, had brought him almost to a point of cheerfulness. As such, he did not reflect on Miss Elizabeth's muddy boots and petticoats, nor on the doubtful necessity of the occasion justifying her coming so far alone, but rather on the brilliancy which the exercise had given to her complexion. Not even her rhotic vowels or plosive consonants had vexed him this morning, although he refrained from mentioning that to the colonel.

In fact, he voiced almost none of these thoughts. "She looked well," he stated with a blank expression. "Her face was alight from her walk. It becomes her."

"It does so," laughed the colonel. "If Miss Bennet is as ill as the apothecary suggested, I imagine Miss Elizabeth will be here some days. Bingley will never stand for having Jane left without her beloved sister. I suggest, Fitz, that you try to find those manners you drill so solidly into your students, for you shall need use of them yourself whilst Miss Elizabeth is in our midst."

Colonel Fitzwilliam's guess was correct. Charles had not been back in the parlour for five minutes before he announced that Elizabeth must stay until Jane was quite recovered.

For some reason this both bothered and intrigued Darcy; he had no desire to have to feign politeness for a stranger he deemed so inconsequential, and yet something about her fascinated him. It could not be her accent; that was quite plebeian and ordinary, nothing like those fascinating Welsh fisherfolk in the Irish Sea. Was it the quality of her voice that had captured his attention? Perhaps. He must think on it later. But now, Charles' voice quite interrupted his thoughts.

"I must send a carriage to Longbourn immediately," his friend announced to the room. "The ladies will require a trunk for a stay of several days' duration. And I must set up the adjoining room for Miss Elizabeth, for she will wish to be close to her sister." He paced between the fireplace and the bright windows as he spoke, and Darcy had to fight the urge to push his friend into a chair to still him.

Caroline did not suppress her urge. "Do stop pacing, Charles. You are quite unsettling me. Besides, why should Eliza stay? Are we not almost sisters with dear Jane? Surely Louisa and I can take care of her every bit as well as can Eliza." Her eyes narrowed as she pronounced the name. "It will be no hardship for me to provide such superior care as only a well-bred woman can do." She turned her gaze to Darcy and simpered.

"Caroline, I really do think—" Charles began, but his words were interrupted immediately.

"Don't be silly, Charles. Whatever does Eliza have to offer that I do not? She is merely a peasant, after all, no matter her father's estate. She will likely have poor Jane's stars read by an astrologer and then will apply boar's bile to the soles of her feet when the moon is new. Such are the ways of the country, are they not?"

"Not in my part of the country." Darcy had not meant to respond, but found the words coming of their own volition, "Recall, Pemberley is far further removed from the sophistication of London than is Meryton." He found his patience for Caroline Bingley—limited at the best of times—was particularly short now. The same humours that had revealed Elizabeth Bennet's simple prettiness this morning had also exacerbated Caroline's faults, and he found her malicious comments particularly unbecoming.

It seemed he was not the only one so bothered. "You speak nonsense, Caroline!" her brother informed her, his voice tight. "Miss Elizabeth is a well-educated young woman, and you have met Mr. Jones from the village apothecary. He is as sensible a man as ever I have encountered, and is expert in the latest medical information. He will advise Miss Elizabeth on how best to care for Jane, and she will do so most admirably, I am sure."

"But Charles—"

"Enough whining, Caroline. Elizabeth is Jane's sister. Jane is ill and needs the comfort of familiarity to rest most easily. With your *admirable*," he stressed the word, "care, Jane would feel the need to be on her best manners, and could not rest and sleep as she ought. My mind is quite made up."

"Surely Professor Darcy agrees with me," Caroline tried one last time. "Explain to him how much better it would be were Eliza to return home," she batted her lashes.

"Your brother is correct." He knew he disappointed her as he turned traitor to her wishes, but cared little. "Miss Bennet will have many years to grow comfortable in your company, but now she needs her sister's care. Your visits will, I do believe, be welcome, but it is Miss Elizabeth who will give her comfort."

Caroline narrowed her eyes and straightened the lines of her fashionable frock. "If that is your thought on the matter, how can I protest it? Eliza shall be made welcome here, for all that I wish her home. She is sweet enough, but not of our class, is she Colonel?"

The colonel said nothing, and merely raised his eyebrows at Darcy. Darcy could almost hear his thoughts: The nerve of the woman, to suggest that she, born to a merchant family and only a single generation from the stain of trade, were somehow closer in rank to the second son of an earl than was the daughter of a hereditary gentleman whose family had held the land for centuries! Richard was no stickler for the rigidities of societal hierarchy, but Darcy knew he could only be astounded at Caroline's assessment.

Allowing his cousin to retain his pride in silence, Darcy returned, "Miss Eliza Bennet is everything that is proper and genteel, and a lady by birth. And she is soon to be your sister via means of Jane's marriage to your brother." Then, having realised that he had spoken kindly of someone for more than a word or two, he bowed and left the room without a further comment. He could feel the eyes of every other person in the room upon his back, with the sole exception of Mr. Hurst, who had said not a word through the entire exchange, and who most likely thought only of his breakfast.

CREO

Lizzy spent much of the day with Jane, who was indeed comforted by the presence of her most beloved sister and who slept fitfully on and off under the worried eye of her nursemaid. A light luncheon was brought up for both sisters—breads and cheese for Lizzy and nourishing broth for Jane—but a note from Caroline in the late afternoon indicated that Miss Eliza was expected to join the others for dinner. As her trunks had arrived and included suitable clothing, Lizzy had no choice but to acquiesce.

At half past six the knock came summoning her to the dinner table, and Elizabeth made her way downstairs to find the others. Not having dined before at Netherfield, she had some difficulty finding the proper room, and in her explorations, came upon a door that stood ajar. She had her hand ready to settle onto the door handle to enter the room when she overheard Miss Bingley and her sister, Mrs. Hurst, conversing within. Elizabeth was about to leave immediately, loath to overhear a private conversation, when she heard her name mentioned. As much as her mind told her to retreat, her feet refused to obey.

"Jane Bennet is really a very sweet girl," Caroline was saying, "and I am glad with all my heart that she is well settled, but with such a father and mother, and such low connections, I'm afraid there is little chance for the other sisters, even the inestimable Eliza. Her eyes might be bright, as dear Darcy says, but she has no conversation, no style, no taste, and little beauty. And her manners!"

"Oh, these country manners!" Mrs. Hurst agreed, her voice an echo of Caroline's. "Charles might find them charming, but really, they are most unsuitable even for the lowest society in Town. And her accent! No matter how she might puff herself up, she gives herself away every time she opens her mouth."

"La, it is dreadful, is it not? To be forever labelled as a country rustic! And even were she from London, her connexions there are even worse!" Caroline tittered. "Their uncle is an attorney in Meryton, and they have another who lives somewhere near Cheapside!" She lowered her voice and whispered loudly, "He is a merchant!"

"Shocking! Too very unfortunate!" came Mrs. Hurst's injured reply. "Whatever was Charles thinking, attaching himself to a family like that? No, it is too late to do anything about Jane, but the other girls... such a pity."

At that moment a bell sounded somewhere, and the conversation ceased. Lizzy could hear the ladies rising from their seats, and she quickly stepped back into the hallway, hoping to look as if she had just arrived from the stairs. As she arranged her features into a look of pleasant indifference, the Bingley sisters emerged from their *tête-à-tête*, and, seeing her, adopted their insincere smiles and guided her to the correct room, chattering away.

But Lizzy heard almost nothing they said.

Was it true? Were they correct? Was she so cruelly marked as they suggested? The Bennets had never employed a governess for their five daughters, and without benefit of a formal education, they were also without benefit of having been taught the speech of the upper classes. Papa sounded like the gentleman he was, but as anybody knows, children will adopt the accent of their community and not of their parents, and Mama sounded very much like every other middle-class mama in the county. No matter their birth and status as gentlewomen, they had grown up as denizens of the village, and sounded every inch the part.

Until this very moment, Lizzy had not realised how her country accent might affect her future. Now, all of a sudden, she became aware of every sound she made. Every syllable, every consonant, every vowel, marked her as unfit for genteel society. With a sensation of dread, she apprehended that as much as she and her upbringing were disparaged here, in this country estate by the daughters of a mere tradesman, so much more would she be once thrust into the midst of a season in Town. How should she act? She must write to Aunt Gardiner immediately, rescinding her agreement to the plan and begging the forgiveness of a favourite aunt and dear friend. She could not subject herself to such humiliation, nor could she expect her friend to lavish such expenses upon her with no chance at all of success. It was hopeless!

These unhappy thoughts were interrupted as they entered the dining room, for Mr. Bingley came up to her immediately and asked after Jane. Feigning calmness, Lizzy assured him that Jane was sleeping comfortably, despite still being quite unwell. Bingley's concern was echoed by Colonel Fitzwilliam, and even the dour Professor Darcy made his good wishes known. "Sleep is a great cure," he stated, "and I am relieved that your sister is comfortable. I beg you convey my further sentiments for her quick recovery."

Now attuned to the nuances and speech and accent, Lizzy listened even more carefully to the professor's carefully modulated accent. She was still smarting from his rude comment at the assembly the week prior, and had no particular liking for the man, but she found herself increasingly enthralled by his voice. His words might not always be pleasant, but they sounded beautiful. What must it be like, she mused, to be able to speak like that?

She hardly spoke at dinner, embarrassed by her speech, although she recognised that by her silence she only reinforced Miss Bingley's contention that she had little conversation. Instead, she spent much time concentrating on the conversation of the others, listening not so much to what they said, but rather how they said it. Now that she was paying attention, she could see how her manners, though perfectly proper in the village, were woefully inadequate for Town. Worse, she became even more aware of how her provincial accent must sound compared to the crystal clear sounds uttered by the elite.

Suddenly she recalled a conversation she had enjoyed whilst dancing the week before. What had Colonel Fitzwilliam said about Professor Darcy? That he taught members of the lower classes to speak like their social superiors? She must find out for herself!

Deciding that she had already been labelled an impertinent girl with no pretensions to real class, she need have no cause to restrain herself and as the main course was coming to an end, she raised her voice and asked, "What is it, exactly, that you do in your field of study, Professor Darcy?"

The professor looked down his patrician nose at her and replied in haughty tones, "We are at the dawn of a new age, Miss Elizabeth. Times are changing, and men who might begin in Kentish Town with twenty pounds a year can end in Park Lane with twenty thousand." His eyes darted quickly towards Mr. Bingley, whose own fortune of a hundred thousand pounds, Lizzy knew, was achieved in just this fashion. "These newly wealthy men want to drop Kentish Town, but they give themselves away with every word. Now, I can teach them, through my art and skill, to speak not as they were, but as they wish themselves to be. I can teach them to move in society."

"Is that true?" These were the first words Mr. Hurst had uttered all night, so enraptured did he seem with the ragout set before him.

"Indeed it is," replied Colonel Fitzwilliam with the enthusiasm of one fully apprised of the professor's abilities. His own beautiful voice was surely approved of by his haughty cousin. "He has a remarkable history of success with people from all walks of life. I recall one young man, hardly a man, dragging himself up from the gutter and with an accent and vocabulary to match, and you would scarcely know him now! In fact, you have almost certainly heard his name, but would never know his origins."

"Do say more, Professor Darcy, for I am most intrigued," said Elizabeth.

"I see no reason to hide my talents," he preened. "I can take ever so lowly a creature, a flower girl for example, with her kerbstone English that will keep her in the gutter to the end of her days, and within three months pass her off as a duchess at an ambassador's garden party."

*Arrogant, insufferable man!* thought Lizzy, but she held her tongue and said only, "How fascinating!"

Mr. Bingley now took over the conversation and spoke volubly on his own great success as a student of the professor, recounting how he had learned to replace the broad and limiting sounds of his native Yorkshire accent with his current cultivated tones.

"Oh Lord, how dreadful it was at that," the professor laughed. Lizzy realised she had never before heard anything resembling joy or playfulness from him and was stunned by the sound. "The challenge we had, eh, Bingley, forcing those troublesome vowels backwards and eliminating the glottal stop from the middle of words."

"Oh, how true, Darcy! Even wairse," he intentionally reverted to his previous pronunciation, making the professor groan, "was leernin' to put oop with yair insistence tha' I add in them pesky consonan's at the ends o' wairds."

"'Words,' Charles, 'wuhhhhds.'"

"Aye, Dercy, 'wairds.'"

Bingley smiled impudently and the colonel roared with laughter, provoking disapproving glares from Miss Bingley and Mrs. Hurst.

"My sisters," Bingley informed Elizabeth in his new cultured accent, "were taught by a governess from a very young age and were sent to the best of schools. I was left to learn with local boys and a tutor until I was sent down to Cambridge. It was there that I met Darcy, who was completing his own studies at the time. He was already an expert in his field and was teaching classes, despite being only four years my senior and still enrolled as a student. He took pity on me for the teasing I suffered and took me on as a protégé, and I was fortunate enough to earn his friendship."

"I am all amazement, Mr. Bingley," Lizzy replied, "for I should never have known from your speech that you were not to the manor born. My congratulations, Professor Darcy, on your inestimable skill."

By now the meal had been consumed, and Miss Bingley stood immediately, suggesting that the ladies withdraw to leave the men to their port and cigars. Mr. Bingley seemed ready to suggest that they all retire, but Caroline seemed insistent on removing Elizabeth from the table. "You know you've been looking forward to trying that new port, Charles. Come, Eliza, I am certain you would not wish to deny the men their after-dinner comforts. We shall await them in the salon for coffee."

Seeing her chance, Lizzy suggested instead that she return upstairs to see to Jane, promising to rejoin the company later in the evening. Caroline was even more pleased at this suggestion, and the company parted ways accordingly.

The following day passed in much the same way. Jane slept ill through the night, but by morning her fever had broken and she was resting peacefully. Exhausted from her night tending to her sister, Lizzy stole out early for a walk in the cool air before taking some tea and toast and finding her own bed for an hour or two. Upon awakening she found Jane much improved and alert, and the sisters passed much of the day talking quietly.

When asked about her evening with the Bingleys and their guests, Lizzy found herself recounting the conversation she had unwittingly overheard between the Bingley sisters. "I hate to admit it," she concluded, "but they are correct. I would be a disaster in London, and I have resolved to write back to our aunt as soon as we are home and explain why I cannot accept after all."

"Surely not, Lizzy," Jane soothed. "You shall be valued for yourself wherever you go, and not for your country accent or country ways."

"No, Jane, it cannot be. You did not hear Miss Bingley and Mrs. Hurst as they spoke. Their words were cruel but true, and I know that I shall meet many more like them in London, far more than the gentler souls who might overlook my origins. I shall be tarred by their brush long before I even have the chance to prove my character."

Jane's lovely face fell as she considered these words. "But is there no hope, Lizzy? Surely there is some remedy..." She lit up as she said, "Why not ask Professor Darcy to help you? I know what he did for Charles, and he is widely considered a formidable expert in this area. You have a quick ear and are intelligent. I am certain he would know just what to do to let you move easily in the upper circles of society!"

*I can take even a flower girl, with her kerbstone English that will keep her in the gutter to the end of her days, and within three months pass her off as a duchess at an ambassador's garden party.*

Those had been Professor Darcy's words, and they reverberated through Elizabeth's head as readily as if she heard them spoken aloud. "Three months..."

"What do you say, Lizzy?"

"Three months! Last night, the professor boasted that he could transform a flower girl into a duchess in three months. I am hardly a flower girl, but I wonder..."

"Oh, Lizzy, it is perfect! I shall ask Charles to plead with him on your behalf! In fact, I shall do so this very day! I am feeling so much improved. Come, help me dress and let us go down for a short while right now, and perhaps I shall talk to Charles immediately! No, do not argue with me, Lizzy. It is for your own good. Now, which dress shall I wear?"

Jane's sojourn downstairs was of short duration, but Mr. Bingley was quite delighted to see her sufficiently recovered to make the attempt, and he was most solicitous of her health and comfort, taking her arm in his for a very short walk in the rose garden, after which he personally arranged the screens by the fire to ensure that she was suitably, but not too, warm. Wishing once more to give the couple some privacy, Lizzy announced that she wished to find something new to read in the library. Bingley promised to summon her, should Jane feel ill, and bade her take her time over his collection.

Upon achieving that room, however, Lizzy discovered that she was not alone, but that Colonel Fitzwilliam and Professor Darcy were seated in the large chairs by the window, engaged in an intense conversation.

"Perhaps you ought to consider Bingley's suggestion after all," the colonel was saying as she entered and made herself known, thereby preventing the professor from replying. The colonel rose and greeted her cheerfully, purposefully ignoring Darcy's scowl at the interruption to their conversation. "What a lovely surprise, Miss Eliza, to see you here. Are you well? And your sister? Excellent, excellent!" Without his eyepatch, which he had removed the previous evening to some remarks of surprise by Caroline, and with his bruises now almost completely faded, he looked the image of a jovial English nobleman, with his long features and fair colouring. "Please," he continued, "may I assist you in your search for a book? I have learned Bingley's library rather well in the time we have been here, and I may have some suggestions!"

Professor Darcy nodded his greeting and bowed slightly, but otherwise seemed somewhat bored by her presence.

Lizzy found a suitable volume and was about to depart when she looked again at the two men, and deciding that she might have no better opportunity to do so, resolved to speak to the professor immediately about Jane's idea.

"Professor Darcy," she began as she turned to face them directly. The colonel's eyebrows rose slightly at her forward address; the professor gazed into the middle distance, his eyes hooded, his jaw lax. "I wish to engage you to teach me to improve my accent."

Darcy gave a visible start and stopped still in his place with his eyes wide; even the colonel, normally so easy to adapt to any circumstances, stared at the young woman who made this statement.

"Teach you, you say? Why on earth would I wish to do that?" He had raised his chin and levelled a piercing gaze at her.

Elizabeth did not waver, nor did she back down. She had taken her first step and was determined in her efforts. "You did say that you are not above giving lessons. I have heard this from others, and I heard it from you, yourself, last night. I wish to take lessons. If you have condescended to teach upstarts from Kentish Town and men from merchant families like Mr. Bingley, you should have no objection to teaching a gentle-born woman such as myself." She kept a steady gaze on him and did not allow him to drop his eyes.

"Why on earth, madam, should you wish for speech lessons? Do you hope to better yourself in society? You are already of the first family in the area; do you wish to alienate your friends by putting on airs?"

"I do not wish to alienate my friends. I wish to be able to move in society in Town." There. She had said it.

"Miss Elizabeth," the colonel asked politely, "what do you mean? Is your father hoping to send you to London?"

"No, not he. My aunt—or rather, my aunt's sister—" She described her relationship to the newly raised baronet and his lady, and added, "Lady Grant has become a dear friend and with her husband's position and new estates, wishes to help me in society. They have offered to provide me with a home for a season and with the funds to outfit myself, as well as a generous increase to my dowry, but I have become all too aware of late that my manners and speech mark me as being of the country, and very much below all the other ladies of the circles in which I am expected to move. And so, Professor, I wish you to teach me to speak and act as they do."

Darcy tilted his head backwards slightly and impaled with her a hard stare. He rose to his feet and regarded her from his superior height, looking once more down his patrician nose. "And what," he demanded, "am I to receive for my efforts? I know your family's situation, Miss Eliza. You are hardly in a position to pay me the amount I usually receive for my efforts."

To this, Elizabeth had no answer. She began to stumble through a reply when the colonel leapt up suddenly and pulled Darcy aside, then whispered at some length into his ear. This monologue was interrupted at intervals by expressions such as "No. Absolutely not," and "You have got to be mad!" but at length these protestations lessened in ferocity and the forbidding head began to nod.

Slowly, Darcy walked back towards Elizabeth, a saturnine look in his dark eyes. "Miss Eliza," said he, "I believe I may accept your request. However, in return I have one of my own. It concerns your payment."

Lizzy was shocked. He could hardly mean....

"I wish you to be my bride."

# Four
## The Arrangement

Now it was Elizabeth's turn to stand unmoving. She felt as if she had turned to stone. What on earth had that infuriating man suggested? He could hardly be serious, and yet there was no indication of mirth in his face. Instead, the face that returned her look was severe in countenance, with no glint of mirth in the eyes and a slight moue of distaste around the mouth. This, she determined, was something far from a joke. Further, this was no romantic proposal, stated so baldly, and with his cousin right next to him. Whatever could this be about? Elizabeth had no particular liking of the professor, and by all indications, he had even less of her; there must be some other meaning to his strange offer. His cool eyes must have taken in her shock, for his expression softened and he quickly began to explain his scheme.

"Please, sit." He showed her to a comfortable chair. "As my cousin unnecessarily reminds me, I am all too frequently the object of many a young woman in Town who wishes to ensnare me in marriage. The true purpose in every one of these cases is for the woman to wed herself to my fortune. I am," he stated as simply as he might comment upon the clouds in the sky, "a very wealthy man.

"I, myself, am never the object of their affections, for as you have seen, I am a misanthrope and a bore, and whilst my manners can be extremely proper, I excel in rudeness. In that, I can see, you agree with me. I have grown tired of fending off these women, and worse, their mothers, at every social event which I am forced to attend. I have also been alerted to the uncomfortable fact that my aunt intends to announce my engagement to her daughter before long. There is, however, a means of bringing an end to all these machinations and that is by becoming engaged to some suitable woman. Namely, you."

Elizabeth blinked. This was not, then, an offer borne of some sudden deep passion or tender love, but of desperation and mercenary coldness. "But we do not like each other enough to be married," she pointed out the simple fact.

"That is true," Darcy countered. "However, we need not actually marry. A public engagement will suffice. At the end of the term we specify, you shall throw me over. This will raise your estimation in the eyes of the *ton*—for how grand you must be to be able to cast me and my wealth aside—and will hopefully lower mine!

"For my part," he continued, ignoring her stuttering protestations, "I shall teach you, as you requested, to speak as a lady of the first circles, to act like one, to be one in every sense of the word. And on my arm, you shall be accepted fully as one. And when, at last, you accept your aunt's offer of a season, you shall be much admired as the finest woman in London."

This was too much for Elizabeth to take in at once. "But how would we proceed? Surely no one here would believe in our faux engagement. They all know me too well to believe that I would accept someone I have known for so little time."

The professor thought for a moment, his brow furrowing slightly as he did so. Elizabeth observed him carefully, taking in the full lips balanced on a crooked finger, the line of concentration above his eyes, the way he sucked in his cheeks as he pondered. He was unpleasant, to be certain, but most fascinating to be around.

He sat up straight with a start. "I have it! We shall start immediately. You will become a regular visitor to Netherfield, at the express request of Caroline as her special guest, and under that guise we can begin your lessons. In time, we will convince your family and friends that we have found affection for each other, and eventually, we shall announce our engagement. Once you have moved to London, where you will stay with

Sir Harrison and Lady Grant, or even with your own aunt and uncle, should you prefer that, we may continue in public. You will no longer require a season, per se, but we can offer the explanation of the necessity of being introduced to London's society as my intended. You then may have your season the following year, should you desire it. By that time, you will have all the social connections you need to make a very good match." He leaned back in his chair and crossed his arms confidently across his chest.

"But do you believe I can learn all the manners and graces and patterns of speech in sufficient time for this?" Elizabeth still was unsure of her thoughts on the scheme.

"Six months, Eliza. Three if you have a good ear and a quick tongue."

"I don't think you can do it, Darcy," the colonel interrupted, "but I'll throw in a wager if you can. Pass her off as the daughter of a duchess at some celebrated ball in six months, and I shall endeavour to see a case of that contraband French cognac you so like make its way to your house. Further, I shall contribute to outfitting her in all the fashions of Town. My allowance from the pater must be put to good use. We shall send for Mrs. Pearce immediately, and take her to London for fittings and a meeting with your sister's dressmaker."

Darcy jumped to his feet and strode over to his cousin. "Let us shake on it, Richard. It is a deal!"

Elizabeth was stunned. The decision had been made, one that concerned her most completely and intimately, and she, it seemed, had little say in it.

"Gentlemen," she protested once she finally was able to speak again, "you have forgotten to consult my wishes!"

"That is true, Darcy. Have you forgotten that Miss Elizabeth might have some feelings about your proposal?" The colonel's concern was sincere.

"Oh no, I don't think so. Not any feelings that we need bother about. Have you, Eliza?" His cheery smile and the quizzical tilt to his head spoke of his utter disregard.

"Well I never! I was mistaken to speak to you. Please forgive me for interrupting your privacy," she stood and turned to leave, but Darcy caught her by the elbow. She flinched at the unexpected physical contact, but remained still.

"No, no, not so fast, Eliza. I have decided that this little endeavour will be of great value to us both. I shall achieve my aim of throwing off the husband-hunters of Town; you shall achieve yours of being able to move in society; and the colonel here will achieve his of procuring for me the cognac his fully intends to drink himself. Don't be missish, Eliza," his marvellous voice grew mesmerising and seductive. "Think of the future. You shall pass as a grand lady, as a duchess. You shall be so admired that even should your custom slip and you revert, momentarily, to your present manners and speech, it shall be seen as something new and wonderful from the highest strata, and everyone will fall over their feet to emulate you. You shall have the pick of the finest men in Town, and you shall marry very, very well. You will even have the opportunity to spend as much time as you wish in my library, perusing my vast collection, and reading at will. Think on it, Eliza! Think on it!"

He waved his hands suggestively as he spoke, and Lizzy was put in mind of the snake charmers she had seen once at an exhibition. But she was no slithering creature to be so manipulated!

"You have decided? You? What gives *you* the right to decide what will be of value to *me*? Have you appointed yourself my lord and master already, when I wished merely to enter into a business arrangement? How dare you!" She would have stamped her foot in indignation, but refused to give him the satisfaction of observing such a typical gesture. Instead she straightened up her posture and intensified her glare.

The colonel was biting his lips and could not suppress a wide grin. "Oh, I am enjoying myself immensely!" he proclaimed to nobody. "You might wish to reconsider, Darcy. This one has fire that will meet yours in equal force. I might be a betting man at times, but I would not wish to wager a penny on which of the two of you would win a battle of wills." He sat back in his chair and made himself comfortable, as if he were about to watch some entertainment.

Darcy, for his part, met Elizabeth's indignation with a sally of his own. "How dare I? I dare by having the means, knowledge, and experience to give you what you want. What you asked for, in fact, only a few moments ago. Have you changed your mind already? Are you so unsteady in your convictions that a mere disagreement over price will send you fleeing? Or are you a woman made of sterner stuff—the sort of woman the *ton* would accept as my betrothed? I, for one, believe it is the latter."

"And, sir, the only way I can prove my mettle is by surrendering to your terms? You sadly underestimate me! I shall be on my way, and shall never bother you again. If my season in Town were to throw me in the paths of others like yourself, I should be glad to have avoided that fate."

Colonel Fitzwilliam lost his valiant attempt to contain his mirth. "Now, now, Miss Bennet," he managed through a barely controlled chortle, "let us see if we can discuss this rationally." He cleared his throat and spoke more seriously and very smoothly. "I shall not expect you to forgive my cousin his rudeness, for he behaves thus willingly and intentionally, and should not be expected to show himself in any other way. However, what he says is true. His skill is remarkable, second only to his conceit, and he can grant you your wish at no cost to you, other than your agreement to have your name linked with his for some months. After that, you will be free to act and move as you please." As Lizzy's eyes reflected the softening of her defiance, he added, "I have recently completed my commission and have no intentions to accept another for some months. I shall, if you desire, locate myself at my cousin's' house whilst you are at your lessons, as a *chaperon* of sorts and to help temper my cousin's less gentlemanly outbursts. He must be master of your instruction, but I shall be your friend when he becomes an ogre. And," he spoke in low and coaxing tones, "I should be pleased to continue our acquaintance."

"Think of the theatre, Eliza," Darcy's beautiful voice purred, "think of the opera. You do enjoy theatre and music do you not? Ah, I thought as much. We shall get a box, and you may enjoy as much art as you desire. And the galleries? The museums? Yes, I knew you were a woman of taste and discretion. You are gentle born and have the makings of a fine lady, Eliza. We need only polish the outside to reflect the treasure within."

Elizabeth could feel herself wavering and knew that she would crumble in the face of this dual assault on her resolution if she did not act immediately. The theatre, the concerts, the lectures, the galleries... these were all such inducements. And while she knew she would never be anything other than a friend to the colonel, she did enjoy his company greatly. "I must think on this, sir," she said as soon as she felt her voice would be steady. "Your claims are beyond what I had expected, and your presumption insulting, but I admit that there are advantages in your scheme as well. I shall inform you as to my decision presently." And she curtseyed and left the room in a hurry before either man could stop her.

CR&

"Well, Richard?" Darcy asked as soon as Elizabeth had closed the door behind her. "How long before she returns to accept our offer?" His smirk was cocky and his tone taunting.

"Fitz, she is a lady. If you wish to have any success in this venture, you must learn to behave yourself. You are accustomed to dealing with merchants and enterprising men of the lower classes who wish to better themselves, but who have been trained from birth to see one such as you as their superior. You have never been tutor to one of your own class. And Miss Elizabeth is of your rank. She is a gentlewoman, born and bred, never mind that she looks and sounds like a country girl of the middle class. She knows her station, and yours, and will not put up with the nonsense you throw at your other clients."

"Nonsense? Richard, you wound me." He threw a hand dramatically over his heart. "I only do what I am paid to do, which is to teach them most effectively. Seeing the results, none have questioned my methods."

"Not the methods of teaching, Darcy, but your general manner. You are rude and obnoxious, and you are proud of it."

"I shall not change my behaviour for one impertinent chit, Richard. I refuse to put on a facade of civility to appease her. You know how I abhor deception. Being anything other than my accustomed self would merely disguise my true character."

"Do you even know how to treat a lady, Darcy?" The colonel was growing serious. "Can you behave as a man of good character around women?"

"There is no such thing as a man of good character around women, Richard." Darcy threw himself into the chair beside the colonel's and took up a cup of coffee that had long since cooled. "I find that I do not rub along well with ladies at all. The moment I let a woman make friends with me, she becomes jealous and suspicious, and starts measuring me for wedding clothes. And the moment I let myself make friends with a woman, I become selfish and tyrannical."

"You are always selfish and tyrannical," the colonel interjected.

"Women upset everything. There is no telling what disasters may occur when you let a woman into your life." He emitted one of his characteristic huffs. "No, if my demeanour is wanting, that is how it must be. I repeat: I refuse to put on airs to disguise my true character."

"Then perhaps, Fitz," the colonel stated baldly, and without a trace of a smile, "your true character is exactly what you ought to consider changing."

☙❧

Elizabeth knew she ought to return to Jane and see how she fared, but she also knew she would not be able to conceal her distress and fury, and thus set off for a brisk walk on the opposite side of the house to where Jane was most likely sitting with her Charles. She was relieved to meet no one on her walk—more of a run, really, such was the energy of her ire—although she did have to choose a different path once when she noticed Mrs. Hurst and Caroline in the far distance.

When she returned to her rooms, her hair in disarray but her temper somewhat under control, it was to find Jane sitting serenely on the chaise by the window, a throw around her pale shoulders and a book in her hands.

"You had a fight with Professor Darcy." Jane offered the observation as a simple statement.

"You know me too well, dear sister. What gave it away?"

"You usually take better care of your hair when you walk, and almost always take a bonnet, but I can see that you have been walking much faster than usual, for your face is red and your breathing still a bit hard. You do that when you are angry. And with whom have you spoken today that would raise your ire, but the professor? Also," she smirked, "Charles told me."

Lizzy was about to respond with some exasperated and possibly unkind comment, but now she allowed her face to fall into a smile. "Oh, Jane, you always know what to say to cheer me up. Yes, I had words with the professor. He is most vexing! And yet, he is, perhaps, the one who can help me best with my problem. He offered a most scandalous suggestion, which I ought to outright refuse, but I must confess that it has merit. Oh, whatever shall I do?"

"Charles only heard of the argument after the fact, and with no details. Whatever did the professor say to upset you so, Lizzy?"

Elizabeth sat carefully on the chaise by her sister and tucked the throw more securely around her, then launched into a recounting of Darcy's offer of a sham engagement as his recompense for teaching her the ways and speech of the upper classes.

"He says it will be of benefit to us both, for it will bring me into the eye of the *ton* and will provide me with a certain cachet once the engagement is broken. Correspondingly, it will do the exact opposite for him, which is what he desires. Tell me it is mad, that I ought to turn around and never look upon that awful man again."

Jane let her eyes drift and lose their direct focus. One who knew her less well than Lizzy might think her to be staring vacantly into the distance, but Lizzy was intimately familiar with the subtleties of Jane's calm features and knew her sister was thinking deeply. "It is not mad, Lizzy. It is, rather, quite ingenious. And it is, as you say, beneficial to both of you. You have already decided to accept, I can see by your face. Now you need only convince yourself that it is the right choice. Charles and I will be in Town much of the time you will be there; you know you can always come to us if you need us. And Aunt Gardiner and Lady Grant will not let you suffer either, nor will the colonel, should matters turn sour."

"*Turn* sour, Jane? They could hardly have started more sour! But yes, I concede, I shall not be alone in Town. Do you really believe it the best course? Whatever will Papa say? Mother, of course, cannot know the truth, for it would be all over England within days, but we must tell Papa. He must know the real reason I am to visit so much at Netherfield, and he will eventually demand an accounting for why I have thrown over the most eligible Professor Darcy of Pemberley when that time inevitably arrives."

"Yes, Papa must know, and our aunt and uncle, and the Grants. They can all be relied upon for their discretion. If Professor Darcy is correct in his estimations and you begin work soon, you can be out in London society shortly after Easter. That will fit well with Lady Grant's proposal to present you in court, and you will be quite the thing once the following season begins. It really is all quite perfect, Lizzy. I think you ought to agree."

"Perfect," she grimaced, "except for the small detail of the annoying Professor Darcy himself! Oh, I find myself dreading a headache which will last six months."

By the end of the following afternoon, Jane was deemed well enough to return to Longbourn, an occasion which Lizzy wished she could celebrate with greater enthusiasm. However, she knew that her return home would be temporary and of short duration. Any joyful anticipation of the promised season in London was well tempered by the certainty of the weeks and months to come in Darcy's company.

She had informed the professor of her decision the very evening after she had spoken to Jane. Darcy had looked triumphant; the colonel quietly pleased. "I shall congratulate myself, Miss Elizabeth," he had purred, "on my great fortune to have the chance to further our friendship." And once more he had kissed her hand in a most genteel fashion. This was the one aspect Lizzy felt she might grow accustomed to quite easily, for it was most pleasant to be treated as such a fine lady.

Darcy had harrumphed and said, "Well, good then. Today is Saturday. We shall start Monday of next week. Be here by ten in the morning." Then he walked out of the room. Elizabeth did not see him again that morning, or even the following day before her and Jane's departure, except for a brief glimpse at church. For this she was thankful. As Jane spent some quiet time with Charles after services and before the carriage arrived to take them and their trunks home, Lizzy found paper and pen and wrote once more to her aunt, outlining this strange scheme and begging for her discretion.

*I must tell you the truth, dear Aunt, for I should not have you under the misconception that I actually like Professor Darcy, much less that I intend to marry him, but I do beg you to keep this to yourself, my uncle, and the Grants, beseeching their secrecy as well. The whole scheme depends on it being believed completely.*

Mr. Bennet, too, was brought in on the secret, of which he did not initially approve, and for a moment threatened to withhold his permission entirely. The scheme was nearly undone before it started, until Jane convinced him how greatly to Lizzy's advantage it would be. It was only when she promised that Lizzy would have complete access to the Bingleys' house in Town, no matter the day or hour, that he relented. The plan seemed to be set into motion.

However, a letter arrived at breakfast the next morning that set the household astir and temporarily replaced her strange plans from the forefront of Lizzy's considerations. The letter was from a certain Mr. Collins, the young parson in line to inherit Longbourn after Mr. Bennet's eventual demise. Mr. Bennet read the letter aloud to all present for the morning meal, a decision which might have put one or more of the ladies present off her eggs. In an obsequious and somewhat pompous manner, the young man introduced himself, apologised for being the means by which the estate would be wrested from the family, and announced his intentions to mend the rift in the family between his father and Mr. Bennet. He concluded by announcing his intention to visit. To wit, he had written that he would arrive on Monday, November 18th, by four o'clock in the afternoon.

"But Mr. Bennet," his wife exclaimed, "that is today!"

"Indeed, Mrs. Bennet, it is. I hope, my dear, that you have ordered a good dinner today for this addition to our family party. This might be a fine thing for our girls."

"Mr. Bennet! How unkind of you to announce this so suddenly! 'Tis most unthoughtful of you. Have you no care for my nerves? Hill, Hill," she cried for her housekeeper. "We must prepare! Oh, there is so much to be done. My poor nerves!"

Suddenly she stopped and turned her gaze to her husband, narrowing her eyes. "What, Mr. Bennet, did you mean by saying 'this might be a fine thing for our girls?'"

"Nothing, my dear, other than that I believe he means to marry one of them." He tossed off these words with an air of indifference, but Lizzy could see the glint in his eye that suggested he knew precisely the effect his pronouncement would have. Neither she nor her father was disappointed.

"Marry one of them! Oh! La! Girls, girls, you must prepare! Oh, what a pity Jane is already engaged, for she would suit admirably. Perhaps Lizzy... she is sensible enough to be a clergyman's wife, if not as pretty as Jane. All of you, be sure to wear your finest frocks, for if this young man takes a liking to one of you, we may keep Longbourn! Lydia, you look to best advantage in pink, and Kitty, in blue. Mary suits green, but not the dress with the ribbon, but rather the one with the lace. Lizzy, you must wear your yellow gown, for you look well in it! Perhaps Mr. Collins will choose to marry you, and then we will all be saved!" How conveniently she forgot about the wealthy Mr. Bingley, now that a lifetime at Longbourn was in sight.

Lizzy exchanged an anxious glance with her father. She knew him well and knew that he shared her thoughts. She would not be at home for dinner, and further, she would soon announce her engagement to Professor Darcy. But they could not divulge this information to Mrs. Bennet! Her silent plea was met with a quiet nod and twitch of her father's lip.

"My dear," Mr. Bennet said after a moment of thought, "Lizzy has had an invitation from Miss Bingley today, and she has already agreed to dine there. We can hardly ask her to refuse the invitation now, after food has been ordered and plans made. Miss Bingley would take it as a cut, and we do wish to remain on the best of terms with Jane's future sister, do we not?"

Lizzy could almost see the visions of Mr. Bingley's grand house and his grand carriages and grand ballroom dancing about her mother's head, replacing the sentimental notion of remaining forever at Longbourn, and Mrs. Bennet immediately cried, "No, of course, Lizzy must go! But why does she not also ask for Jane? Jane is five times prettier than Lizzy, and she is to marry Miss Bingley's brother. Surely she meant to invite Jane instead."

"No, Mama," Jane said softly. "Caroline wishes to know Elizabeth better, and I am still recovering and wish to spend a quiet day at home. Lizzy shall go to Netherfield, and we will all explain her absence to Mr. Collins."

"That we shall," was Mr. Bennet's final word, and he immediately made a great show of calling for the carriage to take Elizabeth to her destination, and set her on the first step towards her new life.

CREO

Elizabeth was ushered into the small study at the far end of the library at exactly ten o'clock. She had arrived some several minutes early, but Forbes, the butler, had requested that she wait in the morning room until precisely the correct time. He opened the door to the study, announced her, and then withdrew, closing the door behind him. Lizzy was left alone with the dark figure behind the desk by the window.

"Good. You are not late," he offered by way of a greeting. "Sit down, Eliza, and let us begin."

"I am very well, thank you, Professor Darcy. Thank you for asking," Elizabeth uttered pointedly. "I did indeed have a most pleasant morning. I hope you were able to enjoy the fine weather before I arrived to keep you at work all day."

Darcy stared at her. "I did not ask you how you were, nor did I inquire about your morning."

"No, and you ought to have done so!" She challenged him with her own fixed gaze. "You claim to be able to teach me the manners of Town, but you show none yourself. Am I, rather, to teach proper behaviour to you? Perhaps I ought to halve my payment, and only agree to be courted by you, rather than be acknowledged as your betrothed."

"You are accustomed to speaking your mind, Eliza."

"I am accustomed to being treated with the respect due my station. If that involves being outspoken, then yes, I confess, I shall not refrain from speaking my mind! And if you will not treat me as a lady, perhaps it is *I* who should teach *you* proper manners!"

Elizabeth expected the professor to anger at this statement. If she was unaccustomed to being treated with disrespect, he must be a hundred times more so. His haughty manner and studied rudeness bespoke a man who accepted correction or chastisement from nobody. But to her great surprise, instead of growing red and exploding at her, the professor began to laugh. His frown dissolved into mirth as his eyes crinkled at the corners, and a deep rich chuckle emerged from his throat. She had heard this laugh once before, and while it disconcerted her for reasons she could not identify, she found it somewhat appealing as well. It hinted at aspects to his character that he did not ordinarily show to the world.

"Well, well, well. The kitten has claws. Richard was right after all. Very well, Eliza." He stood up and walked around the desk to greet her properly. Bowing to the perfect degree, he intoned in his perfect diction, "Miss Elizabeth Bennet, how delightful to see you this morning. I do hope you are well and have spent a pleasant morning thus far." There was something genuine in his smile, a glint of real amusement replacing the accustomed sardonic look in his eyes.

Elizabeth returned his smile with one of her own. "There, that was not so bad, was it Professor Darcy? And how are you today?"

"Ready to get to work," came the curt response. The curmudgeon had returned. "Let us begin with vowels. Yours are not unaccountably awful by general standards, and of course, the local dialect varies only slightly—to the common ear, at least—from the accents of the greater London region, mainly up the estuary, but your vowels do exhibit some influence from the Buckinghamshire dialects and tend alarmingly towards rhotacisation. This must be corrected. Say your vowels."

"If you were a gentleman, you might ask me to sit down, before flinging terms and ideas at me that I cannot begin at this point to comprehend."

Darcy sighed and rolled his eyes. "Indeed. Would you like to sit, Miss Eliza?" She sat. "There, now—as for those vowels...."

"Are you always this rude, Professor Darcy? Do you never take a moment to say something pleasant, to try to learn a little about your students, before starting your lesson?"

He looked quite puzzled. "No. Why on earth should I do that? It seems a complete waste of time."

"You are a most perplexing man, Professor."

"Thank you," he replied. "Now, as I mentioned, while your accent is not as bad as some, it is hardly suitable for society. We will work, and work hard. Remember: You are a human being with a soul and the divine gift of articulate speech. Your native language is the language of Shakespeare and Milton and the Bible..."

"I believe the Bible was first written in Hebrew and Greek, sir."

"Indeed." His answer was cold. "But we did it better."

To this, Lizzy could only stare in disbelief. "Are you always so proud, sir?"

"I have every right to be proud. Where there is real superiority, pride will be always under good regulation."

Lizzy opened her mouth, then closed it again immediately. Finding herself in the quite unusual position of being unable to think of a single arch comment in reply, she decided to give up this train of conversation. "I believe, sir, it is time to commence with my vowels."

# Five
# A Gentleman Comes a-Courting

As Elizabeth toiled at Netherfield, endeavouring to distinguish between two very similar vowels, Jane had the dubious pleasure of welcoming the family's guest to Longbourn. Mr. Collins, as he had written, arrived at exactly four o'clock that afternoon. Upon alighting from the hired chaise which had borne him on the final leg of his journey, he bowed low in a fashion not often seen in men under the age of fifty, and immediately addressed Mr. Bennet in the most overblown and ingratiating terms, after which he performed similar obsequies to the lady of the house. Jane looked upon all of this with her usual unruffled grace, although she heard Lizzy's arch comments in the back of her mind and she took note of her family's reactions to recount when Lizzy returned later in the evening. The two youngest sisters, Kitty and Lydia, merely stared in boredom, for without the glory of a red coat on his back—the mark of an officer in the militia—there was nothing to interest them in a man. Only Mary showed some signs of interest in the newcomer. He was a clergyman recently bestowed with the patronage of the great Lady Catherine de Bourgh of Rosings, in Kent; Mary was of a studious, religious bent herself, and clearly hoped for some hours of conversation with this new-found cousin.

As for the gentleman himself, he was a tall, heavy-looking man of about five and twenty, and he looked over his young cousins with an eye that suggested an interest in more than merely offering an olive branch to the family. Mr. Bennet, it seemed, had been correct when he had suggested that Mr. Collins wished to choose one of the girls for a wife. This was a notion which their mother was most happy to encourage, and as such, urged her girls to converse with their guest. The ladies were ready enough to talk, and neither did Mr. Collins seem inclined to be silent. Mr. Bennet was mostly quiet, as he so often was. Jane imagined this suited him greatly, for he so often had little to say, and Mr. Collins had little with which to recommend himself. After only a few minutes it was clear that Mr. Collins' air was grave and stately, his manners very formal and stiff. Kitty and Lydia looked desperate to be afforded relief from his company; Mary looked like she could not have enough of it.

Although Mary was, perhaps, the least lovely of the Bennet daughters, she had nonetheless inherited something of her mother's youthful beauty. Jane had always supposed that Mary's faults lay not so much in plainness of feature, but in her manner of dress and grooming, which emphasised those characteristics best ignored, and which ignored those features that would be best emphasised. In the right dress, with her hair done softly and without her eyes screwed up constantly as she peered into her books in poor light, she would be as pretty as any of her sisters. Before their guest's arrival, Jane had encouraged Mary to select an attractive frock and had even convinced the girl to try something different with her hair. She smiled now as she observed some success emanating from her efforts, for Mr. Collins seemed flattered by her attention and glanced towards Mary with increasing frequency as he spoke about the values that his patroness, Lady Catherine de Bourgh, would like to see in the rector's wife.

As the family moved to dinner, Mr. Collins' admiration was expressed towards his cousins, whom he extolled for their unrivalled loveliness, as well as towards the dining-room and its furniture. Mrs. Bennet would have been touched if not for the mortifying supposition that her guest were taking account of what would, one day, be his own property. Still, she was not one to look good fortune in the mouth, and she worked to draw her guest's focus towards her choice for his wife. "Smile more, Mary," she whispered into her middle daughter's ear more than once during the meal, when it seemed that Mr. Collins might be tempted to look to the girl as a bride.

All of this Jane observed most keenly, ready to entertain dear Lizzy with the retelling before they retired for bed.

By the time Elizabeth returned home after dinner had been concluded and coffee, tea, and cakes set out in the parlour, it had been all but decided by everyone except, perhaps, Mr. Collins himself, that he would marry Mary. Elizabeth, considered by most to be second in beauty only to Jane, was now tired and somewhat bedraggled and not at all in her best humour, and Mr. Collins' eye flickered only briefly over her form before returning to a serious discussion of some aspect of the Thirty-Nine Articles with Mary.

"Tell me more about him!" Lizzy begged of Jane when they were both upstairs preparing for bed. "He seems... not at all a sensible man," she teased. "Does he improve upon longer exposure?"

Jane smiled in return. "No, not sensible at all. You would have been most amused at his extraordinary deference to Lady Catherine, and at his kind intention of christening, marrying, and burying his parishioners whenever it were required. He is boring and rather silly, but he seems to have taken to Mary, and she might be a good match for him. She is smarter than he, and might be the making of him if she manages him well."

"Jane!" Lizzy admonished, "I have never before heard such criticism of anyone from your lips. You surely have taken a measure of Mr. Collins in the short time he has been here!" Her smile belied her severe words.

Jane was as complacent as ever. "Perhaps I have seen such perfection in Charles that I now measure all men by his standard." She too smiled, a look of such angelic bliss that Lizzy would not say anything to upset her happiness. "But tell me, Lizzy, of your day! What of the esteemed Professor Darcy? Unlike our cousin, does he improve upon further acquaintance?"

"Oh, not at all, not at all!" Elizabeth threw herself back on her bed and laughed. "If anything he grows worse. He is rude and arrogant and absolutely insufferable. He possesses such perfect manners, but chooses not to use them unless taken to task over his lapse. He is supposed to be teaching me the ways of elite society, but I was the one to remind him to greet someone politely, to converse civilly, and to eat with the manners befitting a dining table and not a trough in the barn. And yet..." she trailed off.

"Lizzy?"

"And yet, he is clearly the expert he claims to be. We did little work today on my own speech, but he taught me much about the science of phonetics, and about what marks differences in accent and dialect, not to mention grammatical patterns and word choice. I have much to learn, dear Jane, but as much as I dislike the teacher, I know I shall be well taught."

"And your resolution to pose as his betrothed?"

"Stands firm." She sighed. "It will not be easy to convince the world that we care for each other, but if I can work to soften the professor's harsh character as he works to improve my address, we might pull it off. We just might succeed."

CRSO

Within the week of Mr. Collins' stay at Longbourn, he courted, proposed to, and was accepted by Mary, to the satisfaction of the lady herself, the elation of her mother, and the great relief of her sisters. Mr. Collins was unable to remain past his appointed departure date due to the requirements of his post at the parsonage, but he promised to return as soon as he might arrange matters with the honourable Lady Catherine de Bourgh of Rosings to claim his bride.

Jane and Bingley's nuptials were being planned for the middle of December, after which they would repair to London until the snow melted; only then would they take a wedding trip. Aunt and Uncle Gardiner were often known to visit Longbourn with their family for the Christmas season and now planned to arrive some few days earlier than normal to be present at the wedding. After Christmas, they would take Lizzy back to London with them, ostensibly to spend time with her cousins and to begin procuring a wardrobe in preparation for her season as guest of the Baronet and Lady Grant. No one other than those immediately involved in the plan need know that the true purpose of the visit was to allow her to continue her studies with Professor Darcy, who would, of necessity, be returning to the city himself after Bingley's wedding.

It was hoped that Mr. Collins might be able to return to Hertfordshire during this time as well to wed Mary, but it was understood that his duties as rector to the community in Hunsford might preclude his ability to leave for some weeks immediately before Christmas.

The Bennet household was, as might be expected, in a constant state of activity. With not one, but two daughters to marry off in such a short space of time, Mrs. Bennet found herself in the enviable position amongst her friends of complaining ceaselessly about the many tasks she must undertake and oversee in preparation. Lady Lucas, as she stated to any of her daughters who would hear her, would be quite green, for the latter would do almost anything to see Charlotte wed; at the advanced age of seven and twenty, such an eventuality seemed less and less likely to occur.

All the while menus were being planned and food ordered, lace and silks purchased, and clothing made by the various members and staff of the Bennet household, Lizzy returned again and again to the study at the back of the library in Netherfield to practise her vowels.

"You are punctual again, Eliza. Very good. Now let us begin."

Elizabeth crossed her arms in front of her and glared.

Darcy sighed and rose from his desk. "Good morning, Eliza. How are you this morning? I hope you slept well and are ready to work." He executed an elegant bow.

"I am very well, thank you, Professor. How are you today?"

"Must we do this every time, Eliza? It is most distracting and takes time from our studies."

"Yes, sir. We must. For although our engagement will be merely a pretense, it must nevertheless be believable by our friends and relations. If the world is to believe that I have agreed to marry you, you must treat me accordingly. You must learn to say nice things, to be solicitous of my health and wellbeing, to pretend to care for me."

"You forget, Eliza, that is it I who am the teacher here."

"And *you* forget, Professor Darcy, that you have much to learn as well." She faced him with her hands upon her hips.

Lizzy never knew what words would send the professor into a rage, a fit of the blue devils, or uproarious laughter. His temper was mercurial and he could move from amusement to ire in the blink of an eye. He was thoughtless, rude and quite selfish, but never, Lizzy realised, intentionally cruel. That was something in his favour, which was most welcome since she did have to pretend to love the man.

Now he surprised her by bestowing upon her one of his rare genuine smiles. He was always a handsome man, but when he smiled like this, unaffectedly, sweetly, he became for those few moments the most beautiful man she had ever seen. She must remember this look for those long parties they must of necessity attend, when she would have to feign real delight in his presence. *Remember this smile*, she told herself, *and keep it fast in your mind to safeguard against those moments when you would happily see him dead at the side of the road.*

"You are, as always, correct, Eliza." His voice was gentle. "I have been left alone too long to my own devices and have had no one correct me when my behaviour begins to lapse."

"Begins?" Lizzy caught herself too late. Resigned to her fate, she forged ahead, "Sir, your behaviour seldom does anything other than lapse." Now she waited for the smile to transform into a scowl. Again, he surprised her.

"Yes, so I have been told by my cousin. Bingley would never dare to suggest such a thing, but Richard feels no compunction in recounting to me my many faults. I give you permission, Eliza, to remind me constantly to mind my manners whilst I teach you yours."

That pride! His insufferable pride!

Darcy sat back down at the desk, then, with a pointed expression, asked Miss Bennet most politely if she would care to sit as well. She did so with a gracious 'thank you.'

"Before we start, I believe we have some business to conclude," Darcy now said. "We had outlined the terms of our agreement, but settled on no specifics. We ought to decide when to announce our engagement."

Elizabeth felt herself grow slightly faint. This was the point after which there would be no return. She could run, offer her apologies and flee, but there was something of steel in her backbone, and she knew she would never act thus. She had given her word and she would live by her commitments. And, she admitted to herself, she had come to enjoy some aspects of her lessons, if not the teacher. But Darcy had not finished speaking.

"Yes, we should make the announcement soon. Unless," he now spoke with a concern and tenderness she had never before heard from him, "you have changed your mind. This is a great undertaking that I ask. I will not hold it against you should you wish to reconsider."

Where did that gentleness come from? Until this moment, Lizzy had not considered the professor to have a single bone in his body that might be concerned about the feelings of others. Yet now, without his cousin's guidance even, he had offered her an escape from the scheme.

"I thank you for your consideration, sir," she replied as steadily as she could manage, "but I have no wish to withdraw from our scheme." She allowed her eyes to meet his own and replied simply, "Thank you."

"Then if I may, Eliza, I propose the following. Your sister and my friend wed in two weeks, after which we will all repair to London individually and severally. It is known that you are here at Netherfield often as Caroline's friend; it would not be unreasonable for us to have had many opportunities to speak and become attached to each other. I shall visit your father today to request permission for a formal courtship. I shall do so openly, so your mother will know of my supposed purpose. The news will be about Meryton by dinner time.

"We may then continue courting in London, where you have already engaged to visit your aunt and uncle. This is all quite reasonable and unexceptional. If we announce our engagement by Easter, the progression of our relationship will be seen as quite within the bounds of the expected and will be accepted easily. Does this suit you?"

"You have inquired twice after my feelings about the matter, sir! You have quite outdone yourself. Should I fear that I shall receive no consideration whatsoever tomorrow? That you have met your quota of pleasant words and exceeded it, and there will be no more for a week at least?"

"You delight in vexing me, Eliza. No, perhaps I merely feel moved to say something nice to the lady who will be betrothed to me. Your point is well taken, and indeed, it is no chore to be pleasant to one such as you."

He offered her another smile that lit his dark eyes, and then without another word, drew out the sheets with the diagrams they had been using to explain some aspects of consonant formation at the roof of the mouth.

That afternoon they concluded lessons early and Professor Darcy accompanied Elizabeth back to Longbourn in Bingley's carriage. The colonel declined the invitation to visit, citing some matters of business that had arrived in the morning's post, as well as a letter from his mother wondering if she would ever see him again; Bingley himself was delighted to join the two for the short drive, always pleased for an extra opportunity to see his dear Jane. Miss Bingley and Mrs. Hurst had excused themselves from the outing with the explanation of having to see to dinner. Nobody suffered for their absence.

As expected, the unannounced arrival elicited much excitement and speculation on the parts of those in the house. "Oh, oh, Mr. Bennet, who has come? You must see who has arrived!" could be heard from the driveway as Lizzy was handed down from the carriage by the professor.

Mrs. Bennet greeted Bingley with a curtsey and a kiss on the cheek. She did not seem surprised to see him. But Lizzy stood back and watched as she blinked her eyes in surprise when Professor Darcy walked through the door. She had heard of the professor's uncivil behaviour towards Lizzy at the Meryton assembly some weeks before and had spent no little time in the intervening period chastising her daughter for having anything to do with the man.

"Sir," she looked at him askance, then remembered her manners and curtseyed coldly. Lizzy knew her mother well: she would be polite to the man, but only polite, and even then, only because of his friendship with her future son. The smile Mrs. Bennet plastered onto her face deceived no one, but for once, the professor was too polite to say anything, for which Lizzy was terribly grateful.

"Do come in, gentlemen," Mrs. Bennet cooed in Bingley's direction. "I shall call for some tea. Hill.... Hill!" She began bustling about, organising the seating arrangements. "Here, this sofa is in a lovely spot for afternoon tea; it is well lit but not in the direct line of the sun. Here, let me remove this cushion so you may be more comfortable. Oh, look, there is room for Jane by Mr. Bingley. How do you like your tea, sir? Shall I call for more raspberry preserves with the cakes? Oh. And Mr. Darcy." Her tone changed instantly to one of strained forbearance.

"Professor..." he corrected in a whisper, but Lizzy could hear that he was making an effort to be civil.

"I wished, rather," he announced to Mrs. Bennet, "to have a conference with Mr. Bennet, if he is available." He looked over at Elizabeth and smiled very slightly, and Lizzy felt her cheeks grow red. *Perhaps I am a better actress than I imagined*, she thought to herself.

"Oh, a conference with Mr. Bennet!" the lady of the house cooed, turning her own eyes to Lizzy. "With Mr. Bennet! Indeed! I shall send Hill to see if he is available."

The smug grin on Darcy's face told Elizabeth his very thoughts: this news will be universally known by the time the first star shows itself.

⚭

Darcy was conducted into Mr. Bennet's study a few minutes later. "Well, Professor," the older man greeted him, "do be seated. I imagine I know what this is about. Elizabeth has explained everything."

Elizabeth. She seldom strayed far from his thoughts these days, something not unexpected, since he was teaching her, working with her, for most of the waking hours of the day. Her voice rang through his head, with her dropped consonants and rhotic vowels, chiding him to mind his manners. He had intended to come right to matters of business, stating his decision to have a formal courtship recognised, and then sitting quietly for a few minutes, long enough to let the others believe he had engaged in a real discussion. Instead, he found himself asking after Bennet's health, and that of his family.

If Mr. Bennet were surprised he did not show it. Knowing little of Darcy's propensity towards rudeness, he seemed happy to accept the conversation as the normal behaviour expected of a civilised gentleman. The brief civilities turned to questions about Darcy's estate, and soon the two men were discussing some finer points of crop rotation and the differences in planting times between Hertfordshire and Derbyshire.

At length, they came back to the point of the interview. "Miss Elizabeth and I have decided to engage publicly in an official courtship," Darcy stated, explaining the logical reasoning behind this decision. "Since you are aware of the actual nature of our arrangement, I shall assume there is no objection to having our supposed growing attachment made known. People will expect an engagement within a few months, and we will likely make that announcement around Easter. Have you any objections, sir?"

What objections could Mr. Bennet have? After all, he had given his daughter permission to enter into the agreement. Nevertheless, Darcy felt some compunction to conform to social expectations by making a formal request. He was unprepared for the long, cold stare cast upon him by the older gentleman.

"I cannot object now, and I will not." Gone was Mr. Bennet's sardonic smirk and careless tone. The man's voice was now stern, his eyes hard. "But sir, no matter your rank, your wealth, or your education, if you hurt my daughter, I shall not rest until I have made restitution."

Darcy swallowed and nodded. "Understood, Mr. Bennet. Our ruse is meant for society at large. I have no intentions to harm Miss Eliza in any way whatsoever. She has become..." the thought that had just come to him caught him somewhat off guard, and he had to think about it for a moment. "I have come to think more fondly of her than I ever have of my other students. Despite my slightly abrasive manner on the rare occasion, her wellbeing is of the utmost importance to me."

"And so it should be." There was no misunderstanding his meaning.

At last the two men shook hands, and Darcy returned to the parlour to suffer stoically through the cooings and ravings of Mrs. Bennet and the rest of the family. He sat next to Elizabeth, and said quietly to her, "It is done."

He felt disconcertingly close to Lizzy on the small sofa. She had never been quite so aware of him, no matter how many hours they had spent alone in Bingley's small study. Perhaps it was the cognizance that their supposed courtship was now acknowledged and public. She searched for something innocuous to say to mask her sudden discomposure.

"Mama has gone to request an extra course for dinner. I believe you are expected to stay to dine and gaze dotingly at me all evening. I hope this will not be too much of a chore. Shall I send a note to the colonel inviting him to join us? Would that make you easier?" Her voice was almost a whisper, as to be expected from courting couples, seeking a semblance of privacy in the midst of company.

"No, this was my plan and I shall abide all the indignities that are part and parcel of it." Oblivious to how insulting his words were, he carried on blithely, "I believe I can gaze adoringly at you for long enough to convince your family of my intentions. That should not be beyond my skills." He now looked at her and sputtered, "What have I said?" Then, in quieter tones and more dispassionately, "I have offended you somehow. Well, nothing to be done for it now. How long should I sit here revelling in my success before I may be permitted to go and find Bingley? Where is he? In the back garden, do you think?"

Lizzy sighed as every *soupçon* of her discomposure vanished. This was the Professor Darcy she had come to know; this is what she had agreed to tolerate over the next several months. If she took offence at every unintended slight and display of carelessness or selfishness, she would never be happy until the whole ridiculous affair were called off. Best to tolerate the professor's rudeness and smile while doing it. She could take him to task at another time, when she had the privacy to tell him her true thoughts.

This was an advantage to his unpleasant nature, now that she considered matters. He was rude and churlish, quite unthinking really, and consequently she felt no qualms about returning his abuse syllable for syllable. Had he been a real suitor, she might have accepted some minor slights with Jane's outward complacency, for fear of sending the man running from her independent mind and barbed wit. But with Darcy, she need have no fear of wounding him, for he had as much to gain from the agreement as she did. She could castigate him and correct him and speak her mind quite freely. It was a wondrous thing, really, to be able to take such liberties with a man such as he, with no concerns about repercussions.

But that would come later. Now she had to rely on her own skills to make her mother believe that she were besotted with the unpleasant man. "Five minutes beside me on this sofa ought to suffice. You would wish to tell your friend, after all, that you are to be brothers. For now, however, you may wish to smile at me."

"Five minutes. Right." He drew out his pocket watch and marked the time. Then he turned to Lizzy and smiled. At first, the smile was the smile of an actor upon a stage, but as he caught her eye, the glint in his emerged and his smile became genuine. He reached over and took her hands in his. His fingers were warm on her own, for neither was wearing gloves inside, and she started at the sudden intimate contact. "We are begun, Eliza!" he said proudly. "Here is to our imminent betrothal. May it be fruitful for both of us!" With that, he raised her one hand to his lips and bestowed a gentle kiss on the back, almost as elegantly as the colonel, and just in time for Mrs. Bennet to turn her head and notice it. Yes, it would be all over town by sundown.

CR80

As expected, the news of Lizzy and Darcy's supposed courtship spread quickly. Charlotte Lucas came upon Lizzy the following morning as she was preparing for her ride to Netherfield. "Let me ride with you," she begged of her friend, for I have much to ask!"

Soon the two were seated in the small chaise Lizzy drove when the weather was fair. "What is this news I hear?" Charlotte asked without preamble. "Is it true?"

Lizzy laughed. "I cannot imagine how the news spread, but yes, it is true. Professor Darcy has requested a courtship and I have agreed."

"But you don't like the man!" Charlotte was astounded. "You have always told me how rude he is, how unfeeling and selfish. How can you allow him to court you?"

Lizzy stared into the distance and shrugged her shoulders. "I am not certain. I still do not know whether I like him, but I am willing to spend the time with him to learn more about him. We are not marrying yet. If Charles Bingley has accepted him so completely as a friend, there must be some good in him! And the colonel seems to genuinely enjoy his company too; they are friends as much as cousins. I believe there is good in the man, and I am happy to be allowed to seek it."

"Are you certain, Lizzy, of what you are doing?" Charlotte's concern was obvious. As much as she had always protested that marriage should be a matter of convenience and security rather than romance, she was nonetheless anxious that her dear friend not find herself in an unhappy situation.

"I am very sure, dear Charlotte. 'Tis only a courtship. I have thought about this longer than you can know and am quite confident in my decision."

"Then I must be very happy for you, my friend. I know you are not wed yet, but if that day arrives, I shall celebrate heartily and wish you the greatest joy."

Whilst Lizzy and Charlotte were riding over from Longbourn, Darcy and Richard were talking in the breakfast room at Netherfield. Richard had been occupied with his business all the previous afternoon, and then had been called to confer with the colonel commanding the militia unit stationed in Meryton for the winter. It had been very late when he had finally returned to the house, somewhat foggy from the freely flowing ale that Colonel Forster had ordered for their consumption, and he had not had the opportunity to ask his cousin how matters had progressed until now.

"So Bennet approved, I trust? Now is hardly the time for him to withdraw his support, but she is his daughter, and he must look to her interests."

Darcy nodded and took another sip of his coffee.

"Then I shall warn you, cousin," Richard continued, "that I have taken a liking to Miss Eliza and I will not stand for you treating her ill."

"Why on earth does everyone think I intend to abuse the girl?" Darcy exploded. "Bennet said pretty much the same thing. I am hardly about to beat her senseless and then drop her into the Thames. Do you take me for a monster?"

"I shall reserve judgement on that." The colonel rocked back in his chair and appraised his cousin. Darcy wondered absently whether the chair would tip backwards from the uneven weight upon its legs. "However, since we are on the subject of monsters and men of dubious character, I have some news you may wish to hear." He leaned forward and rested his hands upon the table and waited for his cousin to look up from his steaming coffee before he continued. "Whilst I was conferring last night with Colonel Forster of the militia, I discovered that one of his officers is none other than George Wickham."

Richard sat back and waited for the reaction. He did not have to wait very long.

"Wickham?" Darcy roared, slamming his cup down with sufficient force to spill hot liquid over the table and rattle the china plate holding the morning's pastries. The delicate cup did not break, but only through sheer good luck. "What in blazes is that blackguard doing here? I had thought us well rid of him!"

"It appears he has been here for some weeks," Richard stated calmly, "but since you have hardly been out in society, nor hardly left the estate, it is of little surprise that you have not seen him about the village. Still, he is here. You ought to know."

Darcy reached for a napkin and began mopping up the mess he had made before a footman appeared from nowhere and took over the task, refilling the cup as part of his duties. "Yes, thank you," he replied to his cousin. He spoke with resignation and he calmed somewhat as he inspected his clothing for traces of coffee. "I would rather he be nowhere on Earth, but I would prefer to have the information than not. So he is in the militia now, is he? I suppose I should have wondered what became of him, but I was just too relieved to have him out of my life. Does he know that I am here? Did he see you?"

"From what I know, he did not see me, but it was common knowledge that I was meeting with Forster last night. As for whether he is aware of your presence in the neighbourhood, I cannot say. But you should not assume that the knowledge will remain secret for long. Jane and Bingley marry very soon, and you will be seen at the ball Bingley is hosting next week to celebrate the wedding."

Rubbing his forehead between his eyes, Darcy asked, "How much should I say about him? He will not leave the area without a string of debts and broken hearts—or worse—behind him. The people here deserve to be warned."

The colonel thought for a moment, then said, "I will talk to Forster and explain our history with Wickham, whilst requesting his discretion in publicising particular details. Hopefully that will suffice." He reached into a coat pocket and drew out a letter. "By the way, this came in my package yesterday. It is for you, from Mrs. Pearce."

"Pearce? Why does she write to you and not to me? She is *my* housekeeper, after all."

"It seems," the colonel explained placidly, "that she has done so several times of late, but you seem not to have received or read her missives. She hoped that by sending this to my care, I might entice you to actually read the damned thing."

"Language, Richard, language."

"You just wished someone to blazes, Fitz. I am a soldier. Swearing and uttering profanities is part of my stock in trade. Now, will you read this letter or shall I read it aloud to you?"

"Damn and blast, I shall read it myself." He grabbed the envelope and began skimming the contents. "Pay the accounts, yes, yes... order new linens... send permission to the steward at Pemberley.... Oh no, not this again." He scowled.

"Trouble, Fitz?"

"No, merely an annoyance. I have mentioned to you before of my connection with this group of reformers in Northern Wales." He looked up and waited for Richard's nod, then continued, "They have taken their inspiration from the Quakers and some revolutionary named Robert Owen. Their wealthy patron has procured a large tract of land for them near Conwy, where they have established a cooperative community of some sort. For some unaccountable reason, they have decided that I am a kindred spirit to them, a model of enlightened leadership and a paragon of a new morality. I came across them in the course of my studies, and now they wish me to travel to their remote outpost to give them guidance and inspiration. Why on earth they think this of me, I cannot possibly imagine. Me?" he spat out a short laugh, "Advise Quakers on matters of modern morality? A farce, Richard, a farce! Another one for the rubbish bin. I will respond to Mrs. Pearce later, I promise. At least this eases my temper, for should I happen to think of the scoundrel that is Wickham, I shall cast my mind instead to the presumptuous ignorance of these reformers and laugh myself silly. Now—."

He was interrupted by the footman bearing a note on a silver salver. "Now, it appears, I must go. Eliza has come and duty calls. Be so kind as to entertain her friend Miss Lucas until the carriage can be called to return her to Meryton. There's a good chap." And off he strode, coffee cup in hand, and an unfamiliar smile on his lips.

# Six
## Friends and Strangers

Lizzy paced the small study, a thousand thoughts running through her mind. She had been waiting some minutes in the study with no sign of the professor. This was most unusual; on every other occasion when she had come for her lesson, he had been waiting for her in his accustomed chair behind the large desk. Now, for the first time, she was let into the room alone, and told that the professor would attend her shortly. The sun streamed in through the window and cast a bright glow throughout the room, gilding the honey-blond wooden furniture and illuminating the flowers in the vase on the side table as if from within. Lizzy took the opportunity to survey the room and its ornaments, freed from the disapproving eye of the professor, who would surely chastise her for her distraction and force her back to work. He was a harsh master, tolerant of little, extremely demanding. He would bludgeon her through her exercises again and again until she thought she might break down in tears.

"No, no, no," he would say. "Can you not hear the difference? The sounds are as distinct as night and day. If you can't hear it, you will never be able to say it. Listen, Eliza, listen. Pay attention this time. Again..." And Lizzy would blink back her tears and swallow her mortification and redouble her efforts.

On occasion, the colonel would join them in the study. His presence was always welcome, for he was friendly and amiable where Darcy was curt and dour, and his polite addresses were a blessed remedy to the professor's accustomed rudeness. He would take Darcy to task for some of his more egregious lapses in civility, reminding him that despite everything else, he was a gentleman and ought at least to pretend to the part. On those days, there would be some lightness in the lesson, for the colonel would engage Darcy in banter and *repartée* that would bring some humour to the room, even if it did not lessen the amount or challenge of the work.

Now Lizzy wandered around the study, wondering what it was that had kept the professor, hoping, perhaps, that Colonel Fitzwilliam might accompany him today, but knowing that he would not, for Charlotte had arrived with her. The colonel had taken a liking to Charlotte, and took every opportunity to engage in conversation with her, even encouraging Lizzy to bring her friend along in the mornings. He always behaved very much the gentleman, and would insist on seeing to her comfort until a carriage could be called to drive her home. The two had certainly developed a firm friendship over these past few weeks. Charlotte enjoyed the colonel's humour and colourful tales of his years abroad, and the colonel seemed to enjoy Charlotte's sensible nature and clear view of life.

The friendship could never be more than that—a friendship—for both were most keenly aware of their respective positions in society. As the second son of an earl, the colonel depended on his family's approbation should he wish to retain his allowance from that source, and when he chose to marry, it would have to be to a lady with a large fortune. Although Charlotte's father had been knighted for some minor service to the king, the family's income was quite modest, and Charlotte herself had no fortune at all. Lizzy reflected upon this with regret, for her friend and the colonel seemed to suit rather well, and would be most happy together. Fortunately, the two seemed satisfied at the moment with the relationship they did have, and Lizzy knew that although fate might deny them more, Charlotte could do worse than have a friend and champion highly placed in the military and with intimate links to the aristocracy.

She stood musing over these various subjects, while examining the vista outside the large window behind the desk, when Professor Darcy entered the room at last. He was only fifteen minutes late, but it was so unlike his usual punctuality that it might have been hours.

He did not offer any apologies, but he placed his cup of coffee down on the desk and then handed Lizzy a plate filled with sweet cakes. "I have requested tea. It should arrive shortly," he said. Lizzy was stunned. Never before had Darcy considered, let alone asked, whether she might like something to eat or drink. Rather, she had learned after her first lesson to bring along something to appease her hunger in the middle of the day, in the event that Bingley was out and neither of his sisters thought to offer her luncheon. Professor Darcy himself could go all day without food, and seldom thought to offer his pupil anything to eat; it was only when the colonel was present that a tray of suitable victuals would appear in the study. "I... I thank you, sir," she managed, still taken aback by this unexpected gesture.

Something in her voice must have caught Darcy's attention, for he moved his coffee cup away from the corner of the desk and bowed gracefully. "Good morning, Eliza. It is a pleasure to see you looking so well this morning. I trust you slept well. What plans have you for today after we have concluded our lesson?"

"My goodness, Professor! Are you quite well? You seem to be not quite yourself this morning. You are... polite! First you offer me tea, then you greet me properly without being reminded. Whatever is the matter?" Her voice was light and teasing and her bright eyes shone with amusement.

"Why nothing at all is the matter, dear Eliza. It is a beautiful morning and we are courting, if you recall. I believe I am permitted to be polite to the woman I am courting. Am I not?"

"Of course, Professor, of course. It is just unusual for you."

"I may be old and grumpy, Eliza, but I hope I am still able to learn a thing or two. Perhaps you have proven a good influence on me."

"I should hope so!" she responded. "I could hardly have been a poor one, considering what your manners were before!"

"What on earth is wrong with my manners? They have always been perfect. I merely do not choose always to use them."

"Yes, Professor." Her arched eyebrows left no doubt that her thoughts were very different from her words. However, now was time to work!

"You are doing well to modulate those vowels, Eliza. I heard scarcely a trace of the rhotacisation. Once we achieve London, and you no longer need to switch between proper English and the dialect you are expected to speak with your family and friends, the adoption of new patterns will progress much more quickly."

"Thank you, professor. Shall I recite the poem you assigned to me at our last lesson?"

☙❧

George Wickham had led a charmed life, right up to the time he decided that everything he had was not quite enough.

By his ancestry and parentage alone, he ought to have been born in squalor, destined to live out his miserable existence toiling in the fields of someone else's farm, or carrying slop up and down hundreds of stairs on someone else's estate. But fortune had smiled upon the family when a wealthy landowner recognised the spark of intelligence and signs of diligence in the boy's father and raised him up out of the muck to assist the steward of one of his smaller estates. When Wickham senior proved beyond a doubt that the wealthy landowner had made a wise decision, the landowner gradually bestowed upon him greater and greater responsibilities until he achieved the position of steward-in-chief of the man's primary estate, Pemberley.

This landowner, by chance, himself had a son some few years younger than Wickham senior, and when the old master passed from this world, the new master was pleased to have the man continue his position as steward of Pemberley.

Soon after taking up this position, George Wickham the elder married a young woman from a nearby village and before long had a son, whom the doting parents named George, after his father. This lad was born shortly before the new master's own son, and seeing in him a smart and active lad, with his father's innate intelligence and a charming personality, the master encouraged a friendship between his own heir and his steward's son. And thus, the boy who ought to have been raised between the hedgerows grew up, instead, in the manor house of a large estate, was given an education fit for a gentleman, was allowed to mingle with the children of the aristocracy, and was even sent down to Cambridge with the golden child of Pemberley, Fitzwilliam Henry Darcy himself.

But the young George realised that as much as he was elevated in the world from where he might have been, there were still heights to which he could never aspire. He would never be raised to the ranks of the nobility. He would never dine with his master's brother-in-law, the earl, nor would he be paraded around the ballrooms of London as was the master's son. He would never be looked upon by ranks of beautiful women of high birth, seeking to choose a husband as one might choose a pair of slippers. He would never be master of his own estate.

These vagaries of fate he could well live with. Being an earl entailed duties, headaches, and responsibilities that he had no wish to take up. George the younger had no wish to sit in the House of Lords and listen to endless and excruciatingly dull debates on topics he cared nothing for, nor did he need to be the subject of rumour and speculation on the part of every busybody in England. As for the parade of the ballrooms, that too was a fate better avoided. Being regarded by the silly daughters of overbred society matrons and impecunious lords as a means of support held no appeal to him; there was more fun to be had with the milkmaids and the wenches who worked in the shops and behind the bakeries than with the stiff and haughty daughters of the *ton*. Bedding one of those skirts would be almost as bad as bedding Fitzwilliam, he would think with a shudder: cold, quite unenjoyable, and completely distasteful. As for being master of his own estate, well, who needed that responsibility either? There was more amusement to be had in gaming, drinking, and wenching than in setting up crop rotation schedules and mending broken down tracks and hovels.

What he did desire, and what he believed he deserved, was the *wealth* that so often came with the status of land ownership or nobility. It was due to his father, after all, that Pemberley was so successful an estate. The ten thousand a year that Fuss-Drivelling Darcy was rumoured to have was only possible because of Wickham senior's hard work and effort. And if Darcy was to benefit from his own father's good decisions in hiring the elder Wickham, well, surely George Wickham the younger should benefit even more from having the astute man as his sire!

And that was when the trouble had begun. Young George had been offered the makings of a very good life. With his gentle upbringing and his excellent education, he was expected to find for himself a gentleman's occupation, and the church seemed ideal for the smart and sociable lad. There was even a living attached to Pemberley that was offered to the young man upon his taking orders and the living becoming vacant. He might live very comfortably there, in the knowledge that his patron had done well by him, the son of a peasant-born waif from the dirt.

But a living required some effort and the lifestyle was not to George's liking; nor did the income, comfortable though it might be, seem sufficient to the life George wished to live. His eye was to the thousands, the sort of wealth that would get him carriages and fine clothing, that would allow him to marry well, or better, install a mistress in some discrete apartments somewhere in town while he played the *roué* about the country. This was what he felt he deserved, and this was what he determined he must achieve. And somehow, he resolved, the Darcy family would finance his lifestyle.

The first forays into these attempts to secure a larger bank account took place at university. Wherever there are large gatherings of wealthy and bored young men, there will be shenanigans, and gambling is just one of the milder forms of trouble such a man can find. Wherever there were cards or a race upon which to bet, George Wickham was there, using some of his own modest allowance at first, thereafter announcing that his godfather, Henry George Darcy of Pemberley, would cover the debt. This, of course, was news to the senior Darcy, but he would not let his good name become besmirched by another, and consequently supplied the blunt to meet his obligations.

When gambling proved not to provide the income young Wickham desired, and more to the point, when enough establishments had received notice from Darcy senior not to accept his name as creditor to the young man, he sought other means to fund his existence. School was not to his tastes, and theology certainly not so. Shortly after both his own estimable father and Darcy the elder passed on, Wickham took himself to his old home to meet with his former playmate, now master in his own right of Pemberley and a handful of other smaller holdings around Britain. The new Master Darcy agreed at once to see his childhood friend, and expressed his hopes that, now past the tumultuous years of adolescence, George's character might have improved.

He was proven sadly wrong. George informed Fitzwilliam Darcy that he had no inclination for the church, a sentiment with which Fitzwilliam agreed, and thereupon requested that in lieu of the living, at whatever time it might fall vacant, he be granted a large sum, with which he hoped to support himself for a time while studying law. To this, Fitzwilliam also agreed, and an arrangement was quickly reached wherein all rights to the living were ceded in favour of a bank draught to the effect of three thousand pounds.

The money lasted a year.

When an appeal for the now-vacant living met deaf ears, George realised he had only one more option. If he could not win, beg, or coerce money, he must marry it. His name, however, had become somewhat stained amongst the upper circles of society due to his checkered past and low birth, and so he needed to find a well-dowered lady to wed who might overlook these slight impediments. Fortunately, there was one close to hand, in the person of the sister of the very man who had denied him what he felt ought to be his: Georgiana Darcy of Pemberley. Although much younger than George and her brother, she too had grown up with George as a fixture around the manor house and viewed him as affectionately as a brother; possibly more so, because it had not been he who had assumed the stern role of father-figure and disciplinarian upon the death of her father.

And so, when George discovered that she was out of school and enjoying a holiday at Ramsgate with a companion whom he knew slightly, it was a matter of almost no effort to encounter her, seemingly by accident, woo her with words of love, bribe her companion, and convince the girl to elope with him. Georgiana Darcy was a sweet enough thing, if a bit dull, but her dowry of thirty thousand pounds was far sweeter still. At last, the Darcys would have given him what he clearly felt was his due!

These plans were dashed at the very last moment when Fitzsnivelling Darcy made an unannounced visit to Ramsgate and thereby discovered the planned elopement. His statement that the dowry would be forfeit if he and Georgiana's other guardian did not approve the match was the final nail in the coffin, and Wickham, once more, was deprived of his birthright by the miserable man. Darcy even had the effrontery to criticise George's accent, saying, "For all your education and time amongst good society, you still sound like a farmer."

Wickham burned for revenge, but he could not think what avenue he had yet to try.

Then the perfect plan dropped right into his lap.

For want of any other means of survival, he had accepted a commission in the corps of a militia unit posted in some obscure village in Hertfordshire and was content enough for the time being. The work was not yet too onerous, and there were some very pretty girls in the area, although he had not yet met any whose fortunes might entice him into more than a kiss or a tumble behind the shrubbery.

Then Dame Fortune smiled upon him. One night, not too many weeks after he had arrived, his colonel had called upon a high-ranking officer from the Regulars to consult about a certain matter of discipline, and to his shock and initial horror, that other officer was none other than Colonel Richard Fitzwilliam, cousin to the very Darcy Wickham hoped to destroy. Not wishing to alert the colonel to his presence, Wickham had stayed out of sight, but did begin asking very many questions, the answers to which fascinated him exceedingly.

Colonel Fitzwilliam, rumour told him, was back in England after a lengthy sojourn in the West Indies, and was currently residing in the home of a local gentleman, whose other guest was none other than Darcy! Further, the rumours told him, Darcy had recently been acknowledged as courting a lady from the area. Where there is a courtship, a wedding must surely follow! The rumours were uncertain to exactly what this lady's name might be, but Wickham was determined to discover her identity. If he could find her, he could woo her and win her, and if he might not break Darcy's pocketbook, he might still break Darcy's heart, which would afford equal satisfaction. A bit of bribery might also be possible. The clouds over his future were lifting!

To Wickham's chagrin, the officers of his regiment had not been given quite the freedom they might have had in other times. Colonel Forster was a diligent commanding officer and had more than enough experience with men under his command who ran up debts and caused trouble. Trouble could, and would, occur, of course, but Forster hoped that by keeping a firm hand, he might minimise the damage. The officers were not quite prisoners, but they were kept under Forster's sternest control, and socialising with the local elite was frowned upon; consequently, none of Wickham's fellow officers were certain about the exact social hierarchy of Meryton. Nevertheless, Wickham was persistent in his quest to discover the identity of Darcy's *inamorata*.

What he learned, from a lieutenant who had it from a private who had it from his girl who worked at the dairy behind the bakery in the village, was that the lady was from one of the first families of the area. When asked further about the families in town, Lieutenant Denny was able only to tell him, "The primary landholder here is Bennet, and he does have five daughters, all quite pretty. But to hear them speak, or to see them in the village socialising with the children of merchants and even farmers, you'd never know they were gentry, for they sound and act and behave just as all the other girls in the village. The mother is quite garish and unrefined, always going on about her nerves and trying to marry off her girls. She is quite loud about it, which is how I know. I've heard her in the streets when I've been at the smithy. She is from the area; her brother is an attorney in the village. There's another brother who is a tradesman in Town. The youngest is a delightful flirt, but we have not had the chance to meet, for her family is planning two weddings soon, and the girls have all been needed at home."

Darcy, with all his priggish and snobbish ways, would never allow himself to be linked with a family with such low connections—a family of brash matrons, of flirts with country manners and accents, of small town attorneys and shopkeepers—and consequently, Wickham knew he must look elsewhere for Darcy's lady.

The other grand house in the vicinity was Netherfield Park, where Darcy was staying. This seemed a far more promising situation. The gentleman who was leasing the place had a sister, and a rather pretty one, he believed, and it surely must be she whom Darcy was courting! Why else would a man as fastidious as Darcy willingly sequester himself away in the wilds of Hertfordshire? It must be to court his host's sister! All the pieces fit, and no detail seemed awry. A beautiful young lady of great fortune, and the sister of one of Darcy's dearest friends... who else could it possibly be?

Why, he considered further, he might even attach the lady to himself to the point of wedding her! Her fortune would surely match Georgiana Darcy's dowry; such a sum would be most welcome in Wickham's own pockets. He could break Darcy's heart and make his fortune with one sweeping action. It was perfect!

Two days later, Lieutenant George Wickham presented himself at Netherfield Park, humbly requesting an interview with Professor Darcy. He would not, he knew, gain entrance to the house without some credible business, and his history with the Darcy family was not unknown. Although loath to disclose his presence to Darcy, he nonetheless felt it necessary.

However, fortune smiled upon him once more. Surely his luck was about to change! The house was in an uproar, servants all buzzing about and in a tizzy, for someone had arrived most unexpectedly from London—he could not discover exactly who—and his or her arrival was cause for quite some excitement.

"I am most sorry, sir, but neither Mr. Bingley nor Professor Darcy is available to meet with you at this moment. Perhaps you wish to leave a card?" The butler was polite but insistent.

Not having cards, Wickham was about to make his excuses and leave when a very pretty and rather elegant young woman walked past the entrance hall, just inside the house. This must be Bingley's sister! She turned to say something to the butler when she noticed Wickham standing on the stoop. Wickham knew he was handsome; indeed, his appearance was greatly in his favour, for he had all the best part of beauty, with a fine countenance, a good figure and a very pleasing address. His smart regimentals added to the effect to make him completely charming, and Caroline Bingley stopped in her path and smiled at the man.

At once, he knew that he had won; he need now only fight the battle.

⚬⚭⚬

She ought not to say a word. She ought not to acknowledge his existence. They had not been introduced, and it was quite improper to speak to a stranger thus. In London, with all the eyes of society upon her, she would never deign so much as to glance at him. But today she found herself acting rather out of character. Perhaps it was the country air, or merely the soldier's masculine beauty and most appealing air; Caroline certainly had little enough encouragement from Darcy, and wished to have her own charms confirmed by another. She allowed her eyes to wash over the soldier, then threw all propriety to the wind and approached the door. "Sir, may I help you?" She dismissed the butler with a quick motion of her head. "My brother and his friend are both occupied at the moment, but perhaps I may be of assistance." She kept her face serene and her expression disinterested, but she could easily read the interest in the handsome stranger's eyes. This was the attention she desired!

"Miss Bingley? May I be so bold as to presume?" the soldier asked. She nodded and batted her lashes, allowing a faint smile to adorn her face. "I do hope you will forgive my forwardness and allow me to introduce myself. Lieutenant George Wickham, currently with the militia. Darcy was one of my dearest friends in childhood. His father was my godfather; he quite doted on me, almost as his own son. I had wished to renew my acquaintance with my old friend."

At this, Caroline Bingley smiled more widely, clearly more at ease. "A friend of Mr. Darcy's is no stranger here. Did you have particular business with Mr. Darcy?"

"Oh, no, not at all," Wickham said lightly. "But I see I am interrupting something; I should depart."

"'Tis merely Darcy's housekeeper from Town; he can't quite manage without her. It has always been this way. The poor man is quite lost without strong women to help guide his steps."

"You know Darcy well, then?"

"Oh, yes, dear Darcy," Caroline was eager to embellish upon the nature of her acquaintance with the stern and gruff man. His consequence was sufficient that any acknowledged connection must be seen as a social advantage. "We have been friends—very close and dear friends—for the longest age," she gushed. Despite the unpleasant rumours concerning Mr. Darcy (of whom she felt quite possessive) and Eliza Bennet, she would not deign to dignify the connection with her acknowledgment of it. "He is a most cherished acquaintance, a charming man—quite wealthy, with a splendid estate, as I am certain you are aware."

"Ah, yes, Pemberley!" Wickham matched her enthusiasm. "I spent many happy years there as a child. I quite long for the place when I cannot be there. My childhood memories carry me forward when times are difficult, and I always recall the paternal kindness of old Mr. Darcy. He remembered me always."

This was interesting information! The words were simple enough, but there was meaning behind them. Might this beautiful officer be confessing that he was the natural son of old Darcy? That he had been left well-heeled with the old man's money? That certainly was what he meant. His current occupation, as an officer in the militia, must be more for want of useful employment than for a want of money. Look at Colonel Fitzwilliam, after all. Surely the second son of an earl need not beggar himself to the king merely for food and lodgings. It was a matter of pride and status, to be sure. Such must also be the case with the handsome lieutenant standing before her.

It would be most inappropriate to invite him inside. She was a single woman, he a single man, and they had no common acquaintance hovering to satisfy the dictates of society. And yet, something in the man's bright blue eyes, guileless expression, and wide, sincere smile left Caroline forgetful of everything she had learned. She simpered a moment longer, then dared, "Would you care for some tea? Perhaps Mr. Darcy can be coaxed from his present occupation."

Wickham bowed most elegantly and Caroline felt her heart flutter at the sight. "I would be delighted, Madam," he shook his head sadly, "but I will not impose upon your hospitality at this moment. Perhaps we shall meet again soon. I often exercise my horse on the common before noon."

"Indeed." This was excellent information! "It was a pleasure, Lieutenant Wickham."

As she closed the door behind him, Caroline thought she saw the corner of a wink in those lovely eyes of his. It was always most pleasant to get some air in the mornings after one's duties keeping house were attended to, and the common provided a pleasant prospect. Perhaps a walk on the morrow would be in order. She returned to her previous occupation with a sly smile and a cheerful lilt on her lips.

# Seven
## Lessons

Mrs. Pearce, Darcy's housekeeper from London, had arrived at Netherfield quite unexpectedly to everyone except for the professor himself. He had seen no reason to inform his host, for to his mind, her presence was of no matter to anyone but him and Eliza.

He was, therefore, rather surprised when Bingley seemed somewhat put out by the lady's arrival. The three men were taking their early coffee and toast when a footman with an alarmed face scuttled into the breakfast room and handed his master a note. Bingley glanced at it, then read it more carefully, and finally turned a rather unattractive shade of red as he turned on his friend.

"Darcy, what on earth have you done?"

Darcy paused, his coffee cup halfway between its saucer and his lips. "Done?" His voice was uncharacteristically mild, and he resumed his task of taking his coffee.

"Done." Bingley's voice was not mild. "A carriage has only now arrived from London, a carriage bearing your crest and carrying your housekeeper!"

Darcy returned the cup to the table and dabbed carefully at the corner of his mouth with a linen napkin. "Oh yes, Mrs. Pearce. I sent her a message to come at once." He peered at the sideboard. "Are there any eggs this morning?"

"You asked her to come? Without consulting with me? Darcy, do you know what this means?"

"Why yes, it means that we might take Miss Bennet's measurements so the seamstress in London can begin making her wardrobe. Pearce will only be here for a day or two. She does not eat excessively; she shan't be much bother." He turned to confront his cousin. "Richard, what on earth was that noise? Are you laughing or choking on your tea?"

Bingley, by now, had called over the terrified footman and demanded that he find Bingley's own housekeeper at once. "This is a disaster, Darcy. Caroline will have my head over this. Oh, the trouble this shall give! I must be sure to find Mrs. Pearce suitable accommodations—not so fine as a guest suite; neither so low as the servants' rooms. Oh, and I must reassure my own staff that she is here merely as your housekeeper and as not a threat to anybody's position. They must be told that she holds authority over no one at Netherfield, but that she should be treated with due deference, all the while not being a guest *per se*. Oh, bother Caroline, with her late morning habits. She ought to be dealing with this, not sleeping!

"Tell me, what am I to do with Mrs. Pearce, Darcy? Is she a servant or a guest? How do I treat her? What is her status in the house? We must find her a suitable room!" He repeated these words again and again, waving his arms wildly as he raved, running them through his hair until it fairly stood on end. He was still expositing thus when his own housekeeper entered the breakfast room and quickly took stock of the situation.

"Never you worry yourself, sir," she assured her young employer. "I shall take more than adequate care of our newcomer, never you mind! She may take the room across from my own, for it is quite fine. I have wished to meet her for a long time. She is very highly regarded by those I know. Shall I wake the mistress? No? Leave it all to me!"

Darcy was completely unperturbed by the situation and continued sipping his coffee with equanimity. "Good, you have everything in hand, Bingley," he stood and brushed an errant bread crumb from his coat. "It is time for my lessons to begin. Send Pearce in once she is settled, there's a good man. Come along, Richard. And do stop laughing."

Darcy strode through the hallways with long steps, oblivious to the chaos breaking out around him, and was gratified to find Eliza waiting for him once more. He glanced at his watch; it was only two minutes after ten. He did not consider himself, therefore, late by any real definition of the word, and had no cause to apologise to his student. He did, however, remember to ask her politely after her morning and the health of her family. These meaningless social niceties were becoming something of a habit now, and he seldom required Eliza's pointed looks and promptings, although he also found that he missed her arch comments and the few moments of verbal sparring that inevitably ensued. Never before had he had a student who would dare speak back to him, and he had learned that he rather liked it. Her strength and wit challenged him and sparked something inside him.

Eliza had answered his meaningless questions as these musings flitted through his mind, and he had some notion of responding to her before Richard made his own inquiries. He settled himself in his chair and was leafing through his papers when the door opened and Mrs. Pearce was ushered into the study.

"Professor Darcy," she bobbed her head in a terse curtsey. "You requested my presence."

Richard had leapt to his feet to greet the housekeeper and Eliza, too, had risen from her chair. Darcy remained seated.

In a few words, he introduced his protégée and explained the situation to his housekeeper. "Eliza will be spending much time at Darcy House in the coming months, Mrs. Pearce," he explained, "as both a pupil and as the woman I will announce as my betrothed. Now, do not get yourself excited, for the engagement is a facade to rid myself of unwanted society in Town, but it is a facade the entire household must uphold, and you shall be the only one to know the truth of it."

Darcy watched his cousin guide the older woman to a seat, bemused as always by how the colonel managed to smooth ruffled feathers before they even become ruffled. "We trust your discretion, Mrs. Pearce," Richard bowed his head towards her. "We would not be confiding in you were we not to do so. And of course, I'm certain we do not have to ask for your assistance in preserving Miss Bennet's reputation, for this ruse is temporary and the lady's name must be unblemished."

At Mrs. Pearce's request, Darcy quickly explained the purpose of the ruse, watching as she tutted and shook her head, or sighed in exasperation. "You cannot do this to the girl, Professor," she announced at last. "I cannot be a party to it."

"Oh, it is already done, Mrs. Pearce. I merely need you to ensure that as little damage as possible results." He leaned back in his chair and looked down his nose at the small gathering. "She quite relies on you," he added, nodding his emphasis.

The colonel now took over the attempt to convince the housekeeper. "If Miss Bennet is to reap the benefit of this engagement, she must, of course, emerge with her character completely flawless." He gave the housekeeper a conspiratorial grin. "Under any other circumstances, it would be almost impossible, but we have stronger resources: we have you! In this matter we were *certain* we could rely upon you." His smile broadened.

The older lady grinned back at the colonel. She was, perhaps fifteen years older than him, but Darcy knew she had never been immune to his convivial charm. In true form, Richard reinforced her good opinion of him at that moment by suggesting he call in for some tea. Unused to being served, rather than serving, Mrs. Pearce put up some more token resistance, but eventually agreed to help the gentlemen with their plan. The matter was settled, and the lady now had only to carry out the details.

The main matter for the summons to Meryton, it transpired, was to begin outfitting Eliza with some suitable clothing for London, which task commenced once tea had been served and consumed.

"But I am to stay with my aunt and uncle!" Lizzy furrowed her brow and sat up straight with pride. "My current wardrobe is certainly adequate for that! They are fine people, with whom you would not be ashamed to associate, but they are not so fashionable as to require the latest styles!"

"That may be so, Eliza, but you shall be seen with me, and I require the finest in all I do. Therefore, if we are to be seen out together, at the theatre or taking a ride through the parks, you must look the sort of lady who would catch my eye. You would never do in your current ensembles." Lizzy's mouth gaped open at these cruel words, and Darcy could see that he had offended her. Quickly he added, "Do not be vexed, Eliza. Your general appearance is pleasing enough that one might be quick to forgive any sartorial lapses."

"That is faint praise, Professor Darcy, but praise from you of any sort is meanly given, and I shall accept all scraps." She gazed at him coolly from beneath her thick lashes, and he felt that strange tugging once more. She was a rather pretty thing, and he was beginning to delight in her wit.

Eliza had yet more to say. "All this aside, sir, are we not being presumptuous in providing for a wardrobe for Town? I am hardly ready to be presented in public with you. Whilst we have done much work, I am fully aware that my speech and manners still cry of the country."

"Oh, that is true," the professor ran a hand through his hair to tame an errant lock, "but you shall not speak. You need merely be seen." He turned to his housekeeper, "Now, Mrs. Pearce, measure the girl for a first set of clothing, enough to give the mantua makers a basis on which to begin their task. They can refine their measurements once Eliza comes to Town.

"When she arrives, you will take her and give her a good scrubbing..."

"Professor Darcy!" Eliza protested, while the colonel shouted out, "Fitz!"

"I may be a country girl, Professor, but do not take issue with my ability to clean myself. We have bathing tubs here just as well as in London; we may bathe more often, indeed, for we are out so often in the mud and dust, and not on the dry streets of the city." She peered at him through narrow eyes and raised her chin in defiance. She was delightful!

"Really, Darcy," Richard added, "must you be so rough?"

"Very well, it seems I am shouted down. But Mrs. Pearce, her hair certainly needs attention; arrange to have it cut and styled. What else need we plan?"

By the end of the day, Mrs. Pearce had been tasked with arranging for a wardrobe, an expert in hair styling, a shoe maker, a dancing instructor, a singing teacher, and a specialist in deportment. Since Lizzy would eventually be presented at Court, sponsored by Lady Grant, as well as be seen with the gentleman at all manner of social events around Town, it was imperative that she acquit herself splendidly were she to be accepted as Darcy's intended.

"You plan to keep the girl busy, Fitz!" the colonel chided as they took tea later that afternoon. "Between your lessons and all the activities you have planned for her, she shall barely have time to eat, let alone enjoy the company of her aunt and uncle. Must you work her quite so hard?"

Eliza's expression could only be described as thankful for the colonel's words. "I am vindicated, Professor," she sighed as she sank, exhausted, into her chair. "I have been voicing my concerns over this heavy schedule all day, and you have ignored my every word. Surely you will heed your cousin."

"Nonsense!" Darcy responded with a shake of his head. "A bit of hard work shan't kill you."

"But when shall I see my family? And what of the Grants? You have me busy from dawn to midnight."

"Your cousins may come and visit you at appointed times during the day, if they arrange their schedules with me in advance. I should not wish to remove you completely from your family. See, Eliza, I am not a harsh master at all."

The colonel shrugged in defeat and rolled his eyes, and Mrs. Pearce sighed. Eliza summoned up a smile. "'Tis all for the best, I shall remind myself constantly," she said. Darcy then thought he also heard her mutter something under her breath about cursing him and all his ilk.

Accepting her smile for what it was, Darcy turned to gaze out of the window whilst Eliza muttered more unintelligible things under her breath.

"By blazes, is that who I think it is?" he suddenly burst out.

"What are you talking about, Darcy?" Richard walked over to join him at the window and peered out to where his cousin was staring. "Well, he has some gumption indeed!"

"Wickham?"

"Wickham."

"Who, pray tell, is Wickham?" Eliza asked, before Mrs. Pearce had the opportunity to hush her.

"A most unsavoury sort, Eliza. Do not allow yourself to be caught up in his charming snares. He looks an angel, but he is the very devil himself, mark my words!"

She looked up in alarm. "I would expect such admonishment from the professor. Coming from you, Colonel, it puts this man's character in a different light. I shall take your words to heart, for I have never heard you speak ill of anyone until now. Such condemnation must be richly deserved."

"It is," was all Richard replied.

"What did Wickham think coming here?" Darcy stormed at the window. "Damnation..."

"Professor Darcy! Language!" Mrs. Pearce scolded. "There is a lady present."

Darcy scowled and muttered an insincere apology to Elizabeth, who must surely be growing accustomed to the most ungentlemanly language he so often used. He mumbled under his breath again and stomped across the carpeted floor before coming to a sudden halt. A sly smile stole over his face.

"I say, Mrs. Pearce, have we received any more letters from those Quakers in Wales? The ones with the socialist cooperative based on the new morality and whatever-it-is they do? Yes? Perhaps I shall respond to the next one! I have a most splendid idea." And he refused any further commentary on the matter.

CRISO

Time passed, as it is wont to do, and soon they had arrived at the final few days before Jane's wedding. Lizzy was delighted for her sister, but more than frustrated at her mother. Mrs. Bennet was quite carried away in a fluster of activity, punctuated by attacks of her nerves, which required everybody to cease his or her activities to tend to her, after which she would fly into another tizzy about how nobody was doing any work to prepare but her. Between her mother's demands and Professor Darcy's, Lizzy felt she might well be fit for Bedlam by the day of the nuptials. Eventually she begged off her lessons for the duration, in order to better tend to her mother and to help her sister pack.

Another inducement to this temporary respite from the professor and his lessons was the arrival, two days before the wedding, of the Gardiner family of London. Lizzy had long been looking forward to their visit, and it was to her greatest delight and relief that she saw their carriage rounding the bend in the lane that led to Longbourn. Hopefully she would find some balm for her own overburdened nerves in Aunt Gardiner's calm and sensible company.

The evening the Gardiners arrived, Mrs. Bennet had invited the party from Netherfield to dine, so as to introduce various family members to their new relations. The Hursts begged off, claiming a stomach ailment on the part of Mr. Hurst, and Caroline insisted she must remain behind to help her sister. They were not sorely missed.

Lizzy met the party in the entrance hall to the house, although the rest of the family were gathered in the salon. For some reason, she felt the need to greet the party quietly before the melee. Perhaps it was the desire to acquaint herself with the professor's mood this evening, to determine whether he might be insufferable or endurable, so as better to prepare her relatives. Perhaps, she allowed a part of her to muse, she wished for a moment to converse with him removed from the necessities of public manners. She fussed with a vase for a moment until Mrs. Hill opened the front door and the three gentlemen from Netherfield filled the compact space.

Mr. Bingley sported a great grin and looked quite pleased with himself; he would, after all, be marrying the most beautiful girl in the county in a matter of hours. Colonel Fitzwilliam's smile was of a different sort, broad and generous, radiating his good humour to all around him. But the smile that caused her to catch her breath was Professor Darcy's. As his eyes met hers, he stopped still and allowed a slight smile to creep across his face. It was not proud like Bingley's, nor exuberant like the colonel's, but it was genuine and almost shy, and it reached his dark eyes which glinted their approval.

"Miss Eliza." His voice was almost a whisper, and he bowed deeply. She curtseyed in return and found her feet unable to move as he handed his hat and coat to the waiting footman and crossed the small space to her side. He took her hand in his and raised it to his lips in an elegant kiss, then offered his elbow. "Will you do me the honour of leading me to meet your relations?"

Somehow Lizzy led him through the house, although he knew the way well, to the salon where her family were gathered. As they reached the doorway, the professor stayed her with a hand atop of her own as it rested on his forearm, and he stepped aside to allow Bingley and the colonel to enter first. Such was the ado around the bridegroom's entrance into the salon that Lizzy and Darcy were able to slip into the room relatively unnoticed.

She felt more than saw his eyes scan the room. In a low voice, he whispered, "Who is the couple seated on that green settee? Can those be your London relatives?" Lizzy nodded. "I confess myself surprised," he clucked. "They are much more urbane and sophisticated than I had dared to expect from a family in trade. Do their manners match their appearance?"

Forcing herself not to react to this arrogant question, she began to walk over to her aunt and uncle, who rose as they approached. "They are much younger than I had expected," Darcy whispered in her ear; "Your uncle is much your mother's junior, I see, and your aunt looks not much older than I."

Introductions were made and brief words were exchanged. Then Darcy made his pronouncements. "You, Mr. Gardiner, are an interesting study. London, born and bred, but well educated in Town, before being sent abroad to university. Not Boston... King's?" Gardiner's eyes widened, but he said nothing as the professor continued. "You travel, or have travelled, for your business, and have learned to moderate your speech to be easily understood and approachable wherever you are, but you have spent much of the last decade in London. Were I not to have my particular gifts and talents, I should never imagine you to be anything other than a son of a gentleman with a comfortable but not excessive holding."

Lizzy had warned her uncle about Darcy's blunt manner, and she suppressed a smile at his deliberately stoic expression. When the professor turned to her aunt, however, her uncle gratified her by rolling his eyes heavenward and shaking his head while an amused half-smile flickered on his pleasant face.

The professor inclined his head to Mrs. Gardiner, then listened attentively as she spoke. "My niece has written about you and your talents," the lady told him, "and her claims were not overblown. Your skill is remarkable, for you have pegged my husband down completely!"

With a genteel bow, Darcy stared at the lady, his mouth all but agape, before shaking his head with a slight smile and subjecting her to his analysis. "You are not at all what I had expected," he began.

"How so, sir?" she cocked her head to one side and observed him from the corners of her eyes.

"I had expected you also to have been born into the wealthy merchant class, but no, you are the daughter of a gentleman, raised finely and given a good education as well. You sound every bit the lady of Town. But... I hear the slightest touch of the north. By gum, you are from Derbyshire as well! Near Lambton, if my ears do not deceive me. Now, what estate is there near Lambton other than Pemberley? Not Woolforth... no, not Rushmede... nor Heatheringford... Arlenby! You are the daughter from the Arlenby estate! And of course, Grant is your brother. I might have known! I knew your father when I was a youth, Mrs. Gardiner, and I was very sorry to hear of his unfortunate passing. He was a good and honest man, and you should be proud of your heritage. Now, if your kind husband will permit me to monopolise you for some minutes, I should be most gratified to exchange news about persons we might know in common!"

Mr. Gardiner looked on in amusement, and Lizzy stared, stunned into speechlessness, as the professor took the lady's elbow and led her to a sofa, whereupon he fetched her some tea and sat down beside her for a comfortable chat.

"Close your mouth, Lizzy," her uncle whispered good-naturedly. She did so immediately. "I assume the professor is not always thus?" He gestured to where the tall man was sitting comfortably, but very correctly, engaged in a deep and obviously mutually enjoyable conversation with his wife, sipping tea delicately and nibbling exactly the proper amounts of small cakes.

"No! No, indeed," Lizzy's eyes were wide with amazement. "I have never seen him act this way at all. He talks all the time of the importance of fine manners, but until now, I had not believed him to possess them at all. And I confess, until this moment, I had never heard him utter three polite sentences in succession. I am all astonishment!"

"As you should be," came a friendly voice. The colonel had approached, and Lizzy quickly and very properly introduced him to her uncle. The colonel wore his bright smile, and the two men took to each other immediately. "I see my cousin is determined to destroy his carefully crafted reputation of unsociability," he continued after some initial comments and greetings. "He really does know how to behave in public, Miss Elizabeth, although we see little enough evidence of it at home. What have you done to him to entice him to simper and coo so elegantly to your aunt? You must tell me, so we may replicate the circumstances when needed!"

Turning to Gardiner, the colonel said, "I believe our Miss Elizabeth will be staying at your house when she repairs to London after Christmas. How very pleasant for her, to be happily situated with such fine and caring relations. We will, I am certain, be much in the same company, and I anticipate many a pleasant conversation over brandy or coffee."

As the men talked comfortably together, Lizzy considered the cousins, one so easy and friendly, always with a good word for another, the other so curt and rude, and she was amazed that they were of the same family. Then she considered herself and her own sisters and tittered. Physical traits might be similar within members of a family, but personalities almost never were! Happy that her uncle and Colonel Fitzwilliam were satisfied to be left talking together, she set off in search of Jane and Charles.

⊂୨୫⊃

There were no delays, no complications, no last-minute problems, as Jane and Charles Bingley wed in a simple and meaningful ceremony, conducted by the village vicar who had christened Jane as a babe. A couple as well-matched and even-tempered as the Bingleys must have all the fates working in their favour. Even the weather, normally so unpredictable in the latter part of December, was mild and perfect, with only sufficient high white clouds in the cerulean sky to add a picturesque element to what might otherwise have been too perfect.

Likewise the wedding breakfast was everything it ought to have been. Mrs. Bennet, for all her wailings and affectations and nerves, was a consummate hostess and had managed an exceptional celebration for after the nuptials. In due time, the newlywed couple departed for their house in London, leaving the remaining guests at Netherfield to see to their belongings before departing as they desired over the following days.

Professor Darcy and Colonel Fitzwilliam made a quick stop at Longbourn on their way back to London. Their trunks and belongings had gone on ahead with their personal attendants, leaving only the two men in Darcy's fine carriage. Whilst they took tea with the Bennets, the driver and coachmen took their own refreshments in the kitchen before commencing the chilly ride to town.

Professor Darcy surprised Elizabeth once more by dusting off his fine manners—the ones he had displayed so brilliantly for Mrs. Gardiner—and showing them off to their best advantage. He complimented Mrs. Bennet on a first-rate breakfast ("I have never seen finer, even amongst the first circles in London"), thereby endearing himself eternally to her, and he congratulated Mr. Bennet on acquiring, through Jane, the finest son in England. If he murmured "thus far," no one purported to have heard him. Darcy took a very proper leave of the family, lingering only briefly with Elizabeth, as one might expect of a courting couple still wishing to observe the dictates of propriety. The colonel, however, felt no such compunction and said quietly to her as he prepared to climb into the carriage, "You have been good for our lad. Very good, indeed!" And with that, the men were off.

The Gardiners lingered at Longbourn until just after Christmas, at which time Mr. Gardiner needed to return to his business. Mrs. Gardiner confessed to Lizzy that she and her children were also pleased to be returning to their well-ordered home, but of course said nothing of this to Mrs. Bennet, so proud was she of her exuberant hospitality.

There was one more passenger in the Gardiners' carriage on this return journey, for as planned, Lizzy was to join them for the foreseeable future in London. She kissed her parents and sisters goodbye and promised to write faithfully, and to see Jane as soon as she possibly could. She had taken her leave of Charlotte the previous evening, and was ready for her grand adventure. As she saw her home disappear around the curve of a wooded lane, she realised that she would never return to it as the same person she was now.

She would become someone new in London. That was a certainty: it was the very purpose of this journey. She had mastered enough of the patterns of speech Professor Darcy had set before her to be able to effect a facsimile of the accent of the upper classes with concentration and effort. Until now it had been pretence, as an actor in a play assumes new personae with each production. Now that persona must become real, must take on life and essence. She must assume that new person as her identity henceforth. She might remain the same Lizzy inside, but for all appearances, she would leave a country girl and return, hopefully, a grand lady. The thought was sobering and really rather terrifying.

These thoughts consumed her for the bulk of the journey. Her aunt and uncle spent much of their time on the trip answering the endless questions of their four young children, leaving Lizzy with the solitude, if not silence, in which to ponder her self-selected fate.

The lessons recommended immediately following the arrival of the new year. "I do not believe in allowing my students a long break for the holidays," Professor Darcy had intoned when announcing his plans. "If there is a need for a rest from studying, I question the desire of said student to learn."

Consequently, each morning thereafter he sent a small covered buggy over to the Gardiners' house, which would convey Lizzy as discretely as possible through the streets of London to Darcy House, where her lessons would take place. Every morning the coachman drove her to the mews at the back of the house, to enter through the servants' gate with the deliveries, so as to avoid the public spectacle of a young lady arriving so regularly and unattended at a single gentleman's house. It was all terribly irregular, but the teacher and student were both satisfied by the plans, buttressed by the contingency that should any gossip be spread, Professor Darcy would immediately announce the engagement, thereby preserving Lizzy's good name.

Her buggy arrived early each morning, allowing her to attain Darcy's house by eight o'clock, long before the fashionable world was awake. The professor also did not approve of late mornings. The day began with tea, at the colonel's insistence, where both he and Darcy would instruct her on the finer points of dining in high society in the city. After tea came more lessons in elocution and pronunciation, which Lizzy despised.

CR&SO

"Repeat after me, Eliza: quality, charity, ability." Professor Darcy looked as alert and fresh as he had at eight o'clock, no matter that the lesson had been going on for hours.

Lizzy was feeling much less energetic and had all but given up hope for surviving the morning. "I have repeated it so many times, I can hardly hear the sounds anymore, Professor."

"Then we still have some space within which to work. 'Ability...'"

"Ability... Is that not what I've been saying? I really cannot hear the difference anymore. The sounds all combine into one chaotic morass in my ears. Ability, ability, ability. Quality, charity, humanity, impossibility! They all sound the same!"

"Oh dear, Eliza. You are become much too distraught to learn. Take a drink of water and breathe. Now once again: Listen to the ultimate syllable. Not merely the position of the vowel in the mouth, but the quality of it, the tone, the lilt of the voice, the shortness. 'A-bi-li-tih.'"

"A-bi-li-tee."

"Keep the final vowel shorter, further back. Recall that the sound originates with the French *aigu*, but that it sounds far superior in

English. The sound verges towards the short e sound, but never quite achieves it. 'Ih... ih...' Now... 'A-bil-li-tih.' Better, better. Again. And again."

ↂ

"No, no, no, Eliza. You have it completely wrong. The word is 'gentleman.' The letters are all distinct. Observe the medial consonant blend with the T and the L. You are exploding the T off the roof of your mouth with the surface of your tongue, and letting it combine with some crude approximation of an L. But no, that it not what is done. You must keep the letters separate, no matter the blend. Observe the T: t-t-t. Tip of the tongue on the teeth. Tip, tongue, teeth. T-t-t. Now repeat."

ↂ

These endless, vexing lessons were enough of a chore, as Lizzy endeavoured, sometimes with very limited success, to hear and then reproduce the litany of vowels, or to repeat words over and over without resorting to a medial glottal stop, but when the professor insisted on filling her mouth with marbles and forcing her to recite poetry, she protested.

"Ah cahhn..." she sputtered through the marbles. "Ah cah ha'ee bee..."

"Speak more clearly, Eliza. I cannot understand you at all. This will never do."

"Ah theh Ah cahhn..." she repeated.

"I believe, Fitz, the lady is saying that she can't. She can hardly breathe."

"Oh, no, Richard. I'm not asking her to breathe. Merely to recite the poem:"

Lizzy emptied the marbles into the handkerchief she had in her reticule and immediately flung one at the professor. It hit him on the arm, and the hurt look he flung at her in return would have been pitiable had it not been so well deserved.

"That hurt!" he protested. "What on earth was that for?"

"Fitz, you are too hard on the girl," Richard exclaimed. "If this is so manageable a task, why not show her yourself?"

"Very well," said Darcy, placing a handful of marbles into his own mouth.

He uttered a handful of barely distinguishable syllables before stopping suddenly, his eyes opening wide in shock and alarm. Ridding himself of the rest of the marbles, he gasped, "I believe I swallowed one!"

Despite Richard's howls of laughter and demands for further demonstration, the exercise was not repeated.

ᙢ

After the morning's lessons and a quick lunch, during which time the Gardiner children were permitted to pay a short visit to their cousin in the confines of the back courtyard to the house, the additional tutors would arrive, depending on the day of the week.

On Mondays, Elizabeth glided around the large library with a stack of books on her head, as a stout matron shouted commands at her to improve her posture.

She practiced at the pianoforte on Tuesdays, under the guidance of a rather sweet Italian musician, with Darcy hovering the entire time, glaring at the music master every time he moved too close to Lizzy to correct her hand position or fingering.

On Wednesdays, she would stand still for hours while the dressmakers came and fitted her again and again for a seemingly inexhaustible supply of clothing. Morning dresses, day dresses, evening dresses, ball dresses... Then came the pelisses and wraps and spencers and outerwear for winter, and the boots and shoes and slippers, not to mention the gloves and bonnets and inexpressibles.

On Thursdays the language masters came, one after the other. Lizzy spoke rather good French and had learned Latin and Greek with her father, but a lady of the *ton* was also expected to know some Italian and German, and it was these she must necessarily learn. "No, no, no!" Darcy would shout as he sat and read—or pretended to read—whilst she toiled at her studies. "You have finally perfected that vowel in English, but you must not use it in German. It will not do at all. Listen to Herr Breuger again, and do it his way, not mine!"

On Fridays, the dancing master arrived. "Why do I require lessons for this? I know how to dance, Professor Darcy," she informed him when first told of this set of lessons. "If I recall, we were first introduced at a dance."

"Perhaps so, Eliza, but a country dance in a village's assembly rooms, even at a country house, cannot be held in comparison to a rout or soiree in a duke's grand estate. Your schottische and reel might be adequate for Meryton, but not for finer society. Attend the master; you must also learn the Quadrille and, of course, the Waltz. It is highly scandalous, of course, but it is now danced at every ball, and as a betrothed couple, we will be expected to waltz together. I shall, of course, practice with you." He seemed quite pleased at this pronouncement. Lizzy had heard of the waltz, although she had not seen it performed; still, she knew it involved prolonged contact between the couple dancing, with no changing of partners. She took a deep breath and steadied herself. She ought to have been horrified at the prospect of learning such an intimate dance with the professor, but somehow the thought did not bother as much as she had expected it to.

"Who shall provide the music?" she asked. "Will the tutor bring a pianist?"

"Richard can play. He is reasonably adequate at the pianoforte." Another surprise! She had no notion that the colonel was at all proficient on an instrument, although with his mellifluous voice, it ought not to have been a surprise. She recalled one of her first conversations with the colonel, wherein they had discussed music. Charlotte had certainly made mention of his singing voice over the course of their acquaintance. It would, she decided, be most intriguing to hear the colonel at the keyboard.

Lizzy was suddenly rather eagerly anticipating Fridays.

The dancing master, when he arrived, proved to be a very pleasant man in his middle-thirties, old enough to be commanding and sure, but young enough to have the energy and vigour to perform the steps he taught. Master Hughes, for this was his name, arrived precisely on time—he knew Professor Darcy from previous pupils, and knew that punctuality was *de rigueur!*—and upon being announced, fairly leapt into the room like a *danseur* from a ballet. Somewhat delicate in manner, he moved with a lithe grace, every motion perfectly controlled and a thing of beauty, and Lizzy wondered, for the first time, if she would really be able to achieve the accomplishments the *haut ton* expected her to possess. But Master Hughes proved to be an excellent and encouraging teacher, leaving Lizzy happy with the choice.

"Very good, very good, Miss Bennet!" He minced over to her and, tacitly asking and receiving her permission, adjusted her arms into the correct position. "Turn the wrist just a hair more... there! Oh, Professor Darcy, is she not perfect?" Darcy was most interested in the lesson, but did not exhibit any of the possessiveness he displayed with Signor Rossi, the pianoforte tutor. "Now, Miss Bennet, may I? Oh lovely, darling. Yes, your left foot, just a touch higher... yes, lovely! That will allow you to execute the next step without catching on your gown. Lovely, lovely!"

Colonel Fitzwilliam proved to be a most excellent pianist, and he happily provided the music for these lessons, which Lizzy soon came to enjoy very much. She developed a sweet friendship with the dancing master, whom she thought, in her most private of thoughts, might be a good match for a carpenter she knew in Meryton. But these matters were forbidden and must remain unspoken, and so she attended only to the dance.

At last came the day when they were to learn the dreaded and most highly anticipated waltz. At first, Master Hughes described the steps, and had Lizzy try them alone. "There, Miss Bennet, start from the fifth position, as we learned before, and now, yes, yes, darling, have your right foot in front; the gentleman starts with his left in front. Lovely. Pass your foot forwards into fourth position, and then point the toes on the second beat of the bar. Lovely! Lovely!" After she had perfected the pattern and then executed it to the satisfaction of all with the colonel providing the music, it was time to attempt it with a partner.

Master Hughes offered himself up for the first set of practices. He was a wonderful dancer and with him leading her around the room, Lizzy felt the steps she had just learned become a natural response to the music. So confident was she that she could find no reason to object when Master Hughes suggested that Darcy now take his place, so he could stand back and observe.

But when the professor stepped close and carefully placed his hand between her shoulder blades, Lizzy felt the room begin to sway around her. The proximity of the professor's body impinged on her senses so much more than had the dancing master's. Was it Darcy's height? She had not before realised quite how tall he stood, for now, so close to him, she noticed that her head reached only up to his shoulder, and she could not turn her face up sufficiently to meet his eye without feeling ridiculous. The breath caught in her throat and she might have stiffened briefly, for Darcy stepped back slightly to allow her more space, smirking as he did so. He did not allow his hand to fall from her back and silently offered his other for her to take.

"It is customary, Miss Bennet, for the lady to place her hand on the gentleman's shoulder; however, you may also choose any comfortable place on his upper arm. Lovely!"

Somehow, Lizzy managed her way through the steps of the dance, moving her feet and arms, and pirouetting appropriately around the space in the music room, but her awareness was only on the man who moved with her. His presence was somehow overwhelming, eclipsing every other thing in the room. The touch of his hand now just above her waist, then shifting position to slide up her back, seared through her senses; his other hand, gloveless in the privacy of the house, cradling her own, felt like hot coals and frozen ice, all at once. These sensations had not happened when she danced with Master Hughes... why did the professor affect her so? It must be, she allowed, the threat of censure should she fail, but she could not ignore the very small voice that insisted that perhaps, just perhaps, she found his proximity too pleasant and alluring. *No*, she told the voice, *that would never do*. Their arrangement was one of business and they must, inevitably part ways at its conclusion; besides, she did not like the rude and overbearing man at all! And still she thrilled at the dance and let his careful touch burn her skin.

They stopped moving when the music ended, and Master Hughes made his accustomed coos and compliments, though his words were meaningless sounds to Lizzy's ears. It was only when Professor Darcy turned to her and bowed, murmuring in a deep voice, "You dance beautifully," that she returned to herself and, blushing deeply, answered suitably.

"Thank you, Professor. You are easy to follow. I could have danced all night."

"Let Miss Bennet rest a moment," the colonel called from the keyboard. "She is flushed, and must certainly wish to sit and take some water." Relieved at the respite, Lizzy hurried to the side table where a pitcher and some glasses stood waiting, As she sipped thankfully, she glanced over to the professor, and was not certain whether she was pleased or bothered to see that he, too, looked affected by the dance. Fridays would be, she determined quite interesting indeed!

# Eight
## A New Acquaintance

At last, after so many weeks of repeating vowels and enunciating consonants, practising phrase modulation and rehearsing conversations, Professor Darcy announced that it was time for Elizabeth to be set free into the society of Fashionable London, or at least, be allowed to venture ever-so-tentatively into it, on a very short leash. He had, he declared over luncheon one day before the Italian master arrived, arranged for Eliza and the colonel to take tea the next morning with none other than the Countess Malton.

Lizzy ought to have been confident and assured, and perhaps a few months prior, she would have been so, for the Lizzy of Longbourn had little notion of how inadequately she had been prepared to mingle with the highest ranks. That former Lizzy would have laced up her stays a small degree tighter and held her head high while striding forth to meet the countess, oblivious as to her inadequacies.

But the Lizzy of London was a different Lizzy: more accomplished, to be certain, and better spoken and well-drilled in the minutiae of socially acceptable comportment, but fully aware of what she still lacked. Knowing in theory how to hold a teacup differed so greatly from being presented with one in the company of nobility. Conversation with Darcy and the colonel, no matter how much they might correct her addresses and patterns of speech in the comfort of the familiar library, could not equal the necessity of performing those tasks exactly to perfection in the house of an earl! The colonel and Darcy had grown up in such company and thought little of it, but she, the Lizzy of London, had never been introduced to someone of such exalted rank, and she suddenly, and unaccountably, felt herself shrink from the challenge. Paling, she whispered, "A countess... oh no, sir! I am not ready. I still have so much to learn! I should embarrass you terribly, and I would never be able to redeem myself!"

But the colonel offered a warm, comforting smile, and added in his robust and cheerful voice, "Fear not, dear Eliza. Mother is a pet, and will adore you at once."

"Mother?" She could hear surprise and confusion war in her voice.

"Did I not tell you, Eliza?" the professor quipped in his offhand manner. "The countess is Richard's dear mama. She shall not bite. It is her at-home tomorrow, and she has graciously agreed to host us."

"You might have told me, sir!" Lizzy had to hold onto the table before her, fearing she might swoon. Her face felt drained of all blood and her distress must be obvious, for the colonel called for a glass of water for her. Turning to him she stammered, "I had no notion. I have always only known you as Colonel Fitzwilliam. I did know your father is an earl, but had not heard the name... I..."

"No apologies necessary, Miss Eliza! This really has been a shock to you."

"I know I am not ready. I might have believed, before I met you, that I was equal to all society, but being here in London and learning exactly how much I do not know has been most chastening. The pretty manners my mother taught me are fine enough for the country, or for my aunt and uncle's good company at Gracechurch Street, but they will not nearly do before a countess, even though she be the good colonel's mother!"

"Be easy, Eliza," the colonel's voice was reassuring. "Mother will be kind, and we shall arrive before any other company, so you may become comfortable in her presence. Shall we not, Darcy?" He fixed his eyes on his cousin. Darcy's raised eyebrows and tilted head suggested that this was not something he had planned. He stepped out of the room for a moment, calling to Mrs. Pearce, presumably to arrange for an earlier first meeting.

"Really, Eliza, don't fuss so!" he said as he walked back to his chair, throwing himself upon it in the utmost faith that it would not collapse beneath his assault. "Richard's mother knows all about you and knows what to expect. You are, despite your atrocious accent and background, of a suitable station to take tea with her, especially considering your connection with the colonel and myself. Are you satisfied?" She nodded, although she was still apprehensive.

"Good then," he asserted, sitting up properly for a moment, before leaning forward and resting his chin in his hands, his elbows firmly planted on the tabletop. "Now, remind me what topics are safe for conversation. We have discussed this on several occasions."

Her courage rising with the attempt to intimidate her, Lizzy felt herself grow equal to the occasion. She adopted a very serious expression, so false in its sincerity that the colonel had to suppress a most unmilitary snicker. "Until I am sufficiently immersed in the local society to know of the particular topics to pursue and to avoid, I am to keep to two subjects: the weather and everybody's health. 'Fine day, my lady. How do you do?' Does that meet with your approval, Professor?"

"Yes, yes, very good. It won't do to let yourself go on things in general. This will be safe."

"Will that not restrict her too much, Darcy?"

"Oh, not at all, Richard. No one will want to hear her say much, anyway. Any of your mother's guests will be only too happy to spend the time talking about themselves. All Eliza need do is smile and listen."

Richard looked aggrieved, then nodded. "Sadly, there is some truth in that."

The note Darcy had requested from Mrs. Pearce was written, sealed, and delivered by messenger to Lady Malton that very hour, and a favourable response was received. It was thus that Miss Elizabeth Bennet made her first foray into society the following day, attended by Professor Darcy and Colonel Fitzwilliam, precisely one hour before the countess' official visiting hours were to begin.

Darcy's grand carriage stopped before the front entrance to the townhouse. The journey was only a few short blocks, a distance almost doubled from what a man could manage on foot due to a park between the houses, whose paths could be traversed by pedestrians. Darcy, however, had decided on taking the carriage. His decision was based partly on the wet and unsettled weather, which had been a frequent topic of conversation during his lessons each morning. Arriving in a carriage also gave greater consequence to the visit, as well as having the unintended result of adding to Lizzy's feelings of inadequacy. Within moments of departing the mews behind Darcy House, they had arrived.

Lizzy stepped out of the carriage, assisted by Darcy, and stared at the edifice before her. A few short steps led to a large covered portico, above which massive towering Corinthian columns soared to the upper storeys of the house. A series of modest balconies with decorative iron balustrades adorned the facade of the second storey on either side of the columns, which themselves framed a larger central balcony. These must be the main bedrooms and private sitting room for the earl and countess. The third storey was plainer, with no balconies, although the decorative eye that had envisioned the lower levels of the house had insisted that the stone work remain pristine, allowing the columns to be perfect and impressive in relief. The house was a grand and beautiful thing, far too fine for a country girl of her background, and she began to shake as she stared up at its magnificence.

"Don't be silly, Eliza. It is only a house," Darcy sighed as she trembled against the elbow he had offered her. "You have been in my own home plenty of times and have never quaked like this before!"

"I have never entered through the front of your house, sir," she managed to squeak out, "and your mews and back courtyard are no more intimidating than my uncle's. But this..." she stared up in disbelief, "this is more than I had imagined."

"Be brave, Miss Eliza," the colonel comforted from her other side. "It is just a house, no matter how grand on the exterior, and Mother just a woman, like yourself."

"Hardly!" she whispered, but drew strength from the man's kind words and walked proudly up to the steps, a fine-looking gentleman on either side of her. *Oh, if Lydia could see me now!* she thought with smug humour, and a smile crept over her face.

At that moment, the door opened, and a formally dressed butler stepped forward to greet the arrivals. Lizzy felt a momentary gust of courage and she kept the smile where it was, hoping to act as if being ushered into an earl's house were just part of her daily routine.

A large marble-floored entrance hall greeted her, adorned with columns that matched their Corinthian counterparts on the exterior. The walls were painted a soft eggshell white, which set off the gleaming marble, and a wide semi-circular staircase floated upwards to a balcony on the upper floor, off of which passageways led, presumably to the sitting rooms and main suite. Set into the walls on either side of this marvellous staircase were a series of doorways, through one of which the newcomers were ushered to divest themselves of their winter clothing. The butler and a waiting footman helped the guests with their outer garments and hats, and then led them down a short passageway to the drawing room that led off the main entrance hall.

"Colonel Fitzwilliam, Professor Darcy, and Miss Bennet," the butler declaimed, his voice firm and strong.

A tall, slim woman of about fifty-five years rose from her sofa and walked quickly across the richly carpeted floor. She clasped the colonel on either side of his face and kissed each cheek, in the fashion of the French. "Richard, darling, you have stayed away too long! What does it take to bring you home? Is Darcy's house so much more to your liking than mine, dear?"

"It is, Mother, for Darcy's house often enjoys the presence of Miss Bennet."

All eyes now turned to Lizzy. Mrs. Pearce's efforts with the mantua makers and hair designers had been more successful than anyone might have imagined. Lizzy was dressed exquisitely, with ideal degrees of finery and modesty. Her pale yellow silk dress floated over her figure and fell in perfect folds to the floor, where the tips of her matching shoes could just be seen below the ruffle of her petticoat. Tasteful amounts of lace ornamented her beautifully cut frock, and an elegant necklace of pearls decorated the porcelain skin of her slim neck, matched by ear bobs that dangled delicately from below her coiffure. Her hair, too, was done to perfection. The smile she had managed to maintain lent her an air of good humour and confidence, and her bright eyes shone with excitement and, perhaps, a small amount of terror. She looked marvelous.

"Mother, may I present Miss Elizabeth Bennet. Miss Bennet, Lady Malton, my mother."

With great poise, Lizzy executed an elegant curtsey and greeted the countess. "Lady Malton, how do you do?" Her pronunciation was clear and exact, if slightly too careful to be completely natural. "How kind of you to let me come."

"It is a pleasure, my dear, to have such a charming lady for tea. Richard neglected to tell me how lovely you are. See, Darcy can hardly keep his eyes off of you! And as for you, Fitzwilliam Darcy, you might allow my son to visit his mother on occasion. It is good to see you, Nephew." He also received a kiss on each cheek, looking quite disgruntled at the gesture.

"Always a pleasure, Aunt." He flicked his fingers across his cheek, as if hoping to wipe off the kiss. "Thank you for allowing us the opportunity to be out in society. You know our scheme—"

"Are you so determined, Fitz, to foil Catherine's plot to have you wed Anne, that you would risk this sweet girl's reputation?" The look she gave Lizzy was sympathetic, but also held a note of disapproval that the girl herself would allow the plan.

"'Tis not only Lady Catherine, Aunt. Every scheming mother in Town, and her parade of daughters, like ducklings at the pond! I long to evade them all! And as for Eliza here, how better to make a grand entrance into the first circles than on my arm? And then, when she is the darling of London, she can throw me off." His voice fell at the last few words, almost as if he had not truly considered them before. He paused for a brief moment and furrowed his brow, then resumed his blithe recitation. "She will, of course, be scandalous, but we will arrange for the rumours to work so that she is scandalous in the most delicious ways, and she will be more of a darling than before. There is nothing that can go amiss. But, first, she must have her practice. And that, thanks to you, dear Aunt, is why we are here."

"I see you are committed. Do be seated, Miss Bennet." Lizzy gracefully sat down upon the blue sofa to which the countess had gestured.

"Now, as you have heard, Eliza's accent is quite adequate, but she knows nothing of the idle chatter of silly daughters of dukes and viscounts. Therefore she will limit her conversation to health and weather." The countess looked about to object, but Darcy continued, "I trust I may count on your assistance?"

"If I must, but Darcy—"

Before she could complete her response, the door flew open, and a man strode in. Elizabeth was half-hidden behind the countess and could not immediately take the measure of the newcomer, but she imagined it could only be a resident of the house, and so it turned out to be.

"Alfred," the countess exclaimed, "I had no notion you were to come down for our at-home! You are always 'out' when our guests arrive."

"Mother, Richard, Darcy," he greeted his family. "Richard told me there was to be a special guest today, and I hoped to meet her. Has she arrived? Is she as pretty as Richard intimated? I shall have to be on my best behaviour, I suppose."

The countess stepped aside to reveal Lizzy, who now rose to her feet to greet the stranger and be presented. The gentleman she saw was fine and tall, with all the affectations of the aristocracy. He was very finely dressed, albeit in a selection of hues that the Beau would certainly disparage. Eggshell-white trousers fell in perfect lines to his polished slippers, and a striped blue and gold waistcoat emerged from beneath an exquisitely cut coat of soft mauve. From the lapels of his coat, an elaborate knot decorated an embroidered cravat, which in turn disappeared into collar points so high the man could scarcely turn his head. Lizzy could not help but compare his peacock-bright garb to the professor's understated elegance in black and dark green, or to the colonel's serious military garb of scarlet and brass.

The gentleman's hair was tousled to the ideal degree, which must have taken his valet some considerable time to arrange, and not a single one of those hairs was out of place, but they shone golden and perfect in the bright sunlight that suffused the room. Lizzy could not help but let her eyes flicker over to the professor, whose own mane never quite obeyed his commands of perfection, to the wayward lock that gave the serious Professor Darcy a dash of roguish charm.

The countess made the introductions. "Alfred, Viscount Eynshill. Miss Elizabeth Bennet."

The viscount stood perfectly still, his eyes riveted to Elizabeth. "What vision is this, to transfix me so?" he whispered, turning his entire upper body in his brother's direction—for such were the restrictions of his fashionable collar points—but not allowing his gaze to wander for a moment from Elizabeth's face. Eyes wide, he finally bowed in Lizzy's direction, executing a motion so graceful and effortless that he must have spent hours practicing before a looking glass. "Miss Bennet. A delight. An unfathomable delight."

Lizzy heard a strange noise emanating from the professor that sounded almost like a growl, but she kept her attention on her new acquaintance, as she had been taught to do. "Viscount Eynshill," she pronounced most properly. "How do you do?"

"Oh, Richard, you were right!" the viscount pivoted to face his brother. "She is lovely to behold indeed! You had not told me how much! And Darcy, what other secrets have you been keeping? Why did I only hear of Miss Bennet through my scoundrel brother?"

"Freddy," Darcy nodded his own terse greeting at his cousin, then grew silent. As Lizzy watched, he caught the colonel's eye, then inclined his head slightly towards Alfred. Once the colonel had acknowledged the glance, Darcy shrugged infinitesimally, clearly asking whether the viscount knew about the plan. Richard surreptitiously shook his head in denial, and Darcy grimaced. At length he explained, "Miss Bennet and I were first acquainted in Hertfordshire after Michaelmas, where Richard and I were visiting Bingley. You remember Bingley, I trust."

"The boy from Cambridge? Nice chap, good sense of fashion. I imagine he's a man now as well."

"And recently wed," Richard added with a grin, "To Eliza's... Miss Bennet's sister."

Darcy took over the story. "Miss Bennet is currently in Town visiting family," he omitted their names or stations "and your mother was kind enough to invite her for tea today."

"How wonderful!" Alfred sat next to where Elizabeth had reclaimed her seat and studied her carefully, as if she were a precious ornament that might break if handled too roughly. Darcy took a step backward, a black look on his face, and misjudging his stride, collided with a small table that held a vase full of bright flowers, presumably from a hothouse in the vicinity. The table shook, the vase teetered but did not tip, and Darcy stepped away again with a mortified expression. Never before had Lizzy seen him not in complete control of his circumstances and expressions.

Awkward silence descended on the room, before the countess, with her excellent manners, stated, "We have been enjoying the most fine weather of late, have we not? But now I see clouds coming in. Will it rain, do you think, Miss Bennet?"

Horrified that the attention had once again been cast upon her, Lizzy felt herself unable to think. An innocuous question, otherwise one which she could answer with a witty quip or arch comment and leave people smiling, now seemed as impossible to contemplate as the meaning of the universe. All she could think of was the viscount sitting much too close to her on the sofa, the imposing and intimidating Corinthian columns soaring about the entrance to the house, and Professor Darcy inexplicably stumbling into furniture, and every intelligent thought suddenly abandoned her. Her mouth felt dry and her heart raced, and she felt the weight of the gaze of the four others in the room crushing her to her seat.

Then a slip of a memory crept into her mind, and desperate for something to say, Lizzy declared, "I have not had the opportunity today to examine the barometer, but it has been recorded, by John Dalton, about twenty years ago, that rain most often occurs when the barometer is at its lowest, according to the usual ranges for a region. Therefore, my answer to whether it will or will not rain would best rely on such information, rather than upon my own unformed opinions." She cringed inwardly as she heard herself speak. A simple 'Yes, your Ladyship,' would have sufficed!

She hardly dared look to the others, dreading their reactions, but forced herself to assess the degree of damage she had wreaked. Darcy looked smug; it was he, after all, who had introduced her to Dalton's treatise of *Meteorological Observations and Essays* and his student had studied and learned well. Richard looked confused and kept shooting glances at his mother as if uncertain quite how she would respond. The countess attempted to look interested, and Alfred looked amazed, delighted surprise brightening his face.

"How frightfully interesting!" Alfred burst out. "A bluestocking, Darcy? Why did you not tell me! Are you particularly interested in weather systems, Miss Bennet? I had not thought them of interest to anyone outside the Navy. Perhaps my brother has brought a thing or two back from his long overseas voyages."

Lizzy, once again felt like a rabbit in a snare and found that all her words had deserted her. As she gaped, trying to speak, the countess again took control of the conversation. "Oh, yes, do tell us more about Jamaica, Richard darling. I have only heard a small portion of your tales. You were away so long, you must have so many more."

The colonel gave a quick wink at Lizzy, and immediately began to tell a fantastical story about an excursion he and some of his men had made over the mountains from Kingston, where they were stationed. He told of the dark nights in the rain forest, of the lush vegetation, the cascading mountain streams that opened into deep pools, of the colourful birds and strange fruits, and of the people and villages they encountered. "These were not the slaves working for the plantation owners near the towns—horrid    practice!—but the native men and women, still in the mountains, free as the animals in the forests around them. They were sometimes hostile, often friendly, but always most extremely cautious of us. Though we meant them no harm, they had too often met with others who did, and I blamed them not."

As he spoke, drawing all to him and away from her, Lizzy felt herself grow easier, and hoped that their visit would be over soon. They were expected to remain for tea as other visitors entered to say their hellos and nibble at a biscuit before departing in a socially timely manner, but perhaps none would bother to say more than the most necessary greetings to her.

But Alfred was not satisfied to leave his brother in command. Interrupting him when the colonel paused to take breath, he asked, "And what was the weather there, Richard? Tell us, Miss Bennet, of your impressions of cloud formation in the mountains, such as Richard has just described for us! You must surely have some information, as you are so well informed on barometers." He gazed upon her in rapt anticipation, waiting to hear her speak.

And speak she did, although she knew not whence came the words. In her very careful new accent she explained, "My knowledge of cloud formation in Jamaica is negligible, for my information is gained from studies in Keswick in England; correlations may be drawn, although other meteorological differences might negate any similarities between the regions. However, according to Dalton—" She stopped, all eyes agog upon her.

"How interesting, Miss Bennet," the countess soothed. "Your knowledge is most intriguing; however, it may likely be too involved for many of my guests today." Lizzy apologised most profusely, her eyes begging Darcy to take her away.

"Mother, no!" Alfred interrupted again. "I, for one, am astonished and amazed, and cannot hear enough. One never hears ladies talk of anything other than who took tea with whom, or whether short sleeves will be back in fashion, or deciding whom to cut at the next ball. But Miss Bennet is a breath of fresh air, just delightful! Pray, Miss Bennet, you must tell me more."

"I... I..." Lizzy tried to speak, but torn between Lady Malton's admonition and Viscount Eynshill's encouragement, she felt as a fox torn apart by ravaging hounds. Suddenly, she rose, tripped a curtsey to the countess and blurted out, "I must go." Then, recovering herself to a small degree, added, "So pleased to have met you." Whereupon she darted out of the door before anyone could stop her and desperately sought someone to bring her coat and hat.

CRROD

Darcy watched Alfred leap up as Eliza dashed from the room. "Where is she going, Darcy?" the viscount demanded of his cousin.

"Home, I suppose," Darcy shrugged, no concern in his motions. "My home, that is. Hers is too far to walk, and I don't imagine she will request the carriage. Perhaps she'll find a hack."

Alfred's look became one of horror. "That girl, that delightful girl, alone in a hack? Not bloody likely!" He ignored the gasp of horror from his mother. "I shall follow her and see her safely to her destination!" and he flew out the door in Elizabeth's wake.

Into the shocked silence that followed Alfred's hasty departure, Darcy asked, "Well, Aunt? What do you think?"

"Fitzwilliam Henry Darcy, you cannot be serious?" his aunt spat back at him. Her look needed no such clarification.

"She needs some refinement, to be sure, but—"

"Her accent, Mother, was perfect!" Richard now added cheerfully. "You would not have recognised her from the chit we found in Hertfordshire—"

"Did she not look the part in the dress? I knew I could trust Mrs. Pearce—"

"You have to hear her play the pianoforte. Quite entrancing—"

"We might need to find some other topics to discuss—"

"BOYS!" the countess shouted.

After a long pause, Richard said quietly, "We are not boys, Mother."

"No, indeed, Aunt. We are grown men."

"You," the countess retorted, "are certainly acting like boys. You are behaving like boys who have discovered a mechanical toy or a dog or bird that does interesting tricks and you are exhibiting it like a creature in a zoo."

"What, treat Eliza like a dog?" Darcy was hurt.

"She is a rather pretty bird, though," Richard commented.

This earned him a stern glare from the countess. "Stop right now!" Her voice brooked no refusal. "She is not a puppy, nor is she a bird. She is a girl, a lady from a good family, and a rather sweet one at that. Have a thought for the girl, for her feelings, how mortified she must be, having had the need to run out like that? I shall visit her on my own tomorrow, if you can tell me where she will be, Darcy, and try to give her comfort. But mark my words, *boys*," she emphasised the word 'boys,' "I will not stand for her being your project, with no regards for her opinions on the matter. Am I understood?"

Both men nodded meekly.

"Then absent yourselves. I have guests arriving, and I must be presentable for them." She stood imperiously and glared as the cousins slunk out of the room.

As they walked back across the park to Darcy's house Richard asked, "Is Mother right? Do we really have Eliza's best interests at heart? Or is this, rather, a game for us to enjoy?"

Darcy shrugged, hands balled into the pockets of his greatcoat, his beaver hat perched awkwardly on his proud head. The paths through the park were clear of the snow that still lay on the city, and the rain, which had not quite been discussed to the Countess Malton's satisfaction, began to fall, icy droplets stinging where they met bare skin. Shivering against the onslaught of the elements, Darcy sighed one of his dramatic sighs and replied, sadly, "I do not know anymore, Richard. I just don't know."

◌◌◌

The men arrived home to find Mrs. Pearce pacing the entrance with a sour expression on her face and no good humour in her voice. The rain had intensified during their short walk, and since neither Darcy nor Richard had brought with him an umbrella, both stood dripping icy water on the previously spotless white marble floor. The muddy mess was not the cause of the housekeeper's ire.

"What did you do to her?" she demanded by way of a greeting. "You left less than an hour ago to take tea with the countess, and now she is returned alone, and is sobbing untold tears in the room you allotted to her. Now tell me what happened."

"I cannot say," Darcy shrugged his shoulders again, this time allowing his greatcoat to slip off them and onto the floor. A footman

123

scurried out from his place near the door and retrieved it quickly, to be sent to the maids for laundering and ironing; Darcy would naturally expect it to be immaculate the next time he chose to wear it. Tossing his hat onto a fine chair along another wall, he explained, "We went in to tea, Lady Malton asked after the weather, and the next thing we knew, Eliza was tearing from the room in alarm." He felt genuinely puzzled by the question and this was the only answer he was able to give.

"Do you think, Darcy," the colonel asked as he handed his hat and coat to the waiting footman, "we ought to have given Eliza more warning of our plans? Perhaps asked Mother here for tea, to lessen the girl's discomfort?"

This was a novel suggestion, and to his credit, the professor did not immediately shrug it off as thoughtlessly as he had his coat. His brows furrowed and his mouth gaped slightly as he pondered briefly, chin in hand. "I must think on that. Her comfort had not occurred to me; only her accent had."

There was a bit more respect in Mrs. Pearce's voice when she replied, "Perhaps you ought to make her feelings more of a priority then, Professor. She will only do as well as she is able if she has the confidence to carry off her role. You do, if I may be so bold, tend to think only of yourself, but Miss Bennet is a living, feeling creature, and her feelings count as much as do yours. Sir."

Ignoring the muddy puddles left by his boots, Darcy drifted across the floor to where the door to his study stood ajar. Richard had, by now, divested himself of his outer clothing and boots, and scurried after him, allowing the door to close behind them.

"Fitz?" Richard asked when they were both seated, Darcy's boots now standing on the tile by the fireplace, his feet inelegantly splayed on an ottoman at the foot of his chair. "You are deeper in thought than I have ever seen you, at least while you were not puzzling out a dialect."

"Your mother and Mrs. Pearce both asked after the girl's feelings. I only now realised I ought to ask after my own."

"Whatever are you talking about, Fitz? Your feelings have never burdened you before. Indeed, I have always considered you a veritable pile of stone. Whatever can you—" He stopped short as the realisation of what his cousin might mean struck him. "You don't mean... You and Eliza? But it's just a ruse, a ploy to meet your individual needs. Surely you are not developing feelings for her, are you?"

Shaking his head, Darcy merely said, "That, too, I do not know."

# Nine
## A Welcome Friendship

Lizzy fell onto the bed in the room she had been offered, heedless of damage to her beautiful dress, and wept bitterly. How humiliated she had been, how mortified! She had been unprepared for the immensity of Lady Malton's house, the momentousness of the entire occasion. It might be nothing more than a spot of tea with the colonel's mother to Professor Darcy, an event so commonplace that it was all but meaningless, but not so for her. For all her previous bravado, she was an unsophisticated chit from the country. Her visits to the city had always been to her aunt and uncle's house, a very pleasant and elegant home, to be sure, but nothing like the grand mansions clustered around carefully manicured parks in this part of London.

Mayfair was a very long way from Gracechurch Street, an expanse separated by far more than the three miles of city street. That house... the thought of it sent her shivering once more. She had never before walked up such grand stairs, never before stood before so massive a set of doors, to be admitted by such a formally attired and proper butler. To be sure, Darcy's house was as large, but she always entered from the mews, and the informal manner of its owner was reflected in the less stiff and proper behaviour of the staff. Oh, Darcy would brook no lip or poor work from his household servants, but Mrs. Pearce was the master-in-fact, if not in name, and exact socially dictated observances were rarely practiced.

And then there was the countess herself. Once, Lizzy recalled as she lay sobbing on the bed beneath the counterpane, she had seen a duke. It was during one of her visits to the Gardiners and her uncle and aunt had taken her to a performance at the theatre. They were waiting to make their way through the thronging crowds to take their seats when a hush had come upon the entire waiting audience, and the elaborately dressed bodies had parted as surely as if Moses himself were holding his staff above their heads. Through the pathway they had cleared strode a small party, consisting of a man of middle years, a woman several years his junior, and two or three others, all garbed like princes and princesses. "The Duke of Somerset," Uncle Gardiner had whispered in her ear, and she felt at that moment as unimportant and insignificant as an insect under the great expanse of sky. A countess was not as grand as a duke, to be sure, but the image of being nothing before aristocracy remained seared into her soul, and even knowing that the lady was the genial colonel's mother was not enough to restore to her any equanimity.

When the viscount had seated himself beside her and begun to comment on those silly things she had said, when he had pulled everyone's eyes to her, and gazed at her so intently, it was as if a barrier had broken and every ounce of the confidence she had amassed behind the dam of her courage had drained immediately away. She could do nothing but run, embarrassment and shame trailing her every step. The viscount had tried to stop her, to offer to see her home, but she thanked him—or, she hoped she had managed to do so through her tears—and had run. He had followed her across the square, this she knew, for hearing footsteps, she had turned briefly and seen him, concern etched on his face. But still she had run. She vaguely recalled hearing his voice as she made for the mews, for even on this panicked flight, she had eschewed the front entrance for the comfort of the carriage gate. Had he followed her there? Perhaps, but such was the pain in her breast that she could hardly turn around to acknowledge him. Mrs. Pearce had opened the door at her frantic knock, and Lizzy had thrown herself into the older lady's arms, before retreating to this room to weep away her distress.

Eventually weeping turned to weariness, and Lizzy fell into an unsettled sleep. She awakened some hours later to see the sky had turned dark, the gas lights from the street below reflecting off the raindrops on her window in a myriad of small golden lights. As the drops trickled down the pane of glass, so did the tiny glowing specks contained within them, presenting a mesmerising display in the dark room for her reddened eyes. Her uncle's house, for all its comforts, did not sit on a street with gas lighting, and the effect was new and wondrous to her.

Suddenly she sat up in alarm. Her aunt and uncle! They must be worried about her, for if it were this dark, they must have expected her home long since! She must leave, but oh, she could not face Professor Darcy or the colonel. Where was Mrs. Pearce? That lady alone seemed to care for Lizzy's wellbeing. The colonel was pleasant and amiable, but while he provided some sort of element of civility to the enterprise, he was there to observe his cousin and entertain himself with the progress of the lessons. Under other circumstances, Lizzy thought she and the colonel would be great friends, but his role in the affair was too much delineated by the nature of his bet with Darcy.

As for the professor, his manners improved ever so slightly, but he remained gruff and often rude, and rather selfish in all things, and his interest in her seemed as a project to be completed and admired and not as an independent person with her own thoughts and hopes and experiences. But then there were those moments, rare though they may be, when she wondered if perhaps he did care somewhat for her being: those moments when he was polite and gracious for no reason other than to be pleasant; the times when he glared at the piano master whose hands touched and guided her own; the smiles when he thought she was not looking; the way he had approached her and talked to her after their dance lessons.

But no, she must not read anything into these few suggestions of humanity in the man. She was his student and his co-conspirator, his puppet, his creation. Nothing more.

In her anguish, her thoughts strayed back to Colonel Fitzwilliam's comments about the native communities he encountered in Jamaica, free men and women living in their tribal ways, unlike the African slaves on the plantations. He had seemed so proud of the unbound natives, so scornful of slavery, and yet did he not see that she, Lizzy, was surely as bound up in this scheme as were the slave workers on the plantations? The reasonable part of her mind shouted down these wild notions—she was a free person, enslaved to no one. Had the professor not promised her a dowry, given her the speech of a lady, and the wardrobe to match? But her tears drowned out the tremulous voice of reason, and she despaired anew of ever breaking free of Professor Darcy's machinations. The impossibility of the situation crushed her.

But now she must find Mrs. Pearce. In the half-light filtering in from the windows, she could see no taper to light, nor a bell pull to summon assistance. She crept to the door, resigned to walking down the stairs in search of assistance. She did not fear encountering the men too much, for they were always ensconced in the study, pouring over some treatise on dialect acquisition or a new technique for notating vocal sounds, or dreaming about the possibility of one day capturing sound on a device as an artist captures visual images on canvas. Her goal was not the study, but the kitchen, for there she might find Mrs. Pearce.

Looking through the spy-hole in the bedroom door, she saw the corridor appeared empty. Quietly she opened the door and slipped through, screwing up her eyes against the brightness of the hallway, a shock after the darkness of her room. She had taken only a step, however, when she tripped over something lying across the floor. She caught herself against a wall, and looking down, she saw in horror that the offending object was nothing other than Professor Darcy's long legs.

He was sitting on the floor, leaning against the wall, his legs stretched across the width of the corridor. He scrambled to his feet, apologising profusely for tripping her. "I was dozing... I didn't notice... I thought you had seen me...." She turned her face away from him, afraid of the expression that must be written across it, but he caught her arm and gently turned her around to face him. The softness of his touch stunned her; he had never been so gentle before in all the time she had known him.

"I am sorry, Eliza. I had not thought how trying today must have been. It was inexcusable on my part, and you have every reason to hate me for it. But I do hope you will not hate me; for some reason that would cause me great distress. Forgive me?"

His words stunned her, but his eyes did even more so. She had never seen such sincerity there before, those dark orbs now pleading with her to open her heart just a small amount. Gone was the sardonic glint so often present; gone was the half-smirk of disdain with the world. These eyes, deep brown and really beautiful under their long lashes, were vulnerable and filled with pain. Pain that she could relieve.

For a moment she thought to walk away from him and leave him there in the corridor, but even as her mind commanded her feet to walk away, her heart told her to stay, to forgive him. He had not been deliberately cruel, merely thoughtless. Tea with the countess was as trivial to him as walking into Meryton was to her. It was unfair to condemn him for a sin he had not intended to commit.

Finding strength in the core of her being, she nodded and lowered her eyes. "I forgive you, sir."

"Thank you." The words were whispered, barely loud enough to hear.

"I must... I must send word to my aunt and uncle. They surely have worried about my whereabouts since dusk fell. I am never this late—" she started, recalling her mission.

"Be easy, Eliza. They have been made aware of your present whereabouts. We sent a messenger with a note saying you had taken ill with a minor complaint, a headache—so as not to worry them about that—and that you would remain here for the evening, under the careful eye of Mrs. Pearce. They are satisfied with the arrangements and await word of your health in the morning."

"I thank you." She was able to look him in the eye now. "I, too, must apologise for my behaviour. I thought I was equal to the occasion, but I was mistaken. I felt, all at once, so overwhelmed, I knew not what to say. I am woefully unprepared for a season, I'm afraid." She turned away once more and cast her eyes to the floor.

"Nonsense, Eliza!" he put a finger under her chin and raised it again so her eyes met his. "You were caught unaware. We have been spending so much of our efforts on how you say things and how you move and what accomplishments you ought to possess that we have been neglecting the people and places in which these new talents will be exhibited. We must move from the school room to the drawing room, but we shall do so gradually, at your comfort." He looked intently at her. "At *your* comfort," he repeated. "Will you agree?"

"Aye. Thank you."

"Nonsense!" The sensitive soul that had briefly appeared in his likeness was gone, and he was back to his usual gruff self. "Now, come and play a hand or two at loo. The colonel awaits and Mrs. Pearce is holding your supper. Don't make her wait any longer than necessary."

രുള

The following morning, after another note was sent to the Gardiners by Lizzy herself assuring them of her health, and after a very pleasant breakfast, which only Mrs. Pearce and the colonel attended, Lizzy found herself being summoned into Professor Darcy's private study, a small room off the main library-cum-study area in which most of her lessons had taken place. Walking into the room, she stared astounded at the sheer number of books that lined every inch of spare wall from floor to ceiling, and which were stacked in high piles on tables, chairs, desks and even on the floor.

Ignoring the chaos around him, Darcy sat at his desk, staring at a newspaper, while sipping a steaming black drink that smelled of coffee and distractedly eating from a plate of pastries, whilst crumbs fell unheeded onto his papers. Not looking up, the professor gestured to a chair and mumbled, "Sit, sit," through a mouth full of scone.

There was one chair available that was not stacked with books, a delicate-looking Elizabethan construction opposite the desk to the professor, and Lizzy seated herself gracefully. She sat in silence, waiting for Darcy to complete whatever it was he was doing. After a moment, he looked up and blinked, as if surprised to see her in his private space. Wiping the crumbs from the corner of his mouth with a bare hand, he *hmmmed*, then said, "Oh, yes, Eliza."

"You wished to see me, Professor?" Her accent, by now, was lovely. Every trace of the country was gone, her vowels perfect, her consonants clear and precise, her phrasing lilting and melodious.

He stared a moment longer, then said, "I felt I ought to inform you. The colonel's mother is coming for tea this morning. She wishes to talk with you."

Lizzy felt her face flush red, then drain of all colour. If her heart had stopped beating, it would not have surprised her. What could the countess want, but to scold and chastise, belittle and admonish her for her deplorable behaviour the previous day? She had lost all her composure and had embarrassed herself terribly, dragging Darcy and the colonel with her.

"I... I cannot face her. My shame is too great. She can have nothing good to say, for I comported myself most appallingly yesterday. Please send her my compliments, but I must be gone. I must return to my uncle's house. This will never do." She began to rise to her feet, but Darcy stopped her.

"Oh, Eliza. I have failed you again with my thoughtless words. Let me explain, please." She reluctantly settled back into the chair, although tension reigned in every blink of her eye, every twitch of a hand. "After you departed yesterday, my aunt was most displeased, but," he hastened to add, "not with you. Not at all with you! Rather, her displeasure settled most definitely and uncomfortably upon me and, to a lesser extent, upon Richard. She gave us both a rather severe dressing down, scolding us as if we were both still children. It galls me to admit it, but there's a possibility she may have been right about one or two things."

The arrogance was still there, but the veneer of it thinner now, allowing once more a glimmer of compassion to leak through. For the first time, Lizzy found herself wondering whether the haughty, uncivil curmudgeon was, indeed, the real Professor Darcy, or if a kinder man lurked deep inside the shell he had created around himself.

"Her Ladyship wishes to speak to you not to condemn you," he continued, "but to befriend you. She has suggested that, perhaps, our... my approach has some minor faults." The confession stuck in his throat, but he forced it out. "Will you agree to take tea with her? She truly wishes you no ill."

Lizzy's instinct to run was kept at bay only by the unaccustomed sincerity in his words and in his voice. She had heard that voice once or twice before; she had heard it last night, in the corridor outside her room. It had stopped her flight then, and it stopped it now. She felt some of the tension release itself from her spine and her forehead, and her head nodded slightly of its own accord. "I do not know how I can face her. I am most ashamed."

"She does not see matters that way, Eliza. Believe me. She saw nothing amiss in your actions yesterday other than alarm and being ill-advised by... well, by me. There, I have said it. Now, will you do it or not?"

The screen of rude arrogance slid over the gentle eyes of a moment before, and the gruff professor was making himself heard again, overshadowing the kind man who may have been lurking below the surface. Oddly, Lizzy felt herself rise to his bait. This, she knew, she could confront with her usual headstrong impertinence, and she did so.

"Do you order me around as a servant, sir?" she demanded. "For while your last comment was phrased as a question, it held the import of a command. And I shall not be commanded by the likes of you!"

He threw his head back and laughed, "There's my Eliza! Good girl! Now go and find Mrs. Pearce. She will help you dress."

"I had not agreed, Professor Darcy."

"No, but you will. Run along now. There's a good girl."

She stood and glared at him. "Goodbye, Professor Darcy. I shall send for my belongings." She turned for the door.

Leaping after her, he almost knocked over a pile of books in his attempt to reach the door before her. "You can't just leave!" He edged between her and the door and stood with his back against it, barring her exit.

"And you, sir, can't just order me around. Once more, you have made my decision for me and informed me after the fact of what it should be."

She stood facing him, her breath coming hard and her eyes sparking fire with her sudden determination. She glared at her nemesis as he flung his arms out to block the doorway completely and prevent her escape. His nostrils flared as he leaned back against the egress, a living barricade, his mouth a firm line of determination.

She did not fear him. He might rant and rave, but he had never intentionally done her ill and she somehow knew he would not. He also would not make her escape easy. "You cannot just leave." The words were torn from his chest. "We have... we have our pact, our scheme. You will not abandon me so, will you Eliza?"

She met his gaze and did not back down. As she stared at him, his eyes darkened and his lips parted slightly as his eyes flickered to her mouth. He began to lean forward, then backed away as if burned and squeezed his eyelids closed for a moment as he regulated his breath and his temper.

Then the tension suddenly departed his body, and he collapsed back against the door, his eyes closed in defeat. "Once again, you remind me of my manners, Eliza. Never let it be said that I am a vindictive man. I have offered you every kindness, but I shall not demand recompense. I have no desire to harm you or to force you to act against your will, and if you truly wish to leave, I shall ask Mrs. Pearce to help make the appropriate arrangements. But I will, one last time, beg you to remain. For the colonel. For me."

These words extinguished the flame that fueled Lizzy's ire, and she felt a wave of indecision rush over her. "I do not know..."

"For my aunt?" His voice was smooth, but tinged with desperation. "You may call her Aunt Patricia if you wish. She will not mind, and it will make you easier. I would recommend, however, against calling her Aunty Patsy. That, she will not appreciate."

A smile, small though it was, began to form on Lizzy's face at the thought of the imposing Countess of Malton as Aunty Patsy. She sighed in resignation and stepped back, widening the space between the two. Darcy straightened and returned to his desk as Lizzy took a moment to collect herself. "I shall take tea with her. After that, I cannot say what I will do. But I will not disappoint the countess."

"Thank you, Eliza," he breathed. "Let her be your friend. She is a fine woman, even if she is responsible for Richard." With a curtsey, Lizzy opened the door to finally escape the study, but not before seeing, from the corner of her eye, Darcy fling his head back on his chair, cursing quietly under his breath, and muttering something that sounded like 'What on earth just happened?'

Back upstairs in her room, Lizzy stared blankly at the wardrobe full of lovely gowns as she tried to make sense of the scene in Darcy's private study. He had laughed when she thought he would shout, had been rude and domineering, and just when she thought he would throw her out onto the street, a look had come over him that had shaken her to the core. The intensity in his eyes, as he stood blocking the door, had been terrifying and powerful, but rather than feeling afraid, she had been mesmerised by what she had seen. She had never been afraid of him at all, she realised. Not in his blackest, angriest moods, had he made the first gesture or sound that would cause one to fear. He yelled, he cursed, he insulted, and he ignored, but he never occasioned alarm.

What, then, was that look in his eye? She did not believe him angry. Frightened, desperate, perhaps, but not angry. And if not angry, then what? She relived the moment in her mind. At the moment, she had thought he might reach out and kiss her, but surely that could not be his intention. And, just as before, when he had never given her a moment of apprehension, he had stepped back and let her go. Did he not, then, wish to kiss her after all? No, don't be silly, she chided herself. He never desired it in the first place.

More disturbing was the realisation that she would not have objected if he had kissed her! This was most perplexing, for she was certain that she did not like him. He might have grown on her over the many weeks they had worked together, but surely that was merely because of their enforced proximity, was it not? He could be amusing, to be certain, but he was rude and condescending and really rather handsome. Scolding herself for that last thought, she determined to think no more of the not-a-kiss.

Mrs. Pearce interrupted these roiling and confusing thoughts with a knock at the door. The lady entered and cast her eyes over Lizzy before announcing, "Let us get you ready." Ceding to the inevitable, Lizzy let the older lady guide her focus to the array of gowns before her before summoning the maid to help her dress and do her hair. All the while she worked, the young maid chatted happily about her younger brothers and sisters, about the small village in which she had grown up in Derbyshire, about her new beau who worked in the stables at the duke's house across the square, and a hundred other pleasant and amusing things. "And did ye know, milady," the girl chirped, "that Professor Darcy allows us each an extra half-day off each week, from what's regular? He's a strange one, to be sure, but he is a kind master."

"Really, Millie, Miss Bennet is not interested in that," Mrs. Pearce chided, but from her expression, she was proud of her master's unconventional treatment of his servants. Reluctantly, she added, "I believe this is what brought the professor to the attention of that strange group of reformers in Wales. We were stopped for the day and one of his attendants had the time off to enjoy the local scenery, and there he met with someone or another from the cooperative. Most interested, were they, and poor James nearly had them following him back to the inn. How that would have vexed the professor!" she chuckled.

This, too, was an unexpected side to the professor. At once, so domineering and inconsiderate, while at the same time being a most generous and kind employer. "Has he always been thus?" Lizzy asked.

Mrs. Pearce thought for a moment. "I did not know him as a very young child, but he has always been an unusual person, never one to act according to the dictates of others, but insistent upon making his own rules, according to his own sense of right and wrong, and behaving accordingly.

"Aye, 'tis true," Millie replied. "For 'tis not well known, even amongst the servants here in the house, but Professor Darcy gave Annie Wilkins a whole month off her duties when she married last year, and as a wedding gift, let her and her new man take the cottage he has near Bedford for that time. And for the servants that has childer, he takes on a minder so they can work and not fret about their young'uns. A most unusual master, is he!" And on she spoke, until Lizzy's hair looked as perfect as it ever might. It was uncommon for a servant to talk so freely with her superiors, even in Darcy's very unconventional household, and Lizzy wondered if Mrs. Pearce had allowed the girl to do so in order to provide some pleasant distraction from what must be a rather intimidating morning ahead.

Whether or not the ploy was deliberate, it was successful, and when Lizzy descended the stairs some time later she was much happier and more at ease than she had been when she had gone up to dress. Darcy must have heard her tread on the stairs, for he stood waiting for her at the foot of the grand staircase. He bowed exceedingly politely and offered his arm to walk her into the drawing room. This room was rarely visited, being used only for the social necessities Darcy despised. Lizzy had been in it only once before. It was somewhat old-fashioned in its decor, although it must have been very elegant in its time. The ornamentation was a little too rococo, the decoration a little too Louis-XVI for Lizzy's liking, but the good taste that had gone into its design was apparent. Lizzy gazed up at the cherubs floating on the ceiling in a masterpiece of *trompe-l'oeil*, above walls of feminine pastels and chairs with delicately carved and very thin legs, seemingly unable to take the weight of a normal sized person. As if answering her unasked question, Darcy stated as he threw himself onto one of those chairs, "It was my own mother's favourite room." She understood immediately. He had not touched the space, for it reminded him of his mother. The unexpected sentimentality of this gesture touched her deeply, and she looked at him with fresh eyes.

The room had been aired and the curtains opened to let bright sunlight stream inside. The rains from the day before had abated, and the cheerful light lifted Lizzy's spirits. She hoped, desperately, that she would not be called upon to discuss the weather. Tentatively, she asked, "Professor Darcy, under what restrictions am I this morning?"

"Begging your pardon?" he sounded surprised at the question.

"What might I talk about, and what must I avoid?"

He shook his head sadly. "That was my mistake. One of my mistakes," he corrected. "You are an intelligent woman with excellent understanding. I should never have tried to limit you. This is not a formal call; you are merely having a quiet morning with Richard's mother. You may discuss whatsoever you desire. You will also discover, I believe, that once the artificial dictates of polite society are stripped away, Aunt Patricia is as much a bluestocking as are you. Ask her about her inquiries into steam engines." He winked.

At that moment, the doorbell could be heard, and he excused himself to greet his aunt at the door. "Wait here, Eliza. We shan't be long." A few moments later, Darcy opened the door and led the countess into the room. "I shall go and find Mrs. Pearce to ask for tea. Back in a moment!" He dashed out, closing the door behind him.

"That was not very subtle, was it my dear?" the countess quipped as she lowered herself onto a fragile-looking sofa. "Now, now, do not fret. I can imagine every anguish you put yourself through last night, and likely a few that you did not, and you deserved to suffer through none of them. Eliza... May I call you Eliza? Good. Here is something you ought to know about me. I observe people carefully and make quick decisions about them. I am usually correct in my first assessments, and my first impression of you was to like you very much. So you have no need to fear that I shall see you cut or otherwise disparaged in society. I also wish to know you better. May I take the extreme liberty of asking to be your friend?"

Her handsome face was unstrained, her expression entirely sincere.

"Yes, I would be most honoured, Your Ladyship." Lizzy dipped into a curtsey.

The countess shook her head good-naturedly. "The first rule is that you are not to call me 'Your Ladyship' or 'Lady Malton' or anything so stuffy whilst we are together in private. I insist on the recognition of rank in the appropriate circumstances, but we are to be friends. Can you manage Aunt Patricia? I would like that."

Lizzy looked at the countess closely for the first time. Her eyes were a duplicate of the colonel's in shape and expression, although a lighter colour. They held nothing but kindness, and Lizzy allowed herself to answer, "I would be honoured, Aunt Patricia."

The countess smiled radiantly and settled into her seat. "Good! Now that we have resolved that, our friendship is sure to be a raving success. Please sit." She gestured and waited until Lizzy was perched upon a spindly chair, then continued. "Tell me now, Eliza, more about the cloud formations you started discussing yesterday. It is not, perhaps, a topic most ladies would wish to talk about, but I am fascinated. I grew up in a country estate, for my father did not like Town, and I spent much time observing and trying to predict the weather. Freddy shares my interests. Please, tell me more!"

Tentatively at first, Lizzy began to speak of her studies into the research of John Dalton, and Aunt Patricia responded enthusiastically. By the time Darcy returned with Mrs. Pearce some time later, the two ladies were deep in a spirited discussion about cloud formation and the trade winds. "If I understand correctly," Lizzy was saying as they entered, "the sun constantly heats the earth and the air successively from east to west. The air being heated then expands in different directions to restore an equilibrium of pressure. Because this expansion has a lateral and perpendicular motion, it has a concurrent effect on the barometer, as well as influencing wind strength and direction."

"How fascinating!" Aunt Patricia supplied.

"How charming!" came a voice from behind Darcy and Mrs. Pearce, and Alfred, Viscount Eynshill, strode into the room. "Miss Bennet, a delight to see you again. Once more, I am enthralled by your knowledge and abilities. I must chastise my cousin yet again for hiding you from us for so very long. Really, Darcy, she is a treasure!"

"Freddy," his mother greeted him, "You did not tell me you planned to come by." Her tone was not approving.

"You would only have forbidden me, Mother," he replied with a smile. "And how could I be denied another opportunity to converse with the enchanting Miss Bennet?" He executed an elaborate bow and threw another wicked smile in Lizzy's direction. "I brought these for Miss Bennet." From behind his back he withdrew a bouquet of flowers that perfectly matched the dress she had worn the previous day and presented them to her with a flourish. Lizzy accepted them gracefully and requested a vase be brought. A glance at Darcy's stony face informed her that he was unimpressed.

Watching, as if from a distance, Lizzy took further stock of the viscount. Tall, as were the entire family, with the same light hair as the colonel, he was slightly more handsome and entirely charming. He moved with the ease and grace of long practice, and caught the eye with his elegant demeanour, and Lizzy suppressed a chuckle as he paused before the mirror above the mantelpiece to assess his striking appearance.

The viscount had his brother's amiability and easy nature, but where Richard's pleasant demeanour was overlaid atop the sober and responsible core that comes with the demands of military leadership, Alfred's was pleasantry atop frivolity. It was clear that he loved his clothing, for he wore his finely tailored garb like a model for the clothes-makers' magazines. As with the flowers, he had chosen a waistcoat that matched the yellow of the previous day's frock, and he picked carelessly at the ample lace that extended from his cuffs. If he was a man, like Narcissus, who admired himself too much, he was redeemed because he liked others nearly as much, and sought to befriend where another man might seek to disparage.

Lizzy knew he was a man who could afford to indulge his whims. She knew he need never account for his actions, for his life's work was merely to be the earl and eventually provide an heir. With those two requirements easily managed, he had the luxury to do and act as he pleased. If he did not waste away the family's income, he would be considered a fine example of an English nobleman; if he did fritter it away, he would be thought no worse than most of his breed. It was a career well suited to his temperament.

Despite his foppishness, Lizzy could not help but like him. He was nothing like the serious, deep-thinking men she often found the best company, but his genuine friendliness and lack of condescension endeared him to her almost immediately. That he clearly liked her very much also did not impede her affinity to him. He lowered himself to sit beside her, careful not to disarrange his apparel, and when seated on the long sofa with its old-fashioned and elaborate upholstery, turned his body to face her and offered a friendly comment, then another, and another, until she began to answer in like fashion.

"My brother tells me you are from the country, Miss Bennet, and have not had much experience with society in Town. Yes, yes, Darcy, I know of your little scheme, so you can put that shocked expression back into its box. I forced Richard to tell me all, for I had no other way to decipher the whole situation. Miss Bennet, you are beyond impressive! To have come, green and untried, from a small village in Hertfordshire, to convince us all with your exceptional manners and beautiful speech, is astounding. I would take off my hat to you, but I left it with Mrs. Pearce at the front door. What a smart girl you are! Now, as I was asking..."

He asked about her experiences in the country and how they compared to those in Town; he asked after her aunt and uncle, and far from being shocked at her low connections, proclaimed, "Gardiner! Yes, of Gardiner Mercantile! Fine, upright man he is. He never overcharges, never steers you wrong. You must be proud of the connection! He, himself, guided me to this fine cravat!" He gestured to his embroidered neckcloth, which too matched the yellow of yesterday's gown.

She told him of her four sisters, including flirtatious Lydia, silly Kitty, serious Mary—soon to be the wife of a clergyman in Kent—and Jane, recently wed to Darcy's good friend Bingley. Alfred was amazed that Mary's future husband was none other than his aunt's rector at Hunsford. "Oh, dear Aunt Catherine," he rolled his eyes. "She does like a puppy to pant and pine after her. Is he a puppy, Miss Bennet, always simpering after his master for affection and, if he is most lucky, a treat of some scrap from the table? Oh, do tell more."

And as she spoke, he stared at her with a half-smile and an ever-growing look of besottedness on his aristocratic face. Aunt Patricia started looking concerned. Darcy became most agitated. By the time tea arrived, with Richard trailing after the cart, the professor was most distressed and was hiding it poorly. He paced up and down behind the sofa and wrung his hands, while interrupting the conversation as often as he could.

"Really, Darcy, do settle yourself," his aunt admonished. "We are having a lovely chat, and you are prowling like a tiger in its cage. Now be a dear and pour the tea for us. Eliza is your guest and must not be made to play hostess, and Richard would spill every drop. There's a good lad. Your mother would be proud."

By the time Darcy convinced Richard to drag his brother back to his own home across the square, the viscount had invited Lizzy to walk with him the following afternoon before her lessons, and she had accepted his invitation. Darcy put up a series of objections, all of which Freddy dismissed. "Really, Fitz, you can't be worried about Miss Bennet's reputation. I am hardly the most sensible fellow in town, but neither am I acknowledged as a rake. The lady's name will scarcely be damaged by being seen in the company of Viscount Eynshill in a public park on a sunny day. It would, rather, raise her in the estimation of the *ton*." After some heated argument, Darcy had to agree; nevertheless, he looked quite happy when Freddy and Richard finally bid their farewells and left the room.

Lizzy watched this entire silent discourse with interest. She was in the middle of a most pleasant conversation with the countess, and was even sufficiently comfortable to laugh at Aunt Patricia's description of some awful gown she had seen at the opera the previous week, and for a moment her attention was diverted to the strange interaction between the cousins. What on earth had that been about, she wondered, and only with difficulty returned her focus to the discussion about lace and ribbon.

"Come, Fitz, sit down and join us," his aunt cried, seeing him at the doorway. "We are having a lovely gab. I have offered to guide Eliza for her first several social functions. Instead of your crusty morning lessons, she shall come to me, or I to her, and we shall continue as we are now, woman to woman, as we learn to negotiate the morass that is London society. No, dear, this is not a request. Lovely girl." She patted Lizzy's arm and turned a most pleased expression towards her. "You could not have chosen better."

She left ambiguous the exact meaning of her comment.

# Ten
## The Next Stage

Lady Malton now took over the remainder of Lizzy's education. Whether or not this decision was formal, or whether or not she even informed her nephew of the fact was irrelevant. It was a *fait accompli*, for what Lady Malton decided would happen, happened. Thus, when she informed Darcy that the afternoon lessons must be rearranged according to her schedule, and that the morning lessons were now all but complete, he capitulated without a word of protest.

The countess first ensured that Lizzy was comfortable in her presence. She insisted on being called Lady Malton whilst in public, but assured her young friend that "it is merely to keep up appearances with those I disdain. We shall both know, you and I, and it shall be our little joke." For their first outing, the countess chose to take Lizzy shopping. They would be seen together, and she could introduce "her young friend newly arrived in London from her country estate," whilst allowing Lizzy the opportunity to speak briefly with shopkeepers and be overheard by other ladies of the *ton*, but not needing to engage in serious conversation. Asking the price of a roll of ribbon was well within the young protégée's area of comfort. An additional, if unexpected, benefit to these excursions was an even more expansive wardrobe for Elizabeth, now decorated fully with bonnets and gloves and hair ornaments and stockings, all purchased by Lady Malton, with a deaf ear to all protestation. All she would say is "Nonsense, my dear. It will look lovely with your eyes."

Then came the outings for tea. A visit to Gunter's became a marvellous opportunity to enjoy the sweets and say hello to a wave of elegant women who had to be seen talking to the countess, even for only a moment. A visit to Clarendon's for a fine French meal was next. The ladies were accompanied by Darcy, Richard, Freddy, and even the earl himself, an occasion which only a few days before would have sent Lizzy into fits of terror, but which she now managed with some steadiness of spirit. The earl, Lord Malton, was less openly friendly than were his sons, but he was also the sort to brook no nonsense and his forthright and calm manner reassured his young guest immensely. His very presence amongst the party dining out was a sure sign of his approval, and Lizzy took some confidence in that fact. The countess had drilled her relentlessly on proper city manners whilst dining—these were not so different from what she had learned at Longbourn, varying only in some subtle details—and she felt equal to the task, smiling quietly at her ladyship's constant reassuring nods.

This outing—deemed a great success by the countess—was followed by strolls through the parks, visits to the museums, and evenings at the theatre. At times, Darcy was permitted to join the ladies, and when he did so, he hovered protectively at Lizzy's side, keeping her hand on his arm when possible, and glowering at any men who dared approach. Freddy, too, often begged to join the party, and the ensuing battle of glares between the two men would have been amusing to anyone not intimately caught up in their rivalry. Through all of this, Lizzy's confidence and poise blossomed, and the countess announced after a time that she believed Miss Bennet more than up to any occasion.

Lizzy and her companions were sitting comfortably around the low table in Lady Malton's private salon one afternoon after a chilly stroll through the park, when Darcy announced, "I believe, Eliza, it is time to set the next stage of our plan into effect." He smiled at her and sent a quick sharp stare towards Freddy.

"Our engagement?" This was a surprise! The words reverberated through her head for a minute as she had almost forgotten the purpose of the entire scheme. "So soon, professor? Had we not discussed waiting a while longer? I thought we were to wait until Easter before making the announcement."

Moving next to her on the sofa, he turned his warm gaze to her, "You have progressed so far, learned so much, that I see no need to wait further. I shall send the announcement to *The Times* in the morning..." He stopped himself, then turned to Lizzy and bowed his head. "No. I shall do no such thing until I have discussed it with you, Miss Bennet. This involves you as intimately as it involves me, and I have learned not to assume you will agree to my every whim. Do you wish to consider the change in plans before I take action? I will accede to your wish on this."

"Who is this man" Richard joked from his seat by the fire, "who looks so much like my cousin, but who acts like a gentleman? Surely it can't be Fitz!" He rocked back in the elaborately carved chair, only to be scolded by his mother.

At the same time, Freddy objected, "Are you sure about this, Darcy?" His brows came low over his eyes and he fussed at the lace-edged handkerchief he held in his hands, twisting it to this side and that. "Miss Bennet? I would hate to see you take this step unnecessarily. It seems that Miss Bennet is well accepted in Town already, without this connection..." There was an anguish in his eye that tore at Lizzy's heart, and for a moment, she wished to comfort him. He had been attentive to her, doting even, and his flirtations were obvious and flattering, but he had done little to truly engage her heart. His interest in her seemed as much to bolster his own appearance as hers; he would send a messenger to the house to inquire on the colour of Miss Bennet's frock for the day, and would then appear in a matching waistcoat, or he would parade her around the park with an eye to catching the attention of those he knew, who might wonder at this remarkable young woman on his arm. She was happy to humour these vices, for he was good company and most pleasant to converse with, and she liked him a great deal. That he liked her was evident as well, but she detected no genuine attachment of the heart.

She also wondered, despite his obvious infatuation with her, if what he felt was anything but transitory, the whim of the moment. She knew that Freddy was quite aware of the counterfeit nature of the engagement; if he truly cared, and if his emotions were more than a passing fancy, he would not give up hope. She glanced at him to offer reassurance, but he had turned away towards the mantelpiece and was examining a collection of porcelain figurines.

Darcy, on the other hand, levelled his eyes at her and held her gaze with his own. His was a look of confidence, perhaps of victory. But he, too, must know that this engagement would not be real. He had been increasingly kind and solicitous towards her of late, and she had wondered, more and more, whether there was some real affection growing in his soul. Even now, this quick reversal of his accustomed habit of making decisions on the parts of others demonstrated the existence of a part of him she would not have imagined some months ago. The look of confidence in his eye wavered as she regarded him and became, instead, a look of supplication. "Please..." his expression seemed to beg. "Please..."

Lizzy let her eyes rove back and forth between the two men—her professor and her new friend—and spoke, her voice little more than a whisper. "Freddy, your concern touches me, deeply. However, as you are aware, this scheme is as much to keep Professor Darcy from the sights of the matchmakers as it is for my own benefit. I entered into the plan knowing what it would entail, and I am prepared to meet my obligations. And thank you, Professor Darcy, for considering my feelings on the matter. You are learning as much as am I."

She rose and walked towards the window, where her eyes drifted down to the street below and across the park. The expanse of open space, adorned with a careful latticework of pathways and shrubbery, was a balm to her soul, and her eyes drank deeply of it. She allowed the peace of the scene before her to fill her with a certainty that had not been there a moment before and then, turning back to the others in the room, said, "Yes, I am in accord. You may send out the announcement, Professor."

Darcy looked triumphant; Freddy spun around and looked stunned. Lady Malton and Richard looked on in bemusement. "Well," Richard offered at last, "how are we to commemorate this? I know not whether to celebrate an engagement with champagne or to seal a business arrangement with a handshake."

"Perhaps both, dear," his mother replied. "Call for tea and cakes, there's a good son, and let us begin planning a ball to mark the occasion."

And so it was done. Lizzy was engaged. Not to be married, perhaps, but engaged nonetheless. What she had always imagined would be a momentous occasion, complete with declarations of undying love and promises for the future, was concluded instead with the cool efficiency of an amicable trade negotiation. Was this how her uncle felt upon successfully completing a purchase of a shipment of fine fabric? The certainty that had been present only moments before now deserted her, and Lizzy was left with an empty space at the core of her being, and a dread at what she had just done.

The men were talking amongst themselves over whether or not a ball was necessary, and whether Richard should call for some port. Only the countess seemed to notice Lizzy's distress, and came to her where she stood by the window.

"You are uncertain about this?" The older lady placed a soft hand on Lizzy's shoulder and spoke with the warmth and compassion of a caring friend. "It is not too late to change your mind."

Lizzy shook her head. "No. I am certain. I merely feel..." she paused, not knowing what word could possibly encapsulate the hundreds of emotions roiling through her breast.

"Bereft?" the countess supplied. "You wished to be loved, and you are merely appreciated for what you can bring to an arrangement."

Tears welled in Lizzy's eyes, and she let them fall slowly down her face as she stared back outside for a long time. The peaceful scene had become stark and cold, and she wanted, suddenly, to wrap herself up in a blanket and hide from the world. She felt the countess' presence at her back shift, and then something else, as two warm arms wrapped around her from behind. A shuffling sound suggested that someone was moving, and when she turned her head, she noticed the countess ushering the others out of the room, whilst only Professor Darcy, who possessed the arms currently holding her so warmly, remained.

"Come, talk to me Eliza. We should be celebrating, not crying." Was that tenderness in his voice? It was a new note, and it edged its way into her heart, and before she knew herself, she had turned around in his arms and was weeping into the fabric of his fine coat, her head held securely against his chest. Gentle hands rubbed up and down her back and tentatively caressed the back of her head, fingers tangling in her elaborate hairstyle.

"It was not supposed to be like this," that new voice, so familiar yet so strange, sounded. "I had thought to ask you properly, even if this is only an arrangement. I had thought, perhaps—" He stopped abruptly and stiffened. Then, with a breath, and allowing himself to relax slightly, he continued, "I had even thought, perhaps, to ask you to consider... after a time, of course, during which we would come to know each other better... perhaps not to throw me over after our arrangement is complete. We seem to rub along well together, Eliza. Your presence does not adversely affect my life."

From within the despair that had overwhelmed her from nowhere, a thread of amusement formed. Through the tears, she choked out, "Is that a declaration, Professor Darcy? You ought not to take up a new career as a romantic poet."

"Are you smiling, my Eliza? I do so want you to smile. And... think on it. Do not answer me now, but think on it." His lips carefully touched the top of her head. "I do not speak with the tongue of the poets, although I pronounce their rhymes better than they do, but I do care for you, my dear. No, no, don't respond. Just know that."

The tears had not stopped, but they were lighter now. Her voice thick, she replied, "Thank you, Professor. I shall do so."

Now he stood back, keeping his hands on her shoulders, his arms straight. "You should not call me that anymore, now that we are engaged."

"I can hardly call you Darcy!" she protested.

"Would you call me Fitz? As Richard does when he is most particularly vexed with me? I suspect you will often be vexed with me, and it will suit well."

Her laughter was freer when she replied, "Yes... Fitz. This shall take some getting used to, but I can manage, I believe."

His smile, when it came, was blinding in its brightness, his face glowingly handsome. "I would like, very much, to kiss you. But I shan't unless you allow me. Will you, Eliza? Will you allow me?"

She nodded, dazed at the question, and his head inclined slowly towards her. Then she felt the touch of his lips upon hers, feather-light; she was hardly aware of his caress before he withdrew. His eyes were closed, as if he were sealing the sensation into his memory for eternity. "Thank you," he whispered.

Before any announcement was sent, before the ball was to be planned, Lizzy wished to inform her sister Jane. She had visited Jane and Bingley once or twice over the winter months, but the couple had opted to remove themselves from London at the end of January, and had spent much of their time at Bingley's brother-in-law's small estate in Oxfordshire, the place being abandoned by its owner all winter. Jane had written that while London was lovely, it was too difficult to remain out of the public eye, and that she preferred to spend her first few months as a married woman in the quiet and privacy of the country.

Now the Bingleys had returned for Mary's wedding, which was rapidly approaching, and Lizzy longed to see them. A message was sent and a response received, and the next morning, Lizzy stood at the front door to Bingley's London residence. His sister Caroline had been evicted from the house, leaving Jane the undisputed mistress of the modest but elegant residence.

She had scarcely stepped foot inside when Jane rushed out of the drawing room, crying, "Lizzy!"

"Oh, Jane!" The sisters embraced fiercely, beyond happy to be once more in each other's presence. "Oh, dear Jane! Look at you! You look so well, so content," Lizzy cried. "Are you happy, dearest? Is Charles treating you well?"

"I could not be happier," Jane replied. "Charles is the best of men. We are both so very, very happy! Come now; he is waiting to greet you." Taking her sister by the hand, Jane dragged Lizzy into the drawing room at the front of the house. Bright light streamed in through the window, gilding Bingley's light brown hair in gold as he stood to greet his new sister.

"Elizabeth," he bowed politely before enfolding her in a brief embrace. Her mind flashed to the embrace she had shared with Fitz the afternoon before and her face flushed. Recalling herself to her situation, she greeted Charles with the warmth due a new brother and commented on how lovely Jane looked. "You are good for her, for her beauty is even more now than before."

They took tea, talking about the weather, Oxfordshire, the sad neglect at Hurst's estate, and who had or had not been seen around Town. "Caroline is recently returned," Charles said. "She had gone up to our aunt in Scarborough, for Hurst did not want her in the townhouse after Christmas, but I had a note from her just yesterday asking to stay here once again. I had to tell her no. She has money to take apartments and hire a companion; I cannot be her keeper now that I have dear Jane." He sent a besotted smile across to his bride, and she responded likewise. "Caroline said something about seeing other friends from Meryton in London; do you know what she might mean, Elizabeth?"

"No, not I! I have been quite kept in isolation, between Fitz... I mean, Professor Darcy's lessons and Lady Malton's outings."

"And what of those lessons, Lizzy?" Jane asked, curious. "You sound so very much the lady! I should never have known you, just to hear you speak. And your dress, your very manner of walking, are so elegant and refined. Professor Darcy must be very pleased with your success."

"I feel so very different, Jane, whilst I feel at the same time completely unchanged. It is hard to imagine that I am the same person who left Meryton only a few weeks ago. I had thought myself so worldly and confident and sophisticated before, but now I hardly know myself. I dress like a duchess and I dine with earls, and yet I am, at heart, the girl from the country who fed the pigs in the farmyard and ran through the orchards in John Lucas' old breeches. But I know I can never go back. That is why I hope, so very desperately, that our scheme is successful."

"What of the scheme?" Charles asked. "Is Darcy pleased?"

"Very," Lizzy replied. "In fact, we have decided to announce our engagement earlier than our original intentions. Tomorrow, in fact. Fitz said he will come here shortly to inform you himself. This is something to announce to friends and family before it is read of in the papers."

Jane scrutinised her sister. "Is this good news, Lizzy? I cannot tell if you are pleased or not."

"Neither can I Jane. I believe I am happy, but it is all unsettling, all the more so because..." she let her eyes flick to Charles, who was party to the conversation. "Because," she finished quickly, "it has all been so sudden, not as we had decided at first."

The chimes from the front door sounded, and the three occupants of the drawing room were quiet until, a few moments later, Professor Darcy was announced. Charles leapt up to greet his friend with a slap on the back and a firm handshake, and Jane curtseyed, welcoming him to her home. Darcy responded more civilly than Lizzy had seen since the first encounter with the Gardiners at Longbourn, before walking over to her and taking her hand, then kissing it while gazing into her eyes. "Eliza, my dear," he said softly.

"Oh..." whispered Jane, her head bobbing and her brows rising in realisation of something Lizzy could not quite decipher. Bingley looked on confused, until Jane said something into his ear, at which time he stood, eyes wide, mouth agape.

"We are to congratulate you, Professor," Jane said in her serene way. "Allow me to convey my wishes that matters work themselves out to everyone's best advantage." She bestowed upon him one of her sweetest smiles before turning to her husband. "Charles, why not take Professor Darcy to your study for a drink? It is, I believe, late enough in the day that a celebratory port would not be amiss. I will call down to the kitchen to request a tray. I wish to talk with Lizzy, for I have not seen her in an age! Sisters always need more time together than men will allow without some other occupation." She kissed his cheek, daring the others to be shocked by her brazen actions.

When the men were gone, Jane turned on her sister. "What has happened, Lizzy? Do not hide it, for I see more than you think."

In her beautiful new voice, with her beautiful new sounds, Lizzy described her time in London over the past two months, dwelling on Darcy's behaviour. "He has been acting as if jealous of Freddy—Viscount

Eynshill," she explained at last, "and yesterday, when he told us he wished to announce the engagement early, he was kinder to me than he had ever been before. Afterwards, when we were alone, he even suggested an alteration in our original plans..."

"Tell me, Lizzy. Do not cry, for I am here to share your burden."

Lizzy fell into her sister's arms. "Dear, sweet Jane, always there to lift me up when I have fallen! Oh, Jane, he suggested perhaps not ending the engagement..."

"He loves you, Lizzy? I see how he admires you, although I had not thought him able to love anyone but himself!"

Lizzy shook her head. "No, I do not believe he loves me. He cares for me, and he likes me, but he said nothing about loving me. His proposal, such that it was, included telling me that 'my presence does not adversely affect his life.' What am I to make of that, Jane?" These last words were choked out, somewhere between a sob and a laugh.

"And what did you tell him? Did you accept?" Jane's guileless blue eyes were wide with concern.

"I told him nothing. He requested that I not, but that I think on it over the next months. I believe that now, only after we are officially engaged, he wishes to court me. Oh, I am so confused!"

"And what of you, dearest? Do you like him?"

Chewing her bottom lip, Lizzy replied, "That, I do not quite know. I had not thought it, but there have been moments when I have wondered..." After a breath, she laughed off her distress and turned with a full smile to Jane. "I have many months before I need make that fateful choice. In the meantime, I shall be paraded and danced and exhibited around town like a newly acquired pet from the Orient, and I fully intend to enjoy myself. I shall be on Fitz's arm, with Freddy loping along behind us should I fall, and I am determined to enjoy every moment."

"Then enjoy it you must, Lizzy! Only, I pray that you do not get hurt."

CRSO

George Wickham stepped out of the shadows at the gates to the park. He had been waiting, as he said he would be in the letter he had sent via its circuitous route to the lady he had been wooing. She would arrive soon; she always had before. She seemed to enjoy these secretive assignations almost as much as she claimed to enjoy Wickham's company. The smirk on his face betrayed his own thoughts, which dwelt not so much on the lady's personality, but other aspects of her companionship.

How easy it had been. She had succumbed quickly to his charms, charms which he had applied most thickly for her benefit. Miss Bingley—dear Caroline, as he called her—had been a most willing victim. He thought back to their first meeting at Netherfield those months past, before Bingley married the girl from that other house—what was it? Longsomething? She had batted her eyelashes at his handsome face, and in truth, it was not difficult to respond appropriately, for she was a lovely woman. Lovely in face, at least. Her character, as Wickham had soon discovered, was less lovely, but her character was the least of his concerns.

She had invited him in for tea. A friend of Darcy's must be made welcome! Although he had played the gentleman and declined that particular offer, he had let her know where she might find him, and find him she had. She had most suddenly taken to walking in exactly the location he exercised his horse in the mornings, and after several meetings, so carefully coincidental, she had invited him to meet with her brother on a day when she knew her brother would be out, thereby leaving her with the arduous responsibility of entertaining the handsome officer alone.

They had talked of meaningless, inconsequential matters for a while, before he subtly began his inquiries into her relationship with the gentleman residing in Bingley's home. If his plans to destroy his nemesis were to come to fruition, he must be certain of the man's commitment to the lady. Ruining another man's love would be amusing, to be sure, but not nearly so satisfying as finally wreaking his revenge on the heir to Pemberley.

"Your family must be most intimate with the Darcys," he had said innocently to her as he sipped his tea, "for your brother to invite him here for an indefinite visit. How fortunate to be linked with one of his stature."

"We are most fortunate indeed," she had simpered. "Charles and Darcy—I call him Fitzwilliam, so do forgive me if I slip—became friendly at university, and our families immediately were linked." This was fine news to Wickham's ears, for none of his acquaintance dared call the man by his Christian name. This must signify an attachment.

"I have spent many glorious days at Pemberley," the lady batted her eyes, "which you must know so well. It is a magnificent estate, and I look forward to many more days amongst its splendours. We hope," she added conspiratorially, "to make the connection more formal before long." There was a sly and knowing look in her eye, and Wickham felt emboldened. She did not love the man, of that he was certain, but she dearly wished to be mistress of his estate.

He pressed on, eager to learn more. "Unless he has changed from when last we were together, he is not an easy man to be around. His manners can be quite... abrupt. Is he much improved in your company, Miss Bingley? For only those of us who have known and cared for him from childhood have a true sense of the man inside."

She gave him a coy smile. "His manner is, it is true, difficult for those unaccustomed to him. Charles puts him in his place, and he is always most attentive to me. I do not fear his curt and uncivil ways."

Wickham smiled. This would be an easy conquest indeed. Darcy seemed to care for the lady, especially if the rumours of the courtship were true, but she cared only for his wealth. He would have no difficulty wooing and seducing her and then using the scandal to break Darcy's heart—assuming the man had one. He could even offer to protect the lady's reputation afterwards... for a price! This would be a revenge Wickham could enjoy most thoroughly.

As he had imagined, Caroline responded perfectly to his machinations. He had dropped further hints as to his whereabouts on specific days, and she had happened to be about. He had discovered her own habits and managed, remarkably, to be where she happened to be. He politely held doors for her and handed her into carriages and over thresholds to shops and tea houses, and when, at last, he had whispered words of affection to her, she had looked him directly in the eye and smiled.

After her brother's wedding, she had sadly left Meryton. Her stay in London was short, before she had been forced to spend the frigid months of winter with her aunt in Scarborough. But he had her direction; through a young maid he had bribed, he sent notes to Caroline's own maid, who then delivered and dispatched letters between the two lovers. The affair had grown in intensity despite their separation, and now, at last, Caroline had returned to London, where she had been forced by her brother to take apartments with a companion. The companion, fortunately, was easily evaded through some little mistruth or another, and Wickham had arranged to meet with her here, in the park, whence he would carry her off to his discrete rooms in a less fashionable part of town and complete his seduction. No doubt Caroline still thought to marry Darcy, but her heart would not be broken by his rejection of her. As for Darcy himself, neither lover spoke of him at all. It was enough to know that the man was there in the background, ready to be destroyed by the knowledge of his intended's betrayal!

His reveries at an end, Wickham waited some time more by the gates, until the carriage he awaited arrived. It stopped, and a footman helped a lady descend from its interior. And there she stood, lovely and elegant in the weak light of the cloudy day, eyes glowing with the anticipation of their tryst. He stepped forward and bowing deeply, intoned, "Miss Bingley."

She saw him and smiled, then replied, "Mr. Wickham. Shall we walk?" She dismissed her carriage, asking the footman to return at the appointed time, before taking Wickham's arm. He led her most properly down the main path, then onto a smaller one, and finally, into the deeper wood, where she flung herself at him and kissed him passionately. "George!"

"Caroline," he responded between kisses. "Come with me, my darling. I have a carriage waiting at the other gate, where no one will see us. Oh, Caro..."

# *Eleven*
## *Journeys*

The announcement in the society column of *The Times*, proclaiming to the world the engagement between Miss Elizabeth Bennet of Longbourn, Hertfordshire and Professor Fitzwilliam Darcy of Pemberley, Derbyshire, was published the following day. It was the source of much discussion and amazement in the breakfast rooms of the elite, and a collective sigh of despair could be heard from every match-making mother and single young lady of suitable age in the city. The chatter was everywhere: Who was this girl? Had anybody heard of the family? Someone's sister's brother-in-law had seen Darcy with some girl at the theatre—might it have been her? Was she a great beauty? Exceedingly wealthy? The buzz would not cease.

The one man in town who did not read the announcement was, by a twist of fate, George Wickham. After his tryst, after he had returned Caroline Bingley to her carriage, her hair perhaps not quite as perfect as it had been before, her frock slightly in disarray but unnoticeable under her cloak, he had chanced to come upon an old friend from the gaming tables some years back. A gab on the pavement near the entrance to the park became a longer gab at the Fox and Firkin over some good ale, followed by an impromptu journey out of town to where the horses were being prepared for the first race of the season.

Ale and brandy were consumed in quantity and money was wagered and lost even more liberally, and by the time Wickham returned to his rooms in London three days later, his purse empty and his head full and pounding, the immediate ado over Darcy's engagement had subsided, to be replaced by some scandal from the palace and a rather cryptic article about the Duke of S's wife and the Earl of P and some unusual event at the recent races.

It was two days after this that Wickham's head and stomach had settled sufficiently for him to contemplate a visit to his usual drinking spot, and at last, he finally the news.

"D'ye hear the news, Georgie boy? Yer old pal, Darly or sompin' like dat, he's gettin' hisself leg-shackled!" Wickham knew the man only as Higgins; he was some ten years Wickham's senior, a retired petty naval officer on half-pay, and a regular denizen of the tavern. Although often somewhat in his cups, the man was usually clean and well-enough dressed that he was not to be thought of as a complete reprobate. Mrs. Higgins, whoever she might be, took some care of her wastrel husband, it was clear. Wickham had spent many an evening relating his tale of woe to all who would listen, and Higgins, a good-seeming soul behind his drunkenness, was happy to listen. In turn, he had told his own story, dwelling on the battles he had seen and the final assault on his ship that had left him with his injury, but Wickham had not bothered to pay more attention than was needed to nod, frown, or comment suitably. This was one of Wickham's most valuable skills, he considered: the ability to listen only to what he felt was important, whilst leaving the appreciation of the details and specifics to those whose smaller intellects might need them. A smart man such as he could always supply the details from his imaginings, if ever they were needed.

Taking his flagon over to the table where Higgins sat, Wickham grabbed a chair and placed himself upon it. The man's news intrigued him. "Darcy, you say?"

"Aye," came the affirmation.

"Getting married! Well, this is news indeed! Tell me what you know. I have been out of... town for some days, and had missed this item!" He leaned forward and placed his elbows on the low wooden table, bracing himself above his ale, encouraging his companion to speak.

Always happy to relate gossip, Higgins grinned, belched, and threw back a large gulp of his own ale, before relating all of his meagre information. "'Twas in the newspapers some days back—yesterday, day b'fore, p'rhaps. I didn' read it none meself, but I done hear the nobs talking." The tavern was a fairly respectable spot, as often frequented by gentlemen on their way to some slightly unsavoury entertainment or gaming house as by the more presentable of the underclasses, such as Higgins. Its location, just off the streets that housed more acceptable establishments, with its not-quite-reputable character, allowed these 'nobs' the conceit of feeling they were bashing at the walls of society, living rough, and taking wild risks, all the while never really leaving the safety of their fashionable part of town. It was, in short, a marvellous place to hear gossip.

"So, as I was sayin'" Higgins continued, "these nobs was talkin' 'bout yer man, Darcy, being engaged for a shackling, and how the other one's sister had best start lookin' elsewhere, as should everyone else's."

Wickham suppressed a snicker. Caroline had said nothing at all about this, the little minx! Had she known he would ask when they last met? Or had it been so inconsequential to her, in the light of being with him, George Wickham, that she had not thought to comment? Oh, how Darcy would suffer! "What do you know of the girl?" Wickham asked, feeling he should make the appropriate inquiries, all the while celebrating his triumph.

"Some little thing from the country, they was sayin'. Father or brother or someone has an estate out not too far from town. She must be sompin' mighty pretty to catch his eye like that, and mighty wealthy too! From all ye's said of the man, he wouldn't let hisself go for less than his sister's dowry."

"Then let us raise a glass to him, Higgins," Wickham proclaimed with all good cheer. This was certainly Caroline. His Caroline, the woman he had tumbled only short days before, and whom he would have again, and again, before her wedding... and if he had his luck, even after! Ah, yes, at last things were going his way!

CRITICALLY — ❧

Plans for the ball which would introduce Elizabeth into London society as the future wife of Fitzwilliam Darcy were, by necessity, delayed due to the requirement for the lady to attend her sister's wedding. Mary was, at long last, to wed her cousin, Mr. Collins, after which she would remove to his home at Hunsford in Kent. By a great coincidence, the sort of which was most often expected in novels, but which occur in actual life with a frightening regularity, the living which Mr. Collins held was under the patronage of none other than Lady Catherine de Bourgh, aunt to Darcy, Richard and Freddy, sister to the Earl of Malton. It was Lady Catherine's daughter whom Darcy most specifically did *not* desire to marry, hence his scheme with Elizabeth.

Therefore, it was not considered unusual or unexpected for Darcy to accompany his betrothed to her home in Hertfordshire, where he would reside at Bingley's still-abandoned estate. For the sake of propriety, the couple were accompanied on their journey by Mrs. Pearce and Colonel Fitzwilliam, who had made several pointed comments about looking ever-so-forward to revisiting some former acquaintances in Hertfordshire. Lizzy pretended that she did not realise he was talking about Charlotte Lucas, but she also knew, by off-hand comments and questions about her childhood, that he had not stopped thinking about her friend during the last months in London.

The journey from London to Longbourn was not long: a mere half day in Professor Darcy's large and comfortable carriage saw the party sitting comfortably in the Bennets' sunny front parlour, awaiting tea and biscuits. The professor had insisted upon requesting permission of Lizzy's father concerning their engagement, even though the older gentleman had reluctantly agreed when the plan was first conceived, and even though the announcement had gone out in the newspapers the week before. Afterwards, Darcy related to her in whispered tones the essence of the interview. "Your father seemed quite perplexed at my request," he stated with maddening equanimity. "He granted his second permission easily enough and was almost friendly, offering me brandy, but then he reiterated his threat, namely that I should never sleep easily again were I to hurt you in any way." He sipped at his tea, his eyes fixed on some distant and invisible point. "Why on earth should he think that of me?"

The Bennets were all agog at the transformed Elizabeth. Jane, who was by now accustomed to Lizzy's new speech and manners, was not able to attend the wedding, citing some minor ailment that had all the ladies whispering and tittering in corners; thus there was no one to deflect attention from the phenomenon of the New Elizabeth Bennet. Mary exclaimed at her tales of visiting the museums and the libraries and asked what services were like at Professor Darcy's church. Lydia, echoed by Kitty, gushed and cooed over her gown and bonnet. "Oh, Lizzy, is that silk? Not just the bodice, but the skirt too? Do you wear any muslin at all? How many yards of ribbon are there on the skirt? Look at those tiny satin flowers. Each one would take me a day to make. Is there any lace left at all in the shops after what's gone into this dress? Does everyone wear yellow in Town?"

Mrs. Bennet looked pleased to have her daughter back with her, but perhaps more to triumph over her that it was Mary, two years younger, who was being married, and not Lizzy herself. The matron cast an envious eye at the beautiful frock her daughter wore, and at her finely made pelisse and bonnet, but commented only on her daughter's deportment. "Well, aren't you the high and mighty one now, Lizzy, sounding like a fine lady and acting too good for the rest of us with your society manners? I'm sure we aren't nearly good enough for the likes of you anymore, are we?" It was only much later that she offered her begrudging congratulations to Lizzy and Darcy, well after the latter's interview with Mr. Bennet, when the engagement was announced. "I'm sure you'll be happy in his large estates. Think of the pin money you'll have, and the fine carriages! Do you think Lady Grant will now sponsor Kitty and Lydia for a season instead of you, for you hardly need one now!"

Surprisingly, it was Mr. Collins himself who broke the tension building in the room with a suggestion for a walk. "The weather is fine, most fine today. Even my noble patroness, the honourable Lady Catherine de Bourgh, would declare that this is as fine a day as ever she has seen, and I would not be ashamed to be seen with my bride and her three beautiful sisters."

Indeed, it seemed to Lizzy that she was not the only one to have changed over the past few months. Now that he had found a lady well suited to him and equal to him, Mr. Collins had improved noticeably. He still scattered carefully constructed compliments before him like breadcrumbs before a flock of pretty birds, but they were strewn out of habit and not out of a need to ingratiate himself before everyone. His silly and pompous tone was somewhat more sedate and considered, and more than once, Lizzy saw her sister murmur something into his ear, immediately after which he would blush a furious red and then correct whatever behaviour it had been that had drawn her ire. He would never be a clever or a well-considered man, but under Mary's quiet tutelage, he might be a tolerable one, and he would be, by all appearances, good for her and good to her. It was a most satisfactory alliance!

The day was, in fact, quite lovely, and the stroll under the blue and cloudless sky soon drew the small gathering down the lane towards Meryton. Lydia and Kitty hurried on ahead, hoping to see some of the officers in their red coats about town. The two girls had been most unhappy to have been kept to the house in preparation for the weddings whilst the militia officers were still arriving in town and before their serious training had begun. Although they had been unable to meet any of the dashing young men, they might still look and enjoy the sights. Mary and her future husband walked sedately after them, and Lizzy could hear Mr. Collins as he commented ceaselessly over the blossoms, the height of the corn, the straightness of the hedgerows or the particularly precise flight of the birds in the area as she walked behind him, with Richard on one side of her and Fitz Darcy on the other.

Unsurprisingly, Charlotte was waiting as they walked into town. She must have been alerted by the noisy arrival of the two youngest Bennet sisters, for she had donned her own bonnet and walking boots before leaving her home. She greeted Lizzy with a great embrace, then turned to the gentlemen and curtseyed.

"Professor Darcy," she greeted him with civil politeness, although her smile did not quite reach her eyes. Then she turned to the colonel and her face began to glow. Her cheeks blushed a becoming pink and her eyes sparkled as they echoed the pleased and shy grin that took control of her mouth. Lizzy thought she looked almost pretty. "Colonel Fitzwilliam," she dropped a slightly lower curtsey, and rose to find Richard beaming back at her. Lizzy fought valiantly to suppress her own grin at this silent conversation.

Charlotte pulled her attention away from the colonel and focused it once more upon her friend. "How fine you look, Lizzy! How elegant. Oh, do let me hear you speak! I long to hear what the professor has taught you!" With a laugh, Lizzy obliged as they wandered slowly down the high street, and some minutes were spent in amazement and delight at the transformation. When Lizzy mentioned her engagement to Darcy, the delight was even greater, and the conversation was moved to the small drawing room at Lucas House.

They sat for a short time before Mary suggested it was time to return for dinner, a comment repeated in the most elaborate terms by Mr. Collins.

As they stood to depart, Richard whispered a request to Lizzy, and she nodded. "Charlotte," Lizzy turned to her friend, "we would be honoured if you would accompany us back to Longbourn and dine with us this evening. I fear poor Colonel Fitzwilliam will find no sensible conversation amongst any other member of our present company." She glanced at the colonel, who in turn winked teasingly at Darcy.

Charlotte accepted immediately and ran up to dress. Lizzy smiled at her friend's fortune, but wondered how the countess would accept her son's choice. As an officer in the regulars, Richard drew a respectable salary—not one that would suffice for a lady of his rank, but more than enough for the comfort of a sensible woman like Charlotte, accustomed as she was to her father's modest income. However, should he wish to sell his commission, as he might well do upon taking a wife, he would then be reliant upon his family's charity or his wife's own fortune. There was no purpose to be gained in finding trouble, however, and Lizzy was determined that her friend enjoy whatever friendship Richard might offer her. Taking a moment when they were left in some privacy, Lizzy whispered into Darcy's ear, "You may have a new student before long." He frowned at her and said nothing.

Dinner was pleasant. The Bennets cooed at Lizzy's new manners and speech, and even Professor Darcy proved himself to possess the social graces that he so proudly taught to his students. When, at last, he and his companions from Netherfield departed, taking Charlotte in the carriage to drive her home, the family at Longbourn at last sat together to talk over the evening.

"He is improved, I believe." Mr. Bennet pursed his lips in grudging approval. "He has mellowed these past several weeks. He was always a decent sort underneath it all, but did I detect less arrogance than before?" He sipped from a small glass of sherry and sat back to observe how his family would take his pronouncement.

"La! I believe you are right, Papa," Lydia exclaimed. "I had not noticed particularly, but he did not scowl at me more than once or twice this entire evening!"

"And he entered into pleasant conversation," added Kitty. "I did not think him at all interested in bonnets, but he knows rather a lot about them. He even told me he wished to purchase one for his sister and asked for my advice! Can you believe it?"

"It is vexing to have the trouble of so much company," Mrs. Bennet yawned from her chair, "but it is satisfying when they are such pleasant people. The colonel is such a friendly man, quite unexpected of one with his breeding. You would think him too good for the likes of us, but he is not at all proud. And as for Mr. Darcy..." She ignored Lizzy's whispered correction to "Professor," "Well, he behaved tolerably, I suppose." She smiled at her little joke and murmured something about heading up to her rooms.

Something about their approval made Lizzy smile. She had enjoyed Darcy's company these last few days, and her family's approbation meant more to her than she would have expected. Also unexpected was her reaction to his departure this evening. For so long, she had been with the man from dawn till dark, that now she felt his absence quite keenly. It was only three miles from Longbourn to Netherfield, equal to the distance between Cheapside and Mayfair, but it felt an endless chasm. She had grown so accustomed to his constant presence that without him there, prodding and correcting her, she felt a part of her was missing. With a shock, Lizzy realised that she missed the annoying man! Perhaps, she joked to herself, she ought to consider his proposal more seriously after all!

Mary's wedding, one week later, was a lovely event. If the weather was not quite up to Lady Catherine's standards, it was merely because the grand lady herself were not there to so command it. Nevertheless, the sky was passably blue, with enough wind to rustle the blossoms that had begun to adorn the trees, and with the threatening rain kindly holding off until much later in the day, after everybody had returned to the safety and warmth of his or her abode.

The ceremony was followed by a spectacular breakfast that even Professor Darcy complimented, leaving Mrs. Bennet beaming, after which the newlywed couple were waved off on the first part of their journey. Tonight they would stop in London; on the morrow they would continue on to their home at Hunsford in Kent.

Mr. and Mrs. Gardiner were fortunate enough to be able to attend their niece's wedding and had arrived at Longbourn the day previous. Their plan, as agreed to by Mr. Bennet, was to depart the following afternoon, bearing with them Elizabeth, to continue her preparations for her life in London, and presumably, to become suitably established in society to become Mrs. Darcy.

Darcy's party had also arranged to depart the following afternoon, all the travellers hoping to reach London long before nightfall. As the day progressed, Lizzy observed Charlotte's face growing longer as the hours passed, moving them closer and closer to Richard's departure.

"'Tis a pity they must part so soon," she commented to her aunt as they walked through the small rose garden. "They have become good friends."

Mrs. Gardiner's eyes followed the two as they, too, wandered through the gardens. "They might wish to become more than that, I believe."

"It cannot be, for the colonel has no income of his own, and Charlotte no fortune."

Her aunt gave a chuckle and smiled with her eyes. "Stranger things have been known to happen, Lizzy!"

It was to Lizzy's delight, then, that Aunt Gardiner extended an invitation to Charlotte to accompany the party back to London for a short visit. Richard was at her side when the offer was extended, and his smile was almost wider than Charlotte's. Within moments, a note was written and a message sent to Lucas Lodge, with the hopes that permission would be granted and that Charlotte's trunks would be ready for her by the time the carriages were set to depart.

The final arrangements were made to everybody's satisfaction. In one carriage—the finer of the two, drawn by a matched set of fine horses—sat Darcy, Richard, Lizzy and Charlotte; in the other—sturdy and serviceable, with unmatched but still strong and fine horses—sat the Gardiners and Mrs. Pearce, as well as Darcy's valet. The ladies had become friendly over the weeks of Lizzy's tutoring, and if the men had objections, they were not voiced.

C180

Plans to arrange and host a ball were further delayed by the news that Darcy was needed, as he seemed to be more and more each passing year, by his aunt Catherine to assist in the planning of estate business for the coming year. Whether Lady Catherine was increasingly unable to manage her estate herself, or whether she would grab at any excuse to get Darcy within close enough proximity to her daughter to offer for her at last, no one knew. The summons, however, was quite unambiguous: Lady Catherine required Darcy's assistance, and only Darcy would do.

"She is being ridiculous!" the professor sneered at dinner the day he received the summons. He was dining with his noble aunt and uncle, having been dragged there most unceremoniously by Richard after the latter heard the explosion of oaths and curses that the letter had occasioned. He swallowed far too large a mouthful of wine, and wiped his mouth on the back of his hand, then sheepishly, reached for his napkin to repeat the action in a more polite manner. "Every year I am ordered hence to Rosings, and every year I arrive to discover that her steward had already performed the task more than adequately. There is always one more thing requiring my attention, thereby preventing my return home, and not a single one of these matters is actually important at all. She only wishes to command my time. I shan't go!"

The earl looked over at his nephew and delicately sipped from his own crystal glass, demonstrating how the action ought to be performed. "Now, Fitz, she is your aunt, your own mother's dear sister..."

"And yours, sir, unless my grandparents deceived me." He earned a disapproving glare for that comment, but continued blithely. "And yet, I do not see you rushing out to Kent to help convince the old lady of her mistaken ways."

"Darcy..." his aunt warned. "Have some respect!"

"Aunt Patricia, were I not to have respect, these walls would melt for the brimstone my words would evoke from the netherworld. She cannot force me to attend her; even less can she force me to attend to Anne. My cousin is not my choice for a bride, nor will she ever be, but Aunt Catherine sees only as far as her desire for Pemberley takes her."

Lord Malton raised his eyebrows and rolled his blue eyes heavenward, then conducted an intense but completely silent conversation with his wife, who sat across the table from him. At length, having received her tacit advice and permission to speak his decision, he turned back to his nephew. "Darcy," he sighed, "you shall accommodate her one last time. I shall send her word that after this year, I personally shall endeavour to send my own most trustworthy man of business to oversee her affairs. This will relieve you of the obligation into the future. However, we have not time to set this course of action into being so close to the date, and so you must go. You may also tell your aunt that she is to give up hopes of a union between you and Anne. Surely she must have read the announcement of your engagement. Wave Miss Bennet's success under her nose if you will. I know my sister, and nothing less than a *fait accompli* will convince her to look elsewhere for poor Anne."

"If it is a *fait accompli* she desires, nothing short of ten years wedded bliss and a nursery full of heirs will set her to rights," he grumbled to himself, but accepted his fate this one last time with more mumbled epithets and curses. Then, suddenly brightening, he turned to his cousin and purred, "And Richard shall join me! Think, Richard—a few weeks in the country! 'Twould be charming, and the air would be fresh!"

"A few weeks in the country? With that woman?"

"In the flesh." Darcy's mouth turned down at the notion, but quickly he returned to his initial glee. "Think, Richard: perhaps Eliza can be induced to visit her sister at the parsonage there, and if Eliza goes, she may wish for her friend's companionship. Yes, by gum, it just might do!"

Consequently, a week later, just before Easter, the fine Darcy carriage was once again on the road, transporting Elizabeth, Charlotte, Richard and Darcy through the greening hills south of London towards Rosings, Lady Catherine's grand estate in Kent. The distance was not long, and a half a day's journey saw the travellers delivered to their destination.

It was deemed unreasonable to expect the newlywed Mary Collins to host two guests in her home, which she had just now begun to set up with her new husband whilst adjusting to her role as the parson's wife in the community. Darcy had, therefore, informed his aunt that Miss Bennet and Miss Lucas would require rooms in the manor house. He brushed off all the lady's shocked suggestions that such a thing would bring disaster upon the family and ruin the young women's reputations forever, reminding her that he was a gentleman and that gentlemen are naturally assumed to hold better control over their base instincts than she supposed. *Further*, he wrote, *Miss Lucas and Miss Bennet might share a suite, thereby each serving as chaperone for the other at all times.* It was only when presented with the alternative—Darcy refusing to come—that she relented.

The suite offered to Lizzy and Charlotte was a small set of simply furnished connecting rooms on the distant side of the house to the guest suites, which Lady Catherine might have supposed was a just set-down to their ambitions and a refusal to accept their presence with grace; to the young women themselves, however, the distance from the excessive and ostentatious ornamentation the lady preferred, and from the parts of the house Lady Catherine considered her small duchy, was looked upon much more favourably. Since the lady did not deem that wing of the house—so near the kitchens and storage rooms, so far from the grand entrance—suitable for her own exalted presence, she was also never to be found there, which in turn gave the young women much more freedom and privacy than Lady Catherine might have considered appropriate.

In short, the accommodations were deemed most suitable by all, albeit for very different reasons.

The days at Rosings were spent mostly pleasurably. Each morning Darcy and Richard would take themselves to exercise their administrative duties, which mostly entailed listening to the steward explain his plans for a certain aspect of the estate's management, then nodding and congratulating the man on his wisdom and forethought, followed by the taking of coffee or touring the grounds with the man. Mr. Cromley, the steward, had long since become accustomed to Her Ladyship's insistence on her nephew having nominal authority over the professional manager and he took no insult, enjoying Darcy's rudeness as a welcome change from the stifling politeness of Lady Catherine's company. "I can swear in front of you, sir," he had said once with a wink, "and no one tells me to bugger off for it! Bloody hell, but it's good to be able to cuss every once in a while when dealing with some of these matters!" Darcy had laughed heartily at this, and the men had found a sort of friendship ever since.

Whilst the men were pretending to guide the management of the estate, Lizzy and Charlotte would walk over, or be driven, were the weather to be inclement, to the parsonage, there to visit with Mary. She seemed most content with her lot and proudly showed her sister and friend around her house. It was rather small, but well built and convenient; and everything was fitted up and arranged with a neatness and consistency of which Elizabeth gave Mary all the credit. When Mr. Collins could be forgotten, when he was out tending his garden or his flock, there was really a great air of comfort throughout, and by Mary's evident enjoyment of it, Elizabeth supposed he must be often forgotten.

After their activities each morning, the four visitors would gather for their tea and then would take themselves out to the woods to walk when the air was clear, or to the library, which Lady Catherine never visited, when the skies threatened rain. There, Cousin Anne would sometimes join the gathering of young people. She was small and sickly, with a constant cough and an unnatural pallor, but her pinched face seemed to be more a result of poor health than of poor disposition. Anne was closer to Darcy's age than Lizzy's, but she seemed to possess the worldliness of a child, despite a reasonable intellect and understanding. How long had she been closeted in this house, Lizzy wondered, instead of being allowed to befriend others in the village or at some respectable lady's school? Anne was of a quiet nature; she had little conversation, but attended the others with enthusiasm, and Lizzy again pondered whether the heir to Rosings was in desperate need of the companionship of her peers.

Surprisingly, it was Charlotte and not Lizzy who truly befriended Anne. Lizzy did not dislike Miss de Bourgh, but did not take to her, preferring a more open disposition, or at least, one inclined to some amiability. Charlotte, however, was always sensible and pragmatic, if sometimes too plainly spoken for some people's tastes, and she decided that if Anne would not open her heart to Charlotte, Charlotte must open hers to Anne. In short time, they had established a rapport, and soon afterwards, a nascent friendship. Richard commented once to Lizzy of his wonder as his sickly cousin seemed to develop a personality whilst he watched. Darcy said little, but stood back looking bemused at the actions of both of his cousins.

It was only at dinner on the fifth night of the visit to Rosings that Lizzy realised Lady Catherine was not aware of the engagement. Had Darcy not told her? Or was the grand lady willfully ignorant of what had been on the lips of everyone in London for the past weeks? Anne had certainly known, and the warmth with which she had congratulated the pair—some of the few words she had uttered unprompted—had been genuine. She had as little wish to marry her cousin as he had to marry her.

Regardless, as Lady Catherine stared down the table at her guests as they politely sipped their soup, she announced, "I have had my legal man draw up the paperwork, Darcy, so you may announce your betrothal to Anne at the first ball of the coming season, as I had previously discussed with you. The documents will be ready by your departure, so you may take all the time you require to read them over. I shall be pleased to have this finally settled."

Five sets of eyes darted upwards from their plates to stare at the speaker. Only Anne's companion, Mrs. Jenkins, looked unaffected by this proclamation.

"Mother..." Anne began, echoed by Richard's snort. Half-spoken oaths were interrupted by Darcy.

"Aunt Catherine, call off your man. It shall not happen."

"Nonsense, Darcy, of course it shall. We have been planning this for years. It was your mother's dearest wish."

"Aunt Catherine, my mother's dearest wish for me was to find my own happiness. I love Anne, but not as a wife. I shall not marry her."

"Of course you will. After all, somebody has to take your poor sister in hand. What did happen last summer? You never informed me what became of your trip to Ramsgate, as you ought to have done. As head of the family, I am owed this duty. Now, about Anne..."

"I repeat, Aunt, I shall not marry her." He enunciated each word distinctly and with the precision of an expert marksman.

"Nonsense!" the lady scoffed, flicking her hand as she spoke. "We had decided, had we not, that were you not to have selected your bride by now, you would wed Anne. There is nothing else to it."

"You had decided, Aunt, not I. And you are mistaken in one most important matter: I have selected my bride."

"Yes, of course, Darcy. Anne. It is only natural."

"Aunt Catherine!" Richard bellowed. His voice, normally so refined and pleasant, now took on the tenor of the battlefield, calling hundreds of men to action over the din of battle and artillery fire. "Listen to Darcy. For once!"

The older lady looked askance at her military nephew. "There is no need to shout, Richard, and most certainly not at dinner. I always listen. It is one of my most admired qualities, although there are so many from which to choose." Her expression suggested she had no notion of the unintended irony in her statement.

"Aunt," Darcy continued very quietly, so quietly that all were forced to stop whatever else they were doing to listen. The tight and restrained nature of his voice, normally so careless of convention, brought a frisson of fear into his listeners. "I have chosen my bride, and she is not Anne. Had you read the papers, or the letter I sent to you upon the occasion, you would know that I am engaged to Miss Bennet." His eyes dared her to object.

Instead, Lady Catherine began to laugh. "I had not taken you for a jokester, Darcy! This is most amusing. Most amusing indeed."

The rest of the diners stared at each other around the table, uncertain of what might convince Lady Catherine that Darcy was serious. Then, with a smirk, the gentleman rose from his seat with all the polish and grace of his station, folded his napkin on his chair with exquisite precision, and walked around the table until he was at Lizzy's chair. He helped her to her feet with the utmost decorum, and then, with a wink and a whispered "Forgive me" that only she could hear, he kissed her most passionately. For the first moment, she thought to struggle, then to acquiesce to help Darcy make his point, and then she lost all sense of their audience as she succumbed to the kiss. This was not the gentle flutter of lips that barely touched her own, but a deep and ardent kiss, the kiss of lovers. His arms were around her body, pulling her into his embrace, and her arms, moving without her knowledge, wound themselves about his strong shoulders. It was only the sound of a crystal goblet shattering on the wooden table, having been dropped in shock by the lady of the house, which brought them back to the dining room.

Anne looked on with a hand half covering her gaping mouth, her eyebrows raised in shock, but her eyes wide with delight. Mrs. Jenkins had rushed over to where Lady Catherine pretended to lie in a deep faint, and Richard looked most amused, his eyes constantly flickering towards Charlotte, who feigned not noticing his wistful gaze.

"Aunt," said Darcy at last, "this was no joke." Then he broke into one of his rare, but no less delightful, smiles.

# Twelve
# Understandings and
# Misunderstandings

Dinner ended shortly after Darcy's most indecorous display. Lady Catherine professed herself unfit to continue in this most scandalous company, and she took immediately to her rooms with Mrs. Jenkins in tow. The others elected to conclude their meal in the comfort of the small salon, where they might eat in convivial companionship, rather than at the grand and formal dining table where they had so long suffered under the disapproving and critical eye of Lady Catherine.

Lizzy's head was awash with agitation as these plans were made, and more so when Darcy took her arm to guide her through the house to their destination. "I wish to speak with you in private, out of the hearing of our friends," he whispered, "and intend to take full advantage of this short journey from room to room to do so. With your permission," he added, not quite as an afterthought.

Lizzy could scarcely recall her own name, let alone think of a reason to deny his request, and she nodded her agreement. Darcy tucked her hand over his forearm in a most decorous manner, then rather scandalously placed his free hand over hers. The sensation of this touch of skin on skin brought back memories of their dancing lessons, and the intimacy struck her almost more than that of the kiss. She felt her head grow light.

"Are you well, Eliza?" Darcy asked as he led her from the dining room. She realised that she was leaning rather heavily upon his arm. "Thank you for your forbearance. I shan't apologise, for I regret nothing, having enjoyed that kiss far too much. I cannot wish my actions undone, although I had no desire to distress you. I shall promise not to repeat my actions without your express permission."

Her head still whirled. She suddenly recalled that incident, those weeks past, when she had responded to his imperiousness with ire, and he had looked about to kiss her. She had wondered then what it would be like, to be swept into his arms, to be adored by him. The light peck he had given her when they had decided to announce the engagement had been a tease, a taste of something she had not thought ever to experience, and she was not sure, at that time, whether she truly wished for more. That Darcy sought her approval and her friendship, she knew, but she had not thought, until just now, that he sought her affection at all. A marriage could not thrive on his cool and passionless words of that day—'you do not adversely affect my life'—but this embrace that had so shocked Lady Catherine had betrayed to her something warmer inside the man. Where there was also a meeting of minds, such a fervent kiss could certainly spark the makings of a true marriage.

Once more Lizzy found herself forced to consider his words, his detached and impersonal offer of a true engagement. She had not found herself equal to giving full attention to his offer, for he vexed and intrigued her alternately—and often simultaneously. She had supposed that over the course of their supposed engagement, her heart would make itself known to her, but the notion of actively considering him brought her to the verge of panic. It had been better to let the matter lie for some future pondering. Now, however, with this kiss so fresh in her mind, still felt on her lips, it was not so easy to relegate these thoughts to some far future reckoning.

Lizzy let her attention wander from her companion, but before they entered the salon, where the others were already finding suitable seats to complete their meal, Darcy stopped and pulled her aside, facing her with a hand on each shoulder. There was nothing in his face of the grumpy and arrogant man she so often saw; instead, the rare sight of someone kinder and caring shone through his warm eyes. "Truly, Eliza? Do you hate me now? Please say you don't, that I might hope to one day kiss you again. I really rather lo... like you. Very much. Tell me you don't hate me." He bit slightly at his top lip, the only sign of ill-ease or worry she could see in him.

Oddly she could not meet his eye, as much as she relished the feel of his hands on her arms. He was warm and comforting, despite his often-unpleasant disposition, and she found that for all her new speech and manners and put-on airs, she could be herself in his presence more than with anyone else of her acquaintance with the exception of Jane. Even Charlotte, her very dear friend, saw only a part of Elizabeth Bennet. But Professor Darcy—Fitz—he had seen all of her—her good moods and her bad, her sweetness and her fury—even as she suspected that she was one of a very select few who had had even the smallest glimpse of all of him. And for all of her foibles and her weaknesses, he seemed to like her. What she needed to determine was whether, and how much, she liked him.

She raised her eyes to his through a massive force of will and quietly spoke, "No. I do not hate you. That was... unexpected, but I do not hate you for it."

For a moment she thought he might kiss her again, but instead he pulled her into a quick and fierce embrace before releasing her and silently guiding her into the salon.

Richard was seated beside Charlotte on the sofa by the small table and across from Anne, and he raised his eyebrows questioningly as the couple entered the room. Darcy gave a slight smile and allowed his face to show a trace of relief, which Richard answered with a small pleased smile of his own.

"Would you care to sit, Eliza?" Darcy's voice was soft in her ears as he eased her to a chair by the table, upon which the remains of dinner would soon be set. She accepted the seat, and he pulled one from the other side of the room to place beside her, then sat himself. All through the meal, he was uncharacteristically polite and solicitous, not once uttering a scathing comment or rude remark, or belittling any one or thing which he had recently seen. This was a completely different creature than the man who had sneered at her in Meryton, and Richard made a remark or two about some hitherto-unknown twin who was now impersonating Professor Darcy. Even then, Darcy did nothing but smile complacently at his cousin, arousing still more knowing looks and winks.

The visit to Rosings lasted another week. Lady Catherine no longer took dinner with her guests, claiming illness, although she did command Darcy's presence each morning. What transpired during these meetings no one else was privy to, but Darcy would depart the breakfast table to find his aunt's office looking grim and determined and would return afterwards looking angry and smug, after which he would repair to his rooms for a while and return to his companions with a clean face and a forced smile. "We shall not be returning next year," Lizzy heard him tell Richard once, but within her hearing, at least, said nothing more.

During the afternoons together, the cousins and their guests continued their habit of walking or riding when the weather was pleasant, and Anne was encouraged to join them whenever her health allowed, which was decidedly more often than not. Richard still found himself at Charlotte's side whenever he might arrange it, and Lizzy made an effort to engage Anne in conversation to allow her friend and the colonel time to converse. Darcy's attentions to Lizzy did not abate and she found herself enjoying his company more than she had ever expected. This sojourn was proving most enlightening, and more and more Lizzy thought she might accept Darcy's proposal.

In time, the group had to return to London, Lady Catherine having determined at last that she would get no satisfaction from her nephew. Mary was sad to see her sister leave, but seemed pleased to set about the business of being Mrs. Collins, and Mr. Collins wished his fair cousin Elizabeth the happiest and healthiest of travels, for Lady Catherine would not have poor roads in her part of England, and was most insistent of the finest of wheelwrights for her carriages, which Mr. Darcy and Colonel Fitzwilliam must attend to, for the safety and comfort of their passengers. With heartfelt goodbyes to Anne, and some sincere wishes for her to visit, the group was off once more for Town.

CREO

Upon the return to Town of the couple concerned, Patricia, Lady Malton, immediately set about planning the ball to celebrate the engagement and to introduce Lizzy into society. She was most confident that the young woman would meet all levels of scrutiny, and announced that even were someone to find fault where there was none, her own patronage would more than atone for any back-stabbing behind the scenes. It was now late enough in the year that her ball would be the final grand affair of the season, a capstone, something to be seared into the memories of all fortunate enough to be invited. She seemed determined that it would be a magnificent event.

Darcy, in the meantime, was putting Lizzy through her final paces. He commanded and admonished and corrected as she set about polishing her skills—reciting poetry, walking with stacks of books upon her head to perfect her posture and poise, dancing around the music room, sipping tea without making any extraneous noises, making polite small-talk with the plants, and generally practicing being perfect. His complaints about the exhausting nature of the business were met with cold stares from his student. "This is gruelling indeed," he protested from his comfortable chair as he nibbled upon a biscuit taken from a plate that sat beside him, watching Lizzy as she glided once more across the room. "You have no idea how fagged I am." He ate another biscuit. "Why do you look at me thus, Eliza? What is that look upon your face? Are there crumbs upon my coat? Here, I shall brush them off." He took another biscuit. "Once more. And once again."

Richard attended many of these sessions, as Charlotte was often invited along, and he was showing every evidence of becoming most attached to her. "You know, Fitz," he commented one evening after the ladies had returned to the Gardiners' home, "I am almost contemplating offering for her."

"You cannot be serious!" Darcy burst out and set his brandy glass down with a noticeable crash. "You?"

Richard shrugged and gave an apologetic smile. "I like her. More, I believe, than any woman I have known. She is sensible and we suit. If I had unlimited funds, I would speak immediately."

"You are serious, aren't you?" Darcy rocked back in his chair, shaking his head.

"Without my commission, which I have resolved to relinquish, I have a poor income, but it might be sufficient to support a family. Charlotte is accustomed to economy. I am prepared to live modestly. My only concern is Father," he concluded glumly. "The investments from which my allowance comes are still under Father's control, and should he refuse my choice of bride, he may cut me off without a penny. I will not be in the army forever; even now, I feel myself itching to rid myself of this blasted uniform and settle down. Mother might be swayed, but Father, for all his liberality in some areas, insists on preserving the formalities of rank and blood."

His worries, however, seemed to be put to rest the following week. In the morning's post arrived a letter addressed jointly to the two men from their Aunt Catherine. It had been drafted by her attorney and it conveyed the most astonishing news. It appeared that whilst Lady Catherine had finally come to accept that Darcy had chosen Miss Bennet over her daughter, she had not recognised Richard's growing attachment to Miss Lucas.

In her ire over the presumed rejection of Anne, Lady Catherine de Bourgh had decided to irrevocably deny Darcy the bequest she had intended for him, namely a small estate that the lady had received from her own mother upon her marriage to Sir Lewis. The very existence of this estate was new information to both men, and the loss to Darcy was therefore minimal. What made the decision significant, however, was that Lady Catherine was now deeding it, effective immediately, to Richard. Perhaps she thought that Richard might marry Anne in Darcy's stead. It mattered not. The colonel was now a landholder in his own right, and need depend no more on his father's good will. He could contemplate seriously the prospect of a life with Charlotte.

Darcy had read the letter aloud to his cousin, and they stared at each other over their coffee and morning plates of buttered rolls and marmalade. "Is she joking, Darcy? Is this her way to repay you for your supposed joke about Eliza? She cannot be serious, for I never even knew that Hillford existed until this moment!" Richard was incredulous, not quite able to believe what he had heard from his cousin's mouth just moments before.

"No, I believe she is quite serious," came the reply. "The letter is signed by her attorney, and I know the man's name. He has rooms in London, and is highly regarded. I shall send a messenger immediately for confirmation." He stepped out of the room for a moment to do so, then returned to his coffee.

"Are you not angry, Fitz, to be denied thus?"

Darcy laughed. "Richard, Pemberley is but one of my estates. I can hardly manage what I have, and I am scarcely in need of more income." He scanned the letter once more. "Hillford is small—it will see you about fifteen hundred a year, hardly enough to let you call yourself wealthy, but sufficient for a comfortable life if you live modestly. I shall not miss it, but it will make you independent. I am pleased for you cousin, very pleased." With a chuckle, he rose to clap his cousin on the shoulder in corroboration of his words.

Richard looked stunned still. His mouth hung slightly open, and he shook his head repeatedly, searching for words, until he, too, began to laugh. "The joke, then, seems to be on our aunt... an estate, for me? An independence, free from my father's control... I shall awaken in a moment and discover it is all a dream, and then I shall be bereft... A comfortable income, and my own estate!"

"Do not congratulate yourself until Robbins returns from his mission, but when you do, I shall celebrate with you."

Their wait was not long. It was less than an hour before Robbins returned, leading the attorney in question into the study where the two cousins now waited for Eliza and Charlotte to arrive. Bartholemey—for that was the gentleman's name—confirmed his meeting with Lady Catherine de Bourgh two days previous, stating that he had attempted to convince her to reconsider, but had failed. All of the necessary documentation had been completed and the small property in Bedfordshire now legally belonged to Richard Fitzwilliam, son of the

Earl of Malton, presently colonel in His Majesty's Army. He brought with him a copy of the deed, which he showed the men, and requested that the original remain in his keeping until the details of the transfer were completed. The attorney was duly thanked and compensated for his time, and he departed with a deep bow. As he left the room, the two ladies entered, and they passed each other in the doorway. Eliza raised her eyebrows as the door closed behind the man of law; she had clearly heard what his business had been about, but would not mention the topic unless the colonel raised it first, Darcy was certain.

Darcy could see that Richard was still reeling from the magnitude of the morning's revelations, and consequently the usual banter between cousins and their protégée was subdued. Eliza set about her exercises and final refinements. There was, in truth, little work left to be done. Her accent was perfect, her manners delightful, and with the intrusion of Lady Malton into their plans, her comfort in society had grown immeasurably. Darcy was certain that Miss Bennet would be a tremendous success, that no one would imagine her not to have been raised amongst the highest ranks. He would be proud to have her on his arm. The ball was two weeks away, and she was as prepared as ever she would be.

Seeing his cousin's distracted mood, Darcy suggested they break earlier than accustomed from their morning activities. He left Eliza and Charlotte in the library where they had been working whilst he went in search of Mrs. Pearce to inform her of their change in plans, and summoned Richard to join him, "if you feel the desire to discuss matters." Richard leapt up and followed him out of the room, with a lingering look towards Charlotte.

Darcy strode heavily out of the room, then into the entry hall and down through corridors, dragging Richard behind him and bellowing all the while for Mrs. Pearce. He could picture Eliza in his mind, rolling her eyes heavenward at his uncivilised display, and even considered for a moment ceasing his yelling, but then a young maid, timidly curtseying and apologising for daring to speak, suggested that Mrs. Pearce was downstairs in the kitchens, going over the food accounts. With scarcely a nod to the girl, Darcy pulled Richard behind him as he plunged down the stairs to the lower levels.

"Oh, there you are, Mrs. Pearce. I needed to.... Hullo? What's this?" He turned to stare at Robbins who had just entered from the back way and seemed in need of his master's attentions for a moment. "Yes, Robbins. I shan't bite your head off. Speak."

"Begging your pardon, Professor, but I received a note from Master Bartholemey just now. Pursuant to his visit this morning, he humbly requests a short letter from you, on your stationary and in your hand, if you will, confirming his visit and outlining the matters discussed. It need not be in too much detail, and it is not legally required, but Lady Catherine..."

"Oh, bother, blast and damnation! Yes, yes, I understand. Lady Catherine will make his life a misery in any way she can, so he wishes to protect himself against any foolish whims she may have. Did he send a boy? Have him wait. I shall get to this right now. Mrs. Pearce, feed my cousin some tea whilst he waits, and give Bartholemey's boy a biscuit or some ale, whatever he wants. I shan't be a moment."

The kitchens were directly below Darcy's private study, and rather than taking the circuitous route through the various passageways and in through the study where the ladies were sitting, he elected to dart up the hidden servants' stairs that led directly to his personal room. He had, in fact, designed the space thus, so he might sneak down to the kitchens for a snack at night with minimal inconvenience to his staff, or more importantly, to himself. The door in the study, partly hidden behind a bookcase and a rather precariously leaning pile of tomes, opened smoothly and silently, and Darcy made for his desk in search of his stationary.

His letter was interrupted, however, by the sounds of the women's voices just through the door, which was not completely closed. "...but if a woman is partial to a man, and does not endeavour to conceal it, he must find it out," Eliza was saying. Perhaps she had just walked close enough to the door for her voice to carry, for he had not heard the beginning of her conversation. "It is surely so if they are together often enough, at dinners, or..." now she must have walked away, for her words were lost to vague dulcet tones with no meaning. Darcy sat stone-still at his desk, hardly daring to breathe. What could this mean?

Charlotte, however, must have been sitting on the settee right by the doorway to the private study, for her voice was clear, her words unmuffled. "It may, perhaps, be pleasant to be able to impose on the public in such a case; but it is sometimes a disadvantage to be so *very* guarded. If a woman conceals her affection with the same skill from the object of it, she may lose the opportunity of fixing him."

"Fixing him? Whatever can you mean by that, Charlotte?" Eliza was close to the door again.

"Simply said, she ought to leave no doubt as to her interests in the man if she wishes him to pursue her. There is so much of gratitude or vanity in almost every attachment, that it is not safe to leave any to itself. We can all begin freely -- a slight preference is natural enough; but there are very few of us who have heart enough to be really in love without encouragement." She paused for a moment, during which time Lizzy's voice, but not words, were heard from the far side of the larger room. Then, with finality, Charlotte stated, "In nine cases out of ten, a woman had better show *more* affection than she feels."

This was too much for Darcy to hear. Was this true? Was Charlotte merely hanging around his cousin, flattering him and doting on him, merely to 'fix' him? Had she truly liked him—loved him, really—Darcy would have no trouble standing up for his cousin against the railings he would be sure to garner from his aristocratic family, but now it seemed that Richard was falling in love with a woman who saw him merely as a means to an end, a husband who would provide for her a home and family of her own, but whom she did not truly admire. The morning's news about Richard's new estate would only encourage Charlotte, he reasoned, for now Richard was wealthy—by comparison to the Lucas family if not his own—and would be able to wed where he wished. This must be stopped!

He crept back to the servants' stairs and stumbled down the stairs to where Richard was conversing happily with Mrs. Pearce, tea and cakes at his elbow. Thrusting the hastily-scrawled letter into the messenger boy's hands and shooing him out of the door, he bade Richard follow him once more, eyebrows low over his eyes, his gaze icy and severe, his mouth a thin line. He looked most alarming.

"Good God, Darcy, what is it? Speak, man!" Richard commanded as they entered the butler's office at the far end of the corridors to the kitchen and Darcy clicked shut the door. The walls were crowded with sideboards and built in cabinets containing shelves and drawers, surrounding a large desk and three chairs. Darcy sat, then stood, and then sat again. Richard stared at a chair, but did not take it.

"Richard," Darcy began, not quite knowing how to begin. "Richard, have you offered for Charlotte?"

His cousin stared at him, a mixture of embarrassment and confusion playing with his eyebrows. "No. That is, not yet... I have been giving it the most serious consideration. She is, for my tastes, the best woman I have met, the most suited to my temperament, and she pleases me greatly."

"Do not!"

He blinked as his look become one of shock. "What are you on about, Fitz? This is really no concern of yours."

"I heard them, Richard. Or, rather, I heard her. I heard Charlotte, talking to Eliza. She does not care for you. She merely feigns it so she may 'fix' you, to gain for herself a rich husband and a secure future. You are my cousin and my friend, and I believe you deserve better than that."

"Darcy, you cannot be serious!" He paced around the cramped space. "No, I will not believe it. I have seen her, when she believes no one is watching... I cannot believe that of her at all, and I refuse to listen to you. You must have misheard or misunderstood. And even if she loves me not now, I fancy that I love her, and I will accept her as she is, for love can grow."

"Richard, I do not wish to see you hurt. At the least, think on the matter for a time. I have only your best interests at heart." Sincerity was not a look that was often seen on Darcy, but Richard must have seen it now, for he sadly nodded.

"I will think on it. I do not believe you, but I will take some time and think on it."

Sighing to himself, Darcy resolved that since he could not convince Richard, he must rather work on Charlotte.

Finding time alone with her was much more difficult than speaking privately with Richard. It was no easy matter to arrange a private interview with an unrelated woman, even within one's own home. Charlotte spent her time talking with Eliza or with Richard, or engaged in some activity such as reading or embroidery in the centre of the room. Darcy had about given up on his plan for that day when Mrs. Pearce called to Eliza to meet immediately with the mantua maker, who had just now arrived with some new gowns in need of final alterations. She scurried after Mrs. Pearce, and Darcy asked Richard to look for some volume in his library that he wished to consult. At last he was alone with Charlotte.

"Miss Lucas..." he began. She looked up in a start, for he had scarcely ever been so civil as to refer to her so formally. "Miss Lucas, I must talk to you about Richard." This captured her attention and she looked at him in alarm.

"My cousin has expressed some affection for you," Darcy continued, "and I mean to know whether you would accept him, should he offer for you."

"Really, Professor Darcy!" Her reproof almost matched Eliza's in its sternness. What was it about these Hertfordshire women? "Such matters would be between myself and your cousin. You can have no reason to ask, or to be informed one way or another."

Darcy would not be shaken from his purpose. "I do have my reasons, Miss Lucas. My reasons involve my very real concern for my cousin's happiness." He leveled his well-practiced and much-used haughty glare upon her and spoke in a flat voice. "Yes, Miss Lucas. I won't dissemble. You have learned to expect forthrightness from me, rudeness, even. I'm afraid that this is what you shall hear now. I will speak quickly, before Richard returns, and you will not like what I have to say."

Charlotte sat perfectly still on the sofa, her sewing abandoned upon her lap. "Speak, Professor." Her voice was ice, her eyes narrow.

"My cousin, as I am certain you heard this morning, has come into a bit of property. But do not expect this to be the solution to all your concerns. The property is his, without doubt, and he will have the income from it, but if you accept him, he will lose everything else. He will lose all of his society, all of his family, all of his connections. His father will never accept you, and to be frank, you will never be easy in his father's company. I have seen you with my aunt, Lady Catherine, and with the countess. You are not comfortable in London, and you will never truly feel happy here. You will never fit in; you will never sound like the daughter of an earl; you will never act like the daughter of an earl. Your origins will betray you every time you speak and every time you move, and you will bring shame upon Richard, no matter how you try to avoid it, or no matter how much he might protest to the contrary.

"Further, should Richard marry you, he will be cut off from his relations, and will likely never be accepted in Town, no matter what I may try to do for him. If the earl cuts him off, he will not be welcome at his club, nor will he receive invitations to any events. He will be cut at the theatre and in the coffeehouse and on the street. If he retains his commission, he will never see another promotion: his father will ensure that. Merit is a fine thing, but few men dare defy the Earl of Malton. You do not need to obey my commands, for I am neither your father nor your brother, and you are of age to decide your own fate. But consider my cousin's lot, Miss Lucas: consider whether you truly wish such an unhappy fate for him. Do you understand my meaning?" His eye was baleful upon her, and Charlotte met his cold stare with one of her own, her eyes narrowed now to mere slits. But her cheeks were white, and her lip quivered with repressed emotion.

"I understand you perfectly, Professor Darcy," was all she said.

"Good. Now, I hear Richard return from his task, so I shall leave you with these thoughts. Good day, Miss Lucas." And with these harsh words, he turned and swept from the room.

## Thirteen
## The Ball

It was to Lizzy's unhappy surprise that Charlotte announced that very evening her intention to return to Meryton. She had already made inquiries into taking the mail coach and had requested that her trunks be prepared for departure the following morning. Nothing Lizzy would say could convince her friend to change her mind; appeals to consider the colonel resulted only in soft unshed tears and a refusal to speak.

Lizzy was dumbfounded. Whatever had happened? Had the two had a disagreement? Had he offered, and she refused? Why, then, would Charlotte not speak to her. Had Richard declared that he would not offer for her? That hardly seemed possible, for Richard had been all tenderness and attention towards Charlotte the previous afternoon before they had left Darcy's house for Gracechurch Street, even more so than usual, to Lizzy's eye. Charlotte, however, had seemed most distracted, Lizzy now recalled, but she could not imagine what had occurred to distress her friend so greatly, and to impel her to run from London back to her parents.

With no more information from Charlotte than that her decision—hasty though it might be—was final, Lizzy had no choice but to bid her friend a tearful goodbye as the hackney came to carry her and a footman to the depot where she would get the mail coach. Even the offer of Mr. Gardiner's carriage had been refused and the whole family was most upset. Feeling quite unfit to spend the morning being polite and elegant, Lizzy had sent a note to Professor Darcy, begging off her lessons for the day, a note which was met with stern refusal and the arrival of the man himself at the Gardiners' front door an hour later, demanding that she leave off this sentimental nonsense and join him at once for their planned activities. If not for the inclusion of Lady Malton in their plans, Lizzy would have refused Darcy outright, but she could not behave thus to the countess, and so reluctantly prepared for her day.

The weeks passed quickly, and almost before she knew it, the night of the ball had arrived. Lizzy had spent the previous night at the Malton's fine house, so grand and ornate behind its soaring columns and elegant facade. She had been assigned a maid, one who had been abigail to Lady Malton's own daughter before her marriage a year before, and the evening and day before the ball were spent in final preparations. Lizzy felt like Esther at the king's court, being bathed and oiled and perfumed and coiffed, until she hardly knew herself.

She scarcely recognised the stunning creature who looked back at her from the mirror. Even her recent weeks of tripping around Town with the countess in her fine new gowns and elegant hairstyles had not been enough to prepare her for what she had become. She recalled tales her mother had told her, old French stories, of a young girl transformed by magic into a princess for a ball, and she wondered if the countess were, in truth, her own fairy godmother.

As the abigail stepped away for the final time, Lizzy stared at her reflection. Her hair was cunningly curled and twisted and pinned upon her head, threaded through with the finest silvery-green ribbons and dotted with pearls and the tiniest of silk rosettes. The most delicate of wisps now framed her face, the perfect curls emphasising her fine eyes and the shape of her chin. She wore a trace of kohl around her eyes, enough to draw attention, but not enough to be noticed, and hint of colour on her lips. The result was natural and glowing. Her dress was a work of art, and she cringed to think what it must have cost the professor, who had insisted on taking the whole cost of it. The pale silvery-green silk had been sourced from Uncle Gardiner's own warehouses, and she knew enough about cloth and textiles to understand that the fabric alone was worth more than her entire wardrobe from Longbourn. A small army of expert seamstresses had cut and stitched and ornamented the gown, allowing the darker green ribbons and the dots of pearls, which matched those in her hair, to accentuate and draw the eye, showing her pleasing figure to its best advantage. Earbobs and a necklace of pearl and emerald completed the ensemble, and it was all she could do not to stare at herself all night.

At last there came the knock at her door, summoning her to her fate. Darcy stood there, waiting for her, looking as fine as she had ever seen him in his black formal suit with a dark green waistcoat that matched her ribbons, trimmed in the same silvery-green as her dress. An emerald twinkled in his snowy white cravat, two others at his cuffs. They made a most handsome couple.

"You are lovely," he whispered as they walked slowly down the corridor to the grand staircase. "I have never seen anybody look more beautiful. I am very proud to have you on my arm, and there will be many a jealous man in the ballroom tonight." She blushed at these words and murmured something about his own handsome appearance.

"No one cares for how I look," he snorted. "My clothing is in fashion and I am not covered in mud or horsehair. Unless Brummell decides to appear, all eyes will be on the ladies, of whom you are, undoubtedly, the finest. As for me, if I escape the evening without insulting the ambassador or throwing wine down some sod's neck, it shall be deemed a remarkable success." Just before the corridor opened up into the landing at the top of the grand staircase, he reached out and stopped her with a touch to her wrist. She turned to see what he was about, but the look she perceived in his eyes rooted her to the floor. His eyes were so dark as to be nearly black, and he gazed at her with an intensity that set her heart racing. His lips parted slightly, then closed again and pressed firmly together.

One hand reached out, tentatively, and brushed one of the painstakingly curled ringlets that framed her face. She hardly felt the touch, but the intimacy of the gesture caused her mouth to go dry and she swallowed.

He withdrew his hand, but not his eyes. "I would... that is, I do not dare, but... May I request a kiss? I promise I shall not disarrange your hair, but the touch of your lips will fortify me through much of the inanity I must endure this evening. May I?"

This was the first time since the display at Rosings that he had asked her. Lizzy had wondered, after the fiery passion of that public kiss, whether there had been anything real behind it, or whether it was just another one of Darcy's theatrics designed to shock and importune his aunt. He had, from time to time, been attentive to her, caring, doting even, but the ardour that had fueled the kiss in the dining room at Rosings had not been seen again. Perhaps he had not wished to upset her further, especially after Charlotte's abrupt departure and her own subsequent melancholy; perhaps he simply had not wished to repeat his actions. But now, moments away from presenting all of Fashionable London with his supposed choice for a bride, he was asking—nay, begging—to be permitted a taste of her lips. Was this for his own strength, as he had stated? Or did he merely wish for her to descend the stairs looking like a lady in love, in order to complete the transformation he had effected?

She stood still, not knowing how to respond, not even knowing whether to meet or avoid his eye. His presence pinned her to her spot, and she felt like a butterfly on display, its glorious wings unfurled for the world to admire, but trapped forever in its prison and unable ever to fly again. She felt at once terrified and entranced by the whole affair, and she could not discern her own mind.

"Just one kiss?" he begged. "I shall not ask again, so fear not."

She nodded, or she must have, for he slowly brought his head down to hers and brushed his lips across hers. There was no feather-light touch, nor was there the fire from Rosings, but instead, a sweetness and tenderness that spoke of real affection. Drawing strength from the brief embrace, Lizzy still wondered how she would ever know the true man, or even recognise him if she saw him. He was an enigma, one growing in her heart, but a mystery all the same.

"Come," he whispered when he stepped back to ensure her gown and hair were unscathed. "They are waiting." Silently offering his arm, he led her down the stairs to where Lord and Lady Malton stood in attendance.

Of the ball itself, there is little to be said that cannot be imagined. The guests were numerous and from the highest ranks of society, the food and drink plentiful and of excellent quality, the music delightful and the dancing of the best calibre. Elegant ladies and smartly clad gentleman traced their patterns around the chalked floor, exercising all the skills and habits they had been perfecting since the schoolroom. And through it all, amidst the twinkling diamonds and gleaming brass, surrounded by viscounts and dukes and foreign princes, Elizabeth Bennet swirled her way into society, gliding effortlessly through her dances, charming everybody she met, and entrancing a generation of young men with her beauty and her sweet smile.

She danced with Darcy thrice, including the scandalous waltz, and with Richard and Freddy each twice, leaving little time for the other gentlemen lined up to receive the favour of her arch comments on the room. The news of her engagement to Darcy had been, at first, met with sighs of disappointment from the ladies of the *ton*, but after a glimpse or a short snatch of conversation with Miss Bennet, the eligible bachelors joined the girls in their lamentations. Alfred, Viscount Eynshill, led these men in their collective regret, although he seemed to have a spark in his eye that suggested some secret knowledge.

Only Richard seemed out of sorts that evening. He made the effort to be his accustomed friendly and amiable self, but there was a want of spirit in his laughter and a sadness in his regard that tore at Lizzy's heart.

"What has happened to our hearty colonel?" Lizzy heard as she stood with some new acquaintances at the refreshments table. Lady Malton was holding court, and the others—a viscountess, the wife of an ambassador, and a duke's daughter—were exchanging information on some persons of whom Lizzy knew nothing. Her attention, therefore, was drawn to the voices of the men standing just behind her own party. She could not see them clearly without turning her head, but their words were quite unobscured.

"Old Brass Buttons?" A new voice responded. "Never seen him glum a day in his life, save for when his old dog died. Drank himself under the table that night, but never since. Still, not quite himself tonight, eh?"

"Never seen him like this," responded the first voice. "Puts on a smile for the crowds and whatnot, but we've known him all his life. Something's eating the old boy. Perhaps he's been spending too much time with that prig of a cousin of his."

"More likely crossed in love," came a third voice. "Nothing puts a downer on a man's face like that than losing his lady. Still... could be the cousin. He's enough to sour anyone's temper."

At this point, Lizzy's attention was required once more by the conversation of her own party, but she had to wonder. If Richard's friends had noticed his mood, he must be quite out of sorts indeed.

Whatever had happened between Charlotte and the colonel, therefore, had not been of his doing, or at least, not intentionally so. Lizzy wished with all her being that she might succeed in her quest to discover from Charlotte what had occurred that she might set things to right, for the separation was clearly not Richard's desire. He had even requested that Lizzy write a personal plea to invite Charlotte to the ball, which she had done, but her invitation was met with polite refusal. Neither the news of Jane and Charles' presence, nor the offer of the Malton carriage to transport her to Town was enough to convince her to attend, and for that loss alone, Lizzy felt a pang of regret.

But the night was too magical to dwell on one friend, no matter how dear, and she let herself be swept away, like the girl from the cinders in that old French tale, until the last guests departed shortly before dawn.

The first rays of the new day were beginning to brighten the horizon when Darcy, Richard and Elizabeth finally staggered, exhausted, into the private parlour by Lizzy's suite. A very tired footman had brought up a decanter of port and a pot of hot tea, for the three were far too excited by the whirlwind of the ball to take themselves off to sleep. There was too much to discuss, to many details to be examined, and Lizzy's performance, her first public showing, must be analyzed, step by step, syllable by syllable.

She was the first to enter the room. Her lovely gown still hung in perfect folds from her white shoulders, her pearls and emeralds sparkled in the light, her hair retained its carefully pinned style, but her face was pale from her night of dancing, and her eyes shadowed in the flickering candlelight. She threw her wrap onto the low table by the corner and fell into a soft chair, head collapsing backwards onto her shoulders, eyes too heavy to keep open. Her expression was almost tragic.

Darcy followed her into the room, his face exultant despite his fatigue, and he pulled his finely tailored coat from his back, heedless of the lady sitting before him as he undressed. As he had ordered, a smoking jacket was awaiting him, and he slipped it over his shirtsleeves and waistcoat before tossing the frock coat over the back of the sofa onto which he fell. His actions were echoed by Richard, although the colonel chose not to undress before Elizabeth, electing to remain in his coat instead. His eyes were hooded with fatigue, his face devoid of all emotion.

"I say, Eliza, did you see where I left my slippers?" Darcy asked after a moment. "I had asked for them to be brought with my jacket, but they do not seem to be here." He peered around the room, but did not exert himself enough to rise from the sofa on which he half-sat, half-reclined. "Richard? Have you seen them? No? Alas. Well, thank God that's over!"

Lizzy started at these words but said nothing.

Richard roused himself to speak. "You were not nervous, were you, Darcy? I was, perhaps, for the first five minutes after the duke arrived, but Eliza seemed not nervous at all."

"No, she was not nervous. Quite calm, I should say. But I am most relieved to have the whole thing done. Now we may wait and read of our tremendous success in the society pages, and revel in our accomplishment. Bravo, Richard, I could not have done it without you!"

The colonel straightened himself upon his chair, and nodded once, firmly. "It was indeed a great success, Fitz. You did it! Those long months of work, work, work, all paid off immensely. Ah, is that port? I could do with a tot."

"Be a good girl and pour him some, Eliza." Darcy's voice was a study of indifference.

Too tired to argue, she rose from her chair and did as requested.

The colonel smirked, then extended a hand to take his port with barely a glance at Lizzy. "The congratulations all go to you, Darcy. Truly, a remarkable feat. Not a soul suspected she was anything other than a highborn lady, and they could not fall over their feet fast enough to guess whose daughter or niece she must be. The Earl of Flamborough? The Duke of Wallingford? Perhaps the Marquess of Picton!"

"What a joke that was! The only one who supposed anything other than the cream of the aristocracy was that nasty little man from Cambridge..."

"Your former professor, you said?"

"Indeed! I knew more than he after the first five minutes in his class! He thinks himself such an expert, he who announced in the hearing of the ambassador and the crown prince of whatever country that was, that she could not possibly be English because she was far too well spoken and her manners were too fine. She must, he declared, be a foreign princess! Hah! It was all I could do not to laugh and kiss her soundly then and there. Ah, a remarkable success, Richard. There is always something professional about doing a thing superlatively well."

"You have won your bet, Darcy, and I shall happily pay up. Remarkable job!"

Through this dialogue between the men, Lizzy had been growing steadily more and more angry, but kept her peace. Neither gentleman so much as glanced her way, and neither seemed in the least inclined to compliment the lady herself on her remarkable efforts in the venture. She sank further back into the pillows of her chair, but her face grew tighter and tighter in its expression, and fire began to burn in her eyes.

Darcy took a drink from his glass and yawned deeply, not bothering to cover his mouth. "At last, I can go to bed without dreading tomorrow. This adventure was interesting at first, but after the first few months became an awful bore. Oh, the work on phonetics was fine enough, but there really was no true challenge. After that it was just repetition,

repetition, repetition." He rubbed his eyes. "Well, I ought to find my bed. Where on earth are my damned slippers?"

Neither Richard nor Lizzy commented on his oath as he searched the room once more with his eyes, but still made no effort to raise himself from his sofa.

"I must say, though, Richard, what is wrong with you tonight? You do not seem to revel in our success as you should. By all rights, you should be elated, not sulking.

"I am pleased enough, Fitz," the colonel replied. "I had hoped Charlotte might attend, and I regretted not seeing her." Darcy looked away and Lizzy caught his expression. She sat up a little. "I had asked Eliza to invite her, and when she refused the invitation, I rode to Meryton myself to ask her in person, but she would not even see me. I begged and pleaded, and all I received for my efforts were directions to the inn where I might get a pint of ale to refresh myself before turning back for Town."

Lizzy was now most curious, and most concerned.

"She must," glossed Darcy, still distracted by the search for his errant slippers, "have taken my words to heart then."

At these words, the energy in the room changed dramatically, as Richard and Lizzy both turned their full attention to the professor.

"What did you mean by that, Darcy?" Richard's voice was quiet and menacing; Lizzy could not suppress a gasp.

Darcy brushed off the question with a flick of his hand and attempted to sound unconcerned, but he must have realised he had misspoken. "I may have had a discussion with Miss Lucas before she returned to Meryton," he said.

"What was the matter of the discussion?" Richard's voice had lost its soft edge of fatigue and had taken on instead the crisp and undeniable tone of military authority. Even his cousin was forced to obey it.

"I may have suggested she return home," was all he said.

"Darcy... what on earth have you done?" Richard was standing now, and in two strong steps he stood before his cousin as he lay on the sofa. "What did you say to her? I demand you tell me now!"

In a few sentences, Darcy described his interaction with Charlotte. "She does not love you, Richard. She merely wants your fortune and your name. I overheard her say as much to Eliza, whilst I was in my study at some business."

Lizzy felt every ounce of fatigue drain away, her repressed anger surging to the forefront. "You heard incorrectly Professor Darcy!" she fairly shouted. These were her first words since entering the room, and the sound of her voice shocked the two men. "She never said a word to that effect, and you are most mistaken. If you had eavesdropped on the entire conversation, you would have heard her true expression: that she was talking about Jane, that she was so pleased that Mr. Bingley was able to see through Jane's natural reserve and recognise her feelings, which she keeps so hidden from the world. Whatever you think of Charlotte, she is not the sort to string a man along thus. She is not romantic, it is true, but she would not mislead a suitor, and most particularly not one for whom she cares, even a small amount. How dare you imply such things about my friend?"

"And how dare you interfere in my life? Darcy! I now recall you tried to convince me to throw her off, and I refused. So this was your next tactic: to convince her to abandon me! I repeat: How dare you?" The walls were shaking with the sound of Richard's voice; never had Lizzy heard him so angry.

"I thought only of you, Richard..."

"No. You thought only of yourself, Darcy...."

"As you did tonight," Lizzy added, her rage not one bit abated. "You paraded me around like an exhibit in a zoo, showed me off to all the right people, waltzed me around the room, and then congratulated yourself on your fine performance. Well what about everybody else, Professor Darcy? What about me? I am the one who did all the work. I am the one who practiced my vowels, who recited poetry with stones in my mouth, who walked the corridors of your house with books stacked on my head to improve my posture. What about me? I don't matter at all, I suppose! I won your bet for you after all!"

Darcy looked from Lizzy to Richard and back again, stunned at their reaction. "You matter? You won my bet? How impertinent! I won my bet. You should be pleased—see how well you will do in society now, thanks to me. Really, Eliza, you should run along to bed. You are tired and not thinking clearly. You will see things much better in the morning. Now where are those damned slippers?"

Lizzy looked down and saw the slippers sitting at the foot of the sofa upon which Darcy still sat. She picked them up and hurled them at him, one by one, hitting him quite squarely on the head. "There are your slippers. There, and there! Take your damned slippers and may you never have a day's luck with them! I have never been so humiliated and so angry in all my life." She turned, sobbing, and stumbled towards the door. Richard began to move as though he would go after her, but as he did so, the door opened and Freddy burst through.

"What in blazes is all this noise? I came..." He stopped short at the sight of Lizzy, her face red with anger and wet with tears, and he quickly discerned the source of her fury. "What have you done, Darcy? Shall I kill you now, or call you out? I'm a peer, don't you forget that, and I can see you hang!" He turned back to Lizzy and with a gentleness he had never before shown, put an arm around her shoulders to guide her toward him. "Come, Miss Bennet, let me see you somewhere quiet, and as soon as you wish, I will take you to wherever you want to go." He scowled once more at Darcy and led Lizzy from the room, allowing her to sob helplessly onto his chest.

CRBO

Freddy was as good as his word. He guided Lizzy to her room, summoned her abigail, and instructed the girl to help Lizzy pack, should she wish it. The following day, after a fitful sleep, he personally drove Lizzy and all her belongings to the Gardiners' house, where he stopped in—to the amazement of the neighbours—and waited until he was certain that Miss Bennet was comfortable, and until he had demanded of Mr. Gardiner to be informed the moment Lizzy made any decisions regarding her choice of abode, decisions to travel, or anything else more vital than what colour pelisse to wear with a certain gown.

"I shall not be denied this, sir," he informed Mr. Gardiner in his most imperious tones. "I am a peer of the realm—one day to be Earl of

Malton—and I have it within my power to ease your way in life or reduce you to nothing should you refuse me." He stood up to his full height and puffed out his turquoise-clad chest. "Of course, I would never actually do that," he added conspiratorially, "but I do like the effect it has on people when I so threaten. I do beseech you, sir, to keep me informed of Lizzy's actions. I care frightfully for the girl." Only then, satisfied at last by Gardiner's agreement, based on the latter statement and not the former, did he leave the house, a hundred eyes from surrounding homes and gardens following his carriage as it departed the area.

Thus it transpired that three days later, when Lizzy had declared her intention to return to Longbourn, her uncle sent a message to the viscount, who responded by appearing in person at the house within the half day. He was ushered into the front drawing room by a rather flustered maid, and within moments he was joined by the lady of the house. It was now just past five in the evening, and Gardiner had not yet returned from his office at his place of business, but would most assuredly arrive momentarily. The viscount was offered, and accepted, some brandy and cakes whilst they waited. "We dine as soon as Mr. Gardiner returns," Mrs. Gardiner explained, "and we would be most honoured if you would join us. Our cook is not, I am certain, of the quality of your own, but she provides us with hearty and excellent food, of which there is always plenty."

To her surprise, her guest graciously agreed. This would be a tale for the neighbours! Within a few minutes, Mr. Gardiner returned, and Mrs. Gardiner informed the maid to have another place set at the table. When Lizzy was called to join the family for their meal, she found her aunt and uncle sitting in the salon, engaged in friendly and companionable conversation with their visitor. She stopped at the door, and immediately Freddy leapt up to greet her. "Eliza..." he whispered.

"Freddy." He took her hands in his and kissed both of them. "I had not expected to see you here, of all places..."

"I could not leave you alone, Eliza. Is it true that you wish to return to your family?" He led her to a chair where they could talk quietly, far enough from her aunt and uncle that the conversation might remain private.

"I cannot stay in London. Not now, not after what he did. I cannot face seeing him, nor can I smile prettily at all those people who were there at the ball, and who now must know the truth..." She fought to keep the tears from her eyes. She could not even think of the embarrassment, the humiliation, that she must soon suffer. To have been feted as she was, celebrated as the Professor's chosen bride, introduced by the Countess of Malton, and then the very next day to scuttle off into her corner, could only provoke the most unkind and salubrious gossip. She could not bear to imagine what the ladies, those very ones who had so recently clamoured for Darcy's attention, must be saying about her in their spiteful ways. She knew enough of Caroline Bingley to imagine the direction of their thoughts. Anything else was too painful even to contemplate. And worse, no matter how bad the damage to her reputation, the damage to her heart was still more dire. The tears spilled down her cheeks, to be mopped up by Freddy's lace-edged handkerchief. Her aunt and uncle pretended to see nothing.

"They know nothing, Eliza," Freddy replied. "For all the *ton* is aware, you had a late night, a later morning, and are still sleeping off your success. If you have not been at my mother's house to accept callers, it is due merely to exhaustion and nothing else. Please, stay, for my sake..."

"I cannot, Freddy, and you know it. The truth will out soon enough. How can I bear it?"

"Then allow me to drive you home. Whenever you wish to return, I shall be there with my carriage and a maid. What Richard could not do for Charlotte, I shall do for you."

Lizzy looked up at him. He was a frivolous man, more concerned with his wardrobe than his estates, accustomed to being pampered and fawned over, but he was a good man, and at the moment, this was the one thing she needed most in the world: a friend. He asked nothing of her and offered her kindness and comfort. He could act the pompous viscount and brandish his name and rank about as a buccaneer does his sword, but he was at heart a sweet and honest man, with a generous heart and the willingness to put effort into his generosity. "Thank you, Freddy. I accept."

A date was discussed and agreed upon by all involved, and plans were set underway.

Two days later, the viscount's grand carriage was once again seen on Gracechurch Street, at the very break of day. Two of Gardiner's strongest servants helped Freddy's footmen stow the various trunks and valises onto the back of the conveyance, with an assurance that the remainder of Lizzy's luggage would be sent for immediately, to be transported to Longbourn. Soon enough, the young lady pronounced herself ready, and with tearful goodbyes and promises to her young cousins, she allowed herself to be handed into the carriage. As promised, a maid was waiting in the interior to protect her name, and slowly, the carriage began to move through the busy streets of London. After nearly five months as Darcy's student, she was leaving London. She was abandoning her scheme and the pompous and arrogant professor. She was going home.

# *Fourteen*
## *Home*

Being back at Longbourn was, at first, as much like a dream as had been London when she had first arrived. Everything seemed quite unchanged, yet at the same time completely different. The house, the lands, the farms, the town, were all just as she recalled them. Her mother offered her silly comments and lamented that poor Lizzy had returned without a husband, and whatever became of Mr. Darcy's ten thousand pounds, anyway? But she was certain that Lizzy had enjoyed her many balls and soirees and must surely have returned with some lovely trinkets and with yards and yards of lace and ribbons upon her new gowns. Her sisters, Kitty and Lydia, asked only after what she had brought them, and about the men in London, and whether Lizzy had danced with any officers. Her father, as she had expected, cast a wry eye on the goings-on in the house, and uttered something about finally being able to hear two words of sense at a time, now that she had returned, and retired to his library.

Her arrival had occasioned a great deal of excitement as much for her companion—a viscount no less! Even grander than Professor Darcy!—as for her precipitous homecoming. The carriage had been met by the whole family and many of the servants too, all eager to see the grand conveyance in which she had travelled, and she had been allowed to enter the house first, before even her mother, with Freddy on her arm. Mr. Bennet was not in awe of the viscount, but had comported himself with the dignity appropriate to their guest, and Mrs. Bennet had been so much in awe of him that she had said almost nothing, which suited Lizzy rather well. Freddy had stayed for tea, then for dinner, but had insisted upon beginning his return to Town, keen to take advantage of the lengthening days as they approached summer.

"A viscount, Lizzy! You had not told us! Oh, what riches you shall have! Your sons will be earls!" Nothing she could say would convince her mother that she was not to marry Freddy, and in the end, she rolled her eyes and announced that she needed to see to her unpacking.

After the crowded streets and noise of London, Lizzy revelled in the open spaces of her little corner of Hertfordshire. The morning after her arrival she set off for Meryton, accompanied by her two youngest sisters. She revelled in the mile-long walk, uninterrupted by racing phaetons and curricles, yipping dogs and urchins underfoot, or the bustle of shopkeepers and delivery boys and attending maids. There were no parades of fine ladies exhibiting their elegance in the parks, no displays of the latest manners by the young dandies of Town. On her walks in the park in London, Freddy would have been dancing around her, quipping on the colour of his new coat or on some acquaintance's newly purchased curricle with his monogram embossed upon the leather of the seats that he had commissioned solely to impress a sweetheart. The noise and frippery and chaos had been her constant companions these past months.

Instead, Lizzy now realised how much she had missed the unpretentious and honest farmers who worked her father's land, the friendly boys of the village, the pretty and unspoiled girls on the farms. She waved at the men and women she knew as she walked by, thinking she must go and see Mrs. Wiggins' new babe, must take a basket to Old Mrs. Chancey, must see how Mr. Pollard was managing at the school the vicar had recently established for the town's boys and girls. The sky was clear and blue, and the wildflowers in the meadows and the birds winging from branch to branch all seemed to her as a welcome back, an affirmation that this, not London, was her place.

Oh, there were things and people from Town that she would certainly miss. The opera, the theatre, the museums: these all entranced her and she delighted in them, and was sad to think that they would have to remain rare treats, rather than common engagements, but she could live very well without them. Harder to leave without regret were some of the people she had befriended in London. She truly would miss the good sense and generosity of Lady Malton—forever Aunt Patricia in her mind. She would miss their morning chats over tea, their walks through the crowded streets, and the countess' biting commentary on the ladies and gentlemen they encountered on their daily excursions. She would miss her gentle encouragement and her intelligent and witty conversation.

She would miss Freddy, despite his trivial ways. He might place more importance on the outcome of a horse race on which he had wagered no pennies than on the outcome of the war in Europe; he might ponder more seriously on whether his cuffs ought to extend one-and-a-half or two inches from his coat than on the meaning of the latest lines by Wordsworth or Coleridge. And yet, he had a good and kind heart and he had proven a most worthy companion and a steadfast friend. She had grown to cherish his friendship.

She would also miss Richard. When had the colonel become Richard to her? She hardly knew when he had grown almost as dear to her as a brother. Was it when he began to pay attention to her friend Charlotte? He, who had seen not the plain face or the lost bloom of youth, but the gem that lay within her dear friend, who had been ready to face his family's wrath over his choice because his affection was so deep. He, who had been the counterpoint to Darcy's overbearing and tyrannical ways, who had spread a sheen of civility on all that transpired in that awful study in Darcy House. He too had become a friend, and one whom she would miss dreadfully in time, once the novelty of her return had worn off.

And what of Darcy himself? She hardly even knew what to call him in her innermost thoughts. He was no longer her teacher, and their intimacy had forbidden to her the title of professor. One does not melt into the arms of one's professor as one does one's inamorato, one's betrothed, one's lover. 'Darcy' seemed too formal a name for him now, after their intimacy, and yet she could not countenance calling him by his given name, even in her mind. He would remain "He" until she could clear her thoughts and her memories of the emotional whirlwind that the very thought of him provoked. How could he have kissed her so tenderly one minute, then belittled her the next and cried 'Thank God that's over'? What of his words had been truth and what mere artifice to gain her willingness to further his project? Had those moments of tenderness and vulnerability, when she thought he had revealed his true self, merely been brilliant examples of acting, the world being his stage? She had thought she had seen beneath his veneer of rudeness and disdain into the man beneath, but now, perhaps, she thought that the incivility underlay everything else. He had sought her heart, and she had begun to give it away, before he had trampled on it and left it bleeding in the dirt.

And hers was not the only heart Darcy had broken. Charlotte's too, and Richard's, were victims to his high-handed arrogance. Of Darcy's own heart, she cared little. So much more painful was the damage he had done to others. With these thoughts roiling in her mind, she knew she must see Charlotte, and at least try to explain what had happened. Perhaps, if her friend were willing, she could somehow contact Freddy, her dependable Freddy, and request his assistance in reuniting the two lovers. She hoped that Charlotte was not so destroyed by her encounters with society that she would refuse to attempt a reunion, or that Darcy's cruel words had not damaged her vision of a life with Richard beyond repair.

Lost in thought as she had been, Lizzy had not realised she and her sisters had already achieved the town. She looked around as they crossed the bridge over the small stream that demarcated one boundary of the village. The high street looked as it always had, and the aroma of warm yeasted sweets emanated from Mrs. Johnson's bakery. The sounds of the smithy reached her ears, with the clanging of metal on metal, and from the stables behind the inn a street yonder, she could hear the horses whinnying and the voices of stable hands trying to calm them. Mr. Oldham, the bookseller, had a small table on the street by his door, and her sisters had already started towards the milliner's shop that displayed a series of bonnets in its window. Here, a group of matrons stood talking together as they watched their children run through the streets after a stray dog; there, a small gathering of red-coated officers strutted by the tavern, although its doors would not open for some hours. A handsome young officer doffed his hat and bowed to her sisters as they passed, and they giggled in response, but did not vary from their goal of the new bonnets in Mr. Aberley's window. And there, down the street, around the corner, and another block down, she would find Lucas Lodge and, she hoped, Charlotte. Screwing her courage to the sticking place, she called after her sisters to tell them of her destination, and she set off in search of her friend.

Charlotte was in the kitchens when Lizzy arrived. Seeing her friend, she hastily removed her apron and left the sauce in the capable hands of the young girl who helped with some of the household tasks. "Lizzy!" Charlotte gaped, "When did you return home? I had no notion you were to visit!"

"Not visiting, Charlotte, but here to stay," she sighed. Lizzy took the chair Charlotte offered her, then stood again and asked her friend to walk outside with her. "I am too tired of sitting and being polite. I need to move," she explained.

Charlotte had not heard of the debacle after the ball; Lizzy had been too miserable to put pen to paper, and whilst she thought her mother might inform Lady Lucas that Lizzy was to return to Meryton, the news had not reached Charlotte. Thus, as they walked the lanes that wound in and out of the village, Lizzy opened her heart to her friend and divulged all.

"He loves you, Charlotte," Lizzy said at last, when she reached the point in the tale concerning Richard. "He has been miserable without you, and when he heard what the professor had done, it was only by effort that he did not assault his person. He had thought that you were the one who broke his heart, and it was, instead, his cousin."

Shaking her head, Charlotte let out a puff of breath. "Professor Darcy may have initiated this decision, but he was not wrong in what he said. I am not the colonel's equal, nor will I ever be. I cannot be the wife he needs in society, and he would resent me one day. If he should seek a seat in Parliament, or a position in the government, I would only be a hindrance to him." Her face was grim but resigned, and she fixed her gaze not at her friend but across the fields that lay beyond the hedgerow along which they walked.

"If he truly loves you, that will be nothing to him. He does not desire a seat in parliament, nor a post. He has done his service to his king and country and has no aspirations to any higher position. All he wishes is to be a country gentleman, and a country gentleman requires a sensible and caring wife who will support him in his efforts on his estate and be a good mistress to his tenants. For that position, you are most qualified. If he seeks you out again, promise me you will speak to him." Charlotte looked up in alarm, and Lizzy murmured, "I know he was here and that you refused to meet with him. If he comes back, listen to him. Will you promise me that?"

Though she demurred at first, eventually Lizzy convinced her to at least let the colonel speak. "Yes, Lizzy. For you, I will promise!"

Turning the subject to lighter matters, the two women smiled, their hearts somewhat lighter, and returned to the village along the familiar lanes.

Despite all those aspects of village life that had remained unchanged during Lizzy's sojourn in London, however, there were other areas in which a great deal of change had occurred. As far as Lizzy was concerned, the most notable difference from before she left was the absence of two of her sisters. Mary had always been the quiet one, the one who disdained what she deemed 'foolish chatter,' who would look down her nose at her younger sisters' inanities and flirtations and who would take to the pianoforte or her books of sermons rather than engage in light banter or ambles through the countryside. The plainest of the sisters, more for want of effort and decoration than any real physical defect, she had grown up under the shadow of her two witty and sensible older sisters and been unequal to the spirit and playfulness of the younger. She had made her own space as a devout pedant, although lacking the serious education that would give her opinions weight. She had found her ideal place as Mrs. Collins, where her sermonising would find sympathetic ears in her husband and her serious dogmatism would be admired by Lady Catherine. But, to her surprise, Lizzy found she missed her sister's presence at Longbourn. For all her pontificating and lecturing, Mary had been the voice of sense that often tempered Kitty and Lydia's most extreme bouts of silliness, and her calm nature had soothed their mother where Lizzy's patience wore thin and her other sisters found better things to do. Even those endlessly complicated and poorly executed pieces she endeavoured to learn on the pianoforte were missed, for now the only sounds in the house were her sisters' shouts, her mother's complaints, and the general noises from the servants as they went about their business.

As much as Lizzy found she missed Mary, so much more so did she miss Jane. So short had been the days between Jane's marriage and Lizzy's own departure for London that she scarcely had time to notice that her dearest sister was no longer there, sitting in the salon, humouring her mother, waiting for a good gossip before the firelight when they were preparing for bed. Jane was her confidant, her conscience and her sounding board, the voice of compassion to Lizzy's judgmental tendencies. What would Jane make of the disaster after the ball? What words would she offer in light of the separation of Charlotte and Richard? Lizzy could never ask her, for Jane was married to That Man's close friend, but Lizzy longed for the words of sense and understanding that her dear sister might offer, that they might help soothe her own mind.

But Jane was wed and away in London, mistress of her own household, and Lizzy was here in her old home in Hertfordshire once more. Now, as she strove to find her place anew and re-establish herself in her life at Longbourn, she found she missed Jane's company most dreadfully. Charlotte was a dear friend, it was true, but there were those things one told a sister that one could never divulge to a friend. There were aspects to her, insights into her soul, that Jane alone knew. Jane, and Darcy... No! She must not think of him. She fought those tendrils of thought and forced them from her mind.

Lizzy had also neglected at first to consider how she herself had changed during her months amongst the elite in London. She had learned and practiced her new accent so well that it had become her natural way of speaking now, and whilst she could assume her old patterns of speech if she applied herself, the effort was greater than retaining her crisp and clear aristocratic tones.

The consequences of this had not occurred to her at all, for she had expected to be accepted back into the society of her youth with all the pleasure which she herself anticipated. How sadly her assumptions were dashed when she discovered that her new accent and speech was not seen without contempt. The first instance of this realisation occurred one afternoon, after taking tea with Mrs. Long and her niece Alice, a young woman with whom Lizzy had been friendly since childhood. Tea was a pleasant and cheerful affair, during which the ladies had asked her every possible question about London, which she had answered in her usual arch manner. At the appropriate time, she had risen and taken her leave of the ladies, only to discover that she had forgotten inside the parlor a program from a concert which she had shown to Mrs. Long.

She was about to enter the room to retrieve it when she heard Alice exclaim to her aunt, "Oh, I thought I should never survive the afternoon, listening to Lizzy all high and fine." Then, in the exaggerated tones of mockery, she attempted to mimic Lizzy's fine accent. "'Hoow doo yoo dooooo? Soh verry kayhnd of yoo.' Oh, Aunt Harriet, I thought I would die to hear one more word!" And Mrs. Long laughed and agreed with her niece.

Lizzy stood by the doorway, so shocked and discomfited that she could hardly find her next breath. What wrong had she done these people, whom she had known her entire life, that they must mock her? What had become of former friendship? Was it only here, or was she thought of thus throughout Meryton society, to be an item of derision and amusement? The notion ate at her very soul. She forgot the concert program and turned around immediately, her face white.

Her London manners, too, had become a matter of contention for her. She had not realised how, under both the harsh glare and chastisements of Professor Darcy, and more so, under the gentle guidance of Lady Malton, she had completely adopted the refinements and graces of the upper classes of Town. These, like her new accent, had become second nature to her, as reflexive as breathing, and she could not think of abandoning what had become so much a part of her. She could not find fault with the "country manners" which Mr. Bingley had extolled upon his initial arrival in Hertfordshire, but she saw them now with new eyes, and understood the chasm between her new society and her old, recognised the origins of Darcy's disparaging comments and Caroline's haughty sneers.

Between her new habits and her prolonged absence, fitting back into Meryton society was much more difficult than she had imagined. The invitations were as plentiful as before, but now Lizzy perceived herself as an item of curiosity rather than a friend; she felt as much an exhibit in Meryton as she had been in London—more so, perhaps, for here, her acquaintances knew of her transformation and came to watch her, as a butterfly new from its cocoon, where they had all known the caterpillar. In London, she knew she could blend in and be accepted. In Meryton, that seemed no longer to be possible.

The greatest heartbreak came some three or four weeks after her return, when she came home from early morning visits to some of her father's tenants, to find her mother in cozy conversation with her Aunt Phillips. She was removing her muddy boots in the vestibule by the kitchen entrance to the house, having engaged Mrs. Hill in a moment's discussion over the state of the kitchen garden, and her mother must have mistaken the sound for the routine noise of the servants. As she sat upon the hard wooden bench and untied the laces, her mother's voice came clearly to her through the open doorway.

"I don't know what we shall do about Lizzy, Sister. She has become quite a different person. She was always above us, you know, but since her months in London, I hardly know her. She walks around here, with her high and mighty ways, and looks upon us lesser beings. Us! Her very family! I am quite overcome by this, and it strains at my nerves every day!"

Lizzy was horrified. Was this what her family and friends thought of her? All of her family and friends seemed to have deserted her, with the singular exception of Charlotte, and she was now an outcast amongst her own family, scorned and mocked by those who professed to love her, deemed too grand for the people she had called friends. It was too much to bear, and she left her boots lying on the small rug as she ran up the back stairs to her room and let a flood of tears fall. "What shall become of me?" she wept into her pillow. "Whatever shall become of me?"

This descent into misery was blessedly interrupted some days later by the arrival of two men on horseback. They had driven in from London the previous evening, and after staying the night at Netherfield, had made Longbourn their first stop in the morning.

"Lord Eynshill and Colonel Fitzwilliam," Mrs. Hill announced in some alarm as the two interrupted the Bennet family's breakfast.

"Oh, we are rather too early, are we not?" the colonel asked in alarm, but Lizzy jumped up from her seat and grabbed both men's hands before realising it was most inappropriate to do so. "Richard!" she beamed, "Freddy!" She felt a smile come across her face for the first time in many a day.

Too early to visit or not, the esteem due these two men quickly saw chairs arranged for them, for the very wealthy or high of rank may make their own rules in society and be lauded for them.

"Most dreadfully sorry to barge in like this, Mrs. Bennet," Freddy purred as he accepted the breakfast offered to him, "but I could not wait a moment longer before seeing your lovely daughter Elizabeth once more. What a fine table you set, and not even anticipating guests. You must be the most admired hostess in the area." Then, turning to the master of the house, "Fine estate here, Bennet. You are a fortunate man." Thus, having most efficiently smoothed any feathers ruffled by their unorthodox appearance, the brothers charmed their way into convincing Lizzy to join them on a walk into town.

It was not a difficult task, for more and more, Lizzy found herself an outsider in her family, and was always eager for some means to escape them. The companionship she had found with Richard and Freddy was most pleasing and welcome, and she discovered that she had grown more comfortable with their London ways than with the manners and habits of the good people of Meryton.

"I am most glad to see you, Lizzy," Freddy breathed into her ear as they began their walk. Of her London acquaintances, he was the only one to use the name by which her family and friends called her. She had not, until now, wondered at this. He must have heard her referred to thus by Charlotte and by her aunt and uncle, and had adopted the appellation which she, herself, preferred. He took her hand and placed it upon his forearm. "I have missed your company and bright smile. Have you thought much about me while you have been away? I do hope so!"

Had she missed him? She certainly enjoyed his company and his irrepressible good nature and charm, but had she missed him? Wished daily that he were with her? She was not certain she did. At first, immediately upon her return to Meryton, she had felt his absence, but as the weeks had progressed she had thought less and less of him, except in fond recollection of London and her time there. No, delightful as it was to see him once more, she had not missed him in the manner he meant.

Instead of answering his question, she replied, "I am so very pleased to see you, Freddy! You cannot imagine what a delight it is." He seemed satisfied with that as an answer, and offered his arm as they walked.

Richard's goal, to no one's surprise, was to visit Charlotte. He explained as they walked that he had wrested the entire story from his cousin and had announced that he would accept interference from no one in this matter. "I gave Darcy the tongue-lashing of his life, Eliza. I believe the walls are still ringing from my shouts. I also may have hit him." He rubbed his hand in recollection. "I am not proud of my loss of temper, but neither do I regret it. It was time Darcy got put in his place.

"He was the only son," the colonel continued as they wandered past bright meadows and well-tended farms, "the golden boy, the longed-for heir, and he was treated accordingly. He was afforded the best of everything, but was never taught how to care for people. I do believe this is the first time in his life he has been called to account for his dealing with others. We have laughed at his eccentricities until now and treated them as a bit of a joke, but never before has he acted so heartlessly and given such pain, and so he must be called to account."

Reluctantly, Lizzy asked, "How is the professor managing with the demands of society after the ball? Has he managed to find a good face to present to the spectators?"

It was Freddy who answered. "No, he absconded the very next morning. Packed up his valise, saddled his horse, closed the Town House, and departed, presumably for Pemberley. I doubt very much we shall see him again this side of winter. He has a tendency to sulk."

Gone? Gone from London? That proud, arrogant man who sneered at the dictates of civility and thought nothing of crushing the spirits of people he considered beneath him had left in a pique? Was he embarrassed by his failure—not to pass Lizzy off as equal to the elite, but to sway her mind to his will—or was his abrupt departure due to something else? Did Richard's haranguing cause the rude professor a moment's deep reflection? Or was he genuinely shaken by it? Was there, perhaps, a sliver of humanity in the cold and haughty beast after all? Lizzy thought back to those rare moments when she had glimpsed the vulnerability and sensitivity hidden below the callous layers of disdain and wondered if Darcy was hurting as much as she was.

She had hardly allowed herself to think of him. She refused to give in to the deep desire to recall his kisses, the touch of his hands, the real understanding that had developed between them. She had considered, more than once, accepting his second proposal for a true engagement, and wondered how much she had come to care for the man. When he had disparaged her hard work and reveled in the completion of his project, she had felt her heart shatter in her breast, and resolved to think no more on the man who had created and then destroyed her, but he was there, always there, in her soul, and she knew she would never be free of him. Nor, she realised for the first time, did she wish to be. She missed him.

Richard must have sensed her distress, for he quickly turned the conversation to lighter matters. He chatted happily of his mother, of the flowers at Kew Gardens, and of the horse he considered acquiring from an acquaintance.

"Not that one, Richard," Freddy interrupted. "That horse will never suit. He's strong and well-bred, I grant you, but think of how his coat will clash with the new riding coat Mother had made for you. He is too yellow to match the green of your vestments, and that just will never do. You cannot neglect the importance of such details."

Richard huffed in disdain and rolled his eyes at this, then launched into a recital of his plans to take over the management of Hillford. "'Tis mine now, and I have the responsibility for its prosperity, no matter whether I chose to make it my primary residence or not. I have been thither this past month, learning my way about and meeting the primary tenants. Good people, hard workers." At this sensible adoption of responsibility, it was Freddy who rolled his eyes. Richard ignored him. "The land will prosper under good management, wherever I choose to live. But it would be a grand thing to settle on my own estate, raise a family..." His eyes drifted off to the horizon, and Lizzy knew he was thinking about Charlotte.

They had now reached the town and walked down the high street and around the corner, and were only a few steps from their destination. Lizzy ran the last few steps and rang at the bell. Within ten minutes, Charlotte had joined them, and the foursome walked further down the lanes leading beyond the village.

Richard and Freddy remained for two days, sleeping at Netherfield but spending their days with Lizzy and Charlotte. Their departure, when it occurred, was somewhat precipitous. Freddy announced most suddenly that he wished to attend the races at Ascot. Any attachment he might have felt towards Lizzy was second to his love of thoroughbred horses, so it seemed. Richard also announced that he had better return to London for the nonce to deal with matters of personal business, although his absence would be temporary. He had offered for Charlotte and she had accepted him. He would return shortly to claim his bride.

"I do love him, Lizzy!" she confessed as the men's carriage departed. "I cannot now think that I ever might have accepted a man for the security he offered and nothing more. Now that I have known Richard and heard what my heart has whispered to me, I cannot imagine anything else."

Lizzy hugged her friend, genuinely delighted that there would be a happy ending for at least some of the people drawn into Darcy's plot.

Freddy had continued playing the suitor, but she suspected that he knew as much as she did that the love between them was the love of good friends. She would never feel towards him what Charlotte felt for Richard, nor he towards her. His decision to abscond to Ascot confirmed this notion in her mind.

If it so transpired that he should ask her to marry him, which she increasingly doubted he would ever do, she might accept him, but it would be a marriage of convenience only. The thought made her sad. She might not deserve more, but Freddy certainly did. She did not love him, but she liked him a great deal and wished him all the happiness that fate might give him. Fortunately, this did not seem to be a decision she would have to make in the foreseeable future, and she wished it to remain that way.

Charlotte and Richard's engagement was short, and they were wed three weeks later in London. Richard had returned after only two days, and had borne Charlotte away with him to London, where she would reside with the Count and Countess in order to ensure a suitable residence in the parish; it must be a society wedding, for the groom's father was an earl, after all! The earl was not pleased at his son's choice, but seemed resigned to it and gave his blessing to the couple. All celebrations having been made, the couple set off immediately to Hillford; it would be the first time Charlotte would see the estate that would now be her home and Lizzy dearly hoped the place would meet her expectations and make her happy.

Lizzy had travelled to Town for the wedding, and now, sitting in her uncle's carriage as they returned after the breakfast to Gracechurch Street, she felt completely forlorn. Everybody was gone. Mary was gone, Jane was gone, and now Charlotte was gone. Whilst she was happy for them all, and begrudged them nothing, she could not help the return of sadness that crept through her. She had no more friends in Meryton; those she held dear had moved away, and those she had known less well were all put out by her elegant London ways. She felt quite alone and abandoned.

"What is the matter, Lizzy?" her aunt asked. Mrs. Gardiner had always been a favourite relative; her sensitive soul and perceptive eye now worked to discern the cause of Lizzy's low spirits. "You feel you cannot return home, I believe. Charlotte was your last close friend there, and there is nothing there for you now. Am I correct, my dear?"

"You are always correct, Aunt." A deep sigh emanated from her core as the carriage lurched its way through London's crowded streets.

"Is this a good time, Edward?" her aunt grinned at the man seated on the opposite bench.

Her uncle chuckled conspiratorially and nodded, "I believe it is, my dear. Ask away."

Turning to her niece and grabbing her hands, Mrs. Gardiner spoke. "Your uncle has decided to take a tour in the north, to see the country and to visit my old home at Arlenby. My brother and his wife will be in residence and Lady Grant has most specifically requested that you be included in our party. Come and join us, Lizzy. The change will do you good!"

It was not difficult to convince her. The prospect of travelling with her beloved aunt and uncle was much more welcome than returning to lonely Meryton, and the promise of a long visit with the Grants was delightful. Lizzy very much liked Aunt Gardiner's brother and his wife, and her one regret for the way her adventure in London had ended was the loss of the year under the guidance of Lady Grant. By the time the carriage had finally delivered its passengers to the Gardiners' house, all that remained to be done was to receive Mr. Bennet's blessings for the journey. The future, for the first time in months, was looking brighter.

# *Fifteen*
## *Changing Scenery*

George Wickham sat back in his chair at his favourite tavern and laughed. The afternoon light filtered through the dirty and uneven glass in the windows, further distorted by moiré curtains that might once have been white, but that now had as much character to them as the old man who lived around the long bar at the back of the room. Dust motes floated in the air, catching those rays that had survived the obstacles, glinting like miniscule stars in the half-lit space. The floors and furniture were all old and scarred wood; the walls were plaster, interrupted by shelves, sconces and a large fireplace. It was not quite a respectable establishment, nor was it entirely disrespectable. It was a land in-between, where the classes might meet, where gossip might be exchanged, and where no one quite recalled exactly who had said what to whom the following morning. That the food was acceptable and the ale not watered rendered it even more suitable for the lieutenant, who had just heard something quite delightful from an old companion.

It had been some weeks since he had last seen Caroline. After their last tryst, as she kissed him goodbye behind the curtains of the carriage he had hired, she had explained with a moue of disappointment that a succession of societal and family responsibilities would prevent her from seeing him for a while. No, no, she assured him, this was not a final parting, but a temporary one, made necessary by the demands of her station. She would never say the words or name the people, but Wickham was certain it revolved around her engagement to the miserable Darcy. There would surely be balls, teas, soirees, yawn, yawn, yawn, at which she must appear to dote upon her surly and unpleasant betrothed, while swanning around trying to convince her friends and acquaintances that she genuinely cared for the man, and how happy they would be once they were wed. He could picture her, dripping in the Darcy family jewels—now which ones might he pilfer and sell?—strutting around in some elaborately encrusted gown, looking down her pretty nose at the poor little people who did not have the great luck to be marrying into the Darcy fortune, all while replaying his most particular attentions in her mind. Hah, poor Darcy—cuckolded before he was even wed! Would crusty, boring, unimaginative Darcy ever discover how Caro enjoyed it when...? Ah, yes, he shivered at the recollection. A most pleasant memory indeed. Poor girl to be stuck with that prig. She would undoubtedly always come back to him for her pleasure.

And now, what news had he just heard from Sanderson's lips, but that Darcy had left town! Sanderson's brother was a footman at the Poynters' townhouse, and he had it from the upstairs maid at the Derlains, who had it from the Maltons' very own kitchen maid, that there had been a grand ball to celebrate the engagement and introduce the bride to society, and that afterwards she and Darcy had fought, and both had abandoned London! Some of the details had seemed a tad off, perhaps—surely the bride's name was Miss Caroline and not Miss Elizabeth—but everyone knew how the specifics never survived subsequent retellings intact. It could only be a slip of memory, both being common and rather interchangeable names, and these little inconsistencies bothered him not at all. What was important was that Darcy must have learned of his beloved's betrayal! He had learned of Caroline's faithlessness and he had scuttled out of town like a kitchen pest upon the lighting of a lamp!

Yes, the great Fitzwilliam Darcy had been cast down! Wickham played and replayed various scenarios over in his mind of what must have transpired after the ball, and each one concluded with Caroline informing him that she had been taken and loved by another.

"How could you? How could you choose Wickham over me?" Darcy would say, and Caroline would just laugh and laugh before informing him coolly, "I needed a real man."

And what of Darcy's retreat? Wickham relished the thought of the great master of Pemberley, returning home a broken shadow of a man, tail between his legs. Was his heart broken? Was he destroyed? Was he humiliated, cast down in shame? It mattered not which; it only mattered that the plan was working and Wickham was finally gaining the upper hand. This was the first taste of victory! This was what Wickham had been working towards for so long, and now his schemes were playing out at last. Ah, how he would savour this moment.

He summoned the serving girl over and asked for another pint of the good strong ale, then sat back with a self-satisfied grin on his face to plan the next stage of his assault.

CRSO

Mr. Gardiner had written to Mr. Bennet about the proposed journey northward, and permission had been duly granted. The alacrity with which the response was written and dispatched, so unlike her father's accustomed lackadaisical dithering, suggested to Lizzy that the family was relieved to be rid of her for some time longer. She did not know if this realisation injured her or relieved her to a greater extent.

The ultimate plans were simple and elegant: Lizzy would remain in London with her relatives until the dates of the planned holiday, at which time the carriage would travel to Longbourn, where it would disgorge itself of four Gardiner children and their nursemaid, to be replaced by Lizzy's travelling trunks. Such was deemed most suitable, and such transpired, and in the early days of the summer, the trip was underway.

Although Lizzy had travelled many times south to London, and since had travelled further south still to Kent, this was her first journey northward. Uncle Gardiner often had cause to travel along these roads for his business, and Aunt Gardiner herself was from the north; consequently between the two, they had a multitude of interesting and amusing tales to entertain their guest on the long trip. All along the route, Elizabeth found herself diverted. The changing scenery and topography captured her imagination, and she found amusement at the stopping places and inns where they rested their horses and took meals in observing and inventing stories about their fellow travellers. Along those stretches of the Great North Road that were less than picturesque, she took comfort in the selection of books she had brought along, and the entire adventure was most agreeable and pleasant.

After several days of the tour, during which the travellers stopped at a variety of interesting and beautiful places, they arrived at Arlenby. "This is where I grew up," Mrs. Gardiner told her niece. "There is the village, down that lane, and through those woods is a stream..." She glanced meaningfully at her husband, and Lizzy detected a tale hidden in those simple words. "The house," Mrs. Gardiner continued, "is very old, with parts dating back to the Normans, but the main building, where the family lives, is modern and most comfortable. There, there are the stables, and there the storage facilities and there—" they rounded a small curve in the road and the house came suddenly into view, "There is Arlenby!" The house was a modest manor, with four storeys rising above a beautifully designed lawn, not rambling, but tidy and compact. There were small towers at each of the two front corners to the house, and Mrs. Gardiner pointed to one, saying that the room inside had been her favourite place as a child. The ancient parts to the house were at the back, beyond the new kitchens, and were safe to explore should Lizzy feel the desire to wander through half-ruined rooms during her stay. "If you discover a ghost, please invite it to dinner," Aunt Gardiner teased, "for we would have all residents of the house be happy and pleasant company." Lizzy decided the entire prospect was wonderful.

The travellers were greeted by their hosts, who had been waiting at the main doors.

"Harry!" Mrs. Gardiner cried and flung herself into her brother's arms the moment she had alighted from the carriage. Sir Harry beamed his welcome and greeted his brother Gardiner with the warmth one shows a friend, not merely a relation by marriage. These men had a history and shared adventures, and their mutual respect and admiration was evident.

"Miss Bennet!" Sir Harry greeted Lizzy as she stepped out of the carriage. "How delightful that you were able to join your aunt and uncle. My wife was most pleased to hear of your acceptance." Lady Grant, Lizzy's own friend, echoed these sentiments. "Come, Lizzy, and I shall show you your room, and we may have a great gab like schoolgirls before we are called upon to be ladies again at dinner!"

Three days passed in pleasant companionship. After the growing sense of alienation from her friends and family in Meryton, and the more recent ado around Charlotte and Richard's elaborate wedding, Lizzy reveled in being able to enjoy the easy and intelligent company of her aunt and her friend. Lady Grant had a pretty young daughter, now three years of age, and much time was spent in dressing, undressing, and redressing little Emily's dolls, and creating fantastical stories about fairies, wizards, and the gnomes who lived under the mushrooms in the woods. Lady Grant told her friends that while Sir Harry had been granted a second estate along with his baronetcy, the family had decided to retain Arlenby as their primary residence, for it was here that they felt most at home.

On the fourth day, Aunt Gardiner expressed a wish to travel into the nearby town of Lambton. She had spent much time there as a child, and had several acquaintances she hoped to visit. "There is a very good book shop in the town, Lizzy," Lady Grant said, "and some small but well-stocked shops should you wish to buy presents for your sisters. The town is not large, but it is very prosperous, due to the proximity of several important estates. You must have heard of Pemberley, for that is Professor Darcy's estate."

Lizzy did not know if she paled completely or flushed deep red. All she knew was that, at the sound of the name of Darcy's estate, she felt her head grow light and saw the world spin askew for a moment. She looked up sharply to see whether her reaction had been caught by either of the other two women, but they both had their eyes on young Emily as she pressed another outfit for her dolls into every available hand.

She had known, of course, that Arlenby and Pemberley were within a few short miles of each other, but had not thought to be travelling near enough to the other estate to risk an encounter with its inhabitants. And yet Lambton, the town of which Lady Grant was speaking, relied upon that estate for much of its prosperity, enough that it must be very near indeed. "...only five miles distant, and on good roads," Lady Grant was saying, though the words swam in Lizzy's ears. "but I have not heard that the family is in residence. Miss Darcy is said to be in London now, with her aunt and uncle, and no one has seen the professor in several months."

"Then Professor Darcy is not at his estate?" Lizzy was confused, and slightly concerned, for Richard had told her that Pemberley had been Darcy's intention when he departed London.

"I know not what happens within the walls of the manor house, but from the little rounds of gossip and news-sharing, no one has seen him since the previous summer."

"Oh!" If he were not at Pemberley, where could he be? Ought she to write to Richard to express her concerns about his cousin? Surely he had better information than she, although if the man had wished to vanish, he could send false news to his family. She was loath to disturb the colonel with a letter, for he was recently wed and only now beginning to settle into his newly acquired estate, but she could not write to Freddy—even the most loosely held notions of propriety forbade that—and it would never do to raise such concerns with Lady Malton. But the professor's wellbeing took precedence in her thoughts, and she was resolved. She must inform Richard through a letter to Charlotte, and this she must do at once, for she could not rest easily if she did nothing to alert Darcy's family as to his absence from Pemberley.

She therefore begged a few minutes before the small party would depart for Lambton to write some quick letters, explaining that she would like to put them in the post from the town, and when this wish was granted, hurried to her room to compose her notes. Her words were concise and free from the elaborate artifice so common amongst fashionable circles, and within a very short time her letter was blotted and sealed and the direction clearly inscribed on the outer envelope.

Placing it in her reticule, she laced her boots and donned her bonnet and prepared herself for a visit to the town Darcy might call his own.

It was not a long drive between the Grants' estate and the little town, but it was a most pleasant one. The countryside was striking, its verdant hills contrasting with dramatic crags of rock, and cut through with sparkling streams and rivulets. "Pemberley lies yonder, on the other side of the town," Lady Grant explained as they drove. "We seldom see the family, but they are known in the area for their excellent management and good works. Professor Darcy is regarded as an eccentric and a rather private sort of man, but he lets his charitable actions and care for his lands speak when his own words are lacking. He is, if not beloved, much respected."

Lizzy listened with interest. She had not, heretofore, considered the professor in his role of master of an estate. Seeing him amidst his towers of books and diagrams of vowels, it was difficult to imagine him planning out planting schedules or negotiating compromises between feuding tenants. And yet, seeing the area in which his estate lay, it became clear to her that a great many people depended upon his good management of the land, and the prosperity of the region and of the town which they had just now entered spoke of his success in that endeavour. "Yet another project successfully concluded," she mused somewhat uncharitably, but she was also impressed beyond what she had thought by the diligent exercise of his responsibility and the profits thereof.

The town itself was delightful. Many of the buildings were old, seeming to date back to the time of the Tudors, with their wattle and daub construction, or built of sturdy stone, and the central marketplace stretched along a quickly flowing river, whilst the houses and cottages lay behind, climbing gently up the surrounding hillsides. Lizzy longed to return one day soon with her sketchbook and pencils so she might attempt to capture the picturesque village on paper. She did not claim much merit as an artist, but she enjoyed the exercise and wished to preserve what she could of this lovely scene. She said as much to Lady Grant, and the lady suggested some suitable times for a second visit.

The carriage stopped in front of a well-kept inn, where the passengers alighted. Lady Grant gave some instructions to the coachman and groom, and the carriage then drove off towards the stables where the horses and their drivers would wait until the ladies were ready to return home. "We shall take tea here," Lady Grant gestured to the inn, which housed an elegant tea shop as well as the expected tavern, "after I have completed my business." The lady had already explained her wish to consult with the chandlers and the dressmaker, and wished also to examine patterns for a new set of china which would include Sir Harry's new coat of arms, and thus she departed in one direction with her maid behind her, leaving Lizzy and Mrs. Gardiner to wander in the other to explore the town at leisure.

Lizzy's first stop was the inn, where she left her letter to be sent in that day's post. The innkeeper was a pleasant and friendly man with news about the town and a good word for everyone, and he complimented Miss Bennet on her choice of friends and family, for he remembered Mrs. Gardiner as a lass, spoke kindly of her brother, and had nothing but compliments for Lady Grant. "How fine a lady ye never did see in these here parts, always with a coin for the wee 'uns and a moment for a word wi' their mums and da's, leavin' smiles in her wake." His inn was as clean and well-maintained on the inside as on the out, and Lizzy was happy to know she would return in a few hours to take tea and taste some of the delicious looking cakes set out on a shelf for display.

The shops in the village proved most amenable for a day's distraction. As well as the expected array of baker, apothecary, milliner, and general goods store, Lizzy was delighted to see one shop dedicated to selling chocolates, another specialising in finely crafted woodwork and toys, a well-furnished bookseller, and a tailor's shop with some beautiful and fashionable clothing on display in the window. She hardly knew where to begin, resolving to visit each in turn in hopes of finding some perfect present for each of her sisters and parents. The bookseller, she knew, she would leave till the very last, there to best enjoy her time until she had to leave to meet Lady Grant at the inn.

Mrs. Gardiner kept Lizzy company through much of her exploration, exchanging news with those shopkeepers who remembered her from her youth and asking after children and grandchildren. As they entered the book shop, however, Mrs. Gardiner exclaimed, "I do declare! That is Old Mrs. Broadhead across the street! She was my nursemaid... will you excuse me, Lizzy, if I go to greet an old and dear acquaintance?" Lizzy happily approved of this plan, declaring that she should be more than content to wait in the book shop for Mrs. Gardiner's return.

She had turned to browse some of the newly arrived novels the bookseller had on display when a fellow browser, a respectable-looking woman of middle years, greeted her in most polite terms, and upon hearing Lizzy's friendly response, asked, "Are you an avid reader, Miss?" Lizzy nodded, and the lady added, "I must beg your forgiveness at my forwardness, but I am rather in need of assistance."

"I am your servant," Lizzy smiled warmly at the woman and executed a genteel curtsey.

"I am looking for something diverting for a young woman—only sixteen years old—who is a bit of a shut-in, rather lonely, and in dear need of diversion. My tastes must be far from hers, but you are much closer to her age. Have you read anything you see here that might be suitable?"

While far from an expert in speech and pronunciation, Lizzy had spent enough time working on and discussing such subjects with Professor Darcy that she could recognise in the lady's words the foundation of a good Derbyshire accent, overlaid with a carefully applied veneer of the speech of the elite. The lady made no efforts to hide her origins, but clearly had spent much time in the company of the upper classes, enough to modulate her tones to suit their ears. Was she a local schoolmistress? A spinster aunt or cousin, now companion to the young girl being asked for? Or perhaps an abigail to a fine lady in the vicinity?

When Lizzy paused over the selection of books and considered these questions, the lady spoke further, explaining herself. "My charge is the young miss of the estate where I am housekeeper, a very well-learned young woman, but very shy and in need of something to broaden her interests. If not a respectable novel, is there, perhaps, a travelogue you have read that the proprietor here might have? Or perhaps something of natural history? I have not had the minding of such a young girl since my own lass was that age, and now I am a grandmother, so that was many years gone."

The woman's tone was friendly and her concern for the young woman palpable, and Lizzy was most happy to assist her in finding some appropriate book. She asked more questions about the girl's interests and commented freely and candidly on what of the bookseller's collection she herself had read and would suggest, and the two fell into easy conversation.

As Lizzy saw Mrs. Gardiner emerge from the building across the street, the woman, whose name was Mrs. Reynolds, asked most cautiously, "I may seem most presumptuous, Miss, but I do believe my young charge would very much benefit from your conversation, and might appreciate a visitor. As much as she has closed herself off from the world, she cannot remain without the companionship of those closer to her own age forever. She has only me and her... well, the rest of the staff to amuse her, and it will not do! Might I impose upon you to pay her a visit? If you tell me of your direction, I can have a carriage sent to fetch you and then return you in the evening."

This was hardly what Lizzy had been expecting when she had entered the shop a half hour previous. Uncertain how to respond to such a surprising request, she looked with grateful relief at her aunt, who had just walked in through the shop's door. Seeing Mrs. Reynolds, Aunt Gardiner hurried over with a large smile on her face and greeted the lady warmly. At once, Lizzy felt easier, for if her aunt were friendly with the lady, her request could not be construed as something alarming.

The usual exclamations of surprise and inquiry as to the other's' health were eventually concluded, and Mrs. Reynolds then exclaimed, "My dear Mrs. Gardiner, I had no notion this delightful young lady was your niece. What a treasure, having so sweet a girl amongst your relatives. You must be surely proud of her. I was just asking Miss Bennet if she would do Miss Georgie the honour of visiting with her. The girl is quite withdrawn from society, and I believe she would do well with a friend, even for a short visit or two. Miss Bennet has recommended some books for me to bring home today, and perhaps they might discuss them. You and Lady Grant are most welcome as well."

So Mrs. Reynolds knew Lady Grant, and knew that Mrs. Gardiner was connected with the Grant family! The familiarity and friendliness between the households further eased Lizzy's disquiet, and she now felt rather curious about this young lady who never left her house. She had never heard mention of the Georgie family and wondered if there were some mystery to be solved therein! "Ah, this comes of reading too many novels!" she laughed in her head.

"Is the young lady ill, Mrs. Reynolds?" she asked aloud at a suitable lull in the conversation.

"Nay, not ill in body, but most troubled in spirit. My sweet Miss Georgie has a melancholia that renders her quite unwilling—unable, even—to venture from her rooms. If you can raise her spirits, you will be a miracle worker, a true gift from the heavens."

Mrs. Gardiner left Lizzy with little choice when she nodded furiously, "Then of course, we must attend! I shall inform my sister of our intentions. When would be convenient?"

The following day was settled upon, and the offer of the carriage repeated and then refused, for the Grant carriage would do quite well. Warm greetings of farewell were offered with the knowledge that everyone would meet again the following day.

"How exciting this is, Lizzy!" Mrs. Gardiner gushed as they walked back down the high street towards the inn for tea. "You shall be doing a good turn to a sweet but troubled young girl, and you have just procured an invitation to Pemberley!"

Pemberley? Once again, Lizzy felt herself grow faint. At no point had Mrs. Reynolds mentioned that she was the housekeeper at Pemberley—for Professor Darcy, no less! And who, then, was Miss Georgie? The girl was sixteen, and Darcy only eight and twenty, so certainly not a natural child, but then who? A cousin? A niece? A ward, perhaps? Was that why there had been no mention of the Georgie family. Unless... Could 'Georgie' be the girl's Christian name instead? Georgina or something of the sort? With a sense of horror, she recalled rare and cryptic mentions of a sister, always with the suggestion that the girl was not to be discussed for some reason or another.

Darcy himself had breathed scarcely a word of her. Neither, Lizzy now realised, had he mentioned parents, grandparents, childhood friends, or any other family members with whom she was not herself acquainted. Professor Darcy was a particularly private man, she was coming to understand. What other secrets did he hold so close?

More to the point, how could she possibly visit his estate, walk through his home, partake of his hospitality? Even were he not there, as it seemed he was not, being in his home seemed too intimate an act for one who had abused him and then run off from him so recently. But... Mrs. Reynolds had betrayed no recognition of her name, had not made any little noises of awareness, had raised no eyebrow, nor nodded in cognizance of some familial intimacies. The housekeeper must be as ignorant as to Darcy's goings-on in Town as his Town friends were aware of his affairs in the country. And Miss Georgie, whoever she may be, would also be quite unaware of any previous relationship between the master of the estate and the young woman come to visit with her. She need never know of the alarming sensations borne of hand upon hand, of the heightened awareness of his presence while waltzing, or of those kisses that still fueled her dreams despite her commands that they stop. Shuddering, Lizzy forced those memories away and steeled herself. No, as long as Darcy remained firmly elsewhere, wherever that may be, she could visit with Miss Georgie with complete calmness and equanimity.

Mrs. Gardiner chatted happily about the beauties of Pemberley as they walked back to the inn for their tea, and upon reuniting with Lady Grant, the conversation naturally turned to the estate and the family. "Darcy is an aloof sort, but never unpleasant and always fair in his dealings with tenants and townsfolk alike. Miss Georgie is a very different sort of girl, but she, too, has never occasioned a bad word from anyone," Lady Grant said. Mrs. Gardiner, who knew the family from her childhood, agreed.

"Miss Georgie was only a babe when I left these parts, but her brother was well regarded, though he was but a youth." Ah, so Miss Georgie *was*

Darcy's younger sister, then. "Even then, he had the makings of a good man, no matter what face he showed to the world," she counselled her niece. Despite the wrong he had done Lizzy, Aunt Gardiner had always expressed her thoughts that he was hampered as much by his own insecurities as by his incivility, which he used—so she presumed—to mask a discomfort in society. "Examine the man by his actions as well as by his words, Lizzy. Perhaps when you understand him better, you will see him in a different light."

Lizzy now turned to Lady Grant. "I'm afraid I am at a disadvantage, for I know nothing of this Miss Georgie, whom I am to visit and hopefully help cheer tomorrow. Who is she? What ought I to know?" She turned concerned eyes from her friend to her aunt, and back again, imploring them to divulge their information.

The two ladies looked at each other over the prettily set table in the tea shop with grim faces. Lady Grant took a sip from her delicate china cup and explained, "There is much gossip, most of which we shall ignore. Miss Georgiana Darcy is the professor's sister, some ten years and more his junior. She was always a shy and reserved child, but last year she suffered some great misfortune at the hands of a man. Of course, no one has ever said anything about the affair, but this much seems clear. The nature of her disappointment, I cannot tell you, nor whether it is because of this that she suffers from melancholia. Her brother thought she might do well at school or in London, and it is in London where we all believed her to be. However, if she is home now, those avenues seem not to have been of any help to the girl." She sighed and lowered her eyes to her teacup.

"Poor Georgie," Mrs. Gardiner echoed. "You have also been put upon by a gentleman who ought to have behaved better." She raised her eyebrows at Lizzy and pointedly ignored her sister's inquisitive expression. "You cannot, of course, relate the specifics of your own experience, but she might recognise some common threads and feel comfortable in your presence."

"Now," Lady Grant said with a smile as she finished her final piece of tea cake, "if you are to visit Miss Darcy, you certainly need new gloves! And the haberdasher around the corner has just the thing for you. I saw a pair in his window as I returned from the chandler. Come, Lizzy, I must be allowed to buy some for you."

# Sixteen
## Visiting Pemberley

The following morning dawned cool and misty, but by the time breakfast had been completed and the carriage was prepared, the sky was clearing and the roads were more than fine for the eight-mile journey to Pemberley. With her pale yellow dress, golden spencer with its military-style braiding, and the new bonnet and gloves that Lady Grant has insisted upon purchasing, Lizzy felt her appearance, if not her composure, was suitable for the visit. She had confirmed once more with the housekeeper at Arlenby, who knew and extolled Mrs. Reynolds, that no one had seen or heard from the master in months, and that he most surely was not in residence at his manor house. At this news, despite her unease and concern as to his whereabouts, she felt more confident in her plans.

The journey was pleasant and without incident, and presently they arrived at Pemberley. Lizzy was the only member of the party who had not visited before, and she was amazed at the beauty of the grounds. Where Arlenby was well-kept but compact, the grounds of Pemberley were expansive and spectacular. The road wound through heavy woods, until it broke into a clearing above a valley, on the opposite side of which the magnificent house stood. Behind the house, the hillside rose protectively, further guarded by wooded peaks in the near distance; before the house a lovely stream swelled into a picturesque pond, giving the impression of nature at its finest, displaying the artistry of The Creator. It was a beautiful prospect, and upon seeing it, Lizzy wondered once more about its master. To be proud of such a home was well comprehensible; perhaps, for one raised amidst such natural splendour, the artifice of Town and its glittering denizens was sufficiently distasteful to encourage his disdain and rudeness. She was certain she would never see him again, but perhaps, were she to meet him once more, she might seek to understand the man better.

The carriage drew up before the front entrance to the house, and Mrs. Reynolds rushed from between the great doors to greet the guests. "Lady Grant, we are honoured that you have joined us today. Mrs. Gardiner, a pleasure, as always, and Miss Bennet, I am truly delighted that you have come. Miss Georgie expressed some interest in dressing today, after I described our conversation yesterday; I do hope this bodes well. Come in, come in. I shall conduct you to Miss Georgie's sitting room."

Lizzy hardly knew what to make of this. Miss Georgie had expressed interest in dressing? Was she so ill as to spend most of her days abed? She knew of people with physical ailments who kept to their night clothing and robes, for when one is too weak to rise from bed, one is not expected to dress. But an ailment of the spirits? How dire must it be for a willingness to dress to be such a cause for optimism? Once, Lizzy recalled, she had heard of a young farm girl with a similar affliction, but every attempt to ask after the girl had been met with severe frowns and whispered refusals. That unwelcome frisson of inadequacy that had first assailed her in front of the Malton house in Town now afflicted her once more, and she had to hold herself steady so as not to shake. How could her poor presence possibly help this young lady?

Mrs. Reynolds offered the matrons tea and, in veiled tones, suggested that they not overburden Miss Georgie with too many visitors at once; consequently Lady Grant and Mrs. Gardiner opted to walk the grounds and enjoy the rose garden, after which they would find tea waiting for them in one of the parlours.

"A single guest will be enough for the girl," Mrs. Reynolds nodded, then shook her head sadly. "Come, Miss Bennet, let me show you the way."

"Are you certain this will not do her further harm?" Lizzy's concern was palpable and she wondered if she ought to demur as Mrs. Reynolds led her from the room. "I have no knowledge of what to do or say."

Mrs. Reynolds patted her hand. "You are a sweet and thoughtful young woman; you will know what to say to a young girl who rather desperately needs a friend. Miss Georgie is pleased to see you. You need feel no trepidation at all; only be who you were when we met yesterday." Lizzy blinked back her worries and found a smile for her face.

The housekeeper led her up the grand staircase to the first storey, and then down a hallway, all the while describing Miss Georgie's affliction. "I must prepare you, Miss Bennet," the housekeeper whispered, "so you be not too alarmed at Miss Georgie's state." Before long they entered a suite of rooms that faced the back of the house, overlooking the rose gardens and the hillsides beyond. Despite the bright sunlight, the room was strangely dark, for all but one window remained curtained in heavy swaths of drapery. The walls were light in colour, their exact hue indeterminate in the uneven illumination, and the furnishings modern and elegant. Reclined on a sofa off to one side of the uncurtained window, Lizzy saw a young woman, lit dramatically from the single source of light, an exercise in *chiaroscuro*, like an impression by Caravaggio.

The girl did not rise when Lizzy was ushered inside, nor did she smile, but she raised her head infinitesimally as Mrs. Reynolds made the introductions. "Miss Darcy, allow me to introduce Miss Elizabeth Bennet. Miss Bennet, Miss Georgiana Darcy." Lizzy curtseyed with all the grace she had learned in London. Mrs. Reynolds caught Lizzy's eye and receiving a small nod in response, backed out of the room, closing the door behind her.

"Miss Darcy, it is a great pleasure to make your acquaintance." Lizzy knew from Mrs. Reynolds' information that she would have to take the lead in conversation, regardless of what social conventions might dictate. Not expecting much of a reply, if any, she continued, "I was most pleased to meet with Mrs. Reynolds yesterday at the bookseller, and I hope she conveyed some of our conversation to you. I have a delight in reading novels, and I hoped you might share my interests."

The young girl raised her head a small degree more, and Lizzy took that as encouragement. She chattered about the books she had selected and what had appealed to her about them. As she talked, Miss Darcy seemed to grow somewhat brighter, and her eyes met and held Lizzy's for slightly longer periods over the course of the monologue. At length, Lizzy dared to ask a question, hoping to get the girl to speak. "Do you read much, Miss Darcy? Tell me, what are your favourites?"

Her hopes were borne out as a very quiet voice replied, "I used to read, but have not in some time."

"Pray tell, what was it that entertained you when you did enjoy a book? I am always curious to find new books for my younger sisters."

Slowly, as if the words were being pulled from her with great difficulty, Miss Darcy began to speak of stories she had read and liked. She had been particular to the writings of Mrs. Radcliffe, but now found the horrors the heroines suffered too much to bear. The words came one at a time at first, but after a while, during which time Mrs. Reynolds brought in refreshments, she spoke more easily, although her tone remained colourless and flat.

Looking at the tray of lemonade and cakes, Lizzy dared to ask, "Miss Darcy, would it importune you excessively if I opened another curtain? Such a delightful tray of sweets as this deserves the honour of excellent illumination." She turned wide, hopeful eyes to the girl.

"Yes, that would be fine, Miss Bennet," came the flat reply. Lizzy walked to draw open the heavy drapery, and more sunlight washed its way through the room. The walls could now be seen to be a soft robins-egg blue, with pale yellow foliage printed on the wallpaper. The upholstery matched the yellow, with accents in gold and ivory, lending a classical cast to the decor.

The girl on the sofa, too, was now more fully lit, and Lizzy could see her features with greater clarity. Her hair, which had seemed simply fair before, could be reckoned a light golden brown, which must glow almost blonde in full sunshine. Her skin was very pale, as might be expected from someone who almost never left her rooms, and her eyes were deep brown, like her brother's. Her face was pleasant and sensible, and her features similar to Darcy's, but put together in such a way as to seem feminine and not quite so handsome.

As well as her features, Lizzy could now see the girl's expression. She had expected, perhaps, deep sadness or possibly pain to be written across the young face, but these would have been welcome compared to the completely blank look that was present. Lizzy was reminded of a painting, which once might have been beautiful, but which now had all the colour somehow drained from it. She longed to find a way to return the hues and shades to the work before her, but knew not how. She could only do one thing, which was to keep talking about matters which might interest the girl, to try to draw her back to life.

And so she did. She talked at length about her childhood and her sisters, describing each in the most humorous terms she could, watching Miss Darcy's face for any sign of interest of animation. She described Jane's frustrating pleasantness, Mary's pedantic tendencies and Mr. Collins' worse ones, Kitty's need for attention, and Lydia's silliness and wild spirit. During the latter recital, Miss Darcy cocked her head and widened her eyes, which Lizzy took as a sign to talk further of her youngest sister. This she did, relating in detail some of Lydia's more outrageous adventures with her mother's favourite bonnets, or with the poor cook's supplies of sugar and jam.

At last, as Lizzy was wiping tears of laughter from her own eyes at some of the recollections, Lizzy was rewarded by a twitch of her companion's mouth. It was not a smile, but it was the first sign of emotion she had observed, and it heartened her.

"Come, Miss Darcy, let us take some of these lovely cakes Mrs. Reynold's has brought for us." She walked to the table upon which sat the tray and pondered the selection. "Which should you prefer? This looks to be a fruit cake with currants and," she sniffed, "lavender, and this tart seems to be filled with raspberries and orange. Do you have a preference, or would you like both?" The girl initially declined all offers, but eventually agreed to take a tart and a glass of lemonade.

They sat in silence whilst they enjoyed the food, and Lizzy hoped she had done no wrong by so engaging the girl. But her stories seemed to have lifted Miss Darcy's spirits ever so slightly, and the suggestion of a smile she had seen encouraged her to continue her efforts.

She rose from her seat and walked over to the window once more, now to look out upon the vista. "It is a most pleasant prospect," she said warmly. "I cannot imagine ever tiring of such a view. Will you not come and join me by the window, Miss Darcy, so we may better see these delights? I should enjoy your company."

To her surprise, the young girl rose from her seat and walked, somewhat unsteadily, towards her. It was the first time Miss Darcy had risen from her seat, and at last Lizzy was able to take a better account of the girl. She was tall, like her brother, and though only sixteen, was endowed with a woman's figure. But she did not hold herself straight and proud, and instead rounded her shoulders forward to conceal her bosom and allowed her head to droop on her neck.

Lizzy recalled the countless hours she had spent in London perfecting her posture and deportment, walking around the house with books upon her head as Darcy shouted at her, and knew with a certainty that Miss Darcy had suffered equally, if not more so, in similar exercises. Her natural posture must surely be excellent; this attempt to hide herself away must be another manifestation of whatever had occasioned this lapse into melancholy. She resolved to ask Mrs. Reynolds for whatever information she could; perhaps therein she might find some clue to further help the girl.

Miss Darcy was now standing beside her at the window, shivering despite the pleasant temperature. Spying a wrap that lay across the back of a chair, Lizzy retrieved it and draped it loosely across the girl's back and shoulders, evincing another twitch to the lips and a whispered, "Thank you." For a while they stood, side by side, admiring the view.

Suddenly Miss Darcy spoke, "There is a stream beyond the furthest wing." Lizzy blinked in surprise and stifled a gasp, for it was the first comment the girl had made on her own initiative. "You can see it if you stand on the balcony, and look yonder." Pulling the wrap more securely around her pale and thin shoulders, she opened the French doors and stepped outside, beckoning her guest to join her. She was silent for a very long time, and Lizzy hoped she had not fallen back into her former deep gloom. At last, however, she breathed deeply of the warm summer air, redolent with the scent of the flowers in the garden below. "I have not been here for some time," she said in her flat voice. "The sun warms me."

Lizzy stood next to her new friend and admired the view. The rose gardens were in full display below, and if one stood at the edge of the balcony and looked down, she might see the stone terrace that led from the rooms beneath them—morning rooms? drawing rooms? library, perhaps?—and the wrought iron tables and chairs set out there, on which one might enjoy a lovely vista whilst taking tea or engaging in conversation. The terrace was rimmed with a stone balustrade, and a few short stairs led down to the gardens just at their foot. Past the gardens, which were expansive, a wide swath of green lawn lay like a moat, beyond which the dense woods of the surrounding forests sprang up to climb the protective hillsides.

Following the grassy area towards the direction Miss Darcy had indicated, Lizzy could see where the stream flowed down from the hills, and imagining the path the rivulet must take through the obscuring trees, she let her eyes wander over the wood.

"Is that a building I see there, about half-way up that hill?" she asked, peering at what seemed to be part of a stone cottage, nestled in the trees. Something made her turn her focus to Miss Darcy, and she was surprised to see the faintest glimmer of a smile on the girl's face, the slightest gleam in her otherwise-expressionless eyes.

"Yes. It is a small cottage. It was a favourite of my mother, before she passed, and I spent many happy hours there as a young child. It is close enough to the house that we might come and go as we wished, but once there, we felt as if we were many miles from any other person, in a land of our very own." She paused, lost in memory. "Even after Mama died, my brother would take me there, and we would imagine ourselves to be having adventures." She paused again and stared for some time into the woods.

Her brother. There was no avoiding it, but the mention of her brother disarranged Lizzy's thoughts. Did she wish to learn more about Darcy as a youth and young man, or would it be preferable to forgo all mention and thought of him? This was not a decision for her to make, however, for her primary concern at this moment was the young lady beside her. "Do tell me more, please," Lizzy encouraged, fearing that the girl would drift off into her own thoughts, not to emerge again.

Miss Darcy closed her brown eyes for a moment, then recalled her companion, and resumed her tale in her flat voice. "Sometimes we would pretend to be exploring the wilds of Canada, or the jungles of India. Other times, we would pretend to be lost in the faerie realm, where gnomes and brownies hid beneath every leaf. My brother would call out for Titania and Oberon, and it was there he taught me to speak the language of the pixies."

Lizzy could not stop the short chortle that escaped her in her surprise, and Miss Darcy laughed briefly, a most unexpected sound. "Oh yes, Fitz was a lover of language even then, and he invented some words that were, he told me, how the pixies spoke when alone. Recalling them, they were more akin to the words of our Welsh-born head gardener, but I believed him and thought him the best and cleverest brother in the world." Now she had truly stopped speaking, and she seemed content to remain in companionable silence with her new acquaintance.

They were still there some minutes later when Mrs. Reynolds reappeared to inquire whether the ladies desired more drink or cakes. The housekeeper seemed quite taken aback to see Miss Darcy standing on her balcony and she cast a warm smile at Lizzy. "Thank you," she mouthed, leaving the two to enjoy the lovely day.

Lizzy stayed a short while longer with Miss Darcy, before the girl stifled a yawn and begged Miss Bennet's forgiveness, but she wished to sleep now.

"Thank you for spending the morning with me, Miss Darcy. I enjoyed making your acquaintance." Lizzy spoke with sincerity and was rewarded, once more, by the girl's response.

"I would be pleased were you to come again." Miss Darcy curtseyed and returned to her sofa, whereupon she closed her eyes and seemed to fall into an immediate sleep.

Mrs. Reynolds was waiting as Lizzy departed and closed the door to the sitting room. She took Lizzy by the elbow and guided her back down the corridor to where she might find the other ladies at their tea. "You have worked wonders, Miss Bennet. Miss Georgie has not been outside, even on her balcony, for many a month, long before our departure for Town. We hoped that London might help her regain her spirits, but she grew worse there than she had been here, and consequently we brought her home. But until today, all she has done has been to lie on her bed and sleep, unless forced otherwise. Did she speak to you?"

"Yes, though little. She expressed some interest in the books I suggested, and hoped that I might return to read to her, and I was able to have her speak to me about the cottage in the wood. She also expressed a wish for me to visit again."

"Well, well! That is a turn for the better! To express a desire for anything or an interest in anything—'tis more than we had hoped for, after these long months! Will you return? May I steal you from your family? It would mean so much to all of us!"

In the end, it was agreed upon by Mrs. Gardiner and Lady Grant that Lizzy might come back the following day, and perhaps two days afterwards as well, to visit with the young miss. "'Tis a great thing you do, bringing light back to her eyes. I had hoped only to give her some new companionship, but to see her standing, looking around her with interest, aye, that is a marvelous thing indeed!"

As they waited for the carriage to arrive to drive them home, Mrs. Reynolds offered to conduct the ladies of a short tour of the formal French gardens to the south of the house, out of view of the rose garden. Lady Grant and Mrs. Gardiner were taken by some interesting statuary and they paused to examine it, leaving Lizzy to walk with the housekeeper. "Dare I ask," Lizzy ventured when they were out of hearing of the other ladies, "what happened to poor Miss Darcy to leave her so? Is it a melancholia that emanated from her spirit, or was there some incident that caused this?"

Mrs. Reynold frowned, indecision etched upon her pleasant countenance. At last she let out a breath, saying, "I do not know exactly what transpired, for Miss Georgie will not speak of it to anyone. We fear the worst, but cannot know anything for certain. She was always a shy and retiring child, but last year, she was wooed—against our knowledge and against her brother's wishes—by a young man she knew from childhood. When it was discovered that the man desired only her fortune and not her love, it broke her heart. They were away at a seaside resort, and no one knows if he... importuned her at all, or merely wounded her spirits. Although," she added with a frown, "that is bad enough, to see the girl." At Lizzy's questioning expression, the housekeeper continued, "She will not allow a doctor to see her, and refuses all of the medicines and tonics the apothecary sends up for her. We had tried to hide them in her food, but she can taste them, and will not eat until they are removed. It is a sorely horrid thing to see such a bright child reduced in this way." They continued their walk in silence until the footman arrived to inform them that the carriage was waiting.

The following morning, as arranged, Lizzy travelled back to Pemberley in the Grant's chaise, with only the driver and a maid for company, the lighter vehicle serving to significantly shorten the duration of the trip. Lady Grant had obligations on her own estate, and Mrs. Gardiner wished to visit some of the tenants she had known as a girl. Lizzy was happy for the solitude, for she had much to think on regarding poor Miss Darcy. Without the animated chatter of her aunt and friend, Lizzy was also better able to appreciate the countryside, and she found that repeated exposure only brought more of the beauty of the area to light.

Once again, Mrs. Reynolds stood waiting to greet Miss Darcy's guest, and she conducted her up the stairs to the sitting room, where Miss Darcy was ready for her. To Lizzy's surprise and great pleasure, the drapery had all been pulled open, and the room was awash in sunlight. The soft blues and yellows glowed with iridescent warmth, and the tasteful golden accents caught enough of the sunshine to illuminate the space, as the ornate capitals in a medieval manuscript. Glancing around, Lizzy could see more of the room as well, including, in one far corner, almost hidden behind a Japanese screen, a spinet. Surely Miss Darcy must play! Perhaps she could be coaxed into turning to her music to brighten her spirits!

As well as the room, Miss Darcy, too, was somewhat brighter, and was waiting for her on a chair, rather than half-reclined on the sofa. She rose from her seat when Lizzy entered and greeted her properly, before reclaiming her chair. This was already a marked improvement from the previous day, and Lizzy could feel Mrs. Reynold's approval in every word and gesture. "Ring when you need me. I shall send up some tea and cakes shortly." She patted Lizzy's shoulder and gave her an encouraging smile. Lizzy could not help but smile back. While hardly the actions of a servant—no matter how highly placed—to a guest, the maternal affection she felt from the housekeeper more than atoned for any irregularity in distinction of place.

Again, the professor strode unbidden into her thoughts. In London, too, his household staff had been somewhat unconventional in their behaviour. He was not an ordinary man, to be sure; as demanding as he was, he clearly expected more than the norm in his staff, and he seemed pleased to allow them a fair degree of liberality and freedom in exchange. She found herself considering once more those perplexing facets to the personality she was not quite certain she knew.

But this was not the time to think about the professor. Miss Darcy was here and needed a friend, and Lizzy was determined to offer the girl her full attention.

The morning was quiet but pleasant. Lizzy read from one of the newly purchased novels for a time, and encouraged Miss Darcy to discuss a passage here or a character there, and when it so happened naturally, she allowed the conversation to veer from the text. As the conversation tended in that direction, she told further stories of her childhood in Hertfordshire, and swore Miss Darcy to secrecy at some of the tales that involved running through the fields at midnight in her friend's brother's pilfered breeches. "Mama never did learn why there were mud stains on the ceiling of the front parlour, as much as she swore we were haunted by goblins!" Lizzy laughed in recollection and was gratified to observe her new friend attempt another brief smile.

When Mrs. Reynolds brought the tray of lemonade and cakes, the two young ladies were sitting on opposite sides of the low table, each with a pad of paper and a pencil in hand, attempting to sketch the other. "Oh, Mrs. Reynolds," Lizzy laughed, "you must not look at my sorry efforts, but I have seen some of Miss Darcy's drawings, and I am astounded at her talent. I am certain she is taking a veritable likeness of me!"

"Miss Georgie, back at her drawing! How lovely." The housekeeper beamed. "May I see, my dear? Oh, indeed, it is exactly Miss Bennet's likeness. You must allow her to keep it when it is complete."

"Of course, but perhaps Miss Bennet will allow me to take another drawing, so I may fully remember her kindness when she has returned to her own family. I shall send it to be framed, to hang in the family's sitting room with the paintings of Fitz and..."

She stopped speaking all of a sudden and the liveliness drained from her face.

"What did I do wrong?" Lizzy's eyes begged of Mrs. Reynolds, but the lady closed her eyes and shook her head in warning.

"Later," she mouthed, and Lizzy had no choice but to agree.

The visit ended shortly thereafter, Miss Darcy feeling no longer up to company, but did sincerely express her wish for Lizzy to forgive her and to return soon. And as before, she executed a graceful curtsey and set herself down upon the sofa and closed her eyes to the world.

"Please, forgive me, Mrs. Reynolds! I have no notion of what I did to cause her such pain. What did I do?" Lizzy chewed her lips as the housekeeper sat her down in a small and comfortable room at the back of the house and poured some tea.

"'Twas not you, my dear. 'Twas a memory that neither of us might have stopped. That man, that awful man..."

"The one who is the cause of her current sorrows?"

"Aye, he. Miss Georgie painted his likeness before the trouble, and it hangs beside her brother's portrait in the family's private sitting room. I will have it removed before the lass comes down and sees it. Never fear, it was not your doing. But perhaps it is good that you know more of what bothers her, for you do have a gift of drawing her out. You will forgive her lapse today and return?" The older woman's eyes begged Lizzy's acquiescence, and Lizzy was only too pleased to agree. For all that Miss Darcy was less than cheerful company, Lizzy had taken a definite liking to the girl and wished to be of help.

Over the next two weeks, this ritual was repeated once and again, and Miss Darcy seemed to be brightening ever so gradually, if inconsistently. By the end of the third visit, the two had agreed to be friends and had become Lizzy and Georgie to each other. "I have so longed for a friend," Georgie confessed as they stood outside on the balcony that day. "Fitz hoped to find me companionship in London, but all I saw there was frivolity and artifice, and here, where I am comfortable, I am lonely. How your visits have been a balm for me, dear Lizzy."

Consequently, each day when Lizzy arrived, Georgie smiled in her flat manner and was willing to engage in conversation. Some days were better than others, to be certain, but Mrs. Reynolds never failed to mention after the visit was over how delighted she was with her charge's progress, no matter how subtle.

The mornings would pass in a similar manner. Lizzy would read for a while and the two would discuss the story. Then, whenever the weather was agreeable, she would convince Georgie to join her on the balcony to take in the sunshine and fresh air and observe the roses and the forest from their lofty position. In an attempt to draw the girl's thoughts from her own sorrows, Lizzy suggested a project of knitting items for the tenants' Christmas boxes and she encouraged Georgie to talk about those tenants she knew. Georgie, it transpired, did not know how to knit, but she proved rather skilled at a yarn craft she called *shepherd's knitting*, which used a single needle with a crook at the end to produce the stitches. Despite its rather crude and rustic name, the result was beautiful and delicate, and Georgie showed Lizzy how to make intricate flowers and lovely lace. The project then turned into one in which each taught each other her craft, with the goal of providing even more delightful treats to Pemberley's staff and tenants.

This project was sufficiently useful in raising Georgie from her gloom that, eventually, Lizzy was able to coax her to the spinet in the corner of the room. After many protests, the girl sat herself upon the seat and stretched her long fingers over the keys. She played a note, then a scale, and then tentatively began a simple Clementi sonatina. Lizzy listened with amazement as Georgie's unpracticed fingers milked beautiful music from the ivory keys.

"Your talents are not limited to paper, Georgie! You play most beautifully! I can hear that you have not played for a long time, but you possess a technical mastery I can only dream of acquiring, whilst playing with sensitivity and passion. I am honoured to have heard you. I do hope you will play for me more often!"

The girl blushed a deep red. "I have never played for anybody before, other than my brother and the music master. I am pleased you enjoyed it. Perhaps I shall endeavour to return to my studies so I might one day be brave enough to play at some small event."

This delighted Lizzy, for she heard in the girl's words not the sad reality of the present, but her first burgeoning hopes for the future and an insistence on reaching past her fears. "Then I can only hope to be fortunate enough to be present at your debut!" She beamed and grasped Georgie's hands in her own, giving them a squeeze before allowing the girl to return to her instrument.

*Can it be*, she wondered as she sat in the chaise on her return to Arlenby that afternoon, *that I have actually been of use?* Perhaps, rather than repaying Professor Darcy for his lessons with her supposed betrothal to him, she was instead able to discharge her obligation by helping his sister through the worst of her troubles. That would suit her most well, for no matter how hurt she had been by the professor's betrayal, he had completed his end of the deal.

She thought about him as the vehicle rumbled across the well-tended roads, past streams and hillsides and small hamlets and green fields dotted with flocks of fat and healthy sheep. She had tried once and again to keep him from her thoughts, but it was an impossibility even to attempt such, for all that she spent many hours each day in his house, eating his food, admiring his lands, and befriending his sister.

As much as the professor had scarcely mentioned a word of his sister, she spoke dotingly about him. In all of her reports, he was the best of brothers, for she used words of the utmost affection in describing his beneficence and attributes to her new friend.

The professor, Lizzy reckoned, must be concerned for Georgie, despite so seldom speaking of her; as curmudgeonly and unconventional as he might be, he could be a passionate man, and surely his emotions, whatever they might be, extended to the sister who loved him so dearly. Lizzy could not imagine that her new friend would express such devotion to her brother were he not to return the sentiments in some way! And as the caring brother both Georgie and Mrs. Reynolds portrayed him to be, Georgie's troubles must, in turn, weigh upon him most heavily. Then why, Lizzy wondered, had he not uttered a word of the girl's troubles?

She reflected on what she knew of his character—or rather, what she thought she knew, for it was so changeable. It was almost impossible to know which aspect to the man reflected his essence; he was most difficult to understand! If only she could sketch his nature as easily as Georgie sketched her features, she might have a better knowledge of the real Fitz Darcy.

He could be, in turn, arrogant, careless, condescending, rude, funny, sensitive, gentle and passionate, but underlying it all was a fierce commitment to the people and circumstances around him. To his staff, he showed himself a demanding master, but one who was also kind and generous, allowing them to be individuals and not nameless and faceless servants. To his students, he gave his entire focus and effort, and in turn, he was not satisfied with middling results. As she had seen with Charles Bingley, the professor would not rest until the student had risen to the highest level he could achieve.

Even when it came to his friends, he did everything in his power to see them well-done-by. The consequences were not always positive—she grimaced at the suffering poor Charlotte and Richard had undergone because of Darcy's interference—but she recognised that it was his concern for his cousin's wellbeing that lay behind the debacle. He was totally committed to Richard's best interests, or, at the least, what he believed them to be. Yes, there was a callous arrogance to the whole affair, but it was well-motivated if ill-conceived.

Then a sudden thought came to her, so striking that she gasped aloud, causing her attending maid to ask if she was well. He was equally committed to his sister. He had never mentioned her, but he must feel her pain with every breath. He had done everything in his power for her, and he had failed her.

And then he had met Lizzy. She was his attempt at salvation. Was his complete devotion to his project to create a duchess from a country miss his attempt to atone for his perceived failure of his sister?

And if it were, did the thought please or further distress her?

# Seventeen
# Renewed Acquaintances

Some days later, after their accustomed morning rituals, the two young women were examining Miss Darcy's rather excellent portfolio of drawings when Mrs. Reynolds herself arrived with the tea—it might have been a task for a maid, but the housekeeper was clearly personally concerned about her charge—and Lizzy was praising the artist quite volubly. There was much to praise as well. As Lizzy had already seen, Miss Darcy had a good and natural eye, and her drawings were composed in such a way as to please the viewer and focus the observer's attention on the areas of most interest. She had a gifted hand; her drawings of animals, insects, and flora would have been at home in a naturalist's handbook, so precise were they, and her sketches and portraits of people captured both their outer appearance and their essence perfectly.

Lizzy was, at first, drawn to the portraits of Richard and Freddy. She knew both men well, and it was clear to her eyes how well Georgie had drawn them. There were Freddy's cheerful, slightly mocking eyes, always ready for a laugh, refusing to become serious about any matter. And there was Richard, his face formed for good humour, but with that vein of sober responsibility beneath the amiable exterior. Lizzy complemented Georgie on her work, saying that she could not have imagined better likenesses of the girl's cousins.

"Oh, you know them?" Georgie's eyebrows lifted in amazement, for Lizzy had not before mentioned her time in London and her association with the family. She had no wish to recount her history with Georgie's brother, and less still to explain her own uncertain feelings about him.

"I made their acquaintance in the winter," she dissembled, "and your cousin Richard Fitzwilliam is recently wed to my good friend."

"You are friendly with Charlotte? Richard writes so well of her; Mrs. Reynolds insists on reading his letters to me. I have difficulty finding interest in much of what he says, but he talks so happily of Charlotte that his joy brings some meaning to my own life. Pray, Lizzy, tell me about her!"

This was the curiosity and interest that Lizzy had been hoping for; at that moment, Georgie could be any young woman, poised on the verge of adulthood, eager to meet the world. The girl's eyes were wide with anticipation and she grinned with the notion of particular information. In response, Lizzy felt her own face break into a smile, allowing her brows to rise briefly as she prepared to dispense her secrets.

As she talked, she tried to describe Charlotte to Georgie and the girl sketched at her paper, eventually presenting Lizzy with the result. It was not Charlotte, but the face certainly bore a respectable resemblance to her friend. "You are remarkable!" Lizzy gushed, and Georgie blushed a deep pink that looked most well on her.

Eventually they returned to the portraits. As Georgie flipped through the stack, one by one, Lizzy stopped her at a face that looked familiar. "Who is this man? I know I have seen him before, but I cannot think where."

At once she regretted this question, for the light that had been coming over Georgie's face vanished in an instant, to be replaced by the darkest cloud. It was the same cloud she had seen at their second visit, when Georgie had been visited by memories of the cad who had so abused her.

"Oh, pray forgive me!" Lizzy exclaimed. This portrait clearly evoked terrible memories, and she feared that she would send Georgie once more into the depths of her melancholia. "Do not talk of him, for I see this gives you pain. Let us find another—"

But Georgie stopped her with a soft hand. "No. I wish to talk of him. If you know my cousins, you may know the story anyway...." Lizzy tried to protest that she knew nothing from the cousins, but Georgie would not allow it. "I have known you only a short time, but your kindness to a sad and dull girl such as myself brings me to feel I can unburden myself to you. Mrs. Reynolds, too, must trust you, and the weight of my sins is lying so heavily on my heart. If I can tell you of what I have done, it may ease my burden. I know you will not cast judgement upon me. Please, allow me this!"

The passion that infused these last words alarmed Lizzy, for until this moment, she had only heard the flat and expressionless voice that had matched the blank face. As she stared at Georgie, she also saw, for the first time, real fire in the girl's eyes. "Forgive me if I err," she prayed silently, dreading that her agreement might cause worse damage to the wretched creature beside her on the sofa. To Georgie, she said as calmly as she could manage, "Only speak if it does not distress you; I shan't demand that you finish even a single sentence."

And so Georgie spoke. "The man is the son of my father's old steward. He was a favourite of my father, and a constant playmate to my brother as a child. His name is George Wickham." Lizzy now recalled the man. He had been in the militia in Meryton, a handsome officer in a splendid red coat, with whom her sisters flirted from afar. She had heard his name, but she had not been formally introduced to him during her sporadic residence at Longbourn. She explained this quickly to Georgie, who then continued her sad tale.

"Last year, when I was fifteen, he met me and my companion at Ramsgate, and being an old friend from childhood, my companion allowed us to spend time together. George doted on me and paid me every attention. He convinced me that he loved me. He said we were fated to be together, that providence alone had brought him to where I happened to be, and threw us together once more. Later I discovered that providence went by the name of Mrs. Younge, who was my companion and who was known to Mr. Wickham. But I digress.

"George convinced me to agree to an elopement. He told me that my brother would be distressed at having to set aside the time and resources to plan a wedding, and that he would be much more pleased if the ceremony and festivities could be dispensed with. Knowing Fitz as I do, I had to agree with him, for Fitz is not a lover of society, and is more content on his own than in the midst of a large function. But when Fitz arrived to visit me just days before the elopement was to take place, I had to tell him all. I thought he would be so happy, and so pleased at the trouble we had saved him. Oh, Lizzy, I was so very, very wrong!

"Fitz was furious. He shouted at me for what seemed like hours before he turned his rage on George. And that was when my heart truly broke, for Fitz was right. George did not love me at all. All he wanted was my dowry, and I so nearly succumbed to his plot. When Fitz told him that the dowry was only to be given with his blessing, George spat at him and hissed at me that I could keep my dowry, for he had already ruined me, and that I would be useless to any other man, an object of scorn."

Somewhere in the midst of this breathless recital, tears began to form in the girl's eyes, and now they overflowed the edges of her lashes. She did not sob, nor did she wail, but she let the tears flow unstopped down her face.

This was the matter Mrs. Reynolds had failed to discern. Lizzy had to ask, "Forgive me again, Georgie, but when Mr. Wickham said that he ruined you, did he truly... That is, did he...?" She sighed. There was no polite way to ask, but something in the girl's words made her wonder. "What, exactly, did he do to you?"

The girl wiped her face with a handkerchief and fought back her tears. "Oh, Lizzy, I am so ashamed of what I allowed him. We were alone together, and he said it was expected of courting couples... He... I allowed him to kiss me, on the lips even, and once, he moved his hand to touch my—" she broke off and moved her hand to indicate her bosom. "It is so very, very shameful. I tried to return to my old society in London, but all I could hear were girls who had been my friends and acquaintances talking about those they knew who had been ruined, and how the shame would follow them forever, how they could never wed or be presented or be in good society again, and even though they knew not of my own personal shame, I could not abide it. I had to hide, and that is when the melancholia became so very bad." Now she was starting to sob quietly, releasing emotions held too tightly and for too long.

Still, a question remained. "Georgie, answer me this truthfully. Please. Mr. Wickham did nothing other than kiss you on the mouth and place his hand on your chest?" The girl nodded. "Nothing more?"

"What more is there?" she sobbed, choking out the words between tears and gasps. "I allowed him this, and it is to my eternal shame."

In any other circumstance, Lizzy might have laughed. The relief she felt on the young girl's behalf was tremendous and the sun seemed, suddenly, a little brighter. But she could not laugh, for Georgie's pain was too raw and her innocence too pure. With the steadiest voice she could manage, Lizzy said, "You are not ruined, sweet thing. He misled you. There is much more that he might have done, and still not ruined you. He is a lying cad, a scoundrel of the worst stripes, but he has not ruined you."

Georgie dissolved completely into tears now, and Lizzy gathered her into her arms, allowing the younger girl full vent of her anguish. "But he kissed me... he even used his tongue..."

"Oh, my dear friend, I have been thoroughly kissed too, by a man I thought I liked, and I am not at all ruined. The man's cousins and friends surely know he kissed me thus, and they still are proud to introduce me to their exclusive society. No, you may set your sweet heart at ease, for you are not even slightly tarnished."

"Truly?"

"Truly!"

A great many more tears ensued, but Lizzy felt they were cleansing tears, washing away some of the pain and torment and watering the ground where healing might take root. When Mrs. Reynolds reappeared some time later to take away the tea tray and ask after the two ladies, she found them thus, with Georgie weeping onto Lizzy's shoulder, while Lizzy handed her handkerchiefs to dry her tears and lifted sodden hair from her streaming eyes. The expression on the older woman's face suggested that she was uncertain whether to be alarmed at the tears, or to be relieved that her charge was, at last, releasing the bad humours that fed her melancholia. Lizzy saw her and looked up, mouthing,

"Everything will be alright," and Mrs. Reynolds let out a deep grateful breath.

In time, the weeping abated and Georgie was prevailed upon to take a bit of broth and some bread. Lizzy requested that they take their luncheon on the balcony, for there was sufficient space for a small table and two or three chairs, and this was deemed a good idea by all. The fresh air and sunlight seemed to be healing for the young lady, and might be welcome solace after her cathartic experience that morning. Mrs. Reynolds sat with them for a few moments, enough to convey her maternal concern for Georgie without overstepping her bounds as housekeeper. Then Lizzy and Georgie sat peacefully, watching the birds fly over the wood, catching glimpses of animals as they wandered along the clearing edge of the trees, and enjoying the redolent air of the rose-perfumed garden below.

"Is anybody living in the cottage now?" asked Lizzy after a time. "I have been looking yonder and thought I saw some movement amongst the trees. But, perhaps it was a deer, or even a bird, for it is too far to see clearly, and too hidden by the wood."

"None is there that I know," Georgie replied. Her voice seemed clearer now, though thick from her recent tears, and there was a trace of animation in it. "I have thought, at night, that there might be smoke billowing from the chimney, but I have not looked closely. It might be a groundskeeper, with his maintenance, or it might be birds flying through the air above it."

Happy to keep Georgie's mind on something that cheered her slightly, Lizzy asked more questions about the cottage and the games that were played there, until at last it was time for her to return to Arlenby. The two parted with fervent embraces, and a renewal of Georgie's pledge of friendship. "Perhaps on my next visit we can look through your music," Lizzy teased, "unless you have had any secret assignations with Herr Haydn." The joke was well received and Georgie smiled tentatively and expressed her deep gratitude.

As they walked out of the house, Lizzy requested a moment with Mrs. Reynolds. She had not been asked to keep Georgie's confession secret and thought it best that the caring housekeeper know. She explained the situation as discreetly as she could and expressed her hopes that Georgie might now begin to work her way free from the devils that plagued her since she understood at last that she was not completely ruined after all.

"It will take time, still, Miss Bennet, for her to recover her spirits," the lady warned. Lizzy concurred, but hoped that healing might now begin. "Thank you, Miss Bennet, for telling me," she added as the chaise started moving on its return to Arlenby.

When next Lizzy arrived at Pemberley to visit her friend, it was to find a much improved Georgie waiting for her. The young lady was dressed for the outdoors and walking around her sitting room as Lizzy entered. "I hope you might join me in a short walk through the gardens." Her face was alive with anxious optimism, and she chewed her bottom lip as she took breath. "I feel I might do well with some air. I have not left my rooms in too long, and I feel now I wish to re-enter the world." This was most welcome news, and Lizzy eagerly agreed.

"I also wish to tell you that I have agreed to take the draughts the doctor left for me. Mrs. Reynolds tried a small taste and promised me it is not too foul. There is a tincture of St. John's Wort, and Doctor Trentham promises it will be beneficial. He also suggested taking a tea made with saffron, which is very pretty and rather delicate in flavour. I had my first dose of the St. John's Wort this morning." She bit her lips once more and looked, for a moment, much younger than her sixteen years. "I know it is too soon for the draught to have effect, but I believe I feel better already! The world still feels empty and grey, but now I can sense that there is some colour in it, even if I do not see it yet. I know the colour is there and I shall strive for it." This was better news still, and with a great smile and a gentle hug around the shoulders, Lizzy let her friend lead her down the stairs and through the house towards the terrace below.

The terrace, which ran the entire length of the house on that facing, had doors that opened onto it from several rooms, including the breakfast room, the morning room, and the library. The two exited through the sunny morning room, decorated in pale yellows and greens, seeming an extension of the gardens beyond. Lizzy gazed around the lovely space and commented freely of her appreciation, to which Georgie responded with a quiet thank you, for the colours had been her own choice. "I have forgotten about these things, these simple things that I used to enjoy. I know that one day soon, I will enjoy them again," she stated.

The day was fine and the sun bright but not excessively warm. The two wandered quietly for some time through the rose garden, stopping here to smell a particular variety or there to appreciate some new hybrid of special colour or shape. The garden was an idyllic spot, a true Eden amongst the crags and woods of Derbyshire. There were benches upon which to sit and rest and precisely cut topiary upon which to rest the eyes.

They wandered through a small maze, and from there along the paths towards the far end of the house, near to the wing beyond which the stream curved on its way down from the hills. The sun was shining brightly and Lizzy was grateful for the parasol Georgie had pressed into her hands. She was examining it and the beautiful effect of the sunlight passing through the painted silk with such attention that she almost missed the man who walked around the corner of the wing they were approaching. At first, she thought nothing of him, for he looked, from this distance, to be a gardener or groundskeeper, with his simple trousers, shirt sleeves, and wide-brimmed straw hat. But there was something in the way he moved that arrested her attention.

"Eliza," the familiar, beautiful voice sounded.

Lizzy froze, hardly daring to breathe, whilst at her side, with more enthusiasm and emotion than she might ever have imagined, Georgie cried out, "Fitz!" and ran to her brother, allowing him to enfold her in a ferocious embrace.

CRSO

What was she to make of this, the unexpected return of the disappeared professor? Where had he been hiding? Certainly no one in the house seemed to have been aware of his presence, and yet he was unencumbered with the accoutrements of travel. Had he just arrived, his horse still panting hot air, being walked by a stable hand, his saddlebags being carried into the house by a loyal servant boy? And what of his strange garb? This creature before her, a simulacrum of a gardener, was as far removed from the overdressed gentleman of the London salon as Pemberley was from London. And once again, that old question resurfaced in her mind: Which was the real Professor Darcy?

A more alarming thought, however, was whatever Darcy was to make of her! How would he construe her presence here, walking so companionably with his sister, so at home in his manor house? Would he be angry? Scornful? Would he offer her some subtle but stinging insult, leaving her to slink her way back to Arlenby without so much as a goodbye to Georgie? It took every ounce of courage she could find to turn her head towards him and meet his eye, ready for whatever assault he might fling her way.

But there were no insults, no barbs, no words of dismissal. Instead, he crossed the few paces towards her and bowed as if he were wearing the finest of morning coats and the most fashionable of cravats. He took her hand in his and kissed the back of it so tenderly she thought she might faint. "Eliza," he repeated, his voice soft and full of wonder. "Eliza... I had given up hope of ever seeing you again, but here you are," he gazed around him at his house, his gardens, and the two ladies walking in them, "here, at Pemberley. I must have done something to please the gods, for they have brought you to me, when I could never go to you. Oh, I am grateful to them!"

She ought to hate him, imperious and arrogant man that he was. She ought to turn her head and walk away, cut him and refuse all acknowledgement of him. But her feet could not move, nor could her lips find words with which to repudiate him. He had belittled her and broken her heart, but that heart still beat, and as much as the thought infuriated her, it beat for him. She had been anxious about him, more than she had dared to admit, during those long months during which none knew of his whereabouts; she had denied her conscious mind permission to think about him, but he had crept his way into the depths of her soul, and there he had remained all this time. And where she ought to slap his face or fling some barbed insult at him, all she could do was stare at him, knowing full well that every emotion was writ large upon her face. *Traitor!* She chided her body, but she could not deny that her dearest wish right now was to throw her arms about him and crush him to her.

His eyes, too, were brimming with emotion, and he stared at her with the look of a starving man being offered food. His head shook slightly and he pinched his lips together between his teeth. For a moment, Lizzy thought he might kiss her as his eyes darted from hers to her lips and back again. She started in alarm, wondering if such a daring act would destroy his sister, or conversely, comfort her with the knowledge that a kiss was daring but hardly equal to ruination.

She might have gaped at this notion, or licked her lips, for in a second, Darcy had lowered his head to hers and brushed her mouth so gently with his own. "Oh, I have missed you, Eliza. You cannot know how much."

Who was this man, who looked and spoke so like the Darcy she had known, but who was so very different? Learning his ways would take a lifetime of study; being his wife would never be boring. Had they officially broken off their presumed engagement? What had been revealed to the world? She had not thought to consider him again for a moment, but now Lizzy mused at how interesting life would be, wed in truth to such a man. She might even grow to like him; a small part of her confessed that she may already love him.

These reflections were cut short by Georgie's incredulous tones. "You have met before!" she cried unnecessarily. "Lizzy, why did you not tell me?"

As she sought the words she wanted, Darcy interrupted, "Miss Bennet and I were acquainted in London last winter."

"When you met Richard and Freddy? How wonderful! But why did you not tell me?" Her voice was breathless.

Having had a moment to collect her thoughts, Lizzy replied, "We did not part on the best of terms, and I had no desire to distress you."

"But he kissed you!" The girl turned wide, incredulous eyes towards her brother, then to her friend, her mouth agape. "Lizzy, is this the man who kissed you, but who treated you ill? Oh, I ought to have known. Fitz, what did you do to her?" There was definite fire in the girl's eyes now, and she sounded remarkably like her cousin Richard. Lizzy would gladly have gone through a thousand awful balls and fights with Darcy just to see his young sister coming back to life as she was.

"Georgie, dearest, I treated Miss Bennet abysmally, and I can never expect her to forgive me, but nevertheless I do hope she will try." His eyes bore into Lizzy's as he uttered these words, and she forgot to breathe, trapped as she was in his dark, brooding orbs. "If she will permit me," he continued, "I would like to start working towards atonement now. Pray continue your tour of the gardens, and allow me to exchange this garb for something more appropriate." With another kiss to Lizzy's hand, he bowed again and strode into the house.

His arrival was most assuredly unexpected, for Lizzy could hear cries of "Mr. Darcy!" and "Welcome home, sir," through the open windows of the large house.

"Where did he come from?" Georgie asked, staring after the apparition. "I have not seen him in an age, and yet, here he was, as if he had just come from a walk in the woods." She stopped and turned to look at the woods, beyond the park. "Oh, I think I understand! It was he who has been staying at the cottage!"

And thus it turned out to be. More properly attired, Darcy soon returned to escort the ladies around the park, bringing Mrs. Reynolds with him. "Oh, Mr. Darcy, why did you not tell us you were back?" she badgered him good-naturedly. "Even had you wished to sleep in your mother's cottage, we would gladly have sent food and drink for you. Whatever have you been living on, dear boy? You look quite starved!"

Darcy did look thin, Lizzy agreed, and wondered what he had been doing with himself for the four months they had been apart. Had he been living in the cottage all that time? How had he avoided all notice? She would have to ask him later. For the moment, however, brother and sister had fallen together in their reunion, leaving Lizzy with Mrs. Reynolds. They stood in the shade of a manicured tree as they observed the two Darcys together.

"You have done wonders with Miss Georgie," Mrs. Reynolds said. "I should hardly know her from the wraith of only two weeks ago. The doctor came again, and she would not see him, but she did agree to take the tonic he ordered up. He told me we might expect her spirits to rise and fall unevenly for a while, but as long as she takes her medicine, she is expected to improve over time. How can we thank you, Miss Bennet?"

"In truth, madam, I did little. I merely reassured her that there was hope."

"You coaxed her to confide in you, and let her know that her life was not over, that there was a reason to go on. For that, my dear, we shall be ever grateful."

Presumably Mrs. Reynolds had a moment to convey these same sentiments to Darcy, for later that day, after afternoon tea, he found an excuse to be alone with her, having sent Georgie and Mrs. Reynolds on a quick errand. "I heard what you have done," he murmured as he leaned over her whilst she sorted through music at the pianoforte in the music room. "I have been living, secluded as I was, in the cottage, but not unaware of the goings-on in my house. I knew how low my sister's spirits were when she returned home from Town, and I knew how strongly the melancholia had taken her. The other day, I thought I saw movement on her balcony, and I needed to see what that was about. I can get quite close to the house, do you know, at the edge of the wood, where I can see without being seen. That was when I saw her, standing outside, which she had not done in far too long. And then I saw the other lady, and my heart all but stopped when I saw it was you! I watched the house the entire next day, and there you were again, taking your luncheon with her, on that balcony, and I wondered what angel had descended from above to save my sister.

"When I saw you outside in the garden this morning, I knew I could remain hidden no longer. Mrs. Reynolds explained to me how she met you in Lambton and invited you here without knowing your connection to me. She told me of how you have prevailed on my sister to allow us to help her, and of what Georgie told you about Wickham." He spat out the name as if it were poison in his mouth. "The bastard," he grinned at her, knowing the effect his curse would have, "the bastard convinced her she was ruined by him, that she would never be able to move past their encounter. Heaven knows, I have lost more than one night's sleep over my inability to help her, for my failure to discover what had occurred."

He sighed deeply and rubbed a hand over a furrowed brow. "But you corrected her. I shall presume to kiss you anew, you realise, to show her how a kiss need not be tawdry or destructive to a woman's character."

"Is that the only reason you wish to kiss me, Professor?" There was a teasing laugh in Lizzy's voice as she settled on a piece of music and began to run her fingers up and down the keyboard. The sparkling arpeggios she produced echoed the bubbling lilt in her tone.

"No. By no means is it the only reason. In fact, it is quite secondary to my primary objective. The primary reason is that I enjoy it. I have also now compromised you quite thoroughly, and repeatedly, Eliza. Our presumed engagement has not been called off. Would you consider leaving matters as they are for the present until I have a chance to redeem myself in your eyes?"

Her fingers stopped their exploration of the pianoforte, and the arpeggios and scales ceased. "What are you asking me, Professor?"

"Fitz. We have moved beyond such formalities."

"What are you asking me, Fitz?"

"To consider my proposal. To allow me to prove myself to you. I missed you so desperately, Eliza. I could not eat, nor sleep, but I wished you were near me. Will you give it thought? Please?"

The sensitive, vulnerable man was back. He seemed to be the man most prominent here in the country, in this splendid and prosperous manor house. Far from the artifice of London's glittering society, where falseness was a virtue and sincerity was a vice, the conflicting aspects to the bewildering character seemed to settle a bit, and perhaps the image of the true essence was visible beneath the ennui and disdain.

"I... I shall give it thought," she said at last, to which he did not reply in words, but with his hands, which moved around her to pull her upright and into his embrace, and with his lips, which found hers and silently asking permission, proceeded to kiss her quite soundly.

They were interrupted by Georgie's too-silent return to the room. She carried with her the pile of music which she had been sent to retrieve. "Oh my," she whispered, sending her brother and friend scurrying in separate directions. "I'm so sorry... I did not know... but, how well did you know each other in London?" She looked from one to the other and back again.

"We were friends," Lizzy spoke, at the same time that Darcy announced, "We were engaged to be married."

Georgie stood stunned, allowing the pile of papers she carried to drop to the floor.

# Eighteen
# Unwelcome Company

George Wickham found, to his great astonishment, that he missed Caroline Bingley somewhat. Not, perhaps, for her charm and personality, for those he discovered were more lacking than present, but for her constant and eager willingness to engage in whatever activity he had in mind. In the time they had known each other, she had proved an amusing lover, quick to learn and with an appetite that matched his own. He would regret it when he had to relinquish her, at last, to Darcy. He had considered keeping her on as his plaything, but this would place him too much in the vicinity of his nemesis, and what he wanted was revenge, not prolonged exposure. Further, Caroline was lovely to look at and delightful to bed, but she was a shrew, always ready to speak ill of others if it might further her own ends, too concerned with her place in the world and with what she might do to improve it. Even to him, George Wickham, her seducer and lover, she seldom had a pleasant word, unless she lay entwined with him under the covers in his rented rooms. No, he would find another amenable young woman to satisfy his lusts, one whom he might enjoy for her company outside of the bed chamber, one whom he liked as well as desired. And so much better that would be, for he could then rejoice in the firm knowledge of his success at finally having defeated his old playmate.

But his ultimate victory, while nigh, was not quite complete: first he must find Darcy and watch as he discovered how he had been betrayed. Only then could he enjoy the spectacle as the proud man crumbled at his feet, destroyed by the very people he thought he loved. Ah, that would be sweet victory indeed.

One problem remained: his prey seemed to have vanished. He was not with Caroline. That was certain. Caro was, at present, visiting her aunt in the north, having been sent thither once more by her brother. Why on earth the brother thought this a good idea so soon after the engagement had been announced, Wickham could not fathom, but the wealthy often did very strange things.

During their trysts the previous spring, Caro had related to him a great many details leading to her departure, lamenting her ill treatment at every turn. The apartments Charles had selected for her and her companion were nowhere near adequate in size for a lady of her status. When she complained, her brother suggested that they were the grandest she could afford on the interest from her dowry, but really, could Charles not have paid for better accommodations from his own coffers? Any caring brother ought to have done so! Leaving her to her own devices in this way was quite insupportable, and after all she had done for him over the years! Wickham had been surprised to find a modicum of sympathy for the woman over the abuses she suffered at her brother's hand!

Worse, she had complained, none of her friends would deign to visit her there. The apartments were in a perfectly respectable part of town, despite their modest size and furnishings, and Caro could not think what kept society from her door. It must be the food, she decided. She did not have extensive kitchens, nor did she employ a trained chef as her brother did; therefore, if she wished to entertain and be seen, she must do so from Charles' house. (*All the better*, Wickham considered, *for the funds to come from Charles' pockets than Caro's allowance*. He could see no fault in her plans at all.)

At first she would arrive in the mornings and sit with Dear Jane as she accepted company, presiding as mistress of the house in lieu of the new Mrs. Bingley. She would stay until after dinner, for why should

Charles' chef produce all that food for only two people? And if company should be expected, well surely that company would wish to see Caroline as well!

But these arrangements had their limitations, which the lady had lamented to her lover. When the Bingleys were invited out, Caroline was sent home to her apartments, almost as if she were not wanted. This was unacceptable! If Charles and Jane were to be out in society, she must be as well. How could her brother, whom she had cared for and sacrificed for, neglect her thus?

Wickham had observed that Caro never mentioned Darcy by name; she did not wish to discomfit him with news of her betrothed. It was a sweet action on the part of a rather selfish woman, and he appreciated it. This must be why she did not mention those evenings when she must have been out on Darcy's arm. She never boasted of going to the opera with him, or to some grand society ball, or to cards at his noble relations. It could only be, Wickham considered, that she was protecting his sensibilities.

Once, and only once, had Wickham even dared to ask after Darcy. He had said nothing specific about the engagement or wedding, playing according to Caro's rules, and had merely asked how the gentleman was doing. Caro's response was simple. "Oh, yes, dear Mr. Darcy," she had waved a hand in dismissal and said nothing more. It must be, Wickham assured himself, that Caro did not wish to remind him of her betrothal to another. This left Wickham feeling rather smug and pleased with himself, for after him, what possible good could Darcy be, other than a set of deep pockets? He felt somewhat more kindly towards Caroline at this, for how gratifying it was that when she spent time with him, Caro devoted herself entirely to his pleasure and would not allow other concerns to interfere in their trysts. Perhaps there was more to her than her obvious physical charms after all.

Despite this momentary lapse of her accustomed selfishness, Caroline had often voiced her frustration at her brother's actions. Wickham knew he was adept at reading between the lines, and realised that whether she mentioned the man or not, Caro must think of her betrothed from time to time, at least. Surely, if she were excluded from

Mr. and Mrs. Bingley's engagements, she must still take steps to remain active in society when not on Darcy's arm. This must be why she had abandoned her apartments and returned to Charles' house. Now he and Jane must include her in their plans! And, as Caroline had whispered one lazy afternoon, now she could reassert herself as the true mistress of the house, for poor Jane did not run the household as it ought to be done!

But matters had not proceeded quite as Caro had anticipated. The new Mrs. Bingley had taken exception, it seemed, to her husband's sister always being underfoot and at last, Charles Bingley had grown a spine. Wickham sniggered at the very concept, but it must be so. Caro had always joked about how malleable her brother was, how she could manage to convince him to do anything she desired. Alas, it appeared that Mrs. Bingley had a similar influence over the man, and hers, as his wife, was stronger.

Therefore Caroline was ordered out of the house and up to Scarborough, where she remained, presumably until her wedding.

Wickham could not determine from the letters why Caroline's engagement to Darcy should be so drawn-out. As was her wont, she never mentioned anything relating to Darcy, and her wedding was no exception. Perhaps the man himself had other matters that needed attention before he could devote himself to a wife. His estates must be tended, his business affairs put in order. He might be planning a lengthy wedding trip, and a prolonged absence from his estate would require much advance preparation.

But now Darcy had disappeared and Caroline was gone to her aunt in the north, and corresponding was increasingly difficult. If Caro knew of Darcy's whereabouts, she was silent on the matter. It was, perhaps, time to take other steps. Bringing himself back to the present, Wickham found the old military officer's coat and hat that he had failed to return after his departure from the militia and pulled them on. He checked his appearance in the glass once more, and more than satisfied with his appearance, strode out of the door in search of information.

This information was not easily found at his usual tavern. Higgins, his sometime-confident, was not at his accustomed table, and there was no whisper in the air for Wickham to overhear. But there was Sanderson, over by the window. Wickham bought the man a pint of ale in exchange for rumour, and this proved somewhat lucrative. Sanderson seemed to know something about Colonel Fitzwilliam being in Town rather unexpectedly. The colonel had taken a prolonged leave from his military duties since his marriage and was expected to resign his commission shortly. Why he should be in London was a mystery, but one that could be solved with an appropriate ear at the appropriate door.

What Wickham discovered surprised him. He heard from the kitchen maid at the Duke of Bedford's house, who had it from a chamber maid at the Baron de Morigne, who had it from her beau, a footman for Lord Malton, that someone named Liza had written, concerned that Darcy was not at Pemberley, where everybody thought he ought to be. Who Liza was, he cared little. He knew only that his prey seemed to have vanished. Could he be at Scarborough with Caroline? No, surely not, for if he were so eager to be in his future wife's company, why delay the wedding?

Wickham was also certain that Darcy had not left England at this point, with his wedding approaching. Such news would have reached his ears, of this he was sure. And why, he wondered anew, was the couple separated thus? Could there have been some falling out already over Caro's dalliances? There certainly had been no gossip that he had heard about the engagement being broken. It mattered not. For, as he contemplated affairs, Wickham thought he knew where Darcy was.

He recalled from his childhood a cottage in the woods on the Pemberley estate, and knew well that a man might live there in comfort for a time, if he were prepared to tend to his own needs. Food could be brought in, or purchased in the village by a willing servant or the master himself, in suitable disguise, and none need be any the wiser. Yes, he was certain! That was where Darcy lay concealed, and that was where he, too, must go!

CR80

After discovering her brother and Lizzy in the music room, Georgiana had demanded a full accounting of their past, and Mrs. Reynolds, acting as the mother hen for her adopted brood, had insisted on sitting in on the discussion. Lizzy could do nothing but provide them with the unvarnished truth of the affair, all the while Darcy sat back on a chair in the corner of the room looking distinctly uncomfortable. When she reached the part in the tale about his interference in the blossoming attachment between Richard and Charlotte, both Georgie and Mrs. Reynolds turned their most disapproving eyes upon him.

"Oh, Fitz, what on earth were you thinking? How could you?" Georgie wailed, whilst Mrs. Reynolds chided, "Really, Mr. Darcy, I thought you had been raised better than to make assumptions and go off on that high-handed way of yours! I am most sorely disappointed." Darcy looked as if he wished to disappear through the floor.

Eventually the two decided to allow him to live, since Richard and Charlotte had ended up together, but they were still quite distressed on Lizzy's behalf. "You seem to have forgiven him," Georgie said, "but I do not see quite how. When you told me a gentleman had treated you ill, I had no idea how badly! In truth, I am surprised you even agreed to visit me that first day, knowing that I am his sister. Oh, dear Lizzy, there is so much goodness in you, to befriend a wretch like me, and be associated with a cad like him." She narrowed her eyes and glared sidelong at her brother. "But you did forgive him, did you not? I mean, what I saw suggests..." She blushed a deep red and did not finish her thought.

Laughing, Lizzy replied, "I have such different accounts of your brother, and all from his own actions and behaviour, that I know not exactly what I think. But I am well considering forgiving him at least some of his misdeeds. Oh, do not try to look innocent, Fitz, for we all know you better than that!" she teased. "I suspect he has his redeeming qualities, should we search long and hard enough for them!" This earned a laugh from the assembled company, and the conversation continued.

"What happened after the ball?" Georgie asked. She was sitting at the edge of her sofa, her own woes temporarily forgotten.

"I returned to my aunt and uncle and your brother..."

"Desired some solitude," Darcy concluded.

"No, I know that part," Georgie chided. "I wish to know about the outcome of the ball, what the word has been in Town. Do not scowl at me, Fitz! I was not out in society, but I have ears and I know how the gossipmongers work. Not a single event happens without it being chewed over once and again in every parlor in Town until the next piece of news arrives. What was said about the ball, about your engagement? *That* is what I wish to know!"

Lizzy turned to Darcy and he to her, their eyes meeting. Darcy shrugged. "I honestly cannot tell you, dearest. I had a... discussion with Richard the following morning and immediately left town. The cottage is rather secluded; I have received no news from Town at all. For all that I know of recent events, Bonaparte might have taken London, or given up all of his military ambitions to become a chorus singer at the Opéra. One wonders whether the devil can sing—"

"Nor do I know, Georgie." This was a question Lizzy had asked herself many a time over the past four months. "The engagement was never officially called off, but all of London must know that the very morning after the ball, your brother and I went our separate ways. People surely must assume—"

"Nothing." Mrs. Reynolds exclaimed. "I am certain they assume nothing. I have one or two fingers in the pie of Town gossip, and I have heard nothing. Oh," she turned to Lizzy, "I had no notion when I met you in Lambton that you were Mr. Darcy's betrothed, for my sources of gossip did not reveal that much, but I knew that the professor had entered into an engagement, and that there had been some irregularities after the ball. But that is not enough to set tongues wagging for more than the time it takes for tea to cool."

Lizzy was as yet uncertain. "But it must have been known that we departed in opposite directions, and with no good will towards each other. There could be very few who believed us still to wish to wed."

Mrs. Reynolds, however, demurred. "Not at all, my dear. A tiff, a lover's spat, is quite the expected thing. I do believe, from the time I have spent in London before the most praiseworthy Mrs. Pearce took control of the townhouse, that your little *contretemps* will only have confirmed in the minds of the *ton* that yours is a love-match, and not some arrangement of convenience. Never mind the truth of the matter!" she added as an aside. "No, it is well established that every lady likes to be crossed in love at least once, and most especially by her betrothed. You are most assuredly still engaged, in the eyes of the *ton*, at the very least."

Darcy let out a breath and allowed himself to fall back into his chair. Then his brows flicked upwards quickly and smirk appeared on his face. "What of it, Eliza? Until an announcement is published in the newspapers, telling all that our engagement is at an end and that we are both available for the *ton's* matchmaking efforts once more, we are as good as wed in their estimation. Are we? Do tell me we are!"

Lizzy's response was to roll her eyes at his impertinence, but she knew she had much thinking to do before she could discern her own mind.

"You can hardly expect me to answer you when you speak in that tone, and when your sister and Mrs. Reynolds are in the room!" Her words were accusatory, but her voice soft. "You will have to await my thoughts on the matter."

What was not left to her will, however, was her place of abode in the area. The Gardiners' visit to the area was at an end, for her uncle had business affairs to manage in London, and both sorely missed their children and wished to return to them. However, not a soul connected with the matter wished to remove Lizzy from her new friend Georgie, not when the girl was making such a recovery.

Further, Lizzy knew she could not return to Longbourn, but was reluctant to accept her aunt's sincere invitation to reside with the family on a permanent basis. She adored the Gardiners, but she did not wish to interfere with their happily established family routines. Likewise, Lady Grant was quick to offer her a place with that family, but the objections remained the same; Lizzy was loath to become a burden to amiable couple, no matter how generous and sincere the invitation might be. This was not the offer of a season in Town, where the baronet and his wife would be engaged in their own social whirl, little encumbered by an addition to their party. Here, in the country, Lizzy would be an interloper in the quiet domesticity of their comfortable existence.

Consequently, when Georgie extended the invitation to relocate to Pemberley for the foreseeable future, Lizzy was happy to accept it. "You are my friend and my comfort," Georgie exclaimed, "and your presence here is more to my benefit than yours."

Darcy's presence complicated the matter somewhat, but Lizzy was Georgie's guest, not his, and Mrs. Reynolds' reputation was well enough established in the area and in London that there could be no suggestion of any impropriety. "Miss Georgie and I shall be more than adequate chaperones, Miss Bennet," the older lady informed her, "and it will only be expected that you will wish to learn something of the estate before you assume your role as its mistress. Oh, how well matters have worked themselves out!"

Consequently, as the Gardiners took their leave of the party at Pemberley, Lizzy's trunks arrived at the manor house. Lady Grant and Mrs. Gardiner spirited Lizzy away for a final walk in the gardens, with the intention of assuring themselves that their friend was in complete agreement with the arrangements.

"You are certain you wish this, Lizzy?" Lady Grant asked with worried eyes as they strolled through the maze. "It is not altogether irregular, but I know your history with the professor has not been entirely calm. Are you certain you wish to stay in the same house as he?"

Lizzy was resolute. "He has never given me cause to worry, Lady Grant. He has given me plenty of cause to be angry and irritated and annoyed, but never worried. And I am here with my friend, and she shall protect me against whatever foul words her brother throws my way."

"You are quite set on this plan, then?" her aunt inquired.

At Lizzy's definite nod, Lady Grant declared, "Then I am happy for you. But know this, my dear: You are welcome back at Arlenby at any time. I shall let all my staff know that you are to be admitted and welcomed, no matter the day or hour. We are close at hand, and we shall be your safe refuge if you require it."

For the first time in her life, Lizzy was overwhelmed by the concern and care shown her by her family and friends. Not even in her childhood at Longbourn had she felt so cherished and cared for. At home, her mother always compared her unfavourably to Jane's beauty or Lydia's liveliness, and her father was always, at best, distracted and complacent. Lizzy had been left largely to her own devices. Now she was desired and cared for by not one family, but two. To have two sets of friends and relations all most concerned about her wellbeing was something unknown to her. It was a revelation, and while somewhat disconcerting, Lizzy appreciated what it was to be loved for her own sake by everyone around her.

Thus Lizzy took up residence at Pemberley. How her mother would have been amazed to see her least favourite daughter so well established. She was installed in a small suite of rooms next to Georgie's, with beautiful furnishings and her own sitting room and washing room, and she was treated as well by the excellent staff as was the young Miss Darcy herself.

It did not take long for her to settle into her new routines. As the doctor had predicted, the trajectory of Georgiana's recovery was not smooth and constant. Some days saw her returned almost to the girl she had been before the events of the previous summer, as she laughed and teased with her brother and friend—after she had forgiven them their deception, of course. Other days were more of a reversal, when she rose only with difficulty and could scarcely summon a frown, let alone the first bit of interest in events around her. But the doctor was not concerned, and he could see that overall, she was on her way to recovery. Miss Bennet's constant presence, he also added, was of great benefit in assisting in Miss Darcy's amelioration of spirits, for it had been Miss Bennet who had initiated the young lady's return to health.

Thus, the small group quickly attained a comfortable rhythm in their daily affairs. Lizzy learned her way around the massive house and discovered untold joys in the vast library and music room, Georgie slowly healed and could be seen more and more often downstairs and in conversation with the others, and Darcy set about actively wooing and courting his Eliza, whom he seemed determined to have accept him at last. Lizzy found the latter amusing, but also flattering to a great degree, and she found his efforts touching and pleasing, if perhaps a bit obvious and even laughable at times. Here, in his country home, the professor was a different man, at ease with himself and his companions, full of humour and intelligent conversation, almost devoid of the arrogance and contempt she had seen in Town. All were content.

This idyll of domestic tranquility lasted a week.

The first intimation of trouble ahead came with an innocuous ring at the front door, early on a grey morning. Lizzy had been up for a while and had taken some air in the lovely gardens before the rains would inevitably begin, and she had just taken her breakfast plate when Mrs. Reynolds threw open the door and announced, "Alfred, Viscount Eynshill."

"Freddy!" She leapt up from her chair.

In three long strides, he was there before her. "Elizabeth!" He stood very still as he gazed at her, then pulled her into a hug which he quickly released. "Oh, what an unexpected surprise and joy to see you here! But... what are you doing here? Is everything well with your family? Lady Grant is well? The Gardiners? Oh no... is it Georgiana?" Concern and confusion warred across his pleasant face.

"All is well, Freddy. Everybody is well, even poor Georgie. She improves daily, and will as like as not be downstairs before long to take her chocolate and toast."

"Oh, thank God," he released his breath, his entire body shuddering off suppressed tension. "But then why are you here? I am, of course, more than delighted to see you so soon after my arrival. Oh, I have missed you, Lizzy. London is not the same without you in it. The whole Town pines for you."

Suppressing a laugh at his exaggeration, she replied, "I came here, at first, at the express request of Mrs. Reynolds. She had no notion who I was, besides a lady who enjoyed reading. She believed I might be of some help to Georgiana, and it seems she was correct. I do not know that I did more than anyone else might have done, but your young cousin is much more her old self. When my aunt and uncle returned to London, she and Mrs. Reynolds requested that I stay for a time." She wondered how to approach the topic of her ambiguous relationship with Georgie's brother.

But Freddy spoke before she could. "And what of my cousin, Fitz? Has anyone had word of him? He is well able to fend for himself, but we are concerned, most concerned."

"Your cousin is well," came a voice from the door. The speaker was in Lizzy's sightline, but Freddy had to spin around to reassure himself his identity.

"Darcy, you dog!" he fairly shouted in the anger born of great relief. "Where in blazes have you been? Sorry, Lizzy," he apologised for his oath. "You had us all scared that something terrible had befallen you."

"I never invited you to worry, Freddy." Darcy's eyes were narrow and his voice tight as he glared at the newcomer. Then he took a deep breath and added, "I took shelter in Mother's old cottage. It has a stable for my horse, and I rode not into Lambton for my supplies, but into Berndale, in the valley yonder, where I am not so well known. People see what they expect to see, and dressed as a farmer, and able to take on the local accent at will, I passed quite easily."

"Then why," Freddy demanded, "have you returned now?"

Darcy looked over at Lizzy, and he eased from the doorway into the room. "I had better reasons to return home than to remain in seclusion. I had hidden myself away after that awful ball, after Richard, and then Eliza, and then you had all abused me so badly. No, no, I deserved what you said, and I needed solitude to think. The cottage has always given me comfort, and it beckoned me thither. But then I saw Eliza here, bringing life to my sister, and I felt hope once more."

Freddy eyed his cousin warily. "And what of you, Lizzy? Are you happy with this scoundrel, who treats the most worthy ladies like so much dirt, to be used to suit his will and then to be discarded like yesterday's newspaper? Do you stay for his sake? Do you remain whilst he plays the gentlemen, never knowing when he will turn once more into the selfish and arrogant boor you saw in Town? I was there, Elizabeth, after the ball, and I saw what he did to you."

"Freddy...." Darcy growled.

"What of it, Fitz? Do I not speak truth? Can I allow you to harm this lovely lady once more? Or need I play the gallant knight once again, come to rescue her from the fire-breathing Dragon de Pemberley?" The two men glared at each other, and Lizzy was put in mind of two curs circling each other in anticipation of a fight. She was, indeed, half-afraid that they would come to blows, when to her great gratitude, Georgiana entered the room. It was one of her better days and she looked very well.

Freddy immediately turned his expression to one of joy and greeted the girl with all the love a cousin should hold for another. "Georgie!" he beamed, "You look marvelous, so improved from when you stayed with Mother not so long ago! What a wonderful treat for my tired eyes. How are you feeling, my dear?"

"Freddy!" Georgie launched herself at him, and he caught her and swung her around in a circle as if she were a much younger child. Her feet missed hitting the sideboard upon which the various breakfast dishes sat by inches, and Darcy dashed over to hover protectively over his coffee and eggs. Georgie was bubbling in excitement. "When did you arrive? Surely only moments ago! As you see, I am out of the depths of my darkest moments. I feel almost myself again. Come, let me call for a cup for you so you may take coffee. Or would you prefer tea or chocolate? Did Mrs. Reynolds see you? Has she given you a room? Tell me about your journey!"

Darcy cast one more baleful eye upon his cousin before taking a chair much closer to Lizzy than was strictly necessary and starting in on his own morning meal, allowing Georgie to monopolise the newcomer's time.

With the arrival of Freddy at Pemberley, the mood of the house changed. The easy companionship that had developed between the two Darcy siblings and their guest was suddenly replaced by a tension born of two acknowledged rivals in the same house as the object of their attentions, and Lizzy felt distinctly ill at ease.

Darcy redoubled his efforts in playing the suitor, doting on Lizzy's every word, laughing at her jokes, bringing her drinks and flowers and offering to escort her on walks and drives around the property. He pulled from his library shelves copies of books and poetry he knew she liked, and went to great lengths to engage her in the deep discussions of literature and philosophy in which she had expressed interest.

Freddy, on the other hand, polished his performance as the dashing aristocrat, talking of the delights of Town, of what he could do for her, of how he would ensure that never again would anybody slight her or make fun of her or otherwise treat her as anything less than the jewel she was. "You, my dear Lizzy, are as an emerald—rare and brilliant, with a beauty that transports men to verse. See how well we look together, you and I. I would even purchase you a horse in a colour exactly like your hair! How splendid you would be upon its back! We would be the darlings of London!"

Although somewhat flattered by the attention, Lizzy found it, for the most part, tiring and infuriating, and expressed a wish on more than one occasion to return to Arlenby until the two men could learn to deal amicably together. It was only when she appealed to both men to restrain their rivalry for the sake of Georgiana that matters settled somewhat and an uneasy truce was declared.

The second sign of trouble rode in two days later on a fine black horse.

It was mid-morning, after the company had breakfasted, and they had all repaired to their individual rooms to prepare for the rest of the day. Still uneasy about the tension between Darcy and Freddy, Lizzy had left her chambers to seek out Mrs. Reynolds, hoping to discuss with the sensible housekeeper what to do about the situation.

The housekeeper was not in her offices, but a kitchen maid suggested that she had gone to supervise the cleaning of some of the rooms in the guest wing. Lizzy's route took her past the balcony that presided over the main entrance to the house, and since the sky was clear and the vista fine, she stopped at the great glass doors for a moment to take in the scenery.

It was from there that she saw the horseman approach. He galloped up with a steady and confident seat, and she stood admiring his form on horseback. Then the man pulled his fine steed to a stop and removed his hat, and for the first time Lizzy saw his face. She forgot immediately about Darcy and Freddy and their squabble, and with a gasp, ran off to alert everyone to the identity of the interloper.

# Nineteen
# Retribution

George Wickham had made good time on his journey. He had not made a particular point of rushing, for he was certain his prey would have no thoughts of escape, but neither did he wish to spend too much of his purse on inns and lodging along the way. His horse, a handsome and fine animal, had been hired for the occasion thanks to a generous if unwitting donation from Caroline Bingley. With all her baubles and trinkets, paid for by her wealthy father and doting brother, she would never miss that necklace he had sold, even if the emeralds were genuine and the diamonds not paste. She most likely thought it misplaced, in another chest, or fallen under a carpet during one of their passionate encounters. The funds from that necklace had lasted him several months now, since he had abruptly left the militia in the spring.

All his efforts were about to reach their culmination. He had arrived, at last, before the grand and impressive doors to Pemberley, here to meet his nemesis. For all too long he had been regarded as inferior by the haughty master of this estate; for all too long he had been deprived of what ought rightfully to be his own. Now, at last, there would be retribution. He removed his hat so as to see the entirety of the building, and cast his eye up at the imposing doors—so pitiful, really, made of wood that was easily hewn or burned, despite their grand appearance.

He stifled a triumphant laugh. He had arrived. Fate could no longer be denied.

Alighting from his mount, he straightened his clothing, wiped his forehead and replaced his hat, then approached the entryway. The chimes sounded louder than he recalled from his last visit here, some years past, when he had demanded the Kympton living from Darcy. That time Darcy had denied him. This time would be different.

There, upon the flagstones by the great doors, he waited for what felt like an inordinately long time before a uniformed footman opened the grand portal and asked his name and his business. A mere footman! George Wickham deserved at least a housekeeper, better still a butler. But the residents knew not of his arrival, and he would forgive them this lapse. This particular footman must be newly in Darcy's employ to have to ask his name; surely, everyone who had known him before would recall George Wickham. Of course, he did not recognise the footman, but he never paid much attention to servants, other than for what they could do for him. Neither would Darcy be in residence, but if Wickham were to be seen skulking around the grounds in his surreptitious quest for the cottage, best let it be known that he had come on legitimate business and was merely taking some air and stretching his legs before returning to Town.

"George Wickham, to see Mr. Darcy," he intoned in his most imperious voice, expecting the usual recital about the master not being at home. How surprising, therefore, to be invited inside and led to a small sitting area near what he knew was Darcy's private study.

Well! It seemed the prodigal son had returned. No matter the slight change of venue; his plans could be carried out here just as easily as at the cottage. Better, even, for the great master to be brought low in his own palatial manor house. He sat for a short while, congratulating himself on achieving at last what he had dreamed about for so long. And how pleasant it had been, too, dallying with Caroline. All battles should be this easy and pleasant to fight and win. He sat back on the upholstered wooden chair with a cat-like smile on his face.

"Mr. Darcy will see you, please sir." The same footman ushered Wickham through the set of heavy oak doors and into the study. After the subdued lighting in the room where he had been waiting, the harsh sunlight in the study assaulted his eyes, and he could only make out the shape of his foe, sitting across from him behind a large desk, a bright window to his back, casting his features into shadow. To Wickham's wonder, Darcy was not alone. Seated in an imposing chair, immediately beside the desk, was another man, an aristocrat by the haughty look on his face and his tall and lean figure, with a cold expression in his light eyes. The man looked familiar, although Wickham was fairly certain they had never met. Perhaps it was the lighting; a door just to this other man's side was flanked by two brightly flaming lamps that further cast light behind the stranger, obscuring his features somewhat.

Darcy did not stand, nor did he offer Wickham a seat. "State your business," was all he said. His voice was hard and terse, his expression unreadable. Wickham bristled at the cold nature of the greeting, but Darcy had always been a rude bugger, and rumour had it that he had grown even worse over the past year. Since their last meeting. Ah, yes... dear Georgiana... Wickham recalled that incident with a mixture of embarrassment—for failing and being caught out—and cockiness—for having come so close to his goal.

"Really, Darcy, is that how you treat an old friend?" Wickham purred, disdain oozing in every word.

"If I should happen to meet one, we shall find out. Now state your business." Even here in the depths of the country, miles from anywhere a civilised man would wish to be, Darcy insisted on holding to those haughty and condescending vowels. Could the man never relax?

Wickham looked for a chair, determined to sit even if not invited to do so, but there was none available. The trappings of power had gone to Darcy's head, it seemed. This arrogant hauteur would soon enough be wrested away from him. Looking down his nose at the seated men, Wickham raised his eyebrows and smirked, "I have news of your betrothed."

This got Darcy's attention. He blinked and sat straighter in his chair. His companion did likewise. "Indeed. Speak."

Ah, this was more like it! The mighty were about to fall.

"She has not, I hate to say, been the most faithful to you. In fact, she has been engaging in a dalliance in Town, whilst you have been looking elsewhere." He noticed a flicker of Darcy's eyes towards the man seated next to him. Aha! The rat was getting nervous. The dagger had been plunged. Now all that was left was to twist it. It was all Wickham could do not to lick his lips in glee.

"Go on," Darcy spoke. "How, exactly, do you know my betrothed? I find I am most curious." That cold look in his eye was not, after all, the look of arrogance; it was the look of a man fighting to control his emotions; it could only indicate the greatest distress. This was most satisfying.

"Surely, Darcy, you have a chair for me. 'Tis a long tale, and I should be more comfortable seated." There was no response although the stranger seemed amused. Wickham allowed his regard to wander to this second person. Who was he? So familiar, and yet... he could not place the face at all. Had he seen the man often in Darcy's company, but not been introduced? That must be it! A close friend, perhaps? And if so, how close? Wickham had never taken Darcy for an unnatural, but the very wealthy had their peccadillos, and a great many sins and crimes would be ignored or forgiven amongst the right set. He allowed a sneer to form on his face. Buggery was disgusting to him, but the knowledge of it might be another means to a consistent income, should matters come to a head. Yes, this was excellent information to have.

The cold stare did not abate, and resigned to standing, Wickham continued with his recitation. "I met the lady in Meryton, when I was stationed there. Yes, my old friend, you and your actions have seen me reduced to having to take a commission in the militia. But do not vex yourself about this; there are unforeseen advantages to a smart red coat. I find it attracts the ladies most prodigiously.

"As for your own lady love, I encountered her about town, and she was most particularly friendly towards me. Most friendly, indeed. Her charms are," he paused and scrutinised his nemesis, "distinctive and quite alluring."

"As you say," his victim commented in those annoyingly perfect tones, "but why on earth am I to believe you? You have hardly made your reputation as a teller of truth."

"Ah, but this time, I have proof. Shall I continue?" Darcy waved his long manicured hand in a gesture of invitation. "I have documented every encounter. I can tell you where we met, who might have seen us, and how long our, shall we say our 'encounters' lasted."

"These are evidence only of your ability to fabricate. Have you tangible proof?"

"I have a necklace, a stocking, some other trinkets that are indisputably hers."

"Again, objects can be stolen, or borrowed even, with the help of an untrustworthy servant."

"Yes, but I can describe the lady. All of her. Most very intimately." Wickham now turned his eye fully to the second gentleman in the room. "But are you certain you wish your... companion to hear all these sordid details? For the right price, I can preserve the lady's reputation, if not her virtue." His eyes gleamed as he prepared to twist the dagger.

"Oh, of course," Darcy's tone was nonchalant. "You have not met my cousin, the viscount. Never mind. Continue."

Cousin? This man was his cousin? That was a blow! Well, the aristos were known for all manner of sordid goings-on, but none in authority would truly believe that Darcy was dallying with his cousin. The vision of that particular source of income dissolved before his eyes. Regretful, but hardly instrumental to his plans.

"Very well. As I mentioned," Wickham drawled, his Derbyshire accent growing increasingly more pronounced, "I can tell you rather alarming details about your lady's appearance. Clothed and unclothed. She has a most unusual birthmark, right... well, never mind that. I can describe for you what she likes best, and what she has less appetite for. I can relate to you how she sounds when she is in the throes of her passion, how she cries out and allows her long fingernails to rend the flesh on your back. Oh yes, Darcy, I can tell you all, for I have seen it all." He shifted his weight from one foot to the other and crossed his arms across his chest. He allowed his confidence to show on his face and in his voice. "She is quite ruined, irrevocably so. Yours will not be the first taste of her allurements, and you shall always know that no matter what you do, she shall be thinking of me!"

Strangely, the cool look had never left Darcy's face, and the arrogant man seemed about to speak again when the door behind the viscount flew open and a yellow and golden fireball rushed into the room. The apparition resolved itself as a furious young lady, flashing anger with every gesture as her words flew from her like daggers.

"You are nothing but a liar, George! I would not believe you if you told me the sun had risen in the east this morning. You talk about ruination, but you use the words only to wound and not in truth. Lizzy set me straight, and now I know just how low and despicable you really are. You are a cad and a rat and you should be hauled away in chains!"

Well, well, well! The little kitten had grown claws. And she had mentioned this Lizzy again. A governess? A paid companion? It was irrelevant. "Georgiana, how delightful—" he began, but Darcy cut him off with a flick of his hand.

"Enough with the nonsense, Wickham. Not a soul here believes you. You may have seduced and ruined some poor girl, but nothing you have said convinces me even to bring these accusations before my betrothed. I have complete and utter faith in her, regardless of what tripe you may spill from your soiled lips. Be gone and never let me see you again."

This was too much! Was the man that cold, that he could accept the faithlessness of his future bride so easily? That he had no care that she had been seduced and thoroughly ruined by his own former friend? "I see why Caroline was always so loath even to mention your name," he spat out. "You are the most unfeeling of men. She should better have chosen elsewhere."

Now what was this? Was Darcy laughing? Did Darcy ever laugh? How dare he turn this most serious accusation into a joke? This was no matter for amusement.

"Caroline?" Darcy roared between guffaws. "Well, well, well. Isn't this a pretty pickle you have yourself in now! Caroline Bingley? Oh, Alfred, this is joke indeed! I haven't been this diverted in years. Whatever shall

Richard say? And Charles, oh, poor, poor Charles, to be saddled with this rat as a brother. Oh, this is too diverting by far!"

This was not going as expected! Why was Darcy laughing, and why on earth did he think that Wickham would ever be Charles Bingley's brother? "You are too cruel, Darcy, to make light of your betrothed in this way! Have you no shame, no sense of decency?" Wickham was astounded, and rather confused.

"I have the greatest sense of decency, although you have none at all, it seems." Darcy rose and walked to the open door behind him, then called in the gentlest voice Wickham had ever heard emanate from his stiff and conceited throat. "Eliza, dearest, would you be so kind as to grace us with your presence?"

A rather pretty young woman entered the study, beautifully but not ostentatiously dressed, a model of grace and decorum. Wickham thought he recalled seeing her on several occasions in Meryton. Was this Georgiana's governess? She seemed rather grand for a companion, but Georgiana Darcy always had to have the very best. Had Darcy picked the chit up there, as he might a souvenir from a quaint local shop? But wait... he had called her 'dearest,' his hand was on her back at her waist, and that soft look in his eye...

"Wickham, I shall not sully the lady by offering an introduction, but this, THIS, is my betrothed. You have ruined the wrong woman, and now I shall see you wed to her, should she be in agreement, to atone for your crimes." He sat back in his chair and beamed at the woman next to him; his cousin and sister looked equally amused. Wickham turned to run, but two large and imposing footmen had appeared at the door, and it seemed that escape was impossible. The dagger had been twisted, but it was impaled in the wrong person.

"But.. but..." he sputtered. "This is not possible! Caroline intimated she knew you, suggested she was to be married to you..."

"Caroline has been convinced for years that she would one day be married to me, but she has always been the *only* one who believed it. Until now!" He laughed again, the impudent fool. "At no point has this supposed engagement existed anywhere other than in her mind."

Wickham sputtered for a moment, then exploded, "But... I cannot marry her!" Oh, the horror that would be. Caroline was a fine partner for the bedroom, but much of life existed outside of the bedsheets, and the woman's personality would be a hardship to endure for more than the time it took to remove her clothing. Anxious for a reprieve, Wickham threw out, "I have no income, nothing on which to live! I was relieved of my duties when I failed to reappear after my leave in the spring." Did he really admit that? Oh, how desperate he must be! "Your friend, Bingley, would never allow his dear sister to live in penury!"

"Fear not, Wickham." That look in Darcy's eye was not cool; no, it was ice cold. "I have taken steps on your behalf to ensure your comfortable existence, within limits." He opened a drawer in the desk before him and rifled through some papers before withdrawing an envelope. "This appeared in yesterday's post," Darcy continued. "You see, there is a commune of reformers who have established themselves in a remote part of Wales, an offshoot of some Quaker sect, I believe, with a determination towards societal reform. They have been pestering me endlessly about my thoughts on moral and work reform and the nature of their self-contained community. When I saw you in Meryton—oh yes, I saw you, and knew what you were about—I decided, as a joke, to reply that you, George Wickham, were one of the most innovative moral thinkers in England." Did Darcy's eyes actually twinkle at this? Was such a thing even possible? "They have since decided to devote a portion of their commune's income to supporting you and your wife as you live in and guide their community. The money shall not, of course, be yours, nor shall you retain a penny should you leave, but whilst you remain with them and provide them with the leadership they desire, you will live most comfortably. The choice, Wickham, is yours.

"In the meantime, please make yourself at home in the rooms I shall allot to you in the servants' wing. You are a deserter from the militia, and I have a note from my cousin the colonel to keep you secure should I find you. There you may wait whilst I inform Colonel Fitzwilliam of your whereabouts and my friend Charles Bingley of your recent activities and give him the news about his sister. That should make for some rather interesting conversation at their dinner table, don't you think?" Darcy smiled icily. "Lads, take him to the room I set out. Have a guard at the door at all times, should our guest decide to leave." And that was the end of the interview.

CRSO

Lizzy had been most alarmed when she saw Wickham ride up to the front doors earlier that day. Her own concerns about the rival cousins faded in significance to whatever this unexpected visit might purport, and she had rushed off at once to find Darcy. She knew little from her own experience about Wickham, but from everything she had learned from Georgie, his arrival at this time could have no good will behind it.

She found Darcy in the library, where he had been showing Georgiana some of the excellent books on natural history in his collection. Freddy, too, was in the room, reading through the memoirs he had with him. In other circumstances Lizzy would have tried to speak with Darcy alone, but now time was of the essence, and the few minutes it might take to extricate Darcy from his conversation with Georgie might give Wickham some undeserved advantage in whatever scheme he had in mind. Therefore she had announced to all present that their unwelcome guest had arrived, thus to give them all the most time to prepare.

Knowing what damage her declaration might have caused, she looked immediately to Georgie. Indeed, the young lady's face turned white and she gasped as she took an involuntary step backward, seeming for a moment to collapse inward upon herself. Her brother caught her and held her securely by the shoulders as Lizzy apologised to both with her every expression.

Then the girl cast a glance towards Lizzy and meeting her eye, seemed to take strength from their bond of friendship. She took a deep breath and straightened her back and stepped forward out of her brother's protective embrace. A look of determination replaced that of anxiety, and she raised her chin and flared her nostrils. Lizzy knew immediately that Wickham would have no more power over the young woman.

Darcy, too saw this transformation, and he nodded once, definitively. "Good girl!" he praised her, his voice almost too quiet for Lizzy to hear. "You are free of him."

"This is a problem we will deal with one final time," he announced to the room. He straightened to his full height, and squared his shoulders as his eyes narrowed. "Freddy, come with me. We will present a united front; Wickham's ceaseless lies and accusations will end today."

Georgie tried to insist upon being present at the confrontation, pleading eloquently that she had been wronged and deserved to face her abuser, but Darcy stood firm in his denial. At length, he agreed that Georgie might listen at the door, but should not be seen. "I am most reluctant in this decision, Georgiana. I would not have you harmed anew by this cad's lies. Eliza," he turned to Lizzy now, "I can trust you to stay with her all the while she listens. If you feel her resolve weaken, I charge you to remove her immediately. Georgie, there will be no discussion."

Lizzy agreed. "Your brother is right. You are strong, but your health must take precedence." Darcy nodded again and strode forth through the adjoining door with Freddy like two knights of old charging into battle.

Consequently, as Wickham spewed his venom, Lizzy and her friend stood silently behind the door, listening to every vile word of the bizarre accounting. Lizzy felt herself grow red with anger and embarrassment! Every word the unscrupulous cad uttered was a lie, but oh, she was horrified! How could she bear the shame at what her friends would think of her? She was about to run off when she felt Georgie's hand on her arm. The victim was now victor, and the touch of her hand gave Lizzy strength and confidence. When she spoke, her voice was a whisper in her ear, but no less strong for its quietness. "We do not think this of you for a moment, Lizzy. Not I, not Fitz, and not Freddy. Wickham has never told the truth, and my brother is hardly about to start believing him now."

And so Lizzy had stayed, listening to accusation upon accusation of the vilest nature heaped upon her character, whilst Darcy seemed unconcerned about the whole of it. But as Lizzy grew calmer, Georgie grew more and more angry. At last she could hold the girl back no longer. With a huff that sounded remarkably like her brother's, Georgie wrestled herself from Lizzy's grip and pulled open the door, then dashed headlong into the room beyond to counter the horrid man's abuse.

As the girl railed at her erstwhile tormentor, Lizzy felt her embarrassment turn to pride at Georgie's strength, and she felt her own spine stiffen as she grew equal to the situation. Then, when it became apparent that Wickham was talking about a different person entirely, she felt she might collapse from laughter and relief!

The rest of the interview with Wickham passed in a blur. Georgiana Darcy stood tall and triumphant, George Wickham was cowed and destroyed, and she, herself, vindicated from accusations she had no notion even existed. Perhaps she ought to chastise herself for allowing Georgie to enter the study, but all she could feel, after those horrid words, was profound relief.

And then he had come for her. Quietly, gently, so very much the gentleman after Wickham's venomous poison, Darcy had come for her and guided her into the space so she could face her accuser and watch as he realised the complete destruction of all his evil plans.

Now the drama of the morning was over. Wickham was safely stowed away where he could cause no more harm until Bingley could decide how to proceed, and Darcy was scurrying around and yelling at servants, demanding that an express rider be found, calling for his paper and pen, wondering why there was never coffee when he needed it, and generally making a racket. He would, Lizzy knew, apologise profoundly and sincerely to his servants the following day, for she had seen this happen before. This was part of his character, and nothing would change it. His staff seemed to accept it without the first sign of complaint, for they knew their master well and understood his moods. Lizzy also knew, from discrete and less-discrete inquiries, that despite these sudden rampages of indignation or fury, Darcy's staff were loyal and respectful to a man. For all his blustering and tempestuousness, he was never harsh nor cruel, and treated the lowest scullery maid with the same respect he treated his sister. If this was not much, it at least indicated that he did not think meanly of those in his employ, and his intention was understood and commended.

Slowly, Lizzy was coming to understand what she had observed, both in London and at Pemberley. She had, at first, regarded Darcy's various moods as being almost those of separate men: the arrogant and crusty professor, the sweet and vulnerable friend, the tender and coaxing suitor. But they were all part of the same man, different facets to a fascinating character. His accustomed rudeness made those moments of tender solicitousness all the more poignant; the unforgiving arrogance gave even greater import to those moments when he allowed his sensitive nature to be seen. He was vexing and compelling and really rather wonderful, and as she paced the perimeter of the fine carpet in the morning room, she thought she might very well grow accustomed to these flurries of bluster and tempestuousness.

But he was not the only man who had taken residence in her heart. For there was also Freddy. How could she fail to think most affectionately of Freddy? He had been, since their very first encounter, sweet and steady and reliable. He had been there to support her at every turn, to offer his strength in support or a shoulder to cry upon, and he hung on her every word. Even today, despite his currently strained relationship with his cousin, when the honour of either Miss Bennet or Miss Darcy was at stake, he had put away his rivalry and stood at Darcy's side, ready to support him against whatever Wickham had found to throw their way. Freddy's natural good humour made him excellent company; life with such a man would be most pleasant and free from turmoil. Further, should Freddy offer for her, and should she accept, he would one day make her a countess. This was hardly a reason to wed, but it was not an insignificant detail to consider.

She looked over at him as he toyed with the cards he held in his hand. He had seen her agitation and had offered to divert her, either by taking some air outside or by reading aloud, or by engaging in some conversation on some topic of her choice, but she had suggested he see to Georgie's comfort first. Meeting her glance, he whispered to his cousin and rose to meet Lizzy as she made her circuit around the room. "Lizzy, are you truly well? You heard things today a lady ought never to

RIANA EVERLY

hear." He glanced over to Georgie, who was examining her own cards, and whispered, "I had wished to speak with you in private, and at another time, but perhaps—that is—" He breathed deeply, and then spoke quickly and quietly. "Elizabeth, I know of your arrangement with my cousin, but if you are not happy, I would be most honoured if you would consider my offer in lieu of his. I would be the happiest of men were you to be my wife. I know this is not the time to ask, but if there are rumours flying because of that rat, I can and shall quash them all quite soundly. Do not answer me now; but take your time to consider my offer." He put his bare hand on hers, and let it rest there, with no pressure, no presumption, just his constancy and steady support.

At that moment heavy footsteps were heard approaching the room, and in a moment the door was flung open and Darcy blew in like a storm. "My tasks are complete," he announced to all and sundry. "The letter to Bingley is written and sent off, and Wickham is secure. At last I may sit." He fell into a chair, and then noticed Freddy standing all too close to Lizzy. Leaping up once more from his seat, he announced, "We must have some air. Some exercise will do us all good. Perhaps croquet so I may hit something." He glared at Freddy. The truce was over.

❦

Darcy glowered at his cousin. He had just spent all morning dealing with Wickham; he had no patience now for his rakehell relative to be importuning his lady. A closer glance revealed that Freddy had taken Eliza's hand, and Darcy felt his head swim at what this might mean. Eliza was his, and he would not allow Freddy to wrest her from him. He made some comment about wishing to hit something and strode out of the French doors and onto the terrace beyond, hoping the fresh air of the afternoon would restore him to some semblance of civility, for his sister's sake, and Eliza's, if nothing else.

He sensed, rather than felt, the others follow him onto the terrace, and then down into the rose garden beyond. Eliza was walking with Freddy, but silently, and Georgie seemed confused and ill at ease, despite the tremendous show of strength she had exhibited before Wickham. The awkwardness between the trio grew, until Elizabeth spoke, breaking the tension. "You were wonderful this morning, Georgie. I knew you had such strength in you, but it was a blessing to see it. Do you feel stronger?"

His sister agreed heartily, and began talking rapidly as she sought to order her thoughts. "When I heard him lie about you that way, Lizzy, I could bear it no longer! I could not allow him to destroy anybody else with his duplicity, and most especially not my dear friend." She stopped for a moment to regulate her breath, and continued. "I knew, at that moment, that I had to confront him, and that he would never have power over me again. There is no truth in him, and no beauty, or none in his soul, where it matters," her voice was firm. "He refuses to know himself, and as long as he lives only on the surface, caring only for what is superficially pleasing, he will never be happy. I hate him, but today, for the first time, I am also sorry for him."

She grabbed Eliza's hand and walked resolutely forward to meet the roses in their bloom.

*He refuses to know himself.* Darcy heard the words his sister had spoken, and they bored their way into his spirit. Did he, Fitzwilliam Henry Darcy, Professor of Language and Phonetics, special lecturer at Oxford University, know himself at all? Or was he as vile a creature as Wickham, fixated upon appearances, fated to a life devoid of true happiness? He slowed his step and looked at the three people walking in front of him now, enrapt in their discussion of Georgie's inner strength. Did he possess a fraction of his sister's fortitude? What did he want for himself? What would truly satisfy him?

Did his studies make him happy? They did, he confessed, but to a point only. He delighted in discovering a new vowel shift, or an unusual way of pronouncing a combination of consonants or of documenting subtleties in fricatives. Intellectually, the intricacies of jaw position and sound production were most stimulating, but his studies were only a part of his life. What else was there? He was satisfied, was he not, with Mrs. Pearce in London and Mrs. Reynolds at Pemberley, each seeing to his affairs and managing his life most admirably, whilst he took brandy with Richard or with Charles? But these two men, his closest friends, were now married with their own homes and responsibilities, and he could not devote his life to finding those few moments when he might impinge on their time. No, his happiness had to come from within. He turned his head once more and took in the sight of his sister, glowing for the first time in months, her golden head kissed by the sun and a sense of calmness and animation suffusing her face. Something swelled in his heart, and he nearly stopped walking.

With a start, he realised that what he wished for, more than anything else, was for his family and friends to find their own happiness. This quite astounded him, for he had always considered himself a very selfish creature. His personal wellbeing and luxuries were important to him, and he took them very much for granted, but these were, he now reckoned, what Georgie had termed superficial. True happiness came not from things but from people, from the people he loved. And, with even more of a start, he realised that this was exactly what had happened. He loved. He loved his sister—he would move heaven and earth to see her happy—he loved his cousin, no matter how the man annoyed him, and by God, he loved Elizabeth!

He had been infatuated with her for a while, and had revelled in those stolen kisses and in her impertinence and self-assuredness, but he had grown beyond that, to a point where her happiness meant more to him than his own. He heard her in front of him, talking easily now with Freddy, offering some comments on the weather and the variety of roses and on whether the war in the Americas was detracting from the battles on the continent, as Freddy feigned a look of interest in the topic. For the first time in his life he felt faint. To truly know himself and to truly become settled in his own mind, he had to make a very large sacrifice. The thought of it broke his heart whilst at the same time, it set it free.

# Twenty
## Decisions

After the heightened drama of the confrontation with Wickham and the renewed rivalry between Darcy and Freddy, the remainder of the day took on a most unnatural flavour. An abnormal calm settled upon company, and despite attempts to carry on conversations and activities as per normal, everybody seemed to be acting out his or her own role in a play. Those few moments of candid conversation were rare and ended abruptly, and Lizzy wondered when the four would be able to return to their heretofore comfortable familiarity.

At least, she recognised, Georgiana had come through her ordeal rather unscathed; if anything, the girl was stronger than ever Lizzy had seen her. She spoke freely of her thoughts and feelings about the matter, and Lizzy was most reassured by her liveliness and resolve. Of everybody, Georgie seemed the least affected by the morning's proceedings.

Her own thoughts were less settled. She had so very much upon which to think, so many decisions that must be made, and made soon. She had been placed in a most unusual situation, and it would do nobody good to let it continue for any length of time. For her sake, as well as for Freddy and Darcy, she must come to a resolution, although she knew that at least one heart would be broken in the process.

For what a situation she now found herself in: officially engaged to one man, but courted by and proposed to by another. Both suitors were wealthy and handsome, and both were good men who would make excellent husbands, no matter their very different characters. Taken as an accounting, such as one performs in choosing which field to cultivate, or whether to purchase a new curricle or repair the old, the two men might be weighed rather equally, with a balanced number of positive and negative traits. But this was not a matter to be decided based on reason or logic. Nothing but the deepest love, she had come to understand, would convince her into matrimony, and she had need to spend some time examining her own heart, for she felt great affection for both men.

Regardless of her choice, Darcy had succeeded at his scheme. He had turned a country girl into a lady equal to the highest ranks and ensured his immunity from the matchmakers of Town for at least another season. And as far as she, herself, was concerned, should she wish it, her future was secure. Marriage to either gentleman here at Pemberley would be an entrée into a fine life, and should she reject both, she was certain that she might have her choice of a hundred others in the coming season.

The affair, however, had progressed far beyond schemes and plans and vowels and manners. Hearts were at risk, and true happiness or emotional devastation were the possible outcomes, depending on her decisions. Feigning a headache, she begged off the walk on which they had all begun, and she made for her rooms to lie down and think very carefully about what she wanted. And as she lay there upon her bed, seeing the sunlight filtering in through the light sheer curtains that covered the windows and smelling the rose-scented air from the gardens below, she could hear the muted voices of the others as they completed their rounds of the intricate pathways through the rose bushes. Letting the indistinct sounds provide a cushion for her thoughts, her mind began to clear, and she found that her choice was really not that difficult after all.

CRISO

Dinner that night was a rather subdued affair. The exultation and false cheer after the incident with George Wickham had dissolved, leaving everybody withdrawn into his or her own thoughts. Conversation was almost non-existent, consisting primarily of "please pass the butter," and "the tapers are smoking." The soup, though excellent, may as well have been water, the expertly prepared fowl sawdust. Even the normally ebullient Freddy was quiet and pensive, his customary colourful waistcoat discarded in favour of a dull grey.

The gathering seemed ready to part ways after the meal, to partake of solitary activities or to find oblivion in sleep, but as Georgiana was about to leave the salon where they had taken their tea and sweetmeats, Darcy called upon her to stop.

"I have something to say," he announced, "though it pains me greatly to say it."

Looks of extreme concern passed amongst the other three in the room. What on earth could have happened? Seeing how Darcy was fighting to avoid looking directly at her, Lizzy wondered, briefly, if she was being ejected from the house for some unknown reason. Her initial tenure in the house had been as Georgie's guest, but her status soon changed to that of guest of the master, and he could toss her out as quickly as he could request a different cravat from his valet. Surely he had nothing to say against his sister or cousin. Georgie was blameless in all things, and Freddy's only crime was to care a bit too much for herself. If she had come between the cousins, and if Darcy had recognised her culpability, he would be within his rights to see her gone.

With trepidation, she and the others crept back to the chairs and settees which they had so recently abandoned to await the dire news that Darcy seemed about to impart. Three sets of eyes, anxious and alarmed, focused upon the professor, who ignored them all as he paced up and down, chin in hand and a troubled look upon his face, until Freddy at last called out, "Speak, for heaven's sake, and stop this agony."

Ceasing his restless pacing but not choosing to sit himself, Darcy faced his audience. "Georgie, perhaps what I have to say is not for your ears, but you are intimately involved, and therefore deserve to hear it. Eliza, forgive me for saying in public what ought to be said in private, but here, too, others have interests in this matter, and what I have to say concerns them as well. Afterwards, if you choose to think of me at all, I pray you do so with good will. I could not bear to know that you are alive in the world and thinking ill of me."

Lizzy felt her heart hammer in her chest and her hands grew damp as she clutched at her skirts. This did involve her, and most directly, so it seemed. What disaster was he about to unleash upon her that required so dire a preface? She began to wonder how quickly a message could be sent to the Grants at Arlenby requesting the carriage, or whether she would be forced to walk into Lambton to take a room at the inn for the night. She squirmed in her chair and breathed, "Shall I ask my maid to pack my belongings, Professor?"

He flinched, as if struck by a stone. "Oh, God, no!" he fairly shouted back. "I wish no harm upon you, none at all. Just the opposite. I have thought hard and deeply about matters, and I have come to realise that until now, my concerns have all revolved around myself. I agreed to your request to teach you, Eliza, because the scheme was to my ultimate benefit. I encouraged your association with my Aunt Patricia because it pleased me and furthered my plan. I thought to entice you into a proper engagement because it was what I wished. At no point did I think of you, of your needs. Not even when you shouted at me and abused me after that wretched, damned ball," he ignored Georgie's gasp of shock, "did I think to ask myself what *you* truly desired.

"But today, as we confronted that miserable excuse of a man, Wickham, I perceived at last his real crime, which is unchecked selfishness. Moreover, I dared to examine myself for such a fault. And I found it, oh, how painfully I found it. In my own way, I treated you, my dearest Eliza, as abysmally as Wickham treated first Georgie, and then Caroline, thinking he was harming me. Afterwards, I saw Freddy talking to you, Eliza, and I knew the meaning of his conversation. My heart railed against the very thought of it, black clouds threatened me at the sight, but I knew that in this instance, my wishes must come second to yours."

He squeezed his eyes closed and allowed his head to fall back on his neck before resetting his expression. He seemed to firm his resolve and faced her once again. With tight lips and deep brown eyes that threatened tears, he continued, "Consider my cousin's offer, Eliza. For all that I have grown to esteem you, I cannot stop being the wretch I am, and your happiness means more to me than my own. Freddy can do well by you, and he will make you a better husband than I." Stopping, he turned around and found the nearest chair, into which he fell as if all the strength had suddenly been sapped from his bones. "There. I have said it. I cannot live if you are not happy."

There was silence. No one dared utter a sound and Lizzy felt the loud beating of her heart must resound through the stunned void of the room. She saw, from the corner of her eye, Georgie and Freddy both sitting with mouths agape at the enormity of Darcy's unexpected pronouncement.

All at once the silence was filled with expressions of wonder and alarm. "Fitz, you cannot mean it? Are you giving her up entirely?" Georgie flung herself up from her chair and to her brother's side, whilst Freddy boomed, "I say, Darcy, that's awfully good of you. I had not thought you such a self-sacrificing sort at all." Lizzy alone remained mute as the import of these words reverberated through her head.

So absorbed was she with what she had heard that she did not notice right away that the others were now all looking at her. She came to her senses with a start and tried to speak, but her voice was dry. Immediately, Darcy was there with a small glass of sherry, which she drank rather too quickly. She grew warm, and rose unsteadily to walk towards the windows, now open to allow in the warm summer air.

"What say you then, Lizzy? Do you accept me?" Freddy was at her elbow, tugging at his lace cuffs, eager anticipation written on his noble face. "You would then be sister to Charlotte. I shall order matching garb that we may present the perfect picture when we are about in Town. We shall look so fine together! And think on it—one day you shall be a countess! May that day be long in the coming, for it is a mantle I am in no hurry to take up, but it will, eventually arrive. Will you accept me?"

Turning to take in the room, Lizzy regarded the company set out before her. Freddy was there, as he was always there, willing to please and anxious to be of service, a good man beneath his aura of frivolity. He was by her side now, and would always be there for her, even if his concerns were as much for his horses and cravats as for the sensible management of a household. Georgie sat perfectly still, a statue of shock and amazement, whilst Darcy had turned away from the group. But this time, Lizzy knew in her heart, he had not turned away out of disdain or incivility, but because he could not keep the pain from his face and did not wish to burden his friends with his own personal agony. He lived in broad strokes, and when the veneer of curmudgeonly hauteur was wiped from his visage, he felt deeply and keenly, and his eyes could not lie. His pain was palpable, and she longed to rush over and comfort him, but she knew she had to speak now. This had gone on for too long, and she finally knew her heart.

"Freddy," she turned to the man at her side and took his hand in her own, heedless of the impropriety of the action, "I have come to care for you deeply. You are the best of men, and I am honoured to have received your admiration and your offer. You have always been so good to me, and it was *you* who truly taught me to be a lady." She caught and held his eyes. "For unlike your cousin, you understood that the difference between a country miss and a lady of the highest ranks is not how she *behaves* but how she is *treated*. You have always behaved to me as if I were a duchess, not some scamp from a small estate in the countryside."

Freddy preened, but Lizzy stopped him with the softest touch of a hand upon his forearm.

"But I cannot marry you. I like you tremendously, and I cherish your friendship, but we would not really suit. If I love you, it is as a friend or a cousin, not as a husband. And you do not love me, not in any permanent way. You desire me, perhaps, and you are enamoured of the creature your cousin created, but you do not love me, not in that way. You are a wonderful man and you deserve real affection, and I will not keep you from that. We will always remain friends, I hope. I'm so sorry." She kissed his cheek and stepped away from him.

Freddy's face fell, but with the disappointment of a plan gone wrong and not with the dreadful devastation of a broken heart. Not with the pain his cousin had tried to suppress moments before. He said nothing, but took her hand and bestowed a sweet and delicate kiss just below her fingers, then released her and fell into a chair.

With careful steps, Lizzy walked over to where Darcy stood, his shoulders tense and his breath unsteady. She dared to be bold, and reached out to gently touch his shoulder. He spun around with a haunted look in his eyes, the latent vulnerability now overshadowing every other aspect of his being. He stared at her uncomprehendingly for a moment, then turned away from her once more. She could see tears brimming in his eyes.

"Fitz," she said, so quietly it was almost a whisper. "That was the bravest thing I have ever seen you do, and the noblest. You have put another's interests above your own, even to your own detriment, and you are prepared to suffer to see someone else be happy.

"Today I learned something I had not before understood. I understood what it is to be trusted, entirely and completely. All the while Wickham was slandering me—or the person he thought I was—you never once doubted me. With every new accusation and every assertion of his evidence, your faith in me never wavered. Each vile lie he uttered only made me stronger, for I saw how you had come to know me completely, and you understood that the woman I am would never do the things he said I had done. And that complete faith in me is reflected in the complete faith I have in you. You have never intentionally hurt anybody, and I know you never will. You may be foolish or a tyrant at times, but you are fundamentally a good man who strives to do well by all you deal with."

He began to turn slowly around her, with something akin to hope creeping across his face, and she felt drawn into those deep brown eyes. He did not speak, although his lips moved as if trying to recall how to form words. She continued, "I cannot promise always to be the lady you have worked so hard to create; at times I may forget myself and resort to my country ways..."

"I ought never to have tried to change you!" Darcy exploded, words suddenly returning to him. "You were perfect the way you were." He lingered on the word "perfect" and gazed at her in wonder.

"You did not change me, Fitz. I am who I have always been. The accent and the manners have changed, and for the better, but in essentials, I am who I have ever been. The creature you met in Meryton was more than adequate for the country, but recall: it was I who requested your assistance. And while you have been rude and condescending and surly and a trial to be around at times, you are a fine and decent man beneath it all. Even your gravest errors are made in what you consider to be the interests of others. I know that life with you will not always be easy," she smothered a smile at his hurt look, "but I can think of only one reason a man would willingly give up his deepest-held dreams."

"The reason is that I love you!" he protested. "I love you and wish only for your happiness!"

"True and selfless love... a woman can ask no more than that. If you still want me, I'm yours."

For the longest time, he stared at her, as if he could hardly believe what he had heard and feared that this vision of all he desired would disappear like mist on a summer's morning. "Is this true?" he asked at last. "Can I be dreaming?"

"You are not dreaming, my love, for you are my love. All the while you shouted and ranted, I slowly began to learn of the man beneath the facade, and became fascinated, and whilst here, at Pemberley, I have learned more of you and of the essence inside of you, and I have grown to love you in return."

"Then you will marry me after all?" Wide-eyed, he asked this question.

"I will. Most delightedly."

Before she knew what was happening, Lizzy was swept up into his arms and held tight against his strong chest. She felt his heart beat within his breast, and she sighed in contentment that it beat for her. Her arms now crept around his waist and she felt his face nuzzling in her hair. Her coiffure would be ruined, but she cared not. This was love. It was not passion, although that existed as well, nor was it self-interest, but rather, a deep and abiding love, and her hair be damned (she chuckled to herself at the terrible example her Fitz had shown her), she would revel in his embrace. With a broad smile, she raised her head to gaze at him, and the contentment and sheer happiness on his face was, itself, worth all the tribulations she had gone through.

"Eliza... my Lizzy, may I kiss you now?"

She nodded, her eyes alight with joy.

"Oh, my beautiful one, my darling, my fair Lizzy!" and his lips claimed hers.

# *Epilogue*

"It is a truth universally acknowledged," the tall gentleman said, "that a single man in possession of a good fortune, must be in want of a wife." He took a sip from the goblet of fine brandy he held in his long and manicured hand, and then observed the amber liquid as he swirled it around the inside of the glass, the colours reflecting in the firelight. He sighed the sigh of deep satisfaction. "And how true it is, Charles, how utterly true that is."

"'Tis even so for an impecunious old soldier as myself!" joked the former colonel who occupied the third chair by the fire. "I never knew how much until it was upon me." He raised his own glass, and the three men toasted each other, each revelling in his own great fortune.

The three friends sat in the comfort of Darcy's study in his London townhouse, whilst their wives gathered in the drawing room next door, engaged in deep and delighted conversation about whatever it is that sisters and dear friends discuss when they have not seen each other for some time. Jane Bingley was proudly showing off her latest acquisition, a perfect little boy, now three months old, named Oliver Charles. With his golden curls, rosy cheeks and sparkling blue eyes, the babe was an instant favourite with all who saw him, and Jane was right to be most pleased with her creation. Charles, too, doted on the lad in a manner most unfashionable amongst the haute set, and none could blame him.

Richard had cooed over the child with an unexpected enthusiasm that had his cousin baffled, until it became obvious that his dear

Charlotte would soon be presenting him with an heir as well. If Eliza had a similar secret, she was not yet telling anybody.

Well comfortable with his close friends and in the knowledge of his beloved being only a short few yards away, Darcy allowed himself to relax into pleasant conversation while his mind toyed with the events of the past several months.

Of these events, his own engagement and wedding took primacy in his thoughts. After Freddy's initial disappointment, his cousin had come to see that Lizzy had been quite right and that his affection for her was that of infatuation and friendship, rather than the selfless love that she deserved. The viscount had quickly offered his heartiest congratulations and had promised to do whatever was needed to smooth Lizzy's way during her first season as Mrs. Darcy. He had returned to Town shortly after the wedding with Georgie in tow, and according to rumour—substantiated by Richard—he had become fascinated of late with a young woman who had but recently arrived in London from the colonies. Her father, the third son of a baron, had taken a post in Lower Canada as a young man. Having dwelt in Montreal with his family for the past twenty years, his duties had recalled him to England, and with him came his wife and four children, amongst whom numbered the charming and exotic Miss Helena Hutchison. It was far too early to plan his wedding suit, but Darcy began to hope that there might be a happy ending for his cousin Freddy as well.

Aunt Patricia had been delighted at the news that the false engagement had become real, for she had taken an immediate liking to Elizabeth, which over the course of the countess' ministrations and guidance, had become a genuine attachment. She would, of course, have welcomed Lizzy as a daughter, but was almost as happy to see her as a niece, for it was apparent that this arrangement was of the most satisfaction to everybody. She had continued to squire Lizzy around Town and to introduce her to the right people in the highest circles, and was right now preparing the new Mrs. Darcy for her presentation at court. The former country girl was completely accepted in society as a fine lady, and if none knew of her background, that would be quite acceptable as well.

The wedding itself had been as simple and without ado as was possible for two such people as the esteemed Professor Darcy—nephew to an earl, after all!—and the daughter of Mrs. Bennet. That lady, immediately upon hearing the happy news, had set off for Pemberley and arrived days later with none other than Patricia, Lady Malton. The two set right to work on arranging the wedding and the subsequent celebrations, and only the most strenuous objections by the couple succeeded in tempering any of their plans.

Darcy complained loudly and often about the entire affair, and on several occasions waxed poetic to his betrothed about the relative advantages of eloping to Scotland. "We are, after all, half way there!" he declared more than once. Eliza agreed with him, but reminded him that their suffering was to be of short duration—for they were to be wed within the month—and that other people's happiness depended on their acquiescence. Reluctantly and with no good humour, he agreed to suffer through the elaborate celebrations.

"After all, Fitz, 'tis only the wedding that they are planning," she would remind him once and again, "and we all know that what is truly important is not the wedding but the marriage. And that we shall conduct on our own terms, with no influence by anyone wholly unconnected to ourselves."

In the end, both survived the rites, as well as the attendant trials and tribulations, and were most happy in their new domestic arrangements.

Lost in these pleasant memories, Darcy smiled to himself and allowed the quiet conversation of the others wash over him like the warmth of a good fire on a cold day, soothing and reassuring.

"Tell me, Charles," he asked at last, when the conversation had reached a natural lull, "what is the latest from Caroline and Wickham?"

Charles rolled his eyes and let out a very uncharacteristic huff. "Caroline will forever be a thorn in my side. Fortunately, she is more a thorn in her husband's than in mine, and so I shall survive the experience. She writes nothing but to complain. She is unhappy with the lodgings though they were most comfortable when I travelled thither to see them; she complains of the food, for it is not the finest French fare, but simply good and hearty country cooking. She complains of the society, despite the people being good and honest friendly folk, with nothing but an excellent intention behind every action, and she complains of her husband. She was happy enough to bed him, but not to wed him, and it was only when I informed her that her dowry was not quite large enough to overcome her status as another man's discarded mistress that she agreed. No one forced her into the alliance, any more than anyone forced Wickham. They have made their bed, and I truly believe that if they only decided to be content with their lot, they might be quite happy."

"Then," quipped Richard with a smirk, "there is little else to say. My modest income affords me only half of what they seem to have, if your accounting is accurate, Charles. Their community clearly does them well. And yet I am grown most content indeed with my lot, meagre though it may be. I have enough, and I have Charlotte. What more could I possibly desire? I believe it is the necessity to live exemplary lives that troubles them more than the physical or societal inconveniences they complain about."

"You are correct, sir," Bingley replied. "Where there is no real want of the necessities of life, a willingness to be happy can overcome so many troubles."

"And a simple life can be most pleasing, when one shares it with a partner of one's choice." Richard relaxed into his chair with a most fulfilled smile.

"Enough of my wretched sister, gentlemen. We have more pleasant matters to cheer our spirits! Let us rejoice over our own great fortunes, for we three have the best brides in England," Bingley declared with good cheer, and his companions agreed heartily.

"To the ladies," Darcy raised a toast.

"To the ladies!" the others responded.

Life was good.

# About the Author

Riana Everly was born in South Africa, but has called Canada home since she was eight years old. She has a Master's degree in Medieval Studies and is trained as a classical musician, specialising in Baroque and early Classical music. She first encountered Jane Austen when her father handed her a copy of *Emma* at age 11, and has never looked back.

Riana now lives in Toronto with her family. When she is not writing, she can often be found playing string quartets with friends, biking around the beautiful province of Ontario with her husband, trying to improve her photography, thinking about what to make for dinner, and, of course, reading!

CRXSO

If you enjoyed this novel, please consider posting a review at your favourite bookseller's website.

Riana Everly loves connecting with readers on Facebook. Come and say hello!

Also, be sure to check out her website at rianaeverly.com for sneak peeks at coming works and links to works in progress

RIANA EVERLY

CPSIA information can be obtained
at www.ICGtesting.com
Printed in the USA
BVHW041114060119
537159BV00020B/475/P

9 781775 128328